CONTENTION

A NOVEL OF INTERNATIONAL
SUSPENSE AND INTRIGUE

GARY D. McGUGAN

CONTENTION
A Novel of International Suspense and Intrigue
Copyright © 2023 by Gary D. McGugan

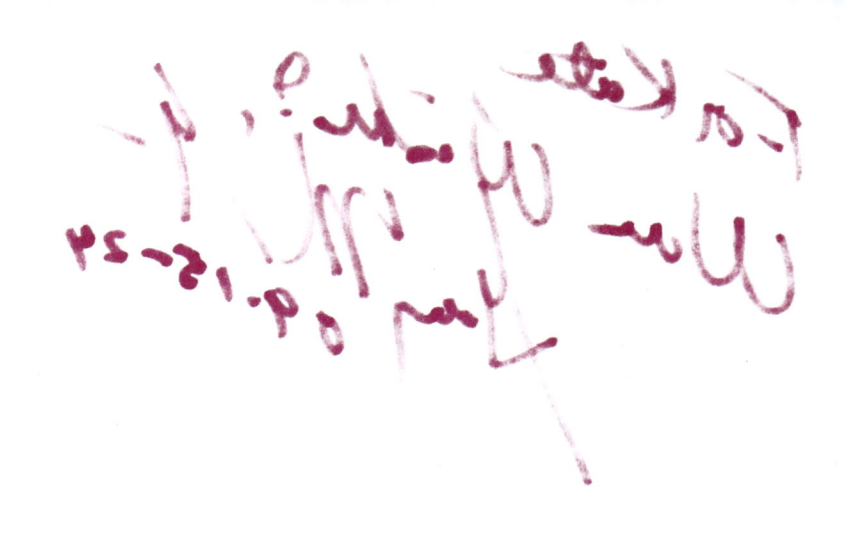

Reprinted August 2024

Cover and book design by Castelane.

No part of this publication may be reproduced, distributed, or transmitted in any form or by any means, including photocopying, recording, or other electronic or mechanical methods, without the prior written permission of the author, except in the case of brief quotations embodied in critical reviews and certain other non-commercial uses permitted by copyright law.

This book is a work of fiction. Names, characters, businesses, organizations, places, events, and incidents are the product of the author's imagination or are used fictitiously. Any resemblance to actual persons, living or dead, events or locales are entirely coincidental.

ISBN 978-1-7779049-6-8 (Paperback)
ISBN 978-1-7779049-7-5 (eBook)
1. FICTION, THRILLERS

Also by Gary D. McGugan

Fiction

Three Weeks Less A Day
The Multima Scheme
Unrelenting Peril
Pernicious Pursuit
A Web of Deceit
A Slippery Shadow
When Power Fails

Non-Fiction

NEEDS Selling Solutions
(Co-Authored with Jeff F. Allen)

What Readers Say About Gary D. McGugan's Books

"There is no point throughout this read where McGugan's audience has the remote chance of getting lost or confused. Rather, he spends just as much time tying loose ends together immediately after each crescendo in the plot before moving on with yet another whammy of a situation." ~ *Diane Lunsford for Feathered Quill*

"As is the case with McGugan's two previous novels, *Three Weeks Less A Day* and *The Multima Scheme,* the plot of *Unrelenting Peril* is tight and complex. McGugan has a gift for well-paced, well-blocked flurries of nail-biting action that all lead up to a surprising finale."
~ *Norm Goldman, Bookpleasures.com*

"The chapters in this fast-paced plot jump from character to character, all interlinked by the hand of fate - some scheming, some grieving, and some learning valuable lessons about how stuff really works in the world beyond the headlines." ~ *Barbara Bamberger Scott, Feathered Quill*

"Gary D McGugan writes in a way that is easily understood and believable in this exciting book. He introduces characters to the story that allows you, the reader, to form a mental picture of what is going on in each scene while we are flown off in private jets to different parts of the world where crimes are plotted and put into operation."
~ *Christopher Anderson for Readers' Favorite*

"What an incredible story. Exciting, suspenseful, and thought-provoking, *A Slippery Shadow* by Gary D. McGugan is one of the best stories I have read." ~ *Natalie Soine for Readers' Favorite*

"I highly recommend all of Gary D. McGugan's books. Though all the stories stand nicely on their own, please do yourself a favor and start at the beginning. The road from the first novel, *Three Weeks Less a Day* to his latest release is an incredible journey." ~ *Sheri Hoyte for Reader Views*

Acknowledgements

Every novel I write is a learning adventure. I start off with my outline of a story I think readers will enjoy, and tell it as effectively as I can. Once a manuscript draft is complete, two excellent writing professionals tell me all the mistakes I've made.

Paula Hurwitz and Val Tobin have worked separately, but together, to help me deliver the novel you're about to read. They did much more than detect mistakes. Both provided valuable suggestions that improved my story meaningfully, and I think you're going to enjoy reading it. I thank both for their dedication and patience. Be sure. If you find any remaining errors or shortcomings, they are entirely mine.

Early in the process, I asked Heather & Dan Lightfoot, and Cathy & Dalton McGugan for their thoughts about the characters and plot. They each provided excellent suggestions that added significant value to the story.

Kim McDougall of Castelane once again delivered a knock-out book cover design and book layout. Every time we work together, I admire her expertise, and unmatched professionalism.

To each of these excellent collaborators, I express heartfelt thanks and appreciation.

ONE

Punta del Este, Uruguay, Wednesday November 16, 2022

After their sullen waiter served steaming coffee, Fidelia Morales might have predicted where the conversation would go next. In the thirty-some years of their tumultuous on-and-off relationship, Howard Knight had never once suggested they dine out on a weekday.

Even for birthdays or anniversary-type celebrations, he invariably maintained that weekends were the only proper time to enjoy dining in a restaurant because there were always more people around and more merriment. She could count on one hand the number of times she'd changed his mind over the years. Yet for tonight, he had suggested *Lo de Tere*, the city's most expensive restaurant and her favorite.

They were one of only three couples in the restaurant. With her security guys included, their group represented almost half of the evening's clientele. Howard had broached the idea for this dinner over a week ago and had confirmed the date and time with her twice since then.

So she'd had lots of time to consider his odd social proposal. Fidelia had also pieced together other out-of-the-ordinary things he'd said or done in recent weeks. There were several. Nothing jumped out, of course, because Howard was indeed a genius and clever enough in his daily habits to avoid behavior that would tip his hand.

The guy was also still handsome, even with graying hair and that stubble he insisted on keeping. His smile had always appealed to her. It suggested a hint of mischief, and his brown eyes still sparkled when he turned on the charm.

He rarely used the gym membership she'd bought him for Christmas last year, but he liked to walk. He'd traipse up and down the beach every day, regardless of the weather, so his body remained trim and fit.

They still had decent sex from time to time, but she'd been the instigator every time over the past three months. Of late, he'd also spent much more time than usual squirreled away in his tiny office with his laptop. Yet it seemed he had ever fewer suggestions for ways she could make more money.

During the miracle recovery of the stock markets after a pandemic plunge, he'd traded furiously on exchanges around the world and doubled the hundred million she'd given him to invest. She suspected he had about the same amount in a personal account stashed away in the Cayman Islands, so he'd probably doubled his cache, too.

Fidelia also mentally tallied the hundreds of millions more dollars his ideas had earned for The Organization. He had an astounding knowledge of cryptocurrencies and ways they could circumvent government regulators and exchanges. He'd taught her unsavory associates around the globe how to steal more money than she'd dreamed possible. However, he had already warned her they'd seen the last easy gains from crypto. He strongly recommended that she pull out much of The Organization's illicit money before it all plummeted.

She followed his advice and sold off their positions before the markets crashed again. Other investors lost billions, and some of the weaker crypto funds collapsed into bankruptcy. She owed him big, and she knew it. But Howard never once looked for a pat on the back or a thank you. So, she guessed he was hatching some new scheme that didn't involve The Organization, something he'd like to do somewhere else.

And that's where there might be a problem. She had big plans, too. More than a decade before, Giancarlo Mareno—the guy who'd run The Organization before her—dreamed of taking over the American conglomerate Multima Corporation. Back then, they came within a whisker of getting it until Howard made one fatal mistake that cost them control of the prized company.

For a while, Fidelia had lost interest in his dream. But Multima had doubled in size in the past six years and had become even more attractive. If The Organization gained control of Multima, it could use the company to move illicit money easily around the world. More crucial, she saw it as a ticket to respectability. Luigi Fortissimo in New York also seemed eager to seize the company to increase his influence in the US and thought he'd found a way to get control. Would it be possible to marry whatever Howard had brewing with her grand scheme?

"I've got an idea," he began. "We shouldn't talk too much about it here, but if you're willing to consider a proposal, I'll share all the details with you at the house."

"Okay, but if we can't discuss it, what did you bring me here for?"

"We can talk about the big picture. We should just save the details for a more private setting." Howard glanced casually around the room before nodding knowingly.

"I want to create a new venture on the Caribbean Island of Aruba. I'd like you to reward me for the half-billion dollars I've earned for you and The Organization by cutting the chain again. You know what we have isn't love, although the sex is always outstanding. Two years ago, you forced me to stay with you here in Uruguay. I had little choice, and I'll concede that you made our time together pleasant. But, I need some space."

It tempted Fidelia to feign surprise, disappointment, or even anger, but it wasn't worth the effort. She'd already decided to give him another chance at some degree of "freedom". But she needed to find a viable means of ensuring his release didn't evolve into cooperation with the FBI or some other international law enforcement agency. It wouldn't be easy. He'd failed that test twice.

"I understand," she replied casually. "Your timing couldn't be better. I need to focus on the US for a while. Luigi's anxious to take a run at some source of revenue he hasn't shared with me yet. I hope he's working on a plan to get Multima Corporation, and I want to be sure he gets it this time."

She paused and leaned back, hoping the idea might tempt him, but he showed no interest in redeeming himself. So she instantly steeled her tone and manner, sweeping back a shock of her long hair to show she meant business.

"Okay, tell me about your scheme when we get home this evening. Let's suppose I agree it's good for The Organization. In that case, I have no objection to you working from Aruba, provided you swear on your life you'll have no contact with the FBI or anyone else that tries to enforce laws. If you won't accept that pre-condition, or I don't like your idea, you may not wake up tomorrow morning."

To underscore her displeasure, she stood up from the table, gathered her bag from the floor, and signaled the bodyguards seated two tables over to follow them to the car.

Howard Knight got her message loud and clear. She didn't speak to him in the rear seat of their BMW SUV during the fifteen-minute chauffeured drive back to her house near the beach, and he knew better than to try.

It was all part of his strategy. He understood Fidelia well and was confident the brief lapse needed for their trip home would be all she required to think through her alternatives and priorities. She was the most pragmatic person Howard had ever encountered, unburdened by the principles or values of most ordinary people.

The nugget she threw in about Multima Corporation was a surprise. It was probably to tempt him to forget his idea and continue to work with her instead. He'd have to proceed with caution. However, by the time they arrived, he expected she'd realize how much he wanted out, define the parameters his idea had to meet, and calm her emotions so they could have a rational conversation.

At first, she didn't surprise or disappoint. Outside the car, she turned away from Howard to address Mateo Lopez, the more senior of her bodyguards, the guy who also ran her illegal businesses in three South American countries.

"We have some matters to discuss in the secure room. Stay here for instructions when we're finished," she said in her most matter-of-fact tone.

He nodded his understanding and glanced at Howard as he held open the door to the residence. Howard winked in return and managed the outline of a smile.

The secure room was a large office on the ground floor at the back of the sprawling two-story house. During the pandemic, Fidelia had brought a team from the US who tore down two walls, then refurbished the space using the latest materials to block sound, electronic prying, or gunshots. The Organization's American unit assured her she could discuss anything with anyone anywhere in total secrecy from her secure chamber. She used the room often.

Howard followed her silently as they trod through the grand entrance into a luxurious living area, then along another long hallway to a closed door at the end. He took in her long legs and short skirt as they walked. Men always turned for a second look when they passed her. Fidelia was taller than average, her legs shapely and inviting. Those legs were one of the things he'd miss if his idea went well.

She opened the door with a key fob. Wordlessly, she strode to the executive armchair, gracefully eased into it, crossed her legs, and motioned for him to use an unpadded, straight-backed wooden chair facing her.

Then she smiled and held it, saying, "Tell me about your plan."

Howard's hand twitched as an unpleasant sensation pulsed deep in his stomach. Her smile conveyed more than her words. It seemed as if an artist had drawn a thin line on her face as an afterthought, reminding him of the last time she'd looked that way. It was right after she blew out the brains of her long-time boss, Giancarlo Mareno, with one shot aimed directly into his face as he pleaded on his knees for mercy.

Right now, her eyes looked even more intimidating. Usually brown, soft, and welcoming, they hardened like weathered granite. They telegraphed he was probably finished if she didn't like his idea. She'd made no secret that she loathed the idea of him running around free in the world at large. She stared at Howard and waited.

"I may have discovered a new source of revenue, and I'm willing to share it with The Organization," he began. He forced his tone to sound confident despite her hostile manner and flashed a mischievous smile as he finished his opening sentence. To be sure she realized it wasn't to be all about him, he paused until she tilted her head in interest.

"You know cryptocurrencies are on their last legs, and I'm glad you followed my advice and sold when you did. I also know you appreciate the half-billion dollars that decision added to The Organization's coffers."

Howard waited again for her to nod slightly in acknowledgment, watching her eyes soften a notch before he continued. "It's increasingly obvious now that there's a promising future in information."

Her head tilted more, which he read as a tinge of curiosity. So, he carried on. "I want to create a semi-legitimate business model that could generate billions."

"So, what prevents you from doing it?"

"Uruguay's a pleasant country, and I like it in many ways. But I need a place with access to more sophisticated technology, better security, and closer to the Northern Hemisphere's action." He smiled to soften his message.

"And you've always liked warm weather." Her expression was blank, but her tone telegraphed mild derision. "Cut to the chase, Howard. What's the business? How will you make money? And how much do you want from me?"

He took a moment to assess her words and manner. Fidelia was like that sometimes. She showed impatience and said little until she understood the issue. He'd have to keep her interested for long enough to avoid opposition.

"Corporate espionage. A company that steals information for a fee. I'm not asking you for money, but I might need The Organization to run interference from time to time and provide resources occasionally. I'm willing to pay you for those services and cut you a percentage of the action, but I don't need a loan or any investment of your money." When he paused for a breath, Fidelia characteristically asked another question.

"So you got your hundred million from TVB Bank in the Caymans?" She sneered before adding, "Even after your contact, Mr. Fernando, unfortunately jumped from a balcony outside his office?"

"Yes. I can access my personal funds and won't need to ask you for financial help." He emphasized his fiscal independence to allay any concerns Fidelia might have about risks associated with starting a new and unproven venture. "To answer your second question, I plan to make enough money to double my personal wealth without attracting attention from legal authorities. That's why I want Aruba as my base."

"And those resources of The Organization you also want?" Her tone had softened a bit.

"One person to start."

"Klaudia Schäffer won't agree." Fidelia's perceptive mind

surprised and impressed Howard, and he smiled to show it. From the meager information he'd shared, she'd already sensed that he wanted her technology whiz from Germany. He chose his next words carefully and studied her reaction.

"Klaudia's your closest friend, so you know her better than I do. But her little company is struggling. She's learned it takes unique skills to keep a business growing, and you must realize I've spent a lot of time coaching her about her enterprise and its potential."

Howard looked intently into her eyes so there'd be no misunderstanding. She should read the veracity of what he was about to say instantly. That would be crucial.

"Klaudia will probably close her company in Germany, but she still doesn't want to become part of The Organization. You know she objects to you continuing the escort trade and realizes you won't give it up. We've talked about her joining me in Aruba. She wants your blessing, as do I, but she's definitely interested in working with me."

He paused for a few seconds but didn't release his lock on her eyes. Still, they didn't telegraph her thoughts.

"Where do you get customers for this venture?" Her tone sounded warmer, more like curiosity than scorn.

"From what I've learned so far, potential clients might be any large corporations in competitive industries. Political operatives could buy our services. Even charities may want to find out who the big donors to competitor not-for-profits are. As the world gets smaller and more cutthroat, every company's thinking about ways to gain an advantage over the other guys. I'm betting a good number of them will rationalize it's easier, quicker, and cheaper to contract out their information needs than go through all the gyrations themselves."

"Where will you get your spies?" Her tone conveyed interest.

Howard paused to re-assess her mood and any signals she might telegraph with her body. She folded her hands in her lap and seemed slightly less erect than when they'd first sat down. Her toes weren't tapping, so she still had some patience. However, he needed to choose his next words with equal care.

"Klaudia connected with a guy in California who's already in the business and talks about it openly. He has some bad personal habits and has left a trail of evidence that could get him locked away if it falls into the wrong hands, or killed if the right folks find out. He's here in Uruguay. I've met with him a couple times. He wants to work with us, and I'd like you to invite him over for dinner."

Howard reached for a sip of water from a glass on the table and almost spat it out when Fidelia asked. "Is Klaudia here too?"

"We intended to let you know. She just arrived today, and I hoped for your blessing to move forward before bringing her into the equation."

Fidelia had had enough. She stood up and pressed a button on the wall beside her chair, calling for her most trusted bodyguard. He burst through the doorway seconds later. Before he could speak, she barked out her instructions.

"Howard, go with Mateo to Klaudia. Don't call her or alert her you're coming. Bring her back here immediately. No conversations. None. Mateo, bring two others with you to ride shotgun and be sure they both follow my rules—not a fuckin' word till they're back here. How long will you be?"

"Less than an hour," Howard mumbled. He should have expected her to figure out that Klaudia was already nearby. Now she was pissed, and that was never a good thing.

"Let me..."

"That silence rule starts right this second," Fidelia hissed.

TWO

Montreal, Quebec, Friday November 18, 2022

They met on the fifth floor of Montreal's luxurious Four Seasons Hotel in the meeting room *Palais des Possibles,* set up boardroom style. The room could accommodate over forty people, but Suzanne Simpson's group was about half that number.

For over a month, she'd been in Montreal out of necessity.

When Hurricane Ian swept through Southwest Florida in late September, Suzanne's home in Fort Myers flooded with more than two feet of water on the ground floor. As expected, high winds caused minor damage to the well-designed and solidly constructed executive home. But an unprecedented storm surge from the Gulf of Mexico caused the Caloosahatchee River, only yards from her house, to overflow and swamp her home with smelly muck and water, making it uninhabitable for months.

In 2020, a bomb had destroyed Suzanne's home in Atlanta. Afterward, police and insurance investigations delayed starting reconstruction. So, the builder still projected several more months before completion.

Suzanne took advantage of her misfortune and rented a sprawling villa in the Laurentian Mountains just north of the city. She'd been living there since early October and was using this board of directors meeting as an excellent excuse to bring her team up to enjoy the warm hospitality of Montreal. Unfortunately, the meeting was not unfolding as she'd expected.

She felt her face flush slightly. After almost thirty years of playing with the big boys, it still happened every time one of her colleagues floated an idea that put her company at risk. People said the tick of Suzanne Simpson's left eye wasn't visible behind her eyeglasses. Still, it was enough to make her face flush. The women and men looking at her around the large oval table would easily spot her discomfort.

They all knew her well. By now, they should also know she wouldn't react rashly or dismiss the idea. But they would also expect she'd pose some pointed questions before Gordon Goodfellow sat down again. The three women all glanced away before she made eye contact, but the gazes of most of the males lingered. It seemed to take the guys longer to validate their reading of her body language.

Goodfellow noticed he'd lost the full attention of his audience and poured himself a glass of ice water from a nearby pitcher before gulping half of it down in one swallow.

When he cleared his throat and resumed his presentation with a trademark electronic pointer dancing on the screen, he drew everyone's attention to the size of his intended target.

"I realize the magnitude of this acquisition dwarfs any we've considered before." Goodfellow paused to read her reaction, but Suzanne pursed her lips enough to hide any sign of her thoughts. "I'm also aware we'll need to take on massive debt to make it happen, but an acquisition like this comes along only once in an executive's lifetime. We owe it to our shareholders to give the idea careful consideration."

Good. Gordon didn't appear so committed to this latest foray into the corporate jungle that she'd need to immediately overrule him before the others.

They'd worked together for almost two decades, and she liked the guy. She'd mentored him through three major promotions at Multima Corporation, including the one that put him in charge of Supermarkets' operations around the globe. Usually, she read his thoughts and body language well. Still, power was a potent opioid.

"If we can make it happen," he continued, "we'll move from being the tenth largest supermarket in the US to number three. More importantly, our deep analysis of their financials suggests we can improve our business synergies by millions annually. And the timing seems right. Jeffersons Stores isn't faring well in the new, tight labor market with high inflation."

"Why is that, Gordon?" James Fitzgerald barked out the question when the speaker paused for a breath. Her long-time confidant and president of Multima Financial Services often asked questions around the table.

"During the early stages of the pandemic, they had a long gap in leadership. You'll recall their CEO, David Jones, died with his wife when someone bombed their home. The management team fell apart with several defections, and it took almost a year to attract a new CEO. During the pandemic, demand was strong because people were eating at home. They easily generated acceptable results. However, the suppliers were eating them alive with price increases. Eventually, Jeffersons couldn't pass on the increased costs. They're earning almost three percent less than us. If we buy smart—and bring their costs and prices in line with ours—we calculate those synergies alone will bring almost a hundred and fifty million dollars to our bottom line every quarter."

Several directors looked toward the ceiling as they made mental calculations. The woman next to James, Natalia Tenaz, calculated something on her phone and flashed a number to him. James nodded in return but said nothing. Despite the gravity of Gordon's proposal, Suzanne took a moment more than necessary to assess Natalia. James was preparing the younger woman as his replacement at Multima Financial Services, and her business demeanor had improved under the old master's tutelage.

The tight, short skirts were gone, replaced by tasteful pant suits with colors that complimented her Latin skin coloring. A shorter cut that probably saved her significant grooming time had replaced her former long, flowing hairstyle. She sat more erect, observing the other people around the table. Next month's board of directors meeting should be an appropriate time to seek approval for her promotion.

Suzanne's attention swung back to Goodfellow, who continued to sell his idea for another ten minutes, guiding the directors through his business unit's research and conclusions. His story held everyone's attention, and there were no further questions until he completed his PowerPoint overview.

All eyes around the table shifted back to her. She bought some time by asking James Fitzgerald if he had any thoughts on the proposal that he was prepared to share. James held the respect of every director, and Suzanne thought of him as her most trusted advisor.

It turned out he had a strong opinion.

"I'll be candid. It will be hard for me to support any acquisition of Jeffersons Stores with the information you've shared." His tone was soft, almost gentle.

"The deal might have all the merits you outline for Supermarkets' businesses. But it will reduce earnings at Financial Services, perhaps severely. When Multima Corporation borrows ten billion dollars to make the acquisition, our corporate bond rating will drop two full notches. Natalia did a quick calculation, and our borrowing costs will almost double. The Fed is also continuing to raise the bank rate to get inflation under control. We'd have to raise our lending rates more than our customers can pay or lose money on every mortgage and credit-card loan we have out there. For Financial Services, your proposal is a non-starter."

The silence in the room was overpowering. Suzanne couldn't recall the last time James had adopted such an adversarial position, but took a deep breath and prepared herself. She straightened her posture to project authority, folded her hands on the table in front of her, and addressed Gordon directly.

"It looks like your team has more work ahead of them." Suzanne smiled. Her tone projected empathy but was firm.

"There's no doubt your proposal is bold. Your team has done a lot of solid research. The benefits to Supermarkets are clear and impressive, and I sense the timing might be right. But James makes a fair point. If half of our business suffers from accommodating a win for the other half, you're asking the board to add considerable cost and risk to our balance sheet for little or no net gain. We'll need to study it further."

The second Suzanne finished her sentence, the director representing Bank of the Americas blurted out more alarming news.

"It's worse than James and Natalia think. With the Fed's current stance on interest rates, I think Multima's bond rating will drop by over two notches. The rating agencies have become ruthless over the past two quarters. If Multima Corporation adds so much debt now, I fear they might reduce our rating to junk status. If that happens, I'll have to leave the board."

With that devastating pronouncement, Suzanne quickly shifted to a safer, more mundane proposal for the board to improve employee health benefits. Fortunately, they wouldn't need to decide about Goodfellow's bid to acquire Jeffersons Stores that day. More urgent was a need to heal a deep fracture in the board.

Her original goal of improving the board of directors' team

dynamics in Montreal had become more critical with these new disagreements about the potential acquisition of Jeffersons Stores. Suzanne pivoted and tried to use the unique setting and opulent environment to her advantage.

"Let's call it a day for our structured meetings," she said. "Most of you are coping with jet lag. Let's take a break for a few hours. Use the time as you choose. It might be too chilly outdoors, but I invite you to join me for a swim in the heated indoor pool. Or a massage in the spa. You might like to try the Kneipp water therapy room or take in the hotel's beautiful art collection."

Suzanne looked around the table as she spoke, making eye contact and assessing each person's reaction to her menu of activity choices.

"We'll have cars pick us up this evening at eight for the short drive to dinner. Eileen tells me she's arranged an outstanding evening of food and entertainment at one of the city's finest restaurants, *Le Muscadin*."

Smiles broadened, and eyes sparkled around the table as Suzanne finished her summary. The test would be how long those smiles lasted while the high-powered movers and shakers that made up her board interacted informally for several hours in an innovative restaurant she imagined would be unique to most of them.

THREE

Punta del Este, Uruguay, Friday November 18, 2022

Howard Knight felt a tingle of concern spike up the back of his neck. Something was wrong. It had all been too easy so far. However, he managed a grin as he watched Joe Montebank work Fidelia. The American corporate espionage expert was more than good. He was a master. And the way he held Fidelia's rapt attention was a work of art.

A couple days earlier, when she had dispatched Howard to fetch Klaudia and bring her German friend back to the secure room in the house at Punta del Este, the sight of Joe and Fidelia conversing so productively was unimaginable.

That late night he'd dared not defy Fidelia's strict orders to stay silent in the car. Her loyal bodyguards probably itched to use their fists, or worse, to enforce the crime boss's angry instructions. Instead, he could only shrug at Klaudia while Mateo relayed Fidelia's orders not to communicate until they reached her and received her permission.

An ugly confrontation never materialized. Instead, Klaudia had scampered from their SUV the moment the vehicle stopped in the driveway and bounced with resolve up the steps, through the doorway, and down the long hallway to the secure room where Fidelia waited.

When Howard caught up, he found Fidelia and Klaudia in a tight embrace with their lips locked in passion. That was something in their relationship he hadn't previously suspected or detected.

As a result, the dressing down he'd expected from Fidelia instead turned into a monologue from Klaudia, delivered with quiet but unwavering intensity, as Fidelia listened without objection or interruption. Within minutes, The Organization's leader had agreed to everything.

She gave her blessing for Klaudia and Howard to start a new corporate espionage business in Aruba. She'd take 25 percent of the earnings and provide protection in return. They could begin organizing immediately and, of course, she'd have dinner with

Joe Montebank to hear his story and learn more about how their business might work.

That dinner lasted over two hours in Fidelia's well-appointed and comfortable dining room. The antique overhead chandelier still glowed. They had polished off the filet mignon—prepared by the resident chef—nibbled at a succulent dessert, and started their third bottle of fine red wine from Fidelia's special, rarely used cellar.

"You mean to tell me they give you that information just because you ask for it?" Fidelia's tone expressed a combination of surprise and awe.

"They give it to me because I know how to ask for it," Montebank gently corrected her, emphasizing "how" with a shrug and conspiratorial smile. "That's the key to success. Howard and Klaudia will need to learn how to identify the right character traits in those who will ask for the information. I'll train them how to do it, and then I'll teach the successful candidates how to build relationships over the phone to get the info you need."

Howard silently seethed at the conman's style. Words like "train" and "teach" were condescending and unnecessary. Klaudia was equally quiet. When he caught her eye, her eyebrows lifted subtly, conveying surprise at how well things seemed to be progressing. They both watched silently for another few minutes as Fidelia lapped it up. Her next question showed how well the guy had sold her the idea.

"How soon can you start?"

"I have to finish another project, but I can be in Aruba by the first of the year," Montebank said with a wink. Then, without a moment's hesitation, he placed his hand over Fidelia's resting on the table and waited.

Almost instantly, Fidelia pulled back her hand, stood up, and moved a few steps toward an intercom, where she dropped an unexpected bombshell after her bodyguard Mateo replied to her buzz.

"Alright. Here's what we're going to do." She spoke into the intercom but looked at the group around the table. "Mateo, call the crew and have them at the airport in an hour. I'm traveling to New York overnight. Have the pilot file a flight plan to arrive at Teterboro. Let Luigi know and have him meet us at the airport.

Bring your full team. Mr. Montebank will also be joining us."

While waiting for Mateo's confirmation that he understood, she looked directly at Joe Montebank, who only gaped in surprise. Once she heard Mateo's okay, she released her finger on the intercom and swung toward Klaudia.

"You're in charge of the spy business. Do it from Aruba or wherever you choose. You're also responsible for Howard. If I hear even a rumor that he's contacted law enforcement anywhere, you're both history. Even a casual chat with a traffic cop. Got it?"

Klaudia nodded once but said nothing. Fidelia turned to Joe Montebank.

"Go with one of Mateo's men to pick up whatever you have at the hotel and want to bring with you. No calls home. No text messages. No communication with loved ones. Mateo's guy will get you to the airport. We'll talk more on the plane." She dismissed him with a wave and turned to Howard with a glare.

"This is your last chance. You heard me tell Klaudia she's in charge of you, and the new project." Her tone was bitter and threatening. "Make yourself lots of money. Pay me my share. And don't fuck it up this time."

With that crude admonishment, she left Klaudia and Howard still sitting at the table.

They looked at each other in quiet surprise for a moment. Klaudia's lips curled into the slightest smile as her mood shifted.

"It sounds like we'll need to fly commercial," she said. "I'll see about getting us some flights. Why don't you find a place for us to stay for a few days while we get settled in Aruba? A quiet, out-of-the-way spot would be nice, don't you think?"

By the time they left the dining room, Montebank had said a quick goodbye as Mateo's guy pushed him subtly toward the door.

Fidelia walked away from her home. There was no farewell, no hugs, not another word. Only the slam of a door more loudly than necessary.

FOUR

Montreal, Quebec, Friday November 18, 2022

After a succulent dinner in Old Montreal with her board of directors and senior management team, Suzanne Simpson stayed at the Four Seasons rather than travel north an hour by car or fifteen minutes by helicopter.

Shortly after everyone arrived at the hotel, Serge Boisvert rapped gently on the door to her suite before letting himself in with an electronic key. Suzanne was already wearing his favorite among her lingerie, a pink, almost transparent negligee that concealed little.

Dressed for their group dinner, Serge still wore his jacket with an open shirt collar, now with the top three buttons undone to display a few curls of chest hair. His brilliant white teeth drew her attention to his mouth and inviting lips.

She offered him a glass of chilled champagne from an opened bottle nestled in a mountain of ice in a large silver serving bowl. He took it as he gently wrapped an arm around her shoulders, drew her close to his chest, then kissed her. At first, he was gentle as his tongue entered her mouth, almost teasing. Soon, their embrace was unreserved passion. They broke only when Suzanne could no longer breathe.

"Sip your drink and let me catch my breath!" She laughed gleefully as she blurted out her playful admonishment.

Serge followed her instruction and walked further into her room toward a sofa in the living area. He took a tiny sip from the glass. Although he had attended the company affair, their only contact throughout the evening had been one discreet wink as Suzanne entered the restaurant's private room. She still assumed none of the other group members that evening was aware that her chief of security was also her lover.

Serge and Suzanne were long-time friends. Years earlier, he had worked for her when she led the Canadian supermarket chain John George Mortimer bought to bring her into the Multima conglomerate. As she climbed the corporate ladder and moved from Canada to the US, Serge accepted a job with the Royal Canadian

Mounted Police and worked his way up to its senior ranks. They had drifted apart for several years with only periodic contact.

It was a Multima crisis that brought them together again. Two years earlier, Suzanne had begged him to use his connections in law enforcement to investigate Dan Ramirez, her former chief of security. She'd expected it to be an uneventful formality, eliminating him from any involvement in the nasty kidnapping of a European colleague. Instead, it shocked both to learn Ramirez had betrayed his country and Multima Corporation by selling state and company information to Russia.

A few months after Ramirez's arrest, Suzanne offered Serge the top security role at Multima. Soon after, they became lovers, then something more. They'd kept their relationship secret for almost two years, but Suzanne had recently started imagining how she might carefully engineer a public transition of their affair. Their current arrangement was exhausting.

"You look gorgeous and incredibly inviting," Serge began. "But before we take this any further, I need to share some business information with you."

He set his champagne glass on the polished mahogany dining table in her suite and pulled out an armchair at one end, motioning for her to join him there. Reflexively, she pulled her almost transparent negligee more tightly around her as she noticed his tense shoulders and somber expression.

"You remember we discovered that software my predecessor wangled from the CIA? The one that starts recording conversations after detecting certain programmed keywords?" Serge waited until she nodded. "As we agreed, I kept it around. We thought we might need it one day."

Suzanne nodded again, showing a touch of impatience in her expression. He was taking a long time to get to his point while she sat there dressed for an entirely different purpose. To be sure her negligee didn't create a distraction, she crossed her arms and legs.

"As I listened to the discussion in today's board meeting about possibly buying Jeffersons Stores, I decided the situation might warrant a test of the software. We wouldn't want anyone in the meeting leaking word about the possibility of a takeover, would we?" His attempt to inject a little levity failed.

Suzanne instantly became more attentive, tilted her head slightly, and leaned toward him in interest.

"You picked up something?"

Serge nodded soberly and shook his head in a gesture of disgust. "I programmed the words 'Jeffersons,' 'acquisition,' and 'Multima' into the app. I also set the detection area for conversations within a kilometer circumference of the hotel. Just before we all left the hotel for dinner, I got an alert that the recording device had activated. When we got back a few minutes ago, I went to my room and listened to what the software captured."

He reached into his jacket pocket and pulled out a device the size of a phone, set it on the table between them, then, with a flourish, pushed a button.

"She's considering buying Jeffersons," they heard. "Major pushback from Fitzgerald and the director from Bank of the Americas."

Suzanne leaned closer to the phone. Although the voices were distorted electronically, there could be no doubt that Multima was the subject of their conversation. Several questions popped into her mind, but she continued listening before drawing conclusions.

"What's next?" the deeper voice asked.

"She sent him back to the drawing board. Expect nothing soon."

The recording ended there, leaving Serge and Suzanne looking at each other with perplexed expressions.

"Did you pick up either of the phone numbers?"

"No. The conversation was too brief, but I expect they were using burner phones anyway," Serge said. "If they were sophisticated enough to disguise their voices, it's unlikely they'd be careless enough to use traceable phones."

"Right. What are you thinking?"

Serge cleared his throat, glanced over her shoulder, then refocused to meet her eyes directly. "I'm concerned. Someone in the room today is feeding information to somebody. It could be a major investor. Somebody at Jeffersons. Perhaps someone in the business media. Or maybe something more sinister. Organized crime has taken a run at Multima before. We need to take it seriously."

"What do you recommend?" Suzanne leaned back in her chair, signaling a willingness to listen for as long as necessary.

As they sipped their glasses of champagne, minutes turned to more than an hour as Serge explored various steps he could take to glean insight into what was going on in the background of the board of directors' meeting. Suzanne rejected most of them. They were all either too intrusive for her liking or would get outside agencies like police forces involved. Finally, they reached a compromise she could live with.

After finishing a glass of champagne, they agreed to meet again in the morning. He'd need most of the night to put the tracers he wanted to program into the secret software and plant the agreed recording devices around the meeting room where the board would convene again at nine o'clock the following day.

With one last passionate embrace, they said goodnight.

"I'll be back at seven to wire you up before you get dressed," Serge said. His charming smile did little to satisfy her disappointment. Not only was she off to sleep without sexual satisfaction, but her mind was also racing with new challenges. The night could be a long one.

FIVE

Miami, Florida, Saturday November 19, 2022

Fidelia allowed Joe Montebank to enjoy a few hours of the good life on her leased Bombardier 7000 top-of-the-line private jet. Although she had pretended to be enthralled with the guy at dinner earlier, something about him seemed familiar. A couple more hours alone with him might jog her memory.

The posh aircraft impressed her guest. For a few minutes, he tested the cream-colored, plush leather seats that adjusted both cushion and back to almost infinite positions. Throughout, he sported a broad grin like a teenager with a prized new video game.

Of course, she could afford to buy a plane outright, but she preferred to lease. Someone else took care of the maintenance and provisions for depreciation while she could upgrade to the latest version of the jet whenever she chose.

Fidelia didn't bother with an inflight hostess to serve food and drinks, so she offered him the self-service option in the luxuriously appointed air kitchen. More elaborate than the reheating galley on commercial jets, her aircraft featured a microwave and convection oven, a refrigerator, and a coffeemaker. Montebank opened every drawer, checked behind every door, and made enough coffee to stay awake for a week.

She pointed him to the cabin operating guide and lost him for about an hour as he pored over all the high-tech features like the forty-inch television, the international internet access, and a lighting system designed to reduce jet lag.

About three hours after takeoff, she asked him to join her in the alcove at the rear that she used as an office. After he took in all the deluxe custom furniture and advanced technology surrounding her desk, she pointed toward two seats divided by a glass table mounted to the wall.

Fidelia brought her coffee from the desk, slipped off her shoes, and crossed her legs. She let him have a good look before she started. Measuring a guy's attraction before dealing with the business details was always useful. His blue eyes looked hungry.

"I'll drop you off in Miami." It was best to signal this session would be all business. "You can get a flight from there to Los Angeles about an hour after we touch down. Our co-pilot booked you a commercial ticket. He'll give you all the details before we arrive."

She studied his reaction. He camouflaged his disappointment well, but the sparkle in his eyes faded despite the cheerful smile. Still, he smoothly transitioned to his new reality.

"That's great, Fidelia. I appreciate you giving me a ride to Miami. That saves me almost a half day compared to the commercial flights out of Uruguay." He broadened his smile and reactivated the charm in his eyes.

It was time to probe a bit. "Do I correctly detect a hint of an Australian accent?"

"Yes! I grew up in Sydney and lived there until my early twenties. Been a California boy ever since." Her memory refreshed, she became more curious. "What kind of work did you do there?"

"I was a bartender, believe it or not. Had a lot of fun with that job, I did."

"Did you ever come across a restaurant owner named Oliver Williams? He had several locations in Sydney."

It was only an instant. The sparkle in his blue eyes dimmed, then he quickly caught himself.

"I did, actually. Worked for the man for a couple years. Very successful guy."

Fidelia needed no more for now.

He was the one tending bar the night of that orgy the Australian crime boss, Oliver Williams, organized for government officials in the outback. The one that claimed one of her best girls. Neither the police nor The Organization had found her killer.

"I want to be clear about how our new project in Aruba will work," Fidelia shifted gears calmly, with a tone of conviction. "Klaudia will be in charge, like I told everyone earlier. But I want to know everything they do. I expect you'll report to me daily. Who are their customers? How much are they charging clients? Who do they hire to work the phones?" She paused and waited for him to nod his understanding and agreement before she handed him a burner phone.

"Plan to spend about fifteen to twenty minutes with me at the end of every day. Use only this phone. I don't want Klaudia or Howard to know we're chatting and don't want any record of our calls. Do we understand each other?"

Montebank swallowed hard as he nodded again and appeared suitably concerned.

Fidelia paused for a second to reinforce that concern. "You'll also get out of the corporate espionage business. I'll make it worth your while. But you need to agree right now that any business that comes your way—starting January first—will go to Klaudia instead. Tell your customers whatever story you think they'll believe, but make sure you bring the business to Klaudia."

His mouth gaped open, his brow furrowed, and his face lit up scarlet red. Still, he didn't make a sound in protest. He looked scared, and that was exactly the reaction she wanted.

"I'll give you a third of my percentage from Klaudia, which you may recall is twenty-five percent of her total take. That means you'll be getting about eight percent of the total profits. I figure that will be about double what you earned last year if you play your cards right. You'll take home to Mrs. Montebank an amount that will keep her in the lavish lifestyle she demands, and the bank will forgive the hundred grand you owe."

"What ... what ...?" Montebank started to stammer out a question but was lost for words again.

Fidelia filled in the blanks. "Yeah, the savings and loan outfit who finally loaned you the money you were desperate for last year is a unit of ours. I'll fix it so your debt goes away, and they'll give you back that mortgage they took on your house. It'll stay off if you do your job with Klaudia, and you'll become a respectable sort of rich guy."

Montebank's color returned to normal, and the fear in his eyes retreated enough for her to close.

"Tell me you agree to everything, and tell me you'll work your tiny buns off to make Klaudia's company a success."

He nodded once. "I'll do it."

Fidelia waved him back to the plane's front section and stepped back toward the comfortable seat at her desk, punching the number of her current Australian country boss into her phone. Formerly in charge of the country's escort services business, the woman would surely be interested.

As expected, that call took only a few minutes before she ended it and hit the speed dial for Luigi Fortissimo's secure direct line.

He answered on the second ring.

"You were right, Luigi. He agreed to everything. Talk to Smith at your savings and loan. Cancel his mortgage and deduct the amount from this month's remissions to me."

"Okay. I'll handle 'em both." Luigi was usually a man of few words. "But if it wer' me, I wouldn't trust that bastard. He's cheated too many guys too many times." He spoke more slowly than usual, enunciating words more carefully, suppressing his New York working-class accent.

"I get it. Have your guys in LA continue to monitor his personal and office numbers for incoming and outgoing calls. Let's make sure he's not a plant. I also want a list of every business opportunity that comes his way for the next two years. If we find any names that don't show up on Klaudia's client list, Montebank better have a damned good explanation."

"You gonna cover the expense of phone monitoring, too?"

"No Luigi. I will not cover the expense. You're going to handle it because I asked you to do it. Small compensation for me giving you the US market, wouldn't you say?" Her tone had turned frosty. A lack of warmth was exactly what she wanted to convey to Luigi. Fidelia wanted to give him something to think about during the five hours until he met her at the airport in Teterboro, New Jersey.

Luigi had been her unwaveringly loyal personal protector when Fidelia had seized control of The Organization. She generously rewarded that loyalty, delegating to him ownership and control of their US crime business, with only a modest monthly commission to her.

While they met in New York over the next few days, that loyalty might be tested.

SIX

Oranjestad, Aruba, Monday November 21, 2022

When Fidelia split for New York with her private jet, she left Howard and Klaudia to find their way from Punta del Este in Uruguay to Aruba.

One wouldn't expect that to be much of an ordeal.

But, Klaudia was almost in tears of frustration when she reported to Howard the best that she could arrange was a departure from Punta del Este by car to Montevideo at three o'clock Sunday morning to catch a flight from Montevideo at seven fifteen to Bogota, Colombia. From there, they'd board a flight to Panama City, where they'd have a sixteen-hour wait until they departed again for a two-hour flight to Aruba on Monday.

Howard offered to book hotel rooms for a few hours of sleep in Panama and their reservations for a place to stay in Aruba. Of course, it irked both of them that Fidelia had flown almost directly over Aruba in her private jet and could easily have descended for a few minutes to let them off with minimal delay in her schedule.

It had all worked out, though. Both had packed all their belongings in a couple pieces of luggage, dined on an excellent meal prepared by Fidelia's chef, then retired for an early night's sleep Saturday before they started their journey.

Howard had charmed the owner of the small hotel he had booked in Aruba, and she had agreed to meet them at the airport and take them and their luggage directly to her inn.

Sandra of Sandra's Inn replied on the second ring when Howard called her from the arrivals area of the airport once they'd cleared immigration and collected their luggage. She remembered her offer and promised to meet them at the hotel beside the airport in ten minutes.

Klaudia and Howard agreed they should make their way to the designated nearby hotel entrance at a relaxed pace because ten minutes in Caribbean time would probably take longer. They joked and made a friendly wager about the time that would pass before their host arrived.

Howard won. His estimate was closest to the actual thirty minutes they stood in the hot Caribbean late-day sun before Sandra pulled up to the agreed meeting spot in a large, older Jeep with personalized license plates which read TIGER.

When Sandra stepped out of the SUV, she wore a sensible-length dress appropriate for an upscale office. Surprisingly, she also sported less sensible high heels, making her look slightly overdressed for her current role as a driver. She appeared more ready for a dinner engagement, with makeup, long black hair and bright red lipstick. She instantly charmed both her guests when she flashed a smile that showed lots of teeth.

She greeted them in English, but Klaudia had immediately detected a German accent. The women became instant friends with warm hugs and a torrent of laughter as they watched Howard lift and squeeze the luggage into the SUV's dusty rear compartment.

Sandra switched back to English as they readied for departure and insisted Howard sit up front with her.

She announced that she'd point out some highlights on the way to her hotel and assumed the role of tour guide for the fifteen-minute drive from the airport. She drove slowly through the old city center and out to a quiet residential neighborhood, where she parked in a lot suitable for a half-dozen cars across the street from her inn.

Sandra's Inn appeared to blend in with all the other upscale homes along the street.

Had he made some mistake?

But two small signs caught his eye as they dragged their bags closer to a locked gate and fence. One said Sandra's Inn, the accommodation he had booked. Below it, another sign said Bargain Rates Hostel.

Sandra commanded an associate to help Howard with the bags and led her procession down a wide sidewalk, running along the side of what appeared to be a pleasant home and toward its backyard. Where one would expect to see a front lawn in an American subdivision, this place featured an area entirely covered in cement with a half-dozen dogs of various sizes and shapes wandering aimlessly or snoozing on the hard surface in a bit of shade.

As they reached the rear of the building, everything transformed.

A rectangular pool divided the area into four sections. The water was a brilliant turquoise color, reflecting the late afternoon sunshine, its water rippling in a gentle breeze. Behind the pool stood a row of compact rooms painted a basic white with red trim around the windows and doors. Motel-type units. It looked like there were six of them.

Opposite, forming the back of what had at first appeared to be a house, were three doorways. One was marked "Office," hand-painted with faded red letters on a dull white background.

At the opposite end of the pool, several palm trees, cacti, and a few lonely flowers created an alcove for relaxation, with lounge chairs of various sizes and descriptions scattered about the area. There was lots of green, very little of any other color.

Finally, in a shaded area just in front of the pool, a half-dozen people sat in comfortable patio chairs, sipping wine or beer and chatting in two or three different languages. It all created a welcoming atmosphere, but Howard spotted one problem.

Where was the "Unique Penthouse with the Best View of Aruba"—the suite he'd reserved for himself?

Before he could ask Sandra about the apparent discrepancy, she had already reached out, grasped one of each of their hands, and led Klaudia and Howard toward the group clustered under the largest palm. There she made introductions.

She announced that Howard and Klaudia would stay at the inn for two weeks, then individually presented each person by name with a brief description. Some were guests. Others were employees. Some stayed at a nearby hostel. A couple people were simply friends.

Before Howard could ask about the penthouse or check-in procedures, Sandra opened a fresh bottle of red wine. She poured tall glasses for her newly arrived guests before passing around the palm tree, refilling glasses for the expanded group.

"Sit and chat for a while before we get you to your rooms," Sandra insisted.

Klaudia and Howard exchanged quick glances, shrugged, and followed their host's instructions. Within seconds, the welcoming group was posing questions. Where did they come from? How long did they plan to stay in Aruba? And questions about their backgrounds.

Howard was at ease. He had an excellent memory and confidence that he would remember all the lies he told. Klaudia was more reticent. He couldn't be sure whether it was her German reserve or concerns about her ability to remember the details of the stories they were fabricating. But her answers were usually short.

"We're business colleagues," she answered one question. "Here doing research."

Soon, the amiable group realized Klaudia preferred to listen rather than talk, so questions drifted toward Howard for amplification.

"Our research is rather confidential. Our employer doesn't allow us to talk openly about our activities because of intense competition in our industry. We're in the advertising and promotion game. A small outfit based in the US."

With a few more questions and sips of wine, the assembled group eventually broke into separate conversations in multiple languages. The new arrivals leaned back in their lounge chairs, listening and observing as much as possible.

One guest in particular caught Howard's attention. His name was Earl Boyante, an American from Maryland with a bubbling personality, a loud voice, and strong opinions about every subject the group discussed.

Earl had an odd shape. Shorter than average, he carried massive body weight that gave him a profile more round than tall. He walked with a pronounced limp and used a cane whenever he stood. Sandra proudly introduced him as a long-term guest who had spent the entire winter at Sandra's Inn last year and was planning to do the same again this year.

Howard thought the guy might be a useful source of information and made a mental note to chat with him more, privately.

Listening to the conversations, they learned Sandra lived in the section that appeared to be a large residence with her menagerie of dogs, and that the nearby hostel was an addition to the building accessed by the doorway furthest along the back of the house. The hostel had space for up to a dozen students and travelers looking for bargain basement rooms. Howard still saw no evidence of a unique penthouse with a magnificent view.

After about an hour of conversation with the group, Sandra

realized the dinner hour was approaching and instructed the young fellow who had helped with the luggage to guide them to their rooms, starting with Klaudia.

There was no need for more paperwork that evening, she declared. They'd verify passports and complete the check-in process the next morning. With a tug at Klaudia's arm and a few German words, she led her guest toward a room halfway along the complex, at the midpoint of the pool.

"Call me when you're settled in," Klaudia instructed Howard as Sandra tugged her from the comfortable lounge chair.

Minutes later, Sandra returned. In Spanish, she instructed a helpful junior associate to carry their guest's bags upstairs and, with an exaggerated smile, motioned for Howard to follow.

They headed toward the door with a sign above the entrance that read "Office."

Inside the doorway, a counter displayed promotional materials for local sights and a large black cat. Stretched out sleeping, the cat appeared about three feet long and looked to weigh about twenty pounds. It opened one eye to peek at Howard as they reached the narrow stairway Sandra had already started to climb.

Howard followed a few steps behind, using a handrail for balance, given the steep pitch and limited light. Sandra opened the door, entered, and gestured welcomingly for him to follow her into the room.

Howard looked around the tiny area they had entered. There was a small brown sofa on one side of the room. Next to another wall, a faded wood table topped with a small bowl of plastic fruit sat with one padded chair in front. Beyond the table, Howard noticed a tiny toilet, a porcelain sink, and a shower. A blue plastic shower curtain was open. Left of the bathroom was the kitchen, equipped with a refrigerator, a two-burner hotplate, and another sink, this one stainless steel.

Off this main living area, Howard noticed the advertised two bedrooms. Each room was large enough to hold a standard bed, with only enough room to squeeze past the beds to reach small closets clearly added in as an afterthought.

"It's smaller than I expected," Howard said after taking it all in for a couple moments.

"You have a wonderful view." Sandra pointed to the windows in every room that displayed much of the island, including a cruise ship docked in the harbor downtown. "If you're not happy with it, let's discuss it tomorrow after you've had a good sleep."

On that note, Sandra left the room. As she reached the doorway, she added, "Oh, don't forget the light for your apartment is out here in the corridor."

"Aren't you leaving a key to my room?" Howard asked casually.

"Oh, there's no lock on this door. But don't worry. In twenty years we've never had a problem."

Astonished, Howard moved closer to the doorway for a better look. Sure enough, there was no lock on the door. A hole drilled in the door at the factory looked like it had never been used. In a respectful but resolute tone, he gave Sandra instructions.

"Tonight, I have no choice. I believe you when you say there's never been a problem, but I expect to see a good lock on that door before noon tomorrow. Or Klaudia and I are both out of here."

Sandra nodded and formed a hospitable smile before she backed out of the doorway again.

Howard unpacked what he could in the limited closet space and stashed both pieces of his luggage in the other bedroom. With a deep breath, he set off down the narrow staircase to see if Klaudia had fared any better with her room.

Across the pool, she sat outside her unit on a straight chair and waved enthusiastically for Howard to join her.

"How's your room?" Howard whispered.

"Fine. Yours?"

"Let's go have some dinner and I'll tell you all about it."

It was probably the right time to share his trepidation that this Aruba idea might be much more challenging than he'd thought.

SEVEN

Nassau, The Bahamas, Tuesday November 22, 2022

Fidelia Morales didn't make it as far as New York. In the air, just thirty minutes after her stop to drop off Joe Montebank in Miami, the secure communication device she used on the aircraft beeped. It was Luigi.

"Bad news. Just heard from my advance guy at Teterboro. Pokin' around with his connections, found out someb'dy put out a CBP alert 'n there's four FBI scum waitin' for ya."

"What? How the fuck did they know I was coming? You must have a leak among your guys!" Fidelia rarely cursed and seldom used an accusatory tone, but this was serious.

Only Montebank, Klaudia, Howard, and Luigi knew her US destination. Montebank was scared shitless and wouldn't dare cross her this early. Klaudia wouldn't betray her, and it seemed too early for Howard to try something stupid. Only Luigi—or one of his people—would have reason to tip off the FBI, who had then apparently alerted American customs and immigration authorities. She bristled as he continued.

"I know ya wanna' talk a bit. If ya wanna' head over ta' Nassau, I can get my jet and meet ya there. Was headed ta' Teterbora' anyhow. Can be there'n 'bout three hours." The working class accent became more pronounced again.

Fidelia paused for only a few moments to weigh her options. It would be folly to land in New York and hope to avoid alerted US customs and border officials plus a contingent from the FBI. Her US lawyers were the best money could buy, but who knew what either agency wanted with her?

The Organization controlled a successful casino on the Bahamian islands, so she could use the diversion to check out the operation and let the guys there know she was paying attention. She and Luigi could have their meeting in The Bahamas. If Luigi's people could dig up why the authorities might want to see her, they could decide whether she should hang out in The Bahamas for a few days or risk landing in the US, maybe at another airport.

"Okay. Head down to Nassau. But before you leave, find out from your guys inside the FBI and CBP what the hell is going on. And get someone on your security team to find your leak. I'll slip over to Nassau now. Should be there in a half hour. I'll tour the casino, then come back and meet with you on my jet. Park your plane beside mine. Don't clear immigration or anything like that. Got it?"

"Ya, no problem. I'll try ta find out what I can."

"I know you'll do your best, Luigi. But be sure you pull out all the stops. When you get here, I need to know what's going on."

Fidelia buzzed the pilot and gave him his new instructions. A couple minutes later, she felt the aircraft bank and make a wide turn to reverse direction. A few seconds later, the pilot buzzed her to confirm they'd land in Nassau in twenty-seven minutes.

Her next call on the ultra-secure aircraft communication device was to her lawyer in New York. She caught the woman in a cab on her way to the office. Fidelia explained the recent developments and asked the well-connected woman to find out what she could from her contacts in Washington.

The attorney confirmed the wisdom of staying out of the US until she got to the bottom of the issue and laughed as she commented that Nassau was probably a good place to be marooned for a few days while they sorted it all out.

Fidelia didn't laugh. Her tone was polite but formal as she ended the call with her lawyer, advising that she expected the issue to be resolved in hours, not days.

This sort of mess wouldn't happen if Luigi was paying attention.

"Mateo," she called out to her dozing security guy in the seat facing her. "Arrange a car in Nassau to meet us at the jet in a half hour. Don't use Luigi's guys or any of your usual contacts in The Bahamas. Google something if you don't have another source. Tell them we're touring the island and will return to the airport after a couple hours."

With a nod, her bodyguard started punching keys in his phone as Fidelia made another call. She reached Klaudia outdoors, with raucous voices in the background, and issued a new set of instructions to the groggy woman.

After a mild initial protest that Fidelia was asking for too much too soon, her German friend consented. She'd look for a way to digitally latch on to the American devices.

EIGHT

Oranjestad, Aruba, Friday November 25, 2022

Despite Howard's disappointment that his "Unique Penthouse with the Best View of Aruba" more resembled ramshackle accommodations, Klaudia was less unhappy. Conversation at their dinner table that Monday evening had surprised him.

"Sandra's Inn's not a terrible spot," Klaudia said. "The residential neighborhood keeps us off the radar of the authorities in Aruba and away from the throngs of tourists who could complicate our lives. Plus, I like having direct access to young travelers without much money. Remember, Joe Montebank suggested that hungry young people make good espionage candidates."

Howard didn't reply right away. He hadn't yet fully adjusted to Fidelia's dictate that Klaudia was running their show in Aruba and he was a supporting character. He trod lightly.

"You're okay with your room?" he asked after a moment or two of reflection.

"Yeah. It's nothing special, but the bed looks comfortable, the air conditioner works, and Sandra assured me there's hot water. Apparently, my room is the only one in the complex with a water heater." Klaudia giggled. "If you need to come to my room, I'll let you have a hot shower. It's only for a couple weeks, anyway. I'm sure we'll find an apartment or house that works better for us in the longer term."

With his new "boss" comfortable with her temporary living arrangements, Howard focused on the American, Earl Boyante. He sensed the guy had some potential.

Over the next few days, they became new best friends.

Earl had a few basic characteristics. He loved to talk loudly and often. He was as passionate about drinking beer as he was about talking. Beaches and sand were his primary interests in Aruba. His lifestyle was dreadful, but his mind was as sharp as anyone Howard had encountered in his long career.

At Surfside Beach in Oranjestad—the capital of Aruba—folks called Earl the "bucket man" for his propensity to order beers in a metal bucket packed with ice to keep them cool and to share them with everyone in sight. Howard joined him for a few hours every day that week and picked up the tab a couple days.

Each time, the total came to over five hundred US dollars, but the locals loved Earl.

Sandra was another unpolished diamond. Once she became comfortable that Howard and Klaudia were only colleagues, her charm intensified, and she became more daring. Almost every morning, she swam in the pool below Howard's room, shedding a towel before she dove in, then parading nude halfway around the pool to collect it again when she finished her five or six laps.

In only a few days, by getting closer to Sandra and Earl, Howard gleaned more about how the Caribbean island worked than one could have hoped to learn over a period of months.

"PETAR's the key," Howard whispered as they sat in wooden lounge chairs outside Klaudia's room beneath the palm trees a few days later. "It's the telecommunications company here. That's where I changed the SIM cards in our phones so we'd have local numbers."

"The company's sure got lots of offices. It seems I pass a different PETAR location every time I take a walk, regardless of the route. Why's it important for us?"

"If we can get someone inside those offices, we might get access to tons of info stored in their systems. I'm talking about data related to residents here, but we should also be able to tap into information about the thousands of upscale visitors here from both the US and the Netherlands."

His voice rose slightly with enthusiasm as he outlined the potential. Klaudia raised a finger of caution to her lips, and he reverted to a whisper. "I'm thinking we should also be able to listen in on some of those conversations if we can plant recording software that's triggered by specific words."

Klaudia listened but looked off into the distance, either skeptical or distracted. Howard waited for her reply.

"Fidelia wants me to do some listening in the US, too. So far, I'm running into brick walls. I've heard the American CIA has that kind of software, but where could we possibly find the stuff they use?"

"They might already have the basic software on some of the

equipment in those PETAR buildings. Here, it's rumored the telecom outfit cooperates with the CIA. Remember, we're only about twenty miles off the coast of Venezuela. It would make sense for a spy agency to listen in on a rogue government from here." Howard let her digest that possibility before he added a second thought.

"I'm sure Luigi's guys can find us the software in Silicon Valley if we need to install our own. But it would still probably be better to have someone we own inside PETAR."

Klaudia stiffened at his mention of Luigi and shook her head slowly. "No, we can't use Luigi's guys. Think of another way."

Howard tilted his head, showing interest and hoping for more information, but Klaudia didn't explain. Instead, she headed off in a different direction.

"Your new buddy, Earl, probably won't help us penetrate PETAR. I doubt their employees are drinking beer on the beach most days." She paused for an instant and smiled mischievously, without a hint of sarcasm. Then she carried on.

"I think we should focus on Sandra. She claims to have lived here for about twenty years. Speaks some Dutch and has passable Spanish. And she seems to know lots of people here, including folks connected to the police and government. She has her eye on you. Maybe it would be a good time to get to know her better."

"Fair enough. I'll do that," Howard agreed. "Have you made any progress with an office for us here?"

"I've looked at a few locations with the real estate agent Sandra recommended, but nothing seems right. You want to poke around a bit too?"

"Not yet. I'm not sure that'll be useful. But I've got a couple ideas brewing. Let me think about them for a few days. We still have time before Montebank arrives to help us settle in," Howard said.

"Yeah. Joe sent me a text today. He'll fly in on the tenth of January. We should try to have our office ready and a candidate or two for him to work with. I'll spend some time with the hostel crowd over the next few days. One German guy looks like he might have some potential."

NINE

Fort Myers, Florida, Monday November 28, 2022

Thankfully, the fireworks Suzanne had feared on the second day of the board meeting didn't materialize. The directors handled the rest of the agenda quickly and efficiently, with minimal discord, before they set off to various destinations around the globe.

After the sessions, Suzanne waited almost three full days for her security chief, Serge Boisvert, to listen to all the recordings from each of the hidden microphones he'd planted in the meeting room and the cars transporting the individual members to Montreal's west-end airport.

"There's nothing there," he said before she could ask.

"I guess that's good. If somebody is poking around, at least they aren't making it a priority."

Serge raised his eyebrows a shade, then nodded. "That's a logical conclusion, and I don't completely disagree with you. But my understanding of the darker side of human nature tells me the probability that something sinister is going on has just increased." He paused a moment.

"My gut tells me we might have alerted whoever was involved in the first conversation. They probably avoided any additional talk until they could be sure we weren't listening in. With your okay, I'll continue to poke around the airwaves to see if something turns up over the next week or two."

She approved his request, then jumped back into her never-ending workload. With Thanksgiving approaching in the US, Suzanne countered any potential loneliness around missed traditional family get-togethers with her usual devotion to her job. Since John George Mortimer and her mother had died a few years earlier, there were no family members to celebrate a holiday with, so she immersed herself in reports, study, and data as she had for most of her adult life.

As the end of their fiscal year rapidly approached, Suzanne drilled down on details of the proposed plans for each of Multima's businesses. The Supermarkets case alone was over a thousand pages long. Many of those pages were graphs and charts, but the amount of data included was still overwhelming, and it was imperative to understand it all.

Of course, Gordon Goodfellow, the leader of the Supermarkets business, compared his projected profits without acquiring Jeffersons Stores with the robustly rosier results he predicted should they buy the company. Despite the reticence of some on the board to support an acquisition of that magnitude, Suzanne understood why the idea was so appealing to Goodfellow and his management team.

The Multima Financial Services business strategies were predictably conservative, although she detected the handiwork of James Fitzgerald's protégé, Natalia Tenaz. The young woman had caught James's eye from the day she joined the marketing department a decade earlier. For a few years, he affectionately referred to Natalia as his favorite resource in business intelligence. Now he was grooming her to fill his role when he soon retired.

Her research skills and influence were evident as the Financial Services presentation made a strong case for dramatically increasing marketing to Latino Americans. Given her upbringing, that orientation wasn't surprising, but Natalia used solid data and conservative forecasting to predict results no chief executive could ignore.

The young woman's pages devoted to rapid expansion in South America were equally compelling. Suzanne had little difficulty visualizing Natalia around boardroom tables, laying the foundations for a management team to grow Multima's credit card and mortgage businesses in new regions ripe for harvesting.

For, as much as Suzanne appreciated James's expertise and wise counsel, she'd noticed less energy and enthusiasm for his role in the last few months.

The pandemic had been a factor. Like many others, he found it challenging to have his team working remotely, connected only by technology and good intentions. But his age was a factor too. He was three years past traditional retirement age, and he'd already deferred his corporate escape twice at Suzanne's desperate bidding.

After her review, Suzanne asked the business units to polish up their proposals for final approval at the December board meeting.

The copies she returned to each division had dozens of questions, notations, and suggestions in the borders for the teams to consider if they wanted to win her support and persuade the board to move forward. Most poignant was her advice to Goodfellow. She told him to resubmit the business plan without including the acquisition of Jeffersons Stores.

Naturally, she called him first to let him know her thoughts. He protested—as she expected he would, but his resistance wasn't strong. In the end, she guessed he'd also realized the timing of his idea probably made approval unlikely. That happened. Running a company often meant taking a step backward before taking a couple steps forward.

Serge had already celebrated Thanksgiving with his Canadian family in October, a month earlier than the US holiday. So they spent the evenings that long weekend together, and she couldn't remember three more satisfying nights when they left her rented home in the Laurentian Mountains together.

The Multima corporate jet waited for them that Monday morning at nearby Montreal Mirabel Airport.

It was Suzanne's first day of annual visits to as many Multima Supermarkets in the US as her schedule allowed. With over two thousand store locations, visiting more than a handful was impossible. But it was a tradition she'd started a decade earlier when she'd managed the Supermarkets division.

The week after Thanksgiving was an appropriate time to meet employees in person, express her thanks for all their efforts for the company, and boost morale for the busiest sales month of the entire year.

She planned to visit thirty-five stores in five days, spending about an hour at each location. The corporate jet would transport her from city to city at the end of each day, and Serge's security team would handle the ground travel, with rented limos shuttling them between locations within each city. Including the security team and her closest advisors, the entourage would number about a dozen people.

That morning, they flew toward Fort Myers as the sun rose to the east of the city. Suzanne had asked her pilot to request special permission from air traffic control to fly low and slowly over Fort

Myers Beach before landing at the airport. They swung out over the gulf and approached from south of Naples, then headed north along the coastline at the slowest speed possible.

She wanted to see the damage Hurricane Ian had caused to the beautiful and popular golden coast of the Gulf of Mexico. It was one of the deadliest storms in US history, and more than one hundred people had died from the high winds and massive storm surge from the Gulf.

That morning, Suzanne sat in speechless horror as she took in the devastation from the window of her plane. The carnage was everywhere. The storm had pushed entire buildings off their moorings and far ashore with a massive surge of water. Many buildings had collapsed, leaving ugly mounds of twisted remnants of former houses, hotels and stores scattered across the landscape. Although the streets were now clear of debris, mountains of furniture, appliances, and fallen trees still lined both sides of the main roadway on Fort Myers Beach.

In the harbor, dozens of boats piled randomly on top of each other like discarded toys, most destroyed beyond repair. Abandoned cars and trucks sat idle in driveways or spaces that once served as parking lots. Some still had seaweed drying on their hoods and salt residue baked on their sides.

Experts had repaired the causeway bridge to the mainland to make it passable, and dozens of contractors' trucks already dotted the streets that morning. Electric power workers, roofing specialists, handymen, and construction crews were visible from the air, with commercial vehicles of every description scattered across the terrain.

At the end of the beach, the pilot dipped the right wing of the aircraft and headed eastward along the Caloosahatchee River and past Suzanne's home on her right. As the pilot made another tilt of the wings toward the private jet airport, she glimpsed the house. It looked okay from the air, with only a few tiles missing on the roof. Flooding from the surge had now receded, and the broad river looked normal. Still, she knew the interior of the magnificent home built originally for John George Mortimer was anything but normal.

The two feet of water that flooded her home had destroyed everything on the ground level. Workers needed to scour the interior and rip out floors, walls and insulation. It would be months before she could hope to use the place when she visited the Southern US. Her shock and sadness from when she first heard the news about the ravages of the hurricane returned, and a lump suddenly formed in her throat as she turned to Serge.

"It was the right choice to start my annual store visits here in Fort Myers. Many of our team suffered the awful consequences of the storm and now have to rebuild their lives while they work in our stores to serve customers and pay their bills," she said.

Serge nodded somberly, clearly as shocked as she was to witness the extent of the devastation.

"Anything we need to change during the store visits?" Serge planned to accompany the entourage in the background. His would be the voice in the bodyguards' ears when they needed to move on or cut short a meeting.

"Yes. Let's be flexible with the time allowances. I don't want our store staff to feel rushed. Sensitize your people to the trauma. If we run long today, we can make up time somewhere later in the week when emotions are less raw."

Only a few moments later, Suzanne felt the reverse thrust of the engines and heard screeching brakes as the plane's tires met the concrete runway of Page Field. From the window, she could see the airport tarmac for private aircraft was still virtually deserted.

TEN

Nassau, The Bahamas, Tuesday November 29, 2022

Fidelia's surprise visit to the MarBa Casino overlooking a magnificent beach on the island's north side was only the start of a week-long stay in The Bahamas. She knew the general manager from her earlier days managing the global escort businesses for The Organization. MarBa Casino always housed several high-priced women from around the globe because it was only minutes by helicopter or private jet from the wealthy millionaires living on Florida's east coast.

Moments after she entered the casino's door that morning, Juan Liso greeted her effusively with open arms and turned on his charm.

"What brings you to our beautiful island? Will you be able to stay a few days?"

At first, she told him no; she was only there to look around. But Luigi called before they had completed a grand tour of the casino.

"Problems with da jet. Pilots can't get it started. Can't getta mechanic till tomorrow or the next day."

"Seriously? No technicians are available to repair a fifty-million-dollar jet immediately?"

"It's that fuckin' corona. Ever since it started, service is fuckin' awful. Happen'd ta me last month too. Had ta rent one fer a few days."

"Why don't you rent one today?"

"Can't. Tried that at the four private airports 'round the city. None available ta rent till tomorra or da next day. Ya wanna do it by phone?"

Fidelia thought about it for a moment. She needed the meeting to be in person. The Multima scheme was too important. By phone, it was harder to detect his lies. She wanted more than the intensity of his accent to signal truth or intentions, and he knew that.

"No. We haven't seen each other for a while. I'd rather do it in person. Juan is taking great care of me here. The beach is inviting. I might even play the slots for a while. Why don't we make it next Tuesday instead?"

Nothing threw the guy off course more than suggesting that whatever they had to talk about was less urgent than a few days of relaxation in the Caribbean. He didn't disappoint.

"Don' need ta wait dat long. Why don' we do it 'n justa couple days from now? Sure da plane can be fixed by then."

Fidelia detected the exact note of concern she wanted. She'd let him stew for a few more days. It better suited her purposes and gave Klaudia more time to plant her software.

"Next Tuesday will be fine, Luigi." Her tone carefully hid any hint of reassurance. However, she added a bit to be sure he got the message. "But let's make sure you have a plan to be here at nine on Tuesday morning. I don't care if you have to drive to Miami and hire a yacht to bring you over. And send me your November numbers so far, for everything."

Fidelia had relaxed, gambled a little, and studied all the files Luigi had transferred to her within minutes of the call. At 8:52 Tuesday morning, Luigi knocked respectfully on the door of the luxurious penthouse suite Juan Liso had generously offered.

To keep him wondering, she greeted Luigi with a friendly hug. When they finished exchanging air kisses, she planted a more passionate one. His lips didn't part with a gentle probe, so she knew his intentions were only business related.

"Let's sit on the balcony to talk before it gets too hot. Mateo checked. The rooms on this floor and for four floors below this one are all vacant. We can talk openly."

They chatted for over two hours, with Fidelia guiding the conversation's direction. Luigi was always comfortable with that approach, so she used the opportunity to catch up on details about his family, several mutual friends from The Organization, and even a few of the football games he'd watched from his private box at MetLife Stadium.

Although she'd lived in New York, Fidelia never developed a taste for football. She'd never understood the violence and punishment the players used to move a ball back and forth on a 100-yard field to collect points. True, the players earned good money, but elite women working for The Organization did just as well. Her best women made as much as the football stars, usually with far fewer life-altering injuries and less pain.

But Luigi was a fan, so she humored him as he recounted his frustration that the Jets would miss the playoffs again. A Super Bowl remained a far-off and perennially elusive dream.

As the day became hotter and more humid, she glanced at her watch and suggested they move inside. There, Fidelia probed for more details about activities in The Organization's US businesses.

Illicit drug sales had grown during the pandemic and continued to increase as society gradually returned to its more typical ways. With its legalization in New York, and several other states, marijuana sales dipped initially. Luigi had astutely bought up a string of legal dispensaries using numbered companies, letting the previous owners continue to manage their stores if they toed the line.

Sales of habit-forming drugs like cocaine and heroin increased each year. However, Fidelia was growing uncomfortable with the amount of fentanyl the people Luigi sold to were adding to their products. Authorities took more notice when people died.

"How long do you think we have before governments rewrite the rules?" she asked.

"Up 'n Canada, we're gettin' flack. Couple cities started safe dispens'n sites. Take'n away a bit. In da US, crazy fundamentl'st Christians'll never buy in. Business is safe for so long as we'll be 'round."

Fidelia wasn't sure, but she held those thoughts for later and pivoted to an unstated reason for her visit. Luigi likely wasn't prepared, and she expected a more forthright answer.

"Tell me more about your message last month, the one about buying a senator."

Luigi tossed back his head and laughed as he answered. "Rented a senator's prob'ly better. Told ya we gave a hundred grand ta that Republican guy sent by the Shadow b'fore the election in November. Promis'd ta give us warnings 'bout anythin' affect'n our businesses."

Fidelia grit her teeth at mention of the Shadow, a despised rival who meddled in everything from real estate to politics. She should have guessed he was behind this new nonsense.

"You must remember that Giancarlo Mareno always warned us to avoid getting involved with politicians. Said it was a death wish. Why'd you get involved this time?"

"Times change. 'Sides, I worked with Giancarlo a lot more than you. Can tell ya, he had more'n one politician 'n his pocket. All my guys 'greed we needed ta keep tabs on da guys makin' da laws. Figur'd it didn't hurt ta have a line ta the Shadow too."

All right, let's see how stressed you are. "Does your new senator even know who the Shadow is?"

"Naah, thinks it's someb'dy close ta da old president. Can't be sure, though."

Fidelia stood up to show her concern about his cavalier answers to her questions. Luigi had worshipped Mareno and his opinions when he ran The Organization. *What changed?*

"I'm concerned, Luigi. I'm reading stories about your guy. He falsified his resume, took in a lot of money personally that funded his campaign, hangs out with folks they can trace back to us. Do you know about that?"

"That's just da New York Times talkin'. Everbody'll forget in a few days. He already got on a new committee ta make new rules fer crypto. We can make a fortune again soon."

"Howard Knight thinks crypto's almost finished. He recommends we not play there anymore. I think he's right."

"Maybe. But fer the US, I wanna keep my options open." Luigi stood up as he spoke, signaling his impatience as he stomped to the suite's refrigerator and pulled out a beer. "Do what ya want for the rest of the world, but I'm gonna milk this guy ta get a' inside track on crypto 'n make sure the government stays outta the rest of our businesses."

His last words reflected newly found confidence. Fidelia paused and bought some time by adjusting the curtains on the picture window to block some of the shifting sunlight. She'd given Luigi the American market. She wasn't his manager. He paid her the agreed 25 percent commission monthly and never complained. But the information back from her lawyer in Washington wasn't good. Luigi's involvement with the guy ran deeper than he let on, and the senator was a fraud in every way.

"Be careful Luigi. Like Giancarlo, I don't trust a politician to do anything. To me, this guy sounds like trouble. Our relationship is good, and I intend to keep it that way. But if your guy in Congress attracts any unwanted attention for The Organization—from the US government or the Shadow—our deal is off." Her tone hardened as she made the threat, and she closed her lips tightly as she finished the sentence to be sure there could be no doubt about her intentions.

Luigi usually backed off and changed his tune when she gave a direct and unequivocal order. This time he signaled why Multima Corporation was on his radar.

"Another thing we gotta talk about in the new year. We'll get Multima this time, but Sugimori still pays commissions on Jeffersons Stores to ya. Jeffersons is an American company. He's makin' big bucks in my territory. Need ya to find a way to gimme a share." His accent reflected more confidence, and his jaw jutted out as he made the demand. His black eyes fired up more than Fidelia had ever seen.

She raised the bar. "We'll talk about it when I can safely return to the US. You know I'll be fair, but I want this threat hanging over my head from the FBI and CBP gone. Get that fixed. We'll reschedule a date for me to visit. Then we'll talk about Jeffersons."

"I hear ya loud and clear, Fidelia. Let me poke 'round with my guys ta see if there's anythin' ta worry 'bout. OK if I get back ta ya in the new year?"

Fidelia smiled, eased back into the comfortable chair, calmly crossed her legs and continued their review of how The Organization was doing in the US. She didn't raise the question of Multima again, nor did Luigi.

Their discussions were productive, and Fidelia eventually conveyed satisfaction with Luigi's profitable leadership of The Organization's largest source of income. It was clear Luigi would send at least another half-billion dollars from the US to her bank accounts in the coming year.

The sun dipped below the horizon as she said goodbye to a somewhat chastened Luigi before he headed back to the private airport minutes from the casino. Then she set the wheels of her new scheme in motion.

"Mateo, I want to live in Curaçao for a few months. It'll be best for me to keep an eye on Klaudia and Howard from there. Aruba's close and New York's only a few hours away."

She waited for him nod understanding, then expanded her instructions.

"Choose one of your guys to find me a secure place to rent there. Nobody's to know. It doesn't need to be palatial. Enough room for you and your guys to live comfortably in one wing and another wing for a few guests and me with a secure room like we have in Uruguay. Until we can buy one, get them to rent a place for a few months. I plan to use it from the first of the year. And let the pilots know we'll return to Punta del Este tonight, dropping off your guy in Curaçao en route. Let's see if they can be ready to leave by eight."

ELEVEN

Oranjestad, Aruba, Tuesday January 3, 2023

On time, as promised, Joe Montebank trailed Klaudia into the spacious third-floor office they'd rented in Aruba's main city. Both plunked themselves down in the two comfortable office chairs, facing Howard Knight across a massive walnut desk they'd found a few days earlier in the lobby of a hotel on Palm Beach undergoing renovations.

Howard rose to greet them and offered a friendly handshake to the fellow who would teach them to become corporate spies. Then he closed the door to his private office. Earl Boyante had agreed to become their first employee and was hanging out in a separate private office a few steps down the corridor.

The first conversation with Montebank had to be confidential. They needed to test the guy and milk him for as much info as possible before they set him loose on Earl.

Before Howard returned to his chair, Montebank started talking. "I've got some great news to share with you." His smile appeared genuine and broad. His eyes sparkled, and his tone conveyed barely contained enthusiasm. "Last Friday, I got a call from what I think can be your first customer if you want the deal."

"Tell us about it." Howard tried to match Montebank's enthusiasm, but his smile faded as soon as he delivered the words. Skepticism had always been part of his nature.

"The customer is a huge supermarket chain in the US called Jeffersons Stores. They're willing to spend a hundred grand if we can get the info they need by the end of January. Their target's another big chain called Multima Supermarkets. Heard of them?"

Howard and Klaudia exchanged glances without changing their expressions. Of course, they knew Multima. Years earlier, Howard had wormed The Organization into partial ownership of the company and tried to take it over. Unfortunately, John George Mortimer, the CEO at the time, thwarted his scheme. It was the disaster that first caused Howard to flee The Organization and the wrath of its kingpin back then, Giancarlo Mareno. Everyone in the criminal outfit knew about it.

Klaudia recovered first. "Isn't Multima the chain that owns the Farefour stores in Europe?"

"Yep. It's the same conglomerate. They also operate stores in Asia and Latin America but use different brand names. Jeffersons Stores would like to know the names and contact details of every district manager in their retail operations, the chain of command in each of their distribution centers, and the hierarchy of the technology department at the Atlanta headquarters. They plan to go on a hiring binge."

Howard listened impassively and worked to ensure that his body language conveyed nothing. He knew the history behind Jeffersons Stores. The company was owned by an outfit that was a front for the Japanese Yakuza, The Organization's criminal element in Japan. Every few years, somebody in Japan decided their US subsidiary should take a run at Multima Supermarkets. This scheme to get information was probably much more than a hiring binge.

Howard changed the conversation's direction to buy time. "Less than thirty days to collect all that information seems challenging. What did you tell Jeffersons?"

"I told them I'd have to get back to them. I figured if I could meet the folks you plan to hire and get a feel for how quickly we can train them, we could decide if their timeline was realistic or not."

"That makes sense," Klaudia said.

For the next half hour, Klaudia and Howard posed questions to drill down on the specifics of what Jeffersons wanted and how Montebank had arrived at the amount of one hundred thousand dollars as a fee. Both took pains not to reveal the extent of Howard's knowledge about the structure and management of Multima Supermarkets.

Although he'd been out of the loop at Multima for over six years, Howard's almost photographic memory still held thousands of details about the company's management structure and organization charts.

"Did you leave some wiggle room in the fee?" Howard studied Montebank to gauge the truthfulness of his answer.

"Probably. They offered a hundred grand. I told them we needed to work up a detailed estimate after I met with you."

Howard smiled at the answer. Jeffersons' price was going to be over double that amount before they reached any agreement.

"Let's start with your first assessment of a candidate. He's an American named Earl. I think you're going to like him."

When they called him in, it turned out Earl didn't make a good first impression. Montebank's usual smile morphed into a sneer as he surveyed the overweight guy shaking his hand. His gaze scanned Earl's body twice before he said anything. The sneer became a scowl that eventually changed to a frown.

"Tell me about yourself, Earl. What have you been up to lately?"

Disregarding the less-than-respectful initial visual assessment, Earl was undeterred. His smile beamed as he responded in his characteristic booming voice.

"I ran a chain of self-serve storage warehouses for twenty-five years. Had a tow motor run over my left leg a couple years ago that caused a lot of damage. I needed foot, ankle, and knee surgery. Lots of pain and suffering, so I sued the bastards. Won a couple million and decided I don't like Maryland winters anymore. I came across a good deal for accommodations advertised on Airbnb, and I've parked my ass here on the beaches of Aruba for the past few months."

Montebank seemed to like the reply. His initial obvious distaste for the guy appeared to soften. His eyes sparkled again, and his grin spread broadly.

"Have you ever done any phone work?"

"Answered when the phone rang. People inquiring about rates and hours. Complaints. The usual stuff." Earl's eyes brightened. Was he teasing the master?

Howard watched the two spar and parry for about a half hour. Montebank tested the jovial guy's memory by asking questions multiple times in slightly different ways. He pushed back on some of Earl's answers to test his toughness and ability to control his temper. And he used clever devices to confuse and distract their potential candidate.

"You're perfect for the job," Montebank pronounced.

"What are you paying?" Earl shot back with barely a second's hesitation.

They hadn't discussed it, so Howard and Klaudia exchanged uncertain glances before she nodded slightly, deferring to Howard.

"It's a fee-based job. If you get the info we want, we'll pay you twenty thousand. Fail, and I might buy you a beer at the beach one day."

Earl slapped his massive knee and laughed uproariously. "You know my buddies and I would do our best to run your bar bill as close to the fee as possible." He sputtered the last words, proud of his quick retort and jaded sense of humor.

Everyone joined in the laughter for a few seconds before Earl wanted a clarification. "Is what you're asking me to do legal?"

The laughter stopped. No one even smiled. The four people huddled around his desk exchanged glances before Howard ventured a carefully worded reply.

"It's hard to say. Joe here thinks it's borderline. If a victim feels hard done by and finds out who we are, they might sue. If a government discovers what we're doing, they might dig up some statute they can use to prosecute. But the victim might also be embarrassed by us penetrating their security wall. They might not want to cooperate with authorities. Let's assume it's illegal and not get caught."

"How much time are we talking about?" Earl pivoted with seemingly no worry about the possible legal issues. Maybe he was more concerned about how quickly he could return to the beach.

Joe Montebank answered. "We don't know. If you're in, we'll develop a strategy, then get started. How quickly we get the info depends on how good you are."

Klaudia had watched the interaction between the men rather impassively. As the appointed leader of the project, she brought the discussion to a conclusion. "Are you with us, Earl?"

When he smiled and nodded, she summarized the agreement. "Okay, you'll get your twenty thousand dollars when we're satisfied that we've got the information we need. You'll be quiet about what we're doing, especially when you're drinking with your buddies on the beach."

Earl nodded again.

Klaudia looked around the group, took a deep breath and arched her back straight. "Let's start. Earl, you can stay. I want you to help develop the strategy and execute your part. A reminder: Everything we discuss stays within this room. Our target company is the conglomerate Multima Corporation. Howard is a walking encyclopedia about the company and its structure. Tell us where we should begin, Howard."

He sipped his cooling coffee and leaned forward.

"Multima organizes its human resources department into three geographic areas by continent to minimize outside access. They share information only on a need-to-know basis, and everything's password protected around the globe. Besides Earl, we'll need a Mandarin speaker and a European with either German or French skills. Both will also need excellent English. We'll need to find out the current major players on each continent. Lots of folks changed roles during the pandemic, which will help us eventually, but we'll need to dig up some basic stuff first."

TWELVE

Montreal, Quebec, Friday January 13, 2023

After Suzanne Simpson completed her annual goodwill tour of stores during the week after US Thanksgiving, she'd spent entire days back in Canada with her chief financial officer, Pierre Cabot.

He'd only been with the company a couple years but had impressed her repeatedly. With his close-cropped brown hair brushed forward above jet-black eyeglass frames and thick lenses, he looked like a typical financial nerd. But Pierre added value, digging well beyond the numbers the company generated.

Each day, he guided her through his concerns with the annual budgets submitted by the operating divisions. Although they'd addressed the issues she'd highlighted before Thanksgiving, Pierre was still unhappy with some assumptions underlying the resubmitted numbers.

Preparing the final strategic and operating plans for approval by the board of directors was always a little messy, like making sausages some would say. It was also time-consuming and tedious. But they needed to submit a plan the directors could approve and shareholders would accept. Before their break for the festive holidays, Pierre and Suzanne reached a consensus on the details.

Thankfully, with minimal discussion, Multima's board of directors unanimously approved their plan at its year-end meeting.

The moment she adjourned that meeting, Suzanne dashed out the door of Multima's Fort Myers office with Serge chauffeuring her to Page Field, where the Multima corporate jet waited. Fueled, and with all preflight checks completed, the pilots greeted them at the bottom of the stairway.

Within minutes, they headed off to St. Bart's in the Caribbean, alone. Her assistant, Eileen, had found a remote and secluded rental property on the island, and Serge had visited it weeks before to ensure security was adequate.

Mere hours later, they nestled in total privacy in their rented getaway. It was idyllic. The one-acre compound had everything they needed, high above the Caribbean Sea and over an alcove cut into a rocky cliff. Amenities included an outdoor pool, private tennis courts, private access to the beach below, and a magnificent view of the sunset.

Of course, it was far larger than they needed, with its four bedrooms and four bathrooms. They only used one bed and two of the bathrooms, after all.

Suzanne giggled when she recalled she'd brought eight bikinis in a carry-on bag but used only their bottoms occasionally during their twenty-three days in paradise. Her casual near-nudity kept Serge adequately aroused, and he had performed far beyond her expectations.

Early in their stay, she'd shared with him her decision that they should no longer keep their relationship a secret. Together, they plotted the best way to gradually share the news with the Multima corporate community as their bond and affection grew stronger. She even allowed the word 'love' to creep into their conversations.

But, like all good things, the trip ended, and they had just returned to Montreal. Her longer-than-usual break from business had been the most enjoyable and relaxing she could remember. Her face glowed brightly from more than a suntan when she studied herself in a mirror that morning.

She was holding up well despite her age. True, she needed more makeup to hide the wrinkles slowly etching deeper into her skin. A couple pounds had lodged stubbornly midriff, and her thighs felt thicker and heavier than in her younger years. Still, her energy was still high, and her mental acuity remained sharp. And the brief break left her eager to enthusiastically attack the new year with even a bit of joy.

Only minutes later, Suzanne hunkered down in the company's corporate headquarters on Sherbrooke Street in the heart of Montreal. She chose that building because it had a helipad on the roof, making it easy for her to commute from the field next to her new home in the Laurentian Mountains.

A few weeks earlier, Serge had recommended she buy that place instead of continuing to rent because he could more easily incorporate security enhancements on the property and inside the home. Since they still hadn't apprehended whoever had bombed her home in Atlanta a couple years earlier, Serge was adamant she take all precautions and avoid unnecessary risks.

A video conference with her long-time assistant, Eileen Lee, had started the day pleasantly as they reviewed her commitments for the rest of January. Her business reality didn't take long to set in with a vengeance.

"The media coverage has been relentless," Gordon Goodfellow complained.

Suzanne watched his face distort in apparent pain on the widescreen mounted beside her desk. She had prioritized his urgent request for a video conference that morning.

"My media spokesperson has received over a hundred inquiries a day since our last meeting of the board. Even over the holidays, they continued to pour in. Customers are irate about our prices, and the media is egging them on."

"What's changed? We've had this inflation issue for more than a year."

"It's the trend. When everything was going up, folks accepted that food prices had to increase along with everything else. Now that inflation numbers are decreasing—and food prices continue to rise—the media's blaming us. They saw the bump up in our profits last year and assume it's entirely because of the price increases."

"They're not giving you any credit at all for good management," Suzanne teased her long-time associate as she delivered a backhanded compliment. She paused until he shared a smile and relaxed visibly. Then she continued.

"Levity aside, I know you and your team beat up on your suppliers all you could. That episode—when Lepsico refused to ship you any products for over a month—should have shown everyone that you'd pulled out all the stops negotiating with the bastards. What's your PR team recommending?"

"They'd like you to do an interview on *49 Minutes*. They suspect you can allay the concerns of women shoppers better than I can. Your television persona is great, and you can talk to viewers more effectively. I've made my appearances on CNN, MSNBC, and FOX, but focus groups after each appearance just didn't buy our story."

"Okay, let me think about that. We'll need to get Edward involved." Edward Hadley was her vice president of corporate and investor affairs. Earlier, he'd emailed, asking her to appear on the business news network CBNN to talk about the outstanding profits her company was earning for shareholders. It would require delicate balancing to do both. But she had a few more questions.

"In the meantime, can we do more to moderate the price increases?"

"Yeah. We're toying with the idea of locking in all our private label prices for a couple months. Our buyers think we can get most suppliers to play ball. We could absorb minor increases from those who don't for sixty to ninety days before we see any actual pressure on margins," Gordon replied.

"That sounds like a good temporary measure. When do you think your team will decide?" It would be best to know about any development like that before she spoke with Hadley about scheduling a *49 Minutes* interview.

"Our team has already decided to move forward unless you have an objection. They're creating the media releases, ad campaigns, and store promotional stuff right now to launch it before month-end."

"No. I have no objection. You and your team are closest to the suppliers and customers now, but I think we should discuss it with Hadley when we talk about the interview for *49 Minutes*. What does he think will get us the best PR mileage? Should you announce it before or after my interview?"

Gordon had a few more quick updates about the ongoing union negotiations, healthcare insurance rate discussions, and some land purchase complications related to their planned New Mexico expansions. They handled those subjects while the Montreal office receptionist tracked down Edward Hadley somewhere in New York.

"I'd prefer Suzanne do the interview *after* the announcement of a price freeze on private label products," Hadley emphasized. "She can convey that Multima is taking action to help moderate prices in a way I think most customers will find credible."

"How much time do we need to allow between our earnings report and a *49 Minutes* interview?" Suzanne asked.

"I think we should allow a month, at least. You know our operating results are spectacular for shareholders, but we have to expect some negative media coverage related to inflation." Hadley displayed his usual pragmatism with a calm and measured tone.

"Do either of you foresee a problem if we announce the price freeze in January as currently planned?" Goodfellow always liked to eliminate any ambiguity in their discussions.

With everyone on the same page about the interview and price freeze strategy, Suzanne had time for only a sip of coffee before Serge knocked on the door to her office and let himself in. His expression was grave.

"More recording news this morning." Serge plunked down in a chair facing Suzanne's desk and seemed to gather his thoughts before he continued. "You know I had my people plant listening devices on the switchboards of the offices here, the corporate office in Fort Myers, Supermarkets' headquarters in Atlanta, and Financial Services' in Chicago."

Suzanne nodded to confirm she remembered. All the devices had been installed before the December board of directors meeting in case they picked up any suspicious conversations while the directors were in town. The devices had detected nothing.

"I took the liberty of adding a few more code words to the software. In addition to the words 'Jeffersons,' 'acquisition,' and 'Multima,' which I used that night in Montreal, I thought it might be useful to add phrases like 'human resources,' 'change jobs,' and 'more money.' It turns out we got a hit at Financial Services. My people forwarded the file this morning. Someone made a call to an employee in Financial Services. They were looking for information about the structure of the human resources department at Supermarkets."

"Curious." Suzanne acknowledged his concern, although the cause of his worry wasn't clear from that tidbit. She waited for more.

"It gets worse. That employee didn't give him any information, but she agreed to consider his request after the caller offered fifty thousand dollars for the information."

THIRTEEN

Willemstad, Curaçao, Saturday January 21, 2023

It took longer for Fidelia Morales to decide how much of her wardrobe she should bring to the Caribbean island of Curaçao than to buy a luxury property on the coast for 3.8 million US dollars.

Fifty-two days earlier, before her jet had touched down in Uruguay, and hours after leaving Mateo's guy in Curaçao to rent her a place, he sent a listing and video for her to review. Reportedly, it was the most desirable property on the island and fit Fidelia's requirements precisely.

The owner refused to rent it.

Mateo's guy called the following morning using a highly secure network linking a realtor's office in Willemstad with Fidelia in Uruguay and a sheik with extensive oil holdings in Qatar. Fidelia tried to rent the place again, offering up to a quarter million dollars to use the property for three months.

The oil executive quickly realized she was the decision-maker and had finally forced Fidelia to divulge one of her false identities. She picked the one she had used living in New York. Unfortunately, the oil sheik remembered a time several years before when she'd used that identity, and he recognized her.

"I'm not prepared to rent my property for even one night to The Organization. Who knows what kind of sordid orgy you plan to hold there? I'll sell it to you if you're willing to buy. But no rental, at any price."

It tempted her to remind the prince that he himself had arranged an orgy in Geneva for fifty of his closest friends. Fidelia had provided women from all corners of the globe for them to use. Instead, she held her tongue.

"I understand, your highness. The Organization's escort business is no longer something I am involved in. I only need the property for a few months' relaxation, but I'll consider buying your beautiful home if your price is reasonable."

He asked for five million dollars, and she countered with three. After no more than five minutes of haggling, they agreed on 3.8

million, provided the sale closed before the end of January.

That afternoon, they'd finalized the transaction at the opulent offices of HPN Law and Tax in the Otrobanda quarter of Willemstad. The wealthy prince from Qatar handed over the keys to her new luxury home. As she had dreaded, he used the opportunity for one final taunt.

"I hope you don't mind that I kept one copy of the master key, hoping you might forget to change the locks." His vulgar leer caused a shiver to shoot up Fidelia's spine as an image of the bastard's repeated insistence that she take care of him—while a dozen of his friends watched—replayed vividly in her mind.

"The unbridled joy of our last meeting was the only reason I let you steal this home at such a bargain price. I pray we might one day have another magnificent rendezvous, maybe even in your new home."

She resisted a surging temptation to reply, turned toward the shocked realtor, thanked him for closing the transaction, then spun on her heel without further comment and left the office.

A half-dozen steps outside the doorway, Mateo swore angrily. Then he suppressed his anger, looked at her with sympathetic eyes, and calmly asked, "You want me to go back and teach the prince some manners? It'll only take me a minute."

Fidelia shook her head and flashed a smile of gratitude for his thoughtfulness. It was not the first time someone had tried humiliating her with reference to her past escort activities, and it probably wouldn't be the last. She'd find another way to even the score with the prince. Maybe some telling and sordid photos from that orgy in Switzerland would surface at the *Gulf Times* or *The Wall Street Journal*.

Mateo's guy had arranged a car and stood reading something on his phone outside the running vehicle. Inside, Fidelia spotted Mia Vázquez in the rear seat, her gaze locked on her phone. Mia had become her personal assistant a couple years earlier when the ravages of age no longer allowed the woman the generous remuneration of an escort in high demand.

A genuine sweetheart, Mia assisted Fidelia whenever she had extra administrative work needing attention to detail. Usually, her childhood friend handled the work from her family's home in the historic section of San Juan, where she also cared for frail, aging parents with the money she earned.

But that morning, Fidelia wanted Mia close by and had the pilots fly from Uruguay to San Juan instead of directly to Curaçao. On the two-hour flight from Puerto Rico to Willemstad, she'd briefed Mia, Mateo, and his team on the upcoming project and their expected individual roles.

As Fidelia approached the waiting car, she had no doubt Mia was already working on her assigned tasks and would be ready to share her accomplishments when Fidelia asked.

"Tak Takahashi agreed immediately and is taking the time off as vacation. I've booked his flight out of Tokyo tomorrow, and he'll arrive on Monday via San Francisco." Tak took enormous risks when he let Fidelia know about the subterfuge brewing in the executive suites of Suji Corporation. Getting him out of there had been her priority.

"Marie Dependente was actually on holiday in New York, but we found her a flight from Miami tomorrow." That was welcome news. Her plant on the board of Multima's French subsidiary would have valuable insight for the quest to control the conglomerate.

"Nadine Violette takes a flight tonight from Aix-en-Provence to Amsterdam," Mia continued. "Her flight leaves tomorrow morning from Schiphol and arrives here about eleven. Her friend Pierre wants you to call him to explain what's going on."

Pierre Boivin was The Organization's country boss in France, and Nadine was his plaything. She was also Fidelia's eyes and ears about the criminal goings-on in France and Italy.

"Good work. What's happening with Annika?" Fidelia asked.

"I tried her numbers several times. So far, no answer. Should I ask someone to visit her apartment?"

"Not yet. Try Bernadette in Lourdes. She still provides occasional johns for Annika to augment my monthly stipend. Bernadette might know how to reach her."

Annika Wentz had been a constant companion of Giancarlo Mareno after Fidelia first quit The Organization, then escaped to the south of Germany after Mareno's death. Fidelia kept tabs on her but had paid enough to let her live comfortably there until she was needed.

Bernadette was a long-time friend of Klaudia's, dating back to the days her technology whiz was running the escort business in Europe and a useful contact. Fidelia trusted her.

"Finally, I found Fernando Disputas in Atlanta. He hung up on me. Told me to have you call personally if there was something to talk about." Mia's tone was neutral, but her flashing black eyes signaled she was displeased that her fellow countryman and childhood friend had treated her so impolitely.

Fidelia also found his manner had changed somewhat since Giancarlo Mareno had given him freer rein in the Southeast US. But he remained an ally, and she wanted him to play a crucial role in her scheme.

"I'll try him when we get to the property," Fidelia said.

She finished the sentence just as her magnificent new purchase came into view. They drove up a short gravel driveway from the roadway, approaching from the rear of the 8,000-square-foot home. Young palm trees lined the driveway and circled the house.

First, Fidelia walked to the front of the home overlooking a spectacular beach. She breathed in deeply the salty sea air and felt immediately at home. Tall waves broke calmly across the rocks and gravel at the base of a beach accessible by a stairway that led to a man-made sandy beach extending the width of the property about three feet above the waterline at low tide.

She admired the front of her new property while standing beside the forty-foot pool filled with water colored turquoise by strong direct sunshine. The white cement exterior of the home almost glowed in the light, and she couldn't wait to check out the interior.

Of course, she'd watched the realtor's video several times before she decided to buy and knew the house had nine bedrooms and nine bathrooms. It was perfect for hosting her security team and the guests Mia had organized to visit.

The main villa housed five bedrooms and baths. There, she would assign rooms for all the players in her charade. A few steps away from the main structure, Mateo and his guys would have four individual rooms and bathrooms, plus their own entertainment center. She didn't expect them to be busy with either her guests or obtrusive neighbors but was always glad to have them nearby.

As she entered the living area, Fidelia smiled. Subtle beiges and grays of the walls and tiled floors fit well with the casual décor and comfortable furniture.

"Mateo, have your guys bring my luggage to the master bedroom. Mia, you'll have to share a room. Take the room with twin beds for yourself and Annika. Get settled in while I call Disputas." Fidelia made herself comfortable in the room that would become her high-security area in the coming weeks, but none of the equipment Mateo had ordered had arrived yet.

Still, she closed the door and pulled a pricey untraceable phone from her bag that would scramble their voices and prevent recording. Mateo had cautioned her that the island's proximity to both Aruba and Venezuela might invite digital monitoring by anyone from rival criminals to the CIA.

Fernando Disputas answered her call on the third ring.

"It's been a long time," Fernando greeted her before saying hello.

"It has. But not so long. You shouldn't blow off Mia when she calls on my behalf. Let's not repeat that discourtesy, or I might reconsider why I want you to come to Curaçao." She used a tone that was light enough to be considered friendly but left no doubt about her displeasure.

"No discourtesy intended toward either you or Mia. It's just that I'm in delicate contract negotiations right now, and they might think it inappropriate if I take off for a few weeks of vacation in the Caribbean. Mia couldn't tell me how long you wanted me there."

"I get it. No damage was done, and Mia was right. I can't tell you precisely how long I need you here. What I can tell you is that what I have in mind for you will move you out of that union job into a much more important role in The Organization. You won't need to worry about your relationship with the employer or the employees. It's Saturday. Get your team together and sign a new contract with the employer by Tuesday. Take whatever they're offering. We can make it up to the membership in the next round of negotiations."

"Whoa there, Fidelia. You're asking a lot in that mouthful. Is Luigi onside with what you're asking?"

"Luigi doesn't know about this conversation or what I'm asking you to do. And he won't know either. Do I make myself clear?"

"You're putting me in a tough spot, Fidelia."

"I know. But let's remember I put you in the spot you occupy right now. Remember, it was me who begged Giancarlo Mareno to place you in that job, and it was me who had to suck his cock more than once before he agreed. I'm running this outfit now and expect total loyalty. You swore it to me two years ago, and we didn't put a time limit on it."

"I know, Fidelia. And I truly appreciate everything you've done for me, but I need more time. I can't control when the CEO might agree to meet again. I've got a wife and family to stick handle around. And I'll need some time to get my team here onside. They're a devoted bunch and won't take it lightly if we give up everything we're asking for the workers just to get a quick agreement."

"Fernando, my friend, I have full confidence in your extensive skills and your ability to overcome all the challenges you've detailed. I expect you to accomplish everything I've just outlined. I expect you to do it in total secrecy. No one, from your wife to Luigi, can know about this conversation. And I expect you here on Wednesday morning."

"Or else?" His tone seemed to be a mix of fear and skepticism.

She could leave no doubt. "If you don't meet Mateo at the Curaçao airport when Mia has booked your flight to arrive, you'll no longer be the union president representing the employees of Multima Supermarkets in America."

FOURTEEN

Oranjestad, Aruba, Monday January 23, 2023

Dressed in his usual loose T-shirt, baggy shorts and New Balance sneakers, Howard Knight walked from Sandra's Inn to their newly rented office in the heart of Oranjestad. It should only take about twenty minutes to cover that distance, but Earl Boyante was one of his walking companions. The guy swore he wanted to improve his fitness and begged to join Howard on his morning jaunt.

Another walker joined them. A young German fellow named Uwe Müller had agreed to work with them, and today was his first day on the job. The guy claimed to be a chef back home but had been kicking around the island for a few months. He smoked too much marijuana for Howard's liking, but he promised not to use any until they finished their work for the day.

Klaudia wasn't with them for their morning hike. She'd rented an apartment near the office—less than a five-minute walk, she claimed. She'd finally had enough of the poolside crowd at Sandra's Inn and preferred to spend her spare time in or around the office playing with technology.

Joe Montebank didn't join them either. Klaudia had booked him into the pricy Renaissance Resort complex down the street a couple blocks on the waterfront. He liked to gamble and looked forward to a few hours in the casino overnight.

As the three guys strolled toward the harbor area downtown, they kibitzed about Sandra and her odd menagerie of guests. They all chuckled when they told stories about Sandra and her morning swims in the nude. It seems each had peeked out behind the closed curtains of his room more than once to watch her revel in her bodily freedom. Uwe even claimed he'd seen her perform ten or fifteen minutes of yoga at the side of the pool wearing only an expression of delight.

Howard could have used the time better to brief the boys on their tasks for the day, but he thought he'd let them have fun and include Klaudia in the briefing. Fidelia did make it her show, after all.

When they arrived at the third-floor working area, Earl was

panting like a tired old mutt after chasing a rabbit. Uwe thoughtfully shared the bottle of water he had pinched from Sandra's ground-floor office. Within a couple minutes, Earl started breathing normally again, and they all helped themselves to the coffee Klaudia had brewed before their arrival.

They gathered chairs and clustered around Howard's desk for the morning briefing.

Howard had insisted that Joe Montebank keep the details of their work private. Uwe didn't yet seem trustworthy enough to have access to everything, so Joe kept his presentation very general.

"Both of you have a simple task. We want you to show your sparkling personalities by captivating a few people with pleasant conversation. You can choose whatever subjects interest you to keep the people we've assigned to you engaged for as long as possible. Ten or fifteen minutes would be ideal, so we can assess which targets look most promising." He paused for a sip of coffee and waited for nods of understanding from both men.

"Your goal is to establish a rapport that lets you call them back sometime later for the real information we need. All the names are of people in the human resources department of a large multinational company called Multima. Do either of you already know anyone who works for them?"

Joe waited again while his subjects thought about it and looked from one to the other as they affirmed they didn't know anyone who worked for the company.

"OK, no problem. Uwe, your subjects work in the Berlin, Vienna, and Brussels offices of Multima Financial Services. Klaudia already determined they all speak German well. Earl, the names we prepared for you are based in Multima Supermarkets' Atlanta headquarters, their UK offices in Manchester, the Multima Financial Services office in Chicago, and a regional office in Toronto."

Joe paused again to observe their reactions, and Klaudia took advantage of the break to share a thought.

"Like Joe said, you can choose the subjects that keep your assigned contacts engaged, but you'll probably find it easiest to start with what it's like working for the company. Perhaps suggest you're thinking about applying for a job. Ask them how they enjoy their work environment. Use a pretense of business to get them started."

"Brilliant suggestion, Klaudia. Now, do either of you have questions?"

Both seemed comfortable, so they split into two groups. Howard, Joe, and Earl stayed in Howard's office. They put Earl at a round table using a landline phone with software added to make the call untraceable. Klaudia had connected two headsets Howard and Joe could use to listen in on the conversations. Earl wore a more elaborate headset, with a special microphone to block background noise from the room or the street or even the sound of curtains blowing in the breeze from the open windows.

Klaudia and Uwe set up in her work area on the other side of the common area with similar technology. Uwe's conversations would all be in German, so she'd gain the same knowledge from his calls that Howard and Joe would glean from Earl's.

Each caller had about a dozen names. As expected, Earl enjoyed early success. After three rejections from people in the UK subsidiary, a young man engaged in a fifteen-minute conversation. He became downright chatty, volunteering information about jobs currently available with the company, working conditions around the offices or within Multima stores, and salary ranges for the various positions. Skillfully, Earl drew him into conversations about that week's Premier League soccer matches and the release of the new movie *Babylon* a couple weeks before.

After the call, Joe offered praise and gentle criticism to help Earl hone his skills and fully engage with his assigned subjects. By the end of their day, Joe offered high fives and congratulations for three successful completions. Only the Toronto office proved impossible to penetrate.

Uwe found it more challenging. The people in Berlin and Vienna would only engage in the most basic polite conversation, none revealing information about the company, themselves, or their interests. That didn't surprise Klaudia. She knew German speakers usually had conservative natures. It was a common trait that made getting to know them more complex.

Joe Montebank, moving between Earl and Uwe to coach them, offered suggestions and applauded Uwe's efforts to keep contacts on the line slightly longer as the day progressed.

After the third call to people in Multima Financial Services' office in Brussels, Uwe found one person willing to talk. She was Belgian and had a slight accent when she spoke German. She also had a slight accent when she spoke English because part of Joe's coaching involved getting their contacts to use at least a few English phrases. But she engaged for over twenty minutes, so Klaudia offered a brilliant smile and thumbs up as Uwe said goodbye to his only success of the day.

The sun dipped into the Caribbean before they sent Uwe and Earl on their way. For Howard, Klaudia, and Joe, several hours of work remained. They listened to each recording multiple times, dissecting the conversations and rating the quality of the calls. They aimed to determine which three seemed most likely to share the valuable information ordered by Jeffersons Stores.

The stakes were high for their nascent business. Howard had insisted on a fee of four hundred thousand US dollars. Jeffersons finally agreed to pay it, with a 50 percent deposit already transferred to a bank account in the Cayman Islands.

First, though, a sophisticated laboratory in eastern Germany that had once worked for the secret service of the communist government needed a few days to analyze the recordings and determine if artificial intelligence could replicate the desired voices before their next steps. It looked like Klaudia was already thinking ahead to eliminating the need for human callers.

"Intelligent robots seem more desirable and ultimately more secure," she said to Howard after the others left.

FIFTEEN

Chicago, Illinois, Tuesday January 24, 2023

Suzanne watched the reactions of James Fitzgerald and Natalia Tenaz as Serge Boisvert walked them through his discovery of a suspicious call to one of their employees in the human resources department.

James said nothing as Serge provided the background for the recordings, starting with the call following the board of directors meeting in Montreal. Her faithful Financial Services business leader listened intently while his face turned slightly red as Serge played the recording of the employee who was offered fifty thousand dollars for information.

Natalia recognized the voice immediately. "That's Judy Jones. She leads the compensation and benefits team in human resources, our longest-serving manager reporting to the vice president."

Suzanne hoped for more, but Natalia apparently preferred to keep her thoughts to herself until she learned more.

"What are you suggesting we do?" James asked, looking at Serge.

"I don't think we have enough information to draw conclusions at this stage." Serge chose his words carefully and avoided making any direct accusations. "We don't know why she agreed to consider the offer. Was she simply tired of the conversation and looking to be rid of the caller? Is she experiencing personal financial troubles that caused her to pause and genuinely think about the proposal? We don't know."

"I've worked with her closely over the years," Natalia said. "We get together socially for lunch or dinner once or twice a year. She seems happily married to a successful physician, so I doubt financial concerns are a factor."

"How's her morale?" James wanted to know. "Is she satisfied with her role?"

"Seems to be. She leads a couple committees to improve working conditions and morale around the office." Natalia's tone seemed thoughtful and confident, her manner calm and collected.

The executives continued to chat about the odd request, trying to guess who might find that information useful. They all agreed that any competitor would find information about positions and remuneration valuable enough to spend fifty thousand dollars. Natalia speculated that it could be a new company planning to open a financial services business. Serge reminded the group they shouldn't exclude the possibility of organized crime trying to create unwanted mischief, again.

After about an hour of speculation and theorizing, Suzanne got to the real reason for their visit that morning.

"Serge wants to plant recording devices around the office. To be clear, we wanted both of you to know about and support this initiative. I think you agree this matter is serious enough that we can't take any chances. Serge, why don't you explain what you propose?"

For a few minutes, Serge outlined the technology he wanted to plant around the office. He intended to add the application to every phone in the human resources area, including the vice president's. Next, he explained how the software would work and how they'd record only those conversations where any of an extensive list of keywords was used.

Serge cautioned that many recordings might result, and he realized employees might consider those recordings an invasion of their privacy. Finally, he emphasized the need for James and Natalia to keep this conversation private.

"Are those recordings legal?" James asked.

"No. Unless a judge approves it, recording telephone conversations without getting permission from the people being recorded is illegal in Illinois," Serge replied.

"As I thought," James said. "In that case, I can't support your request. The issue is potentially grave. And I respect your desire to use the technology, but I can't support an illegal operation, no matter how important the outcome."

Serge looked toward Suzanne, awaiting her cue on next steps. James's posture on the listening devices was unwelcome but not unexpected. She very much admired the fellow's strong ethics, but they'd developed a backup plan that morning.

"Since this looks like a tough one to resolve, let's take a break before we move on to other things. James, do you have a vacant office Serge can use for the rest of the morning while we continue our discussions here?" Suzanne stood as she spoke.

"Of course." James got the subtle message. He nodded. "Natalia, would you mind showing Serge the way to Albert's old office on the second floor? And introduce him to Bonnie so she can assist with his needs?"

Once Serge and Natalia had left the room, Suzanne turned to face James.

"I thought we had an understanding on this." Her tone signaled disappointment more than an accusation.

"We do." James stretched to look around Suzanne toward the doorway before he continued. "You know I think the world of Natalia, but I have two goals. First, I want to send her a message that we should never compromise our principles, even if that is exactly what I'm about to do. Second, we shouldn't eliminate any suspects this early on, including Natalia."

"Fair enough. But how do we install the listening devices now?"

"I'll propose another break in about an hour and go down to the office where Serge is settling in. I'll coach him to ask Bonnie to bring Reginald Robitali up to meet him. Robitali thinks that Serge is here to do a security inspection of all the communications networks in the building. He'll take Serge to the equipment room, let him in, and leave him there for an hour. Serge can do his thing, and no one will know, including Natalia and Robitali."

When Natalia entered the meeting room again, Suzanne welcomed her return. "Let's all chat about James's planned retirement and Natalia's transition to the role of president."

Natalia beamed while Suzanne forced herself to match the woman's expression of pride and satisfaction.

SIXTEEN

Sint Michiel, Curaçao, Wednesday January 25, 2023

Fidelia woke early that morning and wandered to the window overlooking the beach and waterfront. The sky was partially cloudy, but brilliant sunshine still splashed warmth across the sand and rocks in front of her home. She never grew tired of the sea, the crashing waves, and the soothing breezes.

The sea was always within minutes of her home when she was growing up in Puerto Rico. She'd retreated to the shore often to cope with the challenges of being poor in a place that blocked opportunity at every turn.

This morning in Curaçao held no melancholy, however. Rather, her mood leaned more toward celebratory.

Fernando Disputas had called only hours earlier, at almost midnight in Atlanta, to confirm that Gordon Goodfellow had signed the collective agreement for the Multima Supermarkets' employees. It would be in place for four years.

Disputas had been almost despondent over the concessions he'd had to make to reach an agreement quickly. The deal was so bad he wasn't sure the employees would ratify it in a vote that would take place in the coming weeks. Furthermore, two of his team members had resigned in anger. They'd walked out of the negotiations rather than accommodate Goodfellow's demands after he realized how desperate Disputas was to make a deal.

Fidelia smiled as she looked out over the swimming pool, spotting a couple birds taking a morning bath in one corner. The poor deal Disputas had reached with Multima was irrelevant in the scheme of things. If the employees voted down the terms agreed to by Disputas, the union would have to continue negotiating. If it all worked out as planned, the entire affair would simply be a hiccup, forgotten in a few weeks.

Fidelia was reluctant to dress that morning. She felt free with her naked body soaking in the sunshine from an open window. The idyllic setting tempted her to walk down to the pool, swim nude, or lounge on a chair for a few hours. But that might cause a distraction for her assembled guests. Fidelia had lost all inhibitions about people seeing her undressed too long ago to remember. But the cast she'd assembled in Curaçao was diverse, and it was difficult to predict how they might react. A safer bet was to get dressed and get on with the day.

She checked her watch. It showed a few minutes after seven. Her rented private jet should arrive at Atlanta's Fulton County Airport within the next few minutes to pick up Fernando Disputas. The pilots promised to call Mia on arrival in Atlanta and again on departure, so Fidelia could meet him at the airport in Curaçao later that afternoon.

Meanwhile, Mia had scheduled a small tour bus to cart Fidelia and those guests who'd already arrived around the island. The idea was to help everyone get to know one another and create some camaraderie.

After all, this gang would take high-stakes risks in the coming days.

Although Fidelia and her team were ready and waiting at the agreed time of nine thirty, their transportation didn't arrive until almost ten. Mia seethed with displeasure but wasn't surprised. Caribbean time was whenever the planned activity actually got underway.

Jet lag, immense time differences, and a natural human reserve about meeting new people in a strange place combined to create a group that Fidelia wanted to form into a harmonious team instantly. Fidelia used the delay to let her guests engage with each other.

All but Mia had arrived at various times over the past few days and, so far, had interacted little. Instead, Fidelia had occupied a significant block of each participant's time talking, listening, learning, and plotting.

Tak Takahashi needed the most attention. Fidelia had spent almost the entire morning with him the day before. She'd grilled him on the intelligence from Suji Corporation he'd shared with her, testing him a dozen different ways to be sure his story—including the subtle facts—didn't change. He appeared nervous, so she instructed Mateo to introduce him to all the bodyguards and make him feel welcome and secure.

Marie Dependente had arrived from Paris the day before with

symptoms of a cold. She'd tested negative for COVID, but Fidelia insisted she wear a mask for a few days regardless, then put on her own N95 for their two-hour debriefing session in the evening. When they finished their talk, she made sure the long-time director on the board of Multima's French subsidiary realized she could no longer return to that role after they finished their work in the Caribbean.

Annika Wentz flew in from Barbados. Having been Giancarlo Mareno's long-time companion, Annika could afford to vacation wherever she chose. Luigi kept her on to satisfy well-connected guys who enjoyed a good rollick with a mature woman. Her status in Berlin society gave her privileged access, drawing generous payments from Luigi and a few select private clients.

Their conversation was shorter. Annika mainly shared gossip about her recent trysts with politicians in Washington at Luigi's behest. It became increasingly clear Fortissimo was doing far more to woo right-wing American politicians than he had admitted during their meeting in The Bahamas.

As they stood around in the warming sunshine, waiting, Annika played a great role, laughing and joking with the entire entourage. It was easy to see why powerful politicians and the men around them found her so appealing.

Fidelia glanced over at Nadine Violette, who looked the most tired of the group. Once her plane from Amsterdam had touched down, Fidelia had talked with her until her body time was well into the early hours of that morning. They reviewed all the steps she had taken the previous week in France, Spain, Portugal, and Italy to fortify Fidelia's position with each country's crime bosses. Nadine reported that their loyalty was unquestioned.

Finally, an oversized van arrived. Smaller than expected, it comfortably accommodated only seven passengers, so Mateo brought along just one other bodyguard to keep an eye on Fidelia's safety when they stopped to visit tourist sights or have walkabouts. Everyone in the van dressed like tourists in shorts, comfortable tops, floppy hats, and sandals.

Only Mateo and his guy looked subtly different. They wore high-quality Nikes and bulky pouches around their waists. The belts held water bottles on either side but also inconspicuously concealed small, but deadly, automatic weapons.

Mia served as their tour guide. She'd visited the island once before and remembered her favorite sights well. She instructed the driver to deliver them first to Otrobanda in Willemstad. Then she twisted her slim body in the front seat to face all the other passengers behind.

As they made the fifteen-minute drive into the capital, she delivered a brief overview of the island as a tour guide might.

"People here have two official languages, Dutch and Papiamento. Dutch is a remnant of colonization by the Netherlands and the island's continued status as a constituent country within the Dutch state. Papiamento is the language of the Indigenous people." Mia stopped abruptly, realizing it all sounded staged. She rephrased it all with a self-conscious grin that would disarm even her most vociferous critic.

"Sorry about that. You know I meant to say Curaçao is part of the Netherlands, and there are two official languages. But you'll also hear a lot of Spanish and English. Most immigrants here come from Venezuela—only a few miles away—or Colombia. Most of the tourists speak Dutch or English.

"But I want you to learn one word I heard when I came here the first time. That word is *dushi*. It's a handy word because it has five different meanings. First, it means tasty. When the chef Fidelia hired serves you our meal tonight, tell her it's *dushi*. She'll love you and make even more delicious dishes!

"You also need to know that Antillean men love their women and like to express that love. *Dushi* is a common term of endearment. '*Mi dushi*' means my baby. '*Danki dushi*' means thank you, baby. It's sometimes used even with a stranger. But be careful. People from Curaçao don't always find it appropriate."

Fidelia watched as Mia's audience first laughed, then sat upright at the word of caution. Her emerging tour guide also seemed to sense a change in mood.

"People from Curaçao also use *dushi* like the Portuguese word '*doce*.' *Doce* means sweet or loving. So, people use the word *dushi* to express their love or gratitude for someone. But it's often used to let someone know you find them sexy or attractive."

Mia jumped into her role, her eyelashes flashing seductively. "Both men and women can be *dushi*," she said. "But the best way to use the expression is to describe the island as *dushi*."

There was a reason behind Fidelia's odd request that Mia act as tour guide. She had to build a team that could perform harmoniously under intense pressure and do it instantly. Creating an aura of leadership for Mia, or having her act like a teacher, would give the young guests an anchor and, hopefully, create a space where they would follow her instructions quickly and without question.

Fidelia looked around the van. Her guests all focused on Mia and the sights she pointed out as they traveled towards the port in Willemstad. The massive towers of two cruise ships already peeked through the taller buildings. A few moments later, she recognized landmarks and streets she'd seen when their driver brought her to the offices of HPN Law and Tax in the Otrobanda quarter days earlier.

That thought forced her to suppress a grin of satisfaction. She'd already plotted just revenge on the crass prince from Qatar for his humiliating reference to her previous work. Once this mission was under control, the inconsiderate asshole would find his extensive financial holdings in the US severely depleted. She had the means to do it and took joy from the anticipation.

A beep on Fidelia's phone as she stepped out of the van alerted her to a just-received WhatsApp message. It was the pilot of her private jet. Fernando Disputas had just boarded. They were on the runway and next in line for take-off. Estimated arrival time at Albert Plesman International Airport in Curaçao 13:37. She had about four hours for sightseeing and team building before the star of her new production arrived.

She intended to use the time available fully.

SEVENTEEN

Oranjestad, Aruba, Wednesday January 25, 2023

Howard sipped a second cup of coffee as he leaned on a windowsill in his "penthouse" suite at Sandra's Inn and watched the sun climb. The morning appeared to be another day in Caribbean paradise, and he was content to soak up both caffeine and fresh air as he waited for Earl and Uwe to walk with him to the office in Oranjestad.

A police car parked in the tiny lot across the street caught his eye moments before he heard a disturbance below a window on the other side of his apartment. It seemed to come from the courtyard below. Howard dashed across the tiny room just in time to hear Sandra scream, "That's him! The skinny one with the mustache. He's the German bastard that's been stealing from me for two weeks!"

Standing below the tall palm near the entrance to the courtyard, Uwe froze, then looked around anxiously, seeking a viable escape.

A uniformed policeman put his hand on his holstered gun and nodded toward Uwe, then motioned with the forefinger of his other hand.

"Come over here. We have some questions for you. Don't try anything funny." The officer's voice was tranquil compared to Sandra's angry tirade, but his manner was severe.

A second officer backed away from Sandra, signaling he might expect a chase, but Howard saw no other movement.

"You conniving, no-good drug addict, I hope they shoot you!" Sandra shouted out again in German.

The second officer moved closer to Sandra again, and Howard instinctively looked around to plan his own escape.

The drama continued.

The first officer tried to reassert control. He pointed to Earl, who'd just stepped out of his nearby room, and calmly told him to move along. The matter didn't concern him.

Earl looked as if he might protest but quickly retreated instead. Within seconds, he locked the door to his room and shuffled across the courtyard toward the street.

Howard seized an opportunity to do the same. Leaving his coffee behind, he locked his apartment, dashed down the stairs, casually turned right at ground level, and headed toward the street.

Earl held the gate out of the compound open and laughed nervously as Howard caught up with him.

Together, they walked along the street, comparing their brief observations about the incident. About a half-mile from Sandra's Inn, Howard suggested they pop into a coffee shop.

"There's no need for you to come to the office today," Howard said. "I'll carry on after our coffee. Why don't you go back to Sandra's place and find out what's going on with Uwe?"

For a few minutes, they kibitzed and joked about their morning excitement. Then Howard headed toward his office in town, and Earl returned to Sandra's Inn.

Towards noon, Klaudia motioned for Howard to rush over to her private area in their new downtown office. She appeared both stressed and unhappy as she held a phone to one ear and animatedly waved until he stood up from his desk and moved toward her.

"Earl," she mouthed as Howard approached, motioning for him to sit. "Howard's here now. I'll put you on speaker. Repeat what you just told me."

"They arrested Uwe," Earl announced. "Took him away, but we don't know where."

"What did he do?" Klaudia asked.

"It's a long story." Earl sighed audibly. "Early this morning, Sandra discovered a notice in her mailbox from Away-From-Home, the massive global booking service. That notice confirmed Uwe had canceled his reservation with Sandra's Inn digitally less than fifteen minutes after Sandra had formally checked him into the hostel section."

"So our young friend scammed Sandra." Howard suppressed a grin.

"Yeah. Uwe stayed at Sandra's Inn for almost two weeks free. When she discovered it, Sandra called the local police. They told her they'd received other reports of fraudulently canceled reservations from other establishments. They sent out the two officers who questioned Uwe and took him away without saying where they would hold him."

Howard ordered Earl to spend the afternoon calling police detachments to find out what was happening and promised to figure out a way to pay him some sort of separate fee for his efforts.

After work, Klaudia and Joe Montebank walked back to Sandra's Inn with Howard, clearly alarmed their new contract employee was in trouble with the law and perhaps drawing unwanted attention to their mission.

When they entered the compound, they found Earl and Sandra lounging under the tall palm tree in the courtyard.

"I still hope they shoot the little bastard," Sandra said. Her words slurred slightly. A wine bottle on the stubby, green plastic table between their chairs looked almost empty.

"I got the whole scoop," Earl began. "They're deporting Uwe to the Netherlands tonight."

He paused dramatically and sighed as though preparing to recount details about the loss of a close, lifelong friend. Howard looked inquisitively at Klaudia. She opened her mouth to prompt Earl, when he began the story.

"You know Sandra accused Uwe of fraudulently canceling his Away-From-Home reservation after checking in. Sandra's Inn wasn't his first victim. She found out from the police today that seven other hotels, hostels, or inns reported the same crime, using the same method, over the past two months. Uwe confessed to all eight crimes. But it gets worse."

Earl paused, cleared his throat, and continued. "Uwe was in the country illegally. His passport showed he'd arrived in Aruba in March of last year. He didn't have a visa, so he should have left the country by last June. He worked for cash at odd jobs when he could find them. When he ran out of money, he started the reservation frauds. The police in Aruba didn't think he was worth the trouble of a trial and incarceration, so they got the Dutch authorities to ship him to Amsterdam for the European Union authorities to deal with. I hate to tell you this, but he also told the police he was working for you."

Howard's first inclination was to laugh. The story was both bizarre and humorous. Uwe had shown a rebellious streak, so it didn't surprise him that the young German had run afoul of the law. Klaudia caught Howard's eye and motioned for him to follow her.

They took enough steps to be out of hearing range of the others.

"I see nothing funny about this." Klaudia's tone was not only humorless; it bordered on hostile. "The lab had trouble duplicating the guy's voice for artificial intelligence. They say they need another recording before they can go any further. Now we'll have to start all over again. And who knows how the police will react to him working for us."

With the mood dampened, Sandra and Earl wandered off while Klaudia called an Uber to pick her and Joe up. Howard walked them to the street to chat while they waited.

Joe Montebank's take on their situation was even more discouraging. "You'll have to find more candidates to call different Multima offices. If we go back to those same people with another telephone voice looking to build a relationship, we'll raise suspicion and probably get blocked. I think making our deadline for Jeffersons Stores will be hard."

After quadrupling the original fee Jeffersons Stores intended to pay, Howard understood Montebank's concern. Jeffersons would be more than unhappy with the delay, besides the extra cost. Howard also knew enough about the ruthless Japanese owners behind the supermarket chain. Would he have to beg Fidelia for protection on their new company's first business opportunity?

EIGHTEEN

Montreal, Quebec, Wednesday January 25, 2023

Suzanne tried to return a voicemail message Gordon Goodfellow had left on her phone just before midnight. It was well after she'd shut down for the previous day, and she'd slept soundly for the first night in several. In response, she received a message that Gordon was unavailable but would call her back as soon as possible. That turned out to be late in the morning.

"I completed the union contract last night even though I couldn't reach you for an okay," Gordon said.

Suzanne bristled but kept her tone moderate until she had all the facts. "Why would you sign the agreement so hurriedly?"

"Well, you're probably going to find this hard to believe, but Disputas agreed to every one of the terms you and I had agreed upon. Every. One. I thought it better to get his signature on the document before he changed his mind. We finalized the deal just after one o'clock this morning. That's why I'm running late today. I just woke up."

Suzanne didn't know how to respond at first. There was silence for more than a few seconds. "Let me get this straight. The same guy who has always demanded I become involved in the contract negotiations, so he could try to wheedle yet another concession out of me, this time not only accepted all the conditions you and I agreed upon, he did it without even asking to talk to me?"

"Right. And he agreed to one year longer than the current contract—now until 2027. And the hourly rate is fifty cents better than you and I agreed we'd probably need to accept."

"Why do I smell something amiss here, Gordon?"

"I can't explain it either. Our legal counsel read through the summary of agreed terms with Disputas and his attorney before they drew up the final version. Initially, he pushed back on both the agreement term and the hourly rates. As we neared midnight, he caved on both points."

"I know you're a brilliant negotiator, Gordon, and I don't want to minimize your team's achievement here, but this is totally out of character for the man and the union he represents. What could have happened?"

Suzanne rarely speculated. She dealt in facts, and the facts Gordon Goodfellow presented were indeed helpful to the company. But something wasn't computing for her. Both parties had lots of time remaining before the union would be in a position to strike.

For two years, their employees had loudly demanded significant salary increases to cope with unexpectedly high rates of inflation. Yet the union had essentially adopted a position that would hold its members' compensation at the newly agreed level for almost four more years. It was unheard of.

"We talked about the same thing every time we went to the breakout sessions. The only thing we could surmise was that the assurances we gave them on artificial intelligence and automation might have been more important to the union membership than the salary increases. Again, I realize that's hard to believe, but Disputas mentioned our concessions on those points several times."

"Yeah. I suppose." Suzanne remained unconvinced but was unsure what more she could do at this stage. "Let's sit tight and not make any public announcements yet. Let's wait for Disputas to make the next move. He has to take the agreement to his membership for ratification. Maybe he knows they'll turn it down and give him a more powerful strike mandate."

"Our thinking exactly," Gordon said. "In the meantime, can I bend your ear again on Jeffersons Stores?"

Suzanne inhaled deeply but resisted the temptation to exhale with enough volume to signal her growing impatience with Goodfellow's desire to take over one of his most prominent competitors. Instead, she said she would take a couple minutes to hear him out.

"I had a call Monday from Grace Benedict, the CEO who replaced Dave Jones at Jeffersons. It was a little weird. As her name suggests, she's a little religious. Took a moment to adjust to 'thoughts and prayers' and 'God's will' repeatedly working themselves into our conversation ..."

"And the reason she called?" Suzanne became impatient. The gossip didn't seem to add much to their discourse.

"It seems she heard rumblings of our interest in making an offer to take over the company. She never got directly to the point of her call, although I took several runs at it. She seemed to be fishing to see if there might be a role for her in the acquired company. She also claimed that her board of directors wouldn't adamantly oppose any legitimate offer we made."

Goodfellow gave her some time to mull over that odd comment. She shared her thoughts almost immediately. "They might entertain an offer? We know her board's stacked with directors appointed by Suji Corporation, and we suspect Suji's a front for the criminals who run pachinko parlors over there. Why would they be in a hurry to sell a prime money laundering opportunity?"

It wasn't clear where this conversation was going, and another guest was already waiting outside her office. But Gordon wanted to make another point.

"I hear you and don't disagree with anything you're saying. But here's the catch: One of her friends in Tokyo called her that morning to let her know that Suji Corporation just hired Mizuto Capital to sell all Jeffersons' US real estate holdings. They want to raise five billion or more in cash by selling the properties, and their target is the end of the year."

"Has that news become public?" This was a game changer, if true.

"No. According to Grace's source in Japan, a condition of the contract is total secrecy. The agreement has a multi-million-dollar penalty if any information leaks from Mizuto."

"So how did Grace's source in Japan get the information?"

Gordon Goodfellow laughed uneasily before he answered. "I asked the same question. She says her source is a missionary in Japan. A recent convert to their religious sect confessed to Grace's friend—the evangelical preacher guiding her conversion—that she regularly slept with a senior executive at Mizuto. When this guy asked if there were any other sins she wanted to confess, the woman told him about the secret deal. She didn't know if that qualified as a sin or not."

Gordon barely completed the sentence before he became unable to control his laughter.

Suzanne could no longer resist and joined in before she thought about it and answered. "Grace's story sounds a bit fantastical, but she must genuinely believe this source to risk calling you. Why don't you contact Amber Chan? I recall she had a friend highly placed in Mizuto, someone from her college days."

Amber Chan led Multima Supermarkets' business in China but had studied for two years at the University of Tokyo. Her network of influential contacts in Japan was remarkable.

"I will. In the meantime, am I right to assume this news might be a game-changer for my acquisition project?" Gordon spoke carefully and used a deferential tone.

"It could be. James Fitzgerald might ease his opposition if the value on Jeffersons Stores' balance sheet shifted by five billion from real estate to cash. First, let's see if this rumor has any truth."

NINETEEN

Willemstad, Curaçao, Wednesday January 25, 2023

After Fidelia's day of sightseeing like a tourist and team building like a business executive, she sat beside Fernando Disputas outside Baoase Culinary Beach Restaurant at a resort on the south side of Willemstad.

Mateo's guys had rented the entire restaurant for the evening. It was closed to all other visitors, and only the owner, a server, and one chef worked that night.

Tak Takahashi, Marie Dependente, and Nadine Violette sat at a table with Mia inside the restaurant with Mateo and his guys. Only Annika Wentz was missing from their group dinner. Fidelia's private jet was whisking her to California to execute her first part in the plan.

The evening sky was beautiful. The sun had almost entirely set for the day, and hues of purple and blue created interesting patterns on the cloud formation, contrasting with the parting orange glow. Fidelia and Fernando sat at a table specially prepared on a solid wooden dock extending out over the waterfront behind the restaurant.

The jetty jutted out from the shoreline only inches above the water, and lighted candles, peeking from inside decorative shells of all shapes and sizes, lined both its sides. Another section of the dock, added on to the end, created an area large enough to install a structure surrounding the table. With sheer white netting on the top and sides, diners could either leave the curtains hanging to keep out the mosquitos or tie them back to create a relaxing outdoor refuge. Tonight, someone had tied them back elegantly.

There were only two chairs at the table, looking out over the water on forty-five-degree angles to the square wooden table with a tan table covering. In its center, another candle provided flickering light in the gentle evening breeze. The environment looked perfect.

No one would overhear their conversation. Their spot on the dock was about fifty feet from the building, and Mateo had instructed the waiter to ring a bell from the doorway before he ventured out to serve the important guests at the special table.

Fernando looked uncomfortable. His right eye ticked nervously every few minutes, and he cleared his throat often before speaking or answering a question. His manner was polite, not friendly. When he spoke, his tone was respectful, but his shoulders stooped slightly, more than Fidelia remembered.

It had been over three years since they'd last met in person, and his appearance had changed somewhat during that time. He still had a full head of hair, but it was now more gray than black. Worry lines creased his forehead, and the cheek dimples of his youth had long disappeared as his face gained weight like the rest of his body.

He didn't look obese, but his shape didn't suggest fitness. His Latino coloring was paler than she remembered, and his breathing seemed labored, as if he had a cold. Average in appearance for his middle age, he probably had a dozen or more years of good health before the typical ailments of aging caught up with him.

True, he'd worked well into the previous night negotiating the labor agreement with Multima Supermarkets, then had to meet her jet at the airport in Atlanta early that morning. Even if he slept for a couple hours on the flight, the dark patches below his eyes were justifiably earned. Since Fidelia's command to join her in the Caribbean, he probably hadn't slept well, either. He needed to relax for their dinner to be entirely productive.

"Would you like to pick a bottle of wine to start? I'm sure I'll be fine with whatever you choose." Fidelia rarely drank alcohol. She preferred to keep complete control of her faculties, but she knew Fernando would gulp down most of a bottle without difficulty.

As he surveyed the extensive wine list, they chatted informally, first about the Multima negotiations, then about her day of sightseeing with the rest of the group. She'd forewarned him about their dinner arrangements so he'd understand her desire to meet privately and not be overly concerned about isolating him from the rest of the team. She let him know her motives behind the team building and promised to fill him in on all her plans before they left for her new home after dinner.

CONTENTION

They'd been friends since childhood and attended the same school operated by the Catholic church in San Juan. Fernando was the only student whose grades came close to Fidelia's, but she couldn't recall a single time he scored higher than her in any subject in any year.

In their teens, they had experimented with sex but never considered themselves lovers. It came after the Catholic priests and nuns taught Fidelia it was God's will for her to please both men and women using her mouth, hands and, occasionally, other body orifices designed for the purpose. As a teen, she had selectively conferred His will on a few of the guys in her circle of friends.

It had always amazed her how pliable people became after some enjoyable sexual activity.

That stopped when she moved to New York and studied law at Columbia University. But her friendship with Fernando continued. They exchanged letters occasionally, talked by phone when she could afford to call, saw him when she visited her parents and sponsored him to move to the mainland after he found a job with Multima Supermarkets in Atlanta.

When Fidelia started working for Giancarlo Mareno, he suggested Fernando should become active in the employees' union. He'd help him out. Over the years, Giancarlo met her friend, liked him, and coached him to learn everything possible about how the union operated. In Fernando's late thirties, the crime boss arranged for him to be elected president of the union—a role he'd now held without challenge or interruption for the past twenty-five years.

Over those years, Mareno had gradually drawn Fernando into more of The Organization's activities. Although his union responsibilities took up most of his time, Fernando eventually learned how the backroom gambling and numbers games worked and made sure The Organization got its share of the weekly profits.

When payday loan outfits became respectable, Mareno put Fernando in charge of the Atlanta operations. The old man liked how his Puerto Rican protégé decorated the shops with bright and cheerful colors, taught his employees the art of exemplary customer service, and promptly turned delinquent borrowers over to The Organization's collection services. The business was extraordinarily profitable.

After a few years, Fidelia had suggested Mareno let Fernando work for her. She thought he could build up her escort business in Atlanta like he had the payday loan operations. But Giancarlo wouldn't let him go. At some point, Fernando had also married a niece of the crime boss, and he feared overworking the guy might cause problems at home.

Since Giancarlo's death three years earlier, Fidelia's relationship with Fernando had grown complicated. Of course, he knew she had pulled the trigger to eliminate their long-time crime boss, and he was among the first to profess his loyalty to her. But the tone of their conversations had changed slightly, and she'd felt some distance in their friendship recently.

She'd been patient over the years as the guy evolved. On some level, she understood why Fernando might have conflicting feelings about her leadership of The Organization or remorse about her elimination of the old man. Tonight a proper test started. If he failed, she'd wasted a few hundred thousand dollars and added a multi-million-dollar property to her portfolio.

If he performed adequately, the next stage of her scheme would begin, and his future might brighten beyond his wildest dreams. It would be up to him.

"You haven't given your oath of loyalty formally yet," Fidelia said.

He'd sipped from the wine but wasn't yet fully relaxed. The timing was perfect.

"Is there any question about my loyalty to The Organization?" He sputtered the question, clearly unprepared.

"The oath I'm talking about is to me, not The Organization."

Fernando's expression became puzzled, then concerned. "Have you ever doubted my appreciation for all you've done for me since I came to America?"

"Appreciation and loyalty aren't the same things. It's time for you to show your unquestioned loyalty to me."

Fernando tried to inject some levity into an awkward situation.

"You sound like a certain recent President of the United States when you say that."

"That former president, as you call him, understood how The Organization works. For good reason. Now it's time for you to demonstrate your loyalty. A simple oath is no longer enough." Fidelia smiled as she spoke the words and arched her eyebrow in challenge.

She watched him cringe. Was it fear?

His eyes dropped downward, seemingly unable to meet hers directly. His lips twitched. "I've never played that game. I'm a union leader working on getting the best deals possible for my workers."

"And tomorrow, we'll find out if you have the guts to carry on."

A bell sounded from the building. They turned to watch a server bring their first course on a large silver tray. Both oohed and aahed as the server made a show of displaying giant Caribbean lobster tails dripping with butter, before serving them.

When he was safely back inside the restaurant, Fidelia continued. "Have you ever heard the name Joe Montebank?"

Fernando shook his head.

"Tomorrow, you're going to meet him. Mateo will drive you to the airport at seven. The jet that brought you here will take you to Aruba. You'll arrive about seven thirty and meet a guy named Jose. He owns a car rental agency there and works with us. Then, you'll head to the Renaissance Resort. At about eight thirty, Mr. Montebank will come out of the hotel lobby and look for the white van Jose will be driving. When he opens the door, you'll take him for a ride."

Fernando gasped. For a moment, it looked like he might puke all over the floor. Then he whimpered.

"Take him for a drive where?"

"Somewhere you'll demonstrate your loyalty."

He looked as if he was about to cry. "Fidelia, I don't do that stuff. I'm a union leader."

"Tomorrow, you'll do exactly what I described, or your next stop will be the above-ground cemetery for Catholic Christians on *Caya Ernesto Petronia* in Oranjestad. It's an appropriate spot for people who don't have the guts to show their loyalty."

TWENTY

Oranjestad, Aruba, Thursday January 26, 2023

When Joe Montebank didn't show up at their office that morning, Howard Knight tried his cell phone and room at the Renaissance without success. Klaudia was pissed.

They'd worked late the day and night before to create a new strategy to recover from their loss of the deported Uwe. Montebank had been helpful, and they'd both hoped to make more progress that Thursday morning.

After considering Multima's European organizational structure more carefully, Joe had helped them realize they should switch from building relationships with German and British employees to French speakers in France, Switzerland, and Belgium. There was always a slight chance that the targets in Belgium might have heard something about their previous efforts from their German-speaking colleagues. But they calculated that relations between the two language groups in that country were so factious they could take the risk.

It did complicate the artificial intelligence part of the equation. The company Klaudia had hired in Berlin preferred German and English because their software for those languages was more advanced. The management of the lab was less confident about the outcomes they could produce with French but agreed to try their best.

Klaudia had put them in touch with a technology whiz she knew in France. By the end of the day, that added resource was on a flight from Lille to Berlin. Today, they'd start training her to apply artificial intelligence to the app they were creating.

Unfortunately, Montebank hadn't completed his part of the deal. He was to call a woman in France he'd worked with successfully on an earlier project and try to get her to Aruba pronto. With Joe missing, they didn't know whether he'd found a replacement or not.

"We'd better find another French speaker," Klaudia said to Howard. Her tone now implied more resignation than anger. "You know anyone that might fit?"

"No one. My personal network has evaporated over the past

six years. You were one of the few people I had direct contact with in Europe before I had to leave The Organization. While I've been evading the FBI, Giancarlo Mareno, the Shadow, and Fidelia these past few years, I haven't had time to nurture new relationships with French women, as alluring an idea as that might seem." His tone leaned too much toward sarcasm, so he finished his statement with a rueful grin to soften the message.

"I have a friend from the escort business in Lourdes. Her name is Yvette. She's a madam there now. She is always cheerful, quick-witted, and knows a bit about business. I can see if she might fly over to help us out," Klaudia said.

"Worth trying. Do you remember if her voice sounds young enough to pass for a contemporary colleague of the people we identified?"

Klaudia suddenly bolted upright in her chair. Her face brightened unexpectedly before a broad smile crossed her face, followed by a touch of laughter.

"The question should be, do *you* remember her voice? You met her already in Lourdes when Giancarlo Mareno's men from Spain were chasing you across Europe. She drove you from a cemetery, where you were hiding out, to the private airport there. Don't you remember?"

The pictures formed. Howard's eyes drifted off to a space above Klaudia's head. He couldn't meet her gaze directly as the realization set in that he did remember the woman and her help getting him to the private plane that flew him to Austria. He quickly wiped away an unexpected tear from the corner of his eye and shook his head at the awful memory of what followed.

"That was the day before Mareno ruthlessly killed Janet."

"I'm sorry, Howard. It's a painful memory for you. I should have been more sensitive. I know it was horrible for you to see her murdered so cruelly. If Yvette brings back that unhappiness for you, we can find someone else."

He shook his head several times and leaned back in his chair, still looking for something above Klaudia's head. After holding that position a moment, he slowly lowered his gaze and reached for the coffee cup to his right, buying more time to process his thoughts before replying.

"It's all right. Call Yvette. You're right. She's a nice person who should do well with the phone calls. There's just one thing: she's still part of Fidelia's escort business. Do you think we need to get her buy-in?"

Klaudia thought about it for a few seconds. "You don't want to ask Fidelia for any favors at this early stage, right?"

Howard nodded.

"Then we won't tell Fidelia if Yvette will help us. She's the madam, after all. Surely, she can keep tabs on her girls from here for a few days. I'll handle it if we get any complaints." Klaudia bounced up from her seat and headed toward her private alcove, punching numbers into her phone as she walked.

Howard tried Joe Montebank's phone again. There was no answer and no option to leave a voice message. He tried the Renaissance Resort.

Again, no one responded to the dozen or more rings until the hotel operator noticed and returned to the line. "I'm sorry. There is no answer in that room. May I take a message?"

"No. Please connect me to the front desk."

"I'm looking for one of your guests, an American named Joe Montebank, registered in room 402," Howard said when the front desk answered. "Your operator tried the room, and no one answered. Have you seen him in the hotel this morning?"

"Yes. I saw him just a few minutes ago. He waved to me as he left the hotel."

TWENTY-ONE

Montreal, Quebec, Thursday January 26, 2023

Suzanne had invited James Fitzgerald to join her and Serge via a high-security video conference. It was the least she could do after James' help planting the listening devices in Financial Services' Chicago offices. As soon as Serge had first muttered that they had a problem, she knew she'd need help from the veteran executive at least one more time before he rode off into his retirement sunset.

"We may have provided too many keywords for the software," Serge began. "First, we programmed what we thought would be common words to come up in a conversation with an HR person, words like 'job,' 'position,' 'remuneration,' and so on. Later, we added words like 'research,' 'data,' and 'information.' We got a few thousand hits, so the software recorded far more than we expected."

"I can imagine," James said. "What did you do with it all?"

"There was so much. I assigned a couple experts to listen to all the hits. They finished them last night, and only one stood out as unusual. The caller identified himself as calling from New Jersey. When the analyst listening to the recording prompted the app to determine where in New Jersey, it reported the call untraceable. It was a burner phone."

"How do you know that?" Suzanne asked.

"Not to get too technical, but the software is sophisticated enough to detect a burner phone and provides the analyst with a specific code. It also can detect the region where the call originated by tracing the connection links detected from the transfers for each carrier used to transmit the call. The call that concerns us originated on the Caribbean island of Aruba."

"So the fellow calling said he was from New Jersey, but that data showed him calling from the Caribbean. Could it be he was just there on vacation?"

"Maybe. But he said he was calling from New Jersey during the call and even referred to the weather in Trenton that day," Serge replied. "But what really caught our analyst's attention was the chattiness of the caller. During the ten-minute recording, the caller asked more questions about your employee and her personal circumstances than he did about looking for a job, which was his stated objective."

"I'm sorry, but I'm missing the significance, Serge. What's alarming you?" James displayed courtesy and calm but telegraphed some impatience.

"Our analyst didn't know it until she crosschecked the recordings, but this conversation was with that same employee someone approached earlier about giving information and offering fifty thousand dollars. In fact, in the second call, early in the conversation, she asked the caller if he was calling from the same outfit as the one who offered her some money."

James bit his lip. He took a deep breath and rolled his shoulders a couple times. "What do you recommend? Do we fire her?"

"I'm not sure we have grounds for termination," Suzanne said. "What do you suggest, Serge?"

"I'm not sure she's guilty of anything yet. Her tone in the second recording implied she might be receptive to a money-for-information exchange. I suggest we monitor all her calls, incoming and outgoing. I've got software we can install remotely to do that. We should also restrict and record all her access to databases within the company. I can have someone work with your IT department in Chicago to determine what databases she needs to do her job. We'll monitor those and block her access to any she doesn't need."

TWENTY-TWO

Sint Michiel, Curaçao, Thursday January 26, 2023

Fidelia had used the body-camera technology in Chile three years earlier when Luigi was still her primary protector, before he became her US country boss. It recorded and transmitted to her devices in real time. It wasn't perfect, though. She'd mistakenly concluded that they'd killed Luigi on that mission when the camera died in a gunfight.

She could be reasonably confident that kind of mistake wouldn't recur with Fernando Disputas and his assignment that morning. Mateo had wired him up and tested the equipment before shuttling him to her private jet at the Curaçao airport. They needn't worry about any security checks at the airport. They didn't do that for private flights.

Nor would it be a problem in Aruba. Their guy, Jose, owned an offsite car rental company and was part of The Organization. All his vehicles came from owners located somewhere else. They traveled to the island in freight containers, and then Jose registered them as duly licensed vehicles with the Aruba Tax Department. So, he knew well which government officials were on the payroll. Today, he'd bribe the on-duty Immigration Authority supervisor to ignore the car picking up an arriving passenger in the private jet area.

Fernando switched on the camera before he stepped down from the jet. The sun already shone brightly in a cloudless blue sky, and Fidelia confirmed that the audio and video worked perfectly as the men met and exchanged greetings.

Then she nestled comfortably into her bedroom sofa to watch their performance, reaching for her other phone to handle one more task necessary to set the wheels fully in motion.

The first stop Jose and Disputas made after leaving the airport was a quick exchange of vehicles at the rental company's lot. Fidelia watched on her device as they switched from the small gray sedan the rental guy used at the airport to a plain white van like delivery companies used. It was dusty and without distinctive markings.

Using a burner phone, Fidelia reached Annika Wentz in

California and told her it was time to make her move. She'd already instructed Annika to call the Renaissance Resort in Aruba and ask for Montebank's room.

A moment or two later, he would answer the ringing phone in his room and Annika would read from the script Fidelia had drafted, one they'd rehearsed together until Annika had the ideal tone and emphasis for every word.

"Mr. Montebank, I am calling about your wife. She's fine and we'll let her go unharmed after you have a brief meeting with a gentleman in Aruba. Go downstairs now. Leave through the front door to your right as you exit the lobby. Look for a white van with no markings. Our contact will meet you at the van in five minutes. Don't speak to anyone at the hotel. Don't call the police. If the gentleman doesn't confirm to us that he has met you in five minutes, your wife will suffer."

They'd also choreographed that Annika would hold the burner phone camera in front of Montebank's wife before she ended the conversation and instruct her to tell her husband to do as he was told.

After a glance at her watch, Fidelia shifted her attention back to the video transmitting to her laptop from Disputas in Aruba. They'd concealed the video recorder and a handgun under his bulky shirt. Only a camera lens peeked out, disguised as a button. As instructed, Fernando stood outside the hotel beside the white van, facing the doorway.

When Fidelia spotted their prey on the screen, she calmly spoke into her phone. Montebank was the guy in the blue shirt, leaving the doorway. Disputas heard the confirmation in his ear, motioned toward Montebank, and opened the rear passenger door to the white van for their quarry to get in.

Disputas's voice was just above a whisper. "I'm holding a gun in my pocket and am prepared to use it. We're taking a short drive while we ask you some questions. Cooperate, and your wife will be fine. One wrong move and she'll no longer be fine."

He motioned for his victim to slide across to the seat on the other side. Disputas then jumped in, fumbled with his phone and dialed, his actions staged solely for the benefit of Montebank. When a voice answered, Disputas said only, "I have him. Keep the wife until we have our conversation. I'll call you when we finish."

Montebank started to protest, but Disputas pulled the gun out of his pocket and pointed the weapon directly at his victim. "Shut up."

For the next fifteen minutes, Fidelia heard only howls of wind through open windows and the hum of traffic from outside the vehicle as Jose sped towards their destination. She recognized the landscape from previous visits as they zipped along Route One toward the airport, then slowed for traffic congestion in the roundabout in front of the airport before speeding off again southward toward the small village of Simeon Antonio near both the Caribbean Sea and a national park.

When the road ended, Jose made a right turn onto a poorly maintained road of gravel and stones and drove slowly to its end. From there, the camera picked up a single fishing boat dragged ashore and waiting for them.

As they exited the van, Montebank stiffened upright, eyes darting in every direction. A few seconds passed before he said, his voice hoarse, "What are you doing? What is going on?"

"Just climb into the boat." Disputas tried to disguise his own fear. He'd hated being near open water since he'd almost drowned as a child in Puerto Rico. Still, he needed his victim to cooperate and tried to reassure him. "We want to talk where it's quiet and our conversation can't be recorded."

Montebank was having nothing of it. He jerked his arm away from Disputas's grip on his elbow. "Fuck you! I'm not going anywhere. Ask your fucking questions here, right now."

Disputas lashed out in anger and shock. He yanked the gun from his pocket and took one violent swing at Montebank's face, knocking him into the sand. He landed flat on his back, blood oozing from his lips.

Between Jose and Disputas, they dragged the struggling Montebank to the side of the boat and shoved him in. Jose scurried to the front, released the rope and anchor from the sand, then jumped into the rear of the boat as gentle waves carried it to deeper water off the shoreline.

Montebank recovered enough to spit out a tooth as blood trickled more quickly down his face and onto the bottom of the wooden boat.

Jose started the motor when the water appeared deep enough. They headed out until Fidelia saw only an outline of the shore.

"That's far enough," she said into Disputas's ear after several minutes. "Do your work."

"Why are you in Aruba?" Fernando used a tone that made clear he wasn't simply making conversation.

Montebank didn't reply. His mouth was twisted as he groaned with pain and gripped his jaw tightly. He coughed as some blood seeped down his throat, despite leaning forward and spitting into the bottom of the boat every few moments. "I need water."

"We don't have water. Answer the question, or you'll lose another tooth."

"I'm helping a business partner," Montebank answered.

"Is that business partner working for Jeffersons Stores?"

"I'm not at liberty to divulge that information."

Disputas lashed out with his gun again, hitting Montebank in the same place with more force. His victim didn't see it coming and hadn't even raised a hand to deflect the blow. The power of the impact threw his body toward the side of the boat, tipping it momentarily closer to the waterline.

Fear overcame Fernando. He trembled so violently the camera jumped up and down for over a minute. Fidelia couldn't decide whether he was terrified of drowning in the open sea, or genuinely worried that his victim might not cough up the information he needed to satisfy her. She said nothing and watched.

"Answer my question," Disputas said. "Are you and your partner doing work for Jeffersons Stores?"

Montebank nodded once, then gagged and spat up more blood.

"Who gave you the deal?"

"What? What are you talking about?" Montebank took a few moments to respond but seemed genuinely confused.

"Someone at Jeffersons paid you money to do research. Who was it? How much did they pay?" Disputas's voice was now almost a scream of desperation. He seemed as distraught as Montebank, who appeared to gag as he spoke, as if he might throw up at any moment.

"Her name's Susan Willson. Senior vice president business development. It's no big secret. No big deal. Why the fuck did you have to involve my wife, smash up my face, and create all this drama? All you had to do was ask me! A phone call would have worked."

"How much is she paying you?"

"Four hundred thousand dollars. Half as a deposit. The other half when we deliver the goods."

"And just what are the goods?"

"We're getting her some names and titles of people who work for their competitor—Multima Supermarkets. Again, no big deal. Now get me back to shore." Montebank raised his voice and glared, his eyes huge and menacing.

Disputas paused while he listened to the question Fidelia planted in his ear. Unable to see Fernando's facial expression, she could only guess his precise reaction.

"Wrong answer," Disputas said calmly. "The correct answer involves a gentleman in Japan, and the amount paid was one million dollars."

Montebank blanched and shrunk in size. His eyes darted from side to side. He started to say something, then hesitated.

Disputas appeared to regain his composure. The tenor of his voice sounded more confident—his manner more deliberate—as though he sensed this would soon be all over.

"I'll give you one more chance to answer correctly. If you make another mistake, you'll find your wife's pretty face will have a nasty scar from ear to ear when you see her next."

Montebank's shoulders slumped forward. He spat out more blood, though not in anger. It was more as though he was cleansing his mouth. He took a deep breath. "Whoever you guys are, you're no better than the other bastards. If I tell you anything, they promised to kill my wife in retaliation. You're going to harm her one way or the other, so...."

With one massive thrust from his thighs, Montebank lunged upward into Disputas's face, his arms flailing wildly before his entire body filled the camera lens. Male voices shouted and screamed. Before she could plant a comment in Disputas' ear, she heard a shot, then second and third shots.

The last thing she saw was brilliant blue water approaching the camera lens. No further sounds or images came through.

TWENTY-THREE

Oranjestad, Aruba, Friday January 27, 2023

Joe Montebank didn't show up at their office on Thursday. Nor did he respond to Howard's repeated attempts to reach him by cell or at his hotel.

It wasn't alarming, but it was curious. So, the next morning, Howard set out toward the Renaissance Resort to see if he could learn more in person. Equally curious, Earl Boyante joined him for the thirty-minute walk from Sandra's Inn.

Howard genuinely enjoyed the guy's company, and they kibitzed for most of their walk. The American loved to chat. He entertained with stories from the internet, politics, or his experiences on the island almost non-stop as they walked on the uneven sidewalks or edges of the roadways, headed toward the city center.

He said "hello" to every person they met and waved to every passing car. When Howard inquired why, Earl said he liked to be friendly wherever he traveled.

"With the oncoming cars," he added, "I just think it's harder to hit someone who gives you a wave and a smile." Then he wanted to know what they'd do if Joe never came back to the office.

Everyone realized that without Montebank, they couldn't start the next phase of intelligence-gathering calls, even if an English version of the artificial intelligence software was ready. They now needed a French version to gather accurate European information.

Howard said they'd see what was possible after they'd stopped at the Renaissance Resort and found out when the guy expected to return to the office. After that, Earl could head out to Surfside Beach, just down the road from the resort.

The first sign of trouble was an extraordinary number of police vehicles parked at the resort, blue lights flashing. Howard counted at least seven small SUVs and guessed that number of cars might represent the entire fleet of the Aruba constabulary.

Howard's early-warning antenna sprang up. He gave Earl a nudge when he spotted the activity and pointed toward the resort. "Hear about anything that might explain all those police cars?"

Earl shook his head. "Probably a ruckus with a guest. I hear some of the rich guys occasionally show up in the morning drunk, rowdy and angry after a bad night in their casino down the street."

Maybe. But that many police in one area was never a good thing.

Howard improvised. "I think I'll return to find Joe later when things calm down. Since you'll pass there to get to the beach, why don't you wander by and see what you overhear? Call me from the beach if you get anything."

There was little doubt Earl would poke around, ask a few questions, and probably chat with a police officer or two.

Howard ducked behind a couple delivery vans as he left, heading toward their office. When he glanced back, Earl was waddling up the sidewalk like a hotel guest returning home. Howard carried on at his usual pace and didn't look backward again.

Klaudia stepped in Howard's path when he closed their office's outer door.

"Twitter's abuzz this morning." She treated the social media site as a source of news. She'd started following a couple local journalists from the day they arrived. "Local police found a body in a fishing boat adrift off the coast south of the airport this morning. It had gunshot wounds to the head. Police think the corpse might be an American tourist."

"Have they identified the body? Why do they think it's an American?"

"Nothing official yet. The face is a mess, but it seemed to have some characteristics matching those on a passport photo of an American who arrived earlier this week and was supposed to be staying at the Renaissance Resort."

"You don't think they're talking about Joe, do you? And what sort of crazies are you connected with on that site?"

Klaudia only shrugged in response.

Since there was no point in speculating, and there was nothing they could find out or do until the police announced something official, Howard abruptly changed the subject. "What time is your friend Yvette arriving today?"

Klaudia's stern facial expression reflected her annoyance with his abrupt switch, but her tone didn't signal any offense taken. "She'll be in around six thirty tonight. I'll meet her, get her checked into a small hotel near my place, and have dinner with her. That's why I'm anxious about Joe Montebank. We need him here to start her training tomorrow morning."

Howard was not invited to join them for dinner, but that wasn't unexpected. Meanwhile, they were both eager to find their wayward trainer. Why hadn't Earl called with an update? He glanced at his watch and saw thirty minutes had already passed since he'd left the guy on the sidewalk leading to the Renaissance.

Howard's phone rang, saving him from further conversation with Klaudia. The phone didn't display an incoming number. He let it ring several times as he made his way to his private office. When he answered, it was Fidelia.

"How are things going in the corporate espionage business this morning?" Her tone was uncharacteristically light and chatty.

"It's too early to tell. I just arrived at the office and haven't had my first cup of java yet." His tone sounded neutral, almost suspicious, so he quickly added more. "But it's a beautiful day here in Aruba. How about where you are?"

"It's just above zero and sunny here in New York. I think I'll spend all day inside, envying your weather." She laughed, then quickly added, "But I'm sure you and Klaudia are busy, so I won't take much of your time. How's that character Montebank working out for you?"

Howard didn't answer immediately. He leaned back in his executive chair reflectively. *Didn't she put Klaudia in charge of the espionage business? Why's she really calling?*

He chose his words carefully. "He's doing okay. We're all still confident we can complete that first job for Jeffersons Stores on time." As an afterthought, he added a quick probe. "Would you like me to bring Klaudia into the conversation to get her perspective?"

"No. No. I'll chat with her another time," Fidelia replied, a touch too quickly. "I know the guy impressed you. I had some doubts about him, wondered if he'd show up for work every day, that sort of thing."

Howard paused again before he answered. Gossip was not usually part of his conversations with Fidelia. He glanced at his watch again before he replied. "Yeah, you may have something there. He's shown up every day since he got here, except yesterday.

Disappeared off the radar, and we're hoping he checks in here shortly. You haven't heard from him by any chance, have you?"

"No. No. I was thinking about using him for something else when you're done with him." Her tone sounded too tightly controlled, her answer too vague, but he had no time to reflect on it.

"Sorry, I'm going to have to cut our call short," Howard said. "Some gentlemen in uniform just walked into our office."

TWENTY-FOUR

New York, New York, Friday January 27, 2023

Suzanne had expected Hadley to arrange for the male co-host when it came time for the interview. Instead, Liara Furtamo and her producers offered a televised interview for an upcoming program.

Suzanne's first instinct was to refuse.

The woman had blindsided Suzanne in a TV interview once before, back in the days when Liara had worked with CBNN, the corporate news network. Now she co-hosted the popular program *49 Minutes* on a competing network.

Edward Hadley and Gordon Goodfellow wanted her to do it regardless.

"Here's the thing." Edward always started his arguments with the point he considered most important. "They're going to run the story whether or not they interview you. The profits we announced last week make excellent fodder for them to feed on at the trough of public opinion. Inflation is impacting the life of every American. Some are having trouble buying food and paying rent in the same month. If we leave the story to *49 Minutes* without balancing their perspective, we'll get skewered."

Usually, Edward wasn't an alarmist. He was a seasoned professional who had led Multima's corporate and public relations efforts for over a decade. She always listened to his advice and usually followed it. Both his tone and his message caused her to reflect before responding.

Gordon Goodfellow, who had joined them on Zoom, jumped into the conversation gap. "We know they've got interviews scheduled with the head of Consumers' United, the radical economist Bolshoi Negativ, and hostile senators from both political parties. We desperately need someone reasonable to balance their story."

"If they've already decided to attack us, why do you think anything I say will change the tone or outcome of the program's message?"

"You may be right," Edward countered. "Even assuming you do one of your usual great interviews, the outcome still might not be in our favor. We spend very little money on the TV networks, so they have nothing to fear if they destroy us. But to keep credibility with their viewers and give at least an appearance of balance, they have to allow you enough airtime to tell our story. I'm confident you can effectively sell our message to a portion of the audience, muting any negative impact the program creates."

Suzanne continued twiddling her thumbs below the boardroom table out of the Zoom camera's view. Without making eye contact with Hadley across the table, she bought some more time by reaching for her coffee mug and taking a deliberately long sip. Her eyes avoided the camera and Goodfellow's scrutiny too. Finally, she pursed her lips together a couple times before she chose her words.

"Okay. I'll do it. But I want to establish a few ground rules. First, let's tell them I'd like to do it in their studio in a simple setting. Just a couple comfortable chairs. Second, tell them I have only one hour available for the interview. Last, tell them I want to speak privately with Liara Furtamo before the interview. No cameras. No microphones."

"We can ask," Edward said. He stretched the three words over several long seconds while his eyebrows arched, conveying skepticism about how warmly *49 Minutes* might receive the requests.

An hour later, he circled back with the news that the network had accepted all three of Suzanne's conditions, and she needed to be in New York about four hours later for the recording.

"I know you're bitter about how Liara treated you in that interview a few years ago, but I urge you to consider carefully anything you might say to her privately," he said.

With the Multima jet parked about an hour from Suzanne's Montreal office, she scooted out as soon as Eileen rounded up a hairstylist and make-up artist. Edward Hadley joined them all at the waiting car.

In flight, while the women prepared her for the television cameras, Edward reviewed their talking points until she had key numbers memorized and her arguments ready.

Air traffic control cleared them for landing at Teterboro, New Jersey, without delay, and a car arranged by Serge's team drove up to the stairs of the aircraft as the doorway opened. When Suzanne checked her watch as she entered the studio, fifteen minutes remained before the scheduled interview.

Liara Furtamo greeted her warmly with a broad smile and outstretched hand. "You wanted to have a word privately before we start?" She gestured toward an open doorway, inviting Suzanne to enter.

Edward's words of advice about meeting privately still rang in her ears, and she'd thought about them as they rushed to New York.

"I just have a single request for the interview. At whatever point you think it appropriate, can you ask me what keeps me awake at night?"

Liara replied that she'd be delighted to pose the question and asked if there was anything else Suzanne would like to discuss. She shook her head, then looked Liara directly in the eye as she thanked her.

It took only moments for the studio team to wire Suzanne with the unobtrusive microphone attached to the collar of her jacket and allow the make-up artist and stylist one last pass with powder for her face and a couple squirts of hair spray.

Both high-powered women settled into firm leather chairs set so close together that their knees almost touched.

Liara's first questions followed the playbook Edward Hadley had told her to expect. How would Suzanne explain her company's record profits at a time inflation was making it harder for some Americans to put food on their family's tables? Why couldn't a huge, successful company like Multima absorb some of the rising costs to make it easier for its customers? What was her management team doing to fight inflation?

Speaking simply, Suzanne explained the small profits her company earned on every dollar spent in Multima supermarkets. She reminded Liara about their very public two-month standoff with Lepsico, the beverage and snack food manufacturer. Multima's shelves grew bare because they'd refused to pay the higher prices demanded. Lepsico refused to ship goods until Multima caved under pressure from consumers.

She talked about how the war in Ukraine had impacted global food supply and gas prices while COVID-19 continued to disrupt supply chains. As Edward advised, she avoided business and economics jargon and spoke to her audience using everyday language.

Suzanne outlined the surge in customer purchases of Multima's privately labeled products, which were usually far cheaper than brand names for comparable quality. She also made a plug for the company's recent announcement that Multima would freeze prices for those private labels for a few months.

The interview unfolded almost exactly as Edward Hadley had predicted and Suzanne had rehearsed. She allowed herself the luxury of inhaling a silent, deep breath as Liara consulted her notes for the next question.

The interviewer lifted her head and projected an angelic smile directly at the camera over Suzanne's right ear. "Tell us, Suzanne, if rampaging inflation, angry customers, and negative media coverage don't cause you any significant concerns, what keeps you up at night? Anything?"

The bitch just had to do it, didn't she?

By Liara casting Suzanne's sole request in the most negative light possible, how she framed her response might become the highlight of the entire interview. She took another deep breath, maintained her friendly demeanor, and looked directly into the camera over Liara's left ear.

"Thank you for asking that question. It's a good one and an important one too. The issues you mentioned—inflation and how it affects our customers, perceptions created in the media, and public opinion headwinds—are all important concerns. The good news is that they are all temporary, and because we're talking about them, we'll find suitable solutions for each of them in the coming months. It's what no one seems to talk about that keeps me awake at night."

Suzanne paused for a second or two to let that thought sink in.

"Why can a regional meat-processing firm suddenly buy out all its competitors in a few weeks, then almost double its prices to supermarkets, while not increasing what it pays to farmers by one cent?"

Suzanne maintained a calm tone of voice, but picked up her pace slightly to prevent any interruption to her flow by Liara Furtamo. Without taking a breath, she carried on.

"What forces are behind the surges of violence in the

food industry that started well before COVID-19 and recent inflation? Chicken farms that suddenly burn down without police apprehending any culprits. Small farmers forced to sell their properties for a pittance to wealthy registered corporations identified in sale documents only by numbered names? And why are authorities still without answers about the brutal murder of Jeffersons Stores' CEO and his wife two years ago, or the bombing of my home a few weeks before that?

"Do we suspect unhappy customers are taking these actions? No. I think we'd all agree that only organized, sophisticated, and powerful criminals have the means and the motivation to commit those acts. Their goal should be obvious. If they can control the food supply to a region, a country, or the world, their power and wealth will be unlimited. If we're not careful, our society will become subservient to organized crime, and dysfunctional.

"That's what keeps me awake at night. I challenge both our police and our journalists to investigate these concerns vigorously and root out organized crime before it's too late."

Liara Furtamo remained silent for a moment. Unfortunately, she shut down any further discussion with a tilt of her head and a mischievous smile as she looked directly into the camera over Suzanne's right ear. "Thank you, Suzanne Simpson, for spending a few minutes with us today, defending your company's massive profits, promoting Multima private label products and creating a whole new concern for your customers."

Suzanne maintained her forced smile until a producer announced the end and signaled for the cameras to shut off. With slumped shoulders, Edward Hadley looked down at his shoes or something else on the floor.

TWENTY-FIVE

Sint Michiel, Curaçao, Saturday January 28, 2023

Joe Montebank ended up dead, just as Fidelia expected. Fernando Disputas had failed his test miserably. He wasn't supposed to die, so there would be no further opportunity for him to prove his loyalty. Mateo confirmed both deaths when he finally reached their guy, Jose, in Aruba.

His account had been shocking and dramatic. The men struggled over the handgun Mateo had given to Fernando. Before Jose could react, the gun discharged, shattering Fernando's knee and knocking him backward into the water. Disputas managed to yank the gun from Montebank's grip and fire three shots as he fell overboard. One shot exploded in Montebank's face, killing him instantly.

Blood and brains splattered Montebank's corpse. His remains collapsed backward, with what remained of his head bouncing off a middle wooden seat and onto the bottom of the boat, right next to a large hole created when the bullet exited Fernando's knee. Water was already gushing through the opening, the small boat rapidly sinking.

When he turned his attention to Disputas in the water, Jose noticed blood encircling his struggling form. It looked as if the guy couldn't swim. He would disappear below the waves for multiple seconds at a time, coughing and choking whenever he resurfaced.

According to Jose, from the time he fell overboard, Fernando struggled to survive in the water. Meanwhile, Montebank's body slumped on the bottom of the boat, and water from the hole spread wider and faster. Jose did a quick assessment and got his ass out of there. He claimed he stripped to his underwear and jumped from the bow of the boat pointed toward the shoreline.

A strong swimmer, Jose reported that he never doubted his ability to reach shore safely on his own, but was sure there was no way he could do it trying to drag Disputas to shore. When he called Mateo to explain what happened, he was at his home and had already polished off a mickey of rum.

Fidelia had listened in on Mateo's speakerphone.

"When I got ta shore, had only my underwear. Lost my phone in the water. No shoes. Nothin'. I had ta wander in my underwear till I found some laundry dryin' in a backyard. Fortun'ly, found some jeans that fit and a T-shirt. There were people in the house, so I had ta scoot 'fore they saw me."

"How did you get home?" Mateo asked.

"Waited fer a bus, a local one. Flagged down the driver an' he's a neighbor. Got 'im to drop me off here."

"Have you heard anything from the police? Anyone else see you out there?"

"Don't think so. It's quiet out in that area. That's why I took 'em there, just like you asked."

Mateo looked at Fidelia and arched his brows, momentarily perplexed. She held up one finger and nodded, motioning for him to mute the call.

"Jose, hold a second. I'm putting you on hold while I get some instructions."

Fidelia wasted no time. "Tell him to lie low for the next few days. Just go to work and do his normal stuff. Say nothing to anyone. Stay out of the rum. If the police contact him, he knows nothing about any Americans, a fishing boat, or anything else. Tell him to call you if he hears anything."

She picked up her own secure phone and hit the speed dial for Klaudia. "Any word from Howard yet?"

"No. They just let Earl and me out a few minutes ago. Earl Boyante is a guy we hired for our intelligence work. An American. Stays at the same inn as Howard. He says they interviewed him three times last night and kept his passport when they let him go this morning."

"Did they keep yours too?"

"Yeah. They're not used to this kind of violence on the island and figure both Howard and I have something to do with Montebank's death. Earl said most of the questions they asked him were about the two of us. Do you have a lawyer here I can use?"

"I can find you one, but why would they suspect you?"

"Earl says they're not buying our story. Says they know Montebank wasn't involved in typical market research and has an unsavory reputation in the US. None of the cops said it directly to me, but Earl thinks they're on to the corporate espionage angle."

"Why?"

"A young German we hired was arrested and deported. Apparently, he told them everything he knew."

"How much did he know?"

"Enough. He made a number of calls to targets after his training."

"Shit." Fidelia paused to process the revelation. "So they haven't let you see or talk to Howard yet?"

"Not yet. If they've got Howard, he must be in a separate area. There was only one other woman in a cell next to me. An American. Arrested her late in the night, and she was so drunk she slept on the floor. Never spoke to her, either. They only questioned me for about an hour yesterday, but they detained me all night. Nobody came to my cell today until a policewoman stopped by and said I was good to go."

Fidelia took another moment to assess it all.

It was just as well she'd learned at this stage that Disputas wasn't the right guy. She had alternatives who could work just as well. On the Aruba front, Howard and Klaudia had both dealt with the police in the past. They knew the usual routines and should stay quiet. Jose shouldn't be a problem. This guy, Earl, seemed like the only wild card.

"How much does Earl know about your business?"

"A lot," Klaudia said. "We involved him in most of our meetings. He made the initial calls to the Multima offices in the English-speaking countries. He likes to talk but I don't think he knew enough to be much of a danger, except he's really shaken up with the news about Montebank."

"Okay. Lie low and remind Earl to keep his mouth shut about everything. Plant the seed that what happened to Montebank could happen to him. Call me when you hear from Howard."

Disputas's bungled assignment posed other complications. She'd need to change other critical aspects of her plan.

"Mia, call Annika in California. Tell her that plans have changed, and I need her back here. Mateo, get the pilots ready for a flight to LA to pick her up. Send one of your guys along, just in case."

As both scurried from her room, Fidelia wandered down to the poolside where Nadine Violette stretched out on a comfortable sun chair, tanning her trim body. Her reaction to Fidelia's proposal would determine whether the plan advanced, or Fidelia folded her hand to play a different game another day.

TWENTY-SIX

Oranjestad, Aruba, Monday January 30, 2023

Inside the jail at the police headquarters, Howard had seen only some sort of assistant working since Friday. Over the weekend, that woman carried a tray of food from a nearby restaurant to his tiny twelve-by-twelve cell three times a day. Then she must have gone home, since he saw no one from dusk until dawn.

His cell had no air-conditioning, but there was a small window, covered by steel bars and mounted near the ceiling. Continuous breezes off the ocean provided some measure of relief, but high humidity made comfort elusive.

He didn't see any prisoners in any of the three other cells, and the door from the holding area to the offices remained closed except when the assistant made her regular visits with food trays.

Howard tried to get permission to make a call. The assistant told him a supervisor would return to the office on Monday, and he'd decide when and who Howard could call. She brought him some well-worn paperback books and a couple stale English-language newspapers the first day, but only food and drinks afterward.

As the door opened that morning, Howard didn't bother to rise from his bed. Instead, he sat with his back against the wall, his legs and arms crossed. He looked relaxed, but not arrogant, and smiled at the uniformed officer, who took his time selecting the right key from the dozen or more rattling on an oversized chain.

"No food this morning?" Howard asked.

"We'll figure out food after you have a chat with our chief. He'll decide whether you stay longer."

The officer waved Howard out of the cell and motioned for him to come out. He led the way, and Howard followed as they paraded through the area where he'd spent much of Friday answering the same questions asked a couple dozen different ways.

That morning, a few officers and clerical staff glanced up from their work to watch him pass, each appearing to judge his innocence or guilt. No one spoke, and everyone looked away whenever Howard tried to make eye contact.

After climbing the stairs, the officer led him to a large, comfortable air-conditioned office, then turned and left the room. It was considerably cooler than the stuffy and always-hot temperatures downstairs in the office area and jail cells where they'd held Howard.

A large, dark-skinned man in a pale green, open-collar uniform shirt sat behind a massive steel desk painted brown. He looked up with an impassive expression. About Howard's age, he had slivers of gray in his styled haircut, which still looked predominantly a natural black. His dark eyes looked wise but hid any sign of his intentions.

He pointed to an empty chair in front of his desk. The chair beside it was occupied by one of the detectives who had interrogated Howard before the weekend. That fellow didn't bother to greet their suspect and sat looking downward at his phone.

No one spoke at first. The man behind the desk—presumably the chief—took stock of Howard. When he spoke, there was no introduction or greeting.

"We know your real name is not Stuart McGregor. We also suspect you're not Canadian. Over the weekend, we spoke with the IRCC. Do you know what the IRCC does, sir?"

Howard shook his head. He guessed it had something to do with issuing passports, but if he said that, the next question would probably be to explain what the acronym stood for. He had no idea, so it was better to keep his mouth shut.

"It means 'Immigration, Refugees and Citizenship Canada.' According to the Canadian government, you're not any of those. So who are you? And why are you really in Aruba?"

Over the weekend, Howard had had lots of time to think, and he'd used it wisely.

Eventually, the police would concede he knew nothing about Joe Montebank's murder, but they'd probably look for something else to justify his detention. Did his tourist status prevent him from working on the island? Could they connect Montebank's background in corporate espionage with what they were doing in Aruba? Most important of all, what reaction would Fidelia have?

He'd been a slave of The Organization for his entire adult life. True, Mareno had treated him well for many years. In fact, Howard had thrived as the top financial guy in the criminal element and had accumulated a decent amount of money. A slave or not, things were okay right up to the time of Howard's billion-dollar mistake with Multima Corporation.

Mareno could never forgive a mistake of that magnitude.

Howard had no choice. He'd had to run from both the FBI and The Organization—one to avoid arrest for his criminal activities and the other to avoid death by revenge—making the past seven years the worst of his life.

Imagine that. For over ten percent of his time on earth, he'd been running for his life. Despite Fidelia's decision to cut him some slack and let him live in Aruba, his latest venture had come off the rails in a matter of weeks. He had little doubt this entire mess was part of a ploy she'd concocted to keep him under her controlling thumb.

So, when the Aruba police chief asked his loaded question that morning, Howard was ready. It was risky, but the time felt right. He answered without hesitation.

"I'll give you a name and number to call in Washington. They'll give you whatever information you need."

TWENTY-SEVEN

Montreal, Quebec, Monday January 30, 2023

The outcry from media outlets and viewers of *49 Minutes* was worse than Suzanne had imagined possible. It started within moments of her segment on the Sunday evening show with negative tweets on Twitter and a barrage of nasty comments on Facebook and Instagram. Virtually every post criticized her for casting blame on organized crime for food price inflation despite huge Multima profits.

"Living on another planet." "Dereliction of CEO duty." "Out of touch with reality." Comments were vicious, sometimes obscene, and always critical. Her effort had failed miserably.

Monday morning, newspaper headlines were equally negative. "Smoking Something Before Interview?" the *Chicago Tribune* asked on page one in bold letters. "Corporate Greed Reaches a New Low" the *Toronto Star* claimed. And the *Wall Street Journal* was even less subtle, wondering "Is It Time for a Change at Multima?"

Edward Hadley asked for a few minutes with Suzanne just before noon.

"You'll never hear me say I told you so, but it's pretty grim out there in media land today. We may need to issue a statement or make you available for a press conference. The negative momentum of this thing has taken on a life of its own."

He shook his head as he spoke, but he maintained direct eye contact, as always. He might be discouraged, but the public relations fiasco hadn't defeated him. Still, Suzanne tried to make their conversation easier.

"It was a mistake. I realized that as soon as I watched your reaction at the end of the recording session on Friday. I should have heeded your advice and not raised my personal views. What can I do to clean up the mess?"

"I wish I had a clear path to recommend. Candidly, I don't know. I spoke with Alberto Ferer before I came in. The board isn't happy either. He already had two angry calls from directors this morning. If there's a third call, he'll be over to ask you to convene a special meeting of the board to discuss damage control."

Alberto Ferer was Multima's chief legal officer and secretary of the board of directors. It was he who organized and managed their meetings. Although he was usually a loyal supporter, Alberto took seriously his obligation to the corporation at large—and not just Suzanne, the company's CEO, and largest shareholder.

"Let's bring him over right now," she said, reaching for her phone. She had Ferer on the line after a couple rings. Then she instructed Eileen to bring in James Fitzgerald by Zoom as well. She told them all that she was there to listen.

Within thirty minutes, Suzanne had listened to the comments and concerns of her three advisors and decided to act quickly. They'd call a special meeting of the board of directors for four o'clock that afternoon. The only subject on the agenda would be Suzanne's *49 Minutes* interview and any actions the company should take in response.

When the meeting started, Suzanne made her opening comments with candor and confidence.

"First, let me apologize to each of you for making this meeting necessary. I realize your time is valuable, and I regret my decision to deviate from the strategy and script Edward carefully prepared for me to use in the interview with Liara Furtamo. I'm sorry for that." Suzanne looked at their faces displayed on a large screen, gauging their reactions. Some conveyed sympathy, others appeared angry. She carried on.

"We're getting some extremely negative publicity today and we'll have to wait and see what impact that may or may not have on our sales and share price this week. No one knows yet. But I value your opinions and would like to discuss the possible fallout with you openly and candidly. And I'd like your blunt opinions about any steps I or other members of the management team should take."

Her directors didn't hesitate. One suggested she schedule a media conference for later that day. "Apologize publicly for your outburst on *49 Minutes* and promise that Multima will do everything possible to get retail prices down again, and quickly."

Others weren't so sure. One director from the Midwest asked Suzanne if she was entirely convinced about organized crime trying to worm its way into the food supply chain. When she answered she had no doubt about it, that director argued she should become even more vocal and make it an important cause for the public.

The directors' opinions varied widely. After a half hour of discussion, Suzanne felt tensions build. At times, it was even more intense than the raw emotions around Gordon Goodfellow's proposal to buy Jeffersons Stores, the contentious subject of their November meeting. It became clear there was no consensus on the best course to follow.

Suzanne cut the meeting short before tempers flared further and positions became entrenched. Once the Zoom camera was off, she moved on.

"It's your call, Edward." She turned to her vice president for public and corporate affairs, then stood, signaling the end of their discussion. "If you need me to make a statement, do an interview, whatever. Let me know."

Before Suzanne could move on to anything else, Serge came into her office. The worry lines on his forehead signaled it was not a social visit.

"We just had a hit on the caller to Chicago. They confirmed the fifty thousand-dollar offer to Judy Jones at Financial Services. She agreed to get them a list of all the key decision-makers and field supervisors, worldwide. The caller plans to get back to her in a week to confirm she got the info and where she should deliver it."

TWENTY-EIGHT

Sint Michiel, Curaçao, Tuesday January 31, 2023

The developments in Aruba didn't please Fidelia at all. She hadn't slept well during the night and noticed a slight tremor in her hand as she guided a cup of coffee to her lips that morning. If she wasn't careful, things could spin out of control.

How incompetent Fernando Disputas turned out to be. First, the idiot managed to blow off his knee when Montebank apparently surprised him in the boat. That was bad enough. The stray bullet—or maybe even bullets from the semi-automatic handgun—then blasted a hole in the bottom of the boat, which sank rapidly.

How could she have forgotten the guy didn't know how to swim? Still he went a half mile out into the ocean without a lifejacket.

In the longer term, it was probably better that he failed his test, drowned at sea, and wouldn't be around to fuck up any more assignments. But the shit would probably hit the fan when they finally identified his body. It made everything more complicated.

Fortunately, Mateo had found a guy at the airport in Atlanta who wiped clean all airport records of Fidelia's jet landing and departing the day Disputas left for Curaçao. Over on Aruba, Jose had paid someone he knew in the air traffic control tower to do the same. And one of Mateo's guys was at the airport in Curaçao that morning, completing the same task. It would probably end up costing her about twenty-five grand to clean up all the flight records.

On a more positive note, Annika was back from California.

"You left Montebank's wife okay?" Fidelia felt no guilt about leaving the woman a widow. Only Montebank should feel remorse, if he were alive. The bastard had deserved to have his brains blown out after the way he treated her escort girl in Australia.

Fidelia had seen pictures after they'd found the battered woman in the Outback. He'd mutilated her body after he had his way with her. Fidelia had gagged and almost vomited when she first realized what had happened. Sure, the guy's wife would shed a few tears, but when The Organization forgave Montebank's mortgage, the woman would be debt free. If she found a job, she'd survive and probably find another guy.

"She was a bit of an emotional mess, but I fed her the two pills you gave me. She's probably still sleeping." Annika spoke softly, her eyes lowered. This wasn't the work she enjoyed most.

"Never saw your face?"

"No. I wore an N95 mask the entire time, with this sunhat on." She held it up for Fidelia to see. It flopped down well over her forehead and ears. "And she only got a good look at me with my sunglasses on, too. She won't be able to identify me."

Fidelia took a long look at the woman. Annika still had the magic, even as she approached sixty. Blessed with a naturally trim body, she appealed to guys instantly. Her face showed traces of the usual worry lines that come with age, and she noticed skin drooping slightly under her eyes, but the woman's face looked as vibrant as that of many women years younger. Dark brown eyes still hinted at mystery with enough sparkle to suggest adventure.

"I hope you got some sleep on the jet. I have another job for you," Fidelia said. She called in Mia, explaining to both what was happening next.

"The same private jet that brought you from California will take you over to Aruba at eleven thirty this morning. You'll arrive about noon. Here's a backpack I bought where you can store the things you need to bring. Inside, I've included a swimsuit that should fit you perfectly, but try it before you leave, to be sure."

Mia passed her the vegan leather backpack and Annika pulled out a black, low-cut swimsuit for a quick inspection.

Mia continued the instructions. "We've reserved a room for you at the Aruba Surfside Marina. Take a taxi from the airport. It should take about 10 minutes, and they'll charge you twenty US dollars. Check in using the name Suzy Smith. I already paid for your room, and they won't ask you for ID. Change into your swimwear. When you're ready, head across the street to Surfside Beach. It's less than a five-minute walk."

Fidelia watched intently as Annika nodded understanding, then issued her orders. "Here's a picture of the guy you're going to meet. His name is Earl Boyante, an American. Around the beach they call him 'the bucket man.' He likes to drink beer and they tell me he's extremely social. Get him to your room. Just like you slipped a couple pills in Montebank's wife's drink, do the same with these tablets and Boyante. It'll only take five or ten minutes before he's gone."

Fidelia watched Annika's eyes for any signs of fear or concern. As far as she knew, this would be the first time the woman's assignment included murder. Annika's eyes widened noticeably, and she looked like she was about to ask a question. Instead, she swallowed and averted her eyes downward.

"What's my payment for this assignment?" Her tone hardened.

Maybe she has done this before. "Ten big ones."

"Into my bank account in Cayman before I leave?"

Fidelia turned on her phone and scrolled to a photo, showing the screen to Annika. "It's already in your account. The pilots and plane will stay on the ground. They'll give you a number to call when you're finished. They'll pick you up outside the hotel and take you with them to the jet. You should be back here shortly after darkness sets in tonight."

Earl Boyante would become an unfortunate victim, but there was little choice. He was a wild card who had talked too freely with the police in Aruba already and probably fed them more information about Klaudia and Howard. That pair had enough sense to say nothing to the police, but she had no way of knowing how much Boyante might have learned about her and The Organization's role in their mischief in Aruba.

Cornered, he might eventually connect some dots in the deaths of Montebank and Disputas. Eliminating Boyante, while the police held Howard in custody, would reduce the likelihood of that happening.

First, she needed a rock-solid alibi for Klaudia while Annika did her work.

TWENTY-NINE

Oranjestad, Aruba, Tuesday January 31, 2023

Something suitably impressed the police chief when he dialed the number in Washington that Howard had scribbled on a scrap of paper. He sat more erect as the phone rang.

Howard knew either Agent Burke or Agent Douglass would answer, and it turned out to be Burke. Once the police chief explained that Stuart McGregor had provided the number and asked him to call, he listened for a moment longer. Then he glanced over at Howard, set his phone down on the massive desk, and activated the speaker.

"Are you there McGregor?" Burke's familiar voice asked. Before Howard could lean closer to the phone and answer, Burke added another question. "What's the code?"

"495320651."

"Why have you detained him, Sir?" Burke's tone wasn't friendly but didn't convey annoyance as Howard had feared.

"We checked Mr. McGregor's passport with the Canadian authorities, and they tell us it's fake."

"Why did you need to see his passport?" Now, a touch of annoyance slipped into Burke's question.

"We've had a murder here. The victim was an acquaintance of Mr. McGregor, so we invited the gentleman in for an interview. As a standard practice, we also verified his documentation. That's when we learned it's fraudulent. "

"Fraudulent is a strong word, Chief. McGregor, what do you know about the murder?"

"Nothing at all, Agent Burke." Howard used the FBI agent's name. No one had divulged it over the speaker. It might add validity in a moment or two.

"What evidence of McGregor's involvement do you have, Chief?"

"We understand they were colleagues working on some secret project that neither McGregor nor his cohorts will divulge, but it sounds suspicious."

"Colleagues? Cohorts?"

"Yes. A German woman and an American man working with McGregor also knew the victim. We're not sure yet about their possible roles, but their documents are in order."

Howard waited silently while the FBI agent processed that information. The police chief looked perplexed and glanced toward the detective sitting next to Howard, the one who hadn't yet said a word in the conversation. Probably a minute passed before Burke posed another question.

"McGregor, can you give me one good reason why I shouldn't tell this good Chief to just keep you there and let this all work its way through Aruba's system of justice?"

"I'll give you two, Agent Burke." He used the agent's name again to underscore the code words he knew the guy would understand. "First, I know absolutely nothing about Joe Montebank's apparent murder, and second, I'm ready to come in."

The last phrase was critical. Howard said it slightly louder and pronounced the words succinctly. He waited for Burke's response.

"Okay, Chief. He's one of ours. We have an undercover officer on Curaao. I'll get a guy to fly over today, and he'll sign off on any documentation you need to release Stuart McGregor to our supervision. Are you okay with that?"

The police chief had a few more questions about logistics, and both he and the silent detective made notes as they spoke. Only minutes passed before the call ended and the detective ushered Howard to an air-conditioned office down the hallway.

There, someone ordered a large American breakfast from a restaurant, brought in a few newspapers for Howard to read, and apologized that they couldn't give him back his phone and documents. That would have to wait until the FBI agent from neighboring Curaçao arrived and completed all the paperwork. Then, the fun would begin.

THIRTY

Montreal, Quebec, Wednesday February 1, 2023

To her amazement, sales numbers for Multima Supermarkets remained historically high. Despite widespread media stories about rampant inflation, "obscenely high" Multima profits, and Suzanne's outburst blaming organized crime for meddling in the grocery business on *49 Minutes,* sales for the last two days of January were higher than the average of the preceding twenty-nine days.

Massive digital servers at Supermarkets' headquarters processed billions of numbers only hours after individual sales occurred. Then the systems generated sophisticated reports summarizing each day's sales activities dozens of different ways. Gordon Goodfellow's team in Atlanta analyzed that data every morning, in minute detail, searching for any anomalies or trends.

Suzanne had asked Gordon to circle back with her that morning so they could decide if they might need to take some action to counter any negative fallout from the TV interview. Everything looked fine, but Edward Hadley had joined the Zoom meeting and suggested they schedule a focus group session to validate their impressions. He also remarked cheerfully about how little time they needed for that meeting when they ended the call less than five minutes after it'd started.

"I hope that's an omen for how the rest of this day will go," he called out as he waved goodbye to the other participants.

With a bright smile, Suzanne said she doubted that one good meeting was a predictor of the coming day, and her intuition soon proved accurate. Before she could make a coffee in the Keurig machine in the alcove off her office, Eileen Lee stepped in to let her know Beverly Vonderhausen had already called twice that morning from Washington. She wanted to speak urgently.

It delighted Suzanne that Eileen had moved from Fort Myers to work in the new Montreal headquarters. Today was her assistant's first day working in her new office, and she hadn't yet welcomed her properly.

"First, let me give you a big hug," Suzanne said as she crossed the room to greet her before responding to Eileen's message. "Let's have lunch today. I know a glorious spot that's walking distance from the office, and you can tell me all about your new place. I'll make the reservations for noon."

They laughed at the switch of roles, and Eileen immediately nodded her acceptance. "Put Beverley through as soon as you can reach her."

It was over an hour, and Suzanne had finished three brief meetings, before Eileen called again, connecting the Washington attorney.

"I have some news you will not want to hear. Brace yourself because your *49 Minutes* tirade about organized crime is about to hit close to home. Fernando Disputas's body washed ashore in Aruba overnight. It seems he drowned at sea after someone blew off his left kneecap, gangland style."

Suzanne was speechless. Her hands trembled as she reached for a tissue. The union leader was no friend of hers, but he was someone she'd known for more than a decade, spent countless hours negotiating with, and respected for what he tried to do. To suddenly learn someone had killed him violently struck her in a way she'd never imagined.

"Are you okay, Suzanne?"

"I think so. It's just such a shock." She sniffled, then blew her nose. "What happened?"

"There's nothing official so far. I got a call from someone we often work with at the FBI here in town. She knows we represent you and watched your TV interview with Liara Furtamo on Sunday. She thought she should give you a heads-up. She also expects they'll announce it in a release later today after they notify the family."

"He just signed a new 4-year labor agreement with Gordon Goodfellow last week. Do you think the two events are related somehow?"

"No idea, Suzanne. But I'm guessing the union membership will never ratify whatever agreement he signed."

With promises to keep each other in the loop about any fresh developments, they ended the call. Suzanne buzzed Serge and asked him to meet her immediately.

While she waited, she called Gordon Goodfellow. Had he heard the news? Within seconds, Suzanne breathlessly filled him in on the details provided by Beverley. He listened in silence as she told the story. They promised to keep each other apprised as Serge wandered into her office.

He wore a scowl on his usually handsome face. She asked about that first.

"Judy Jones in human resources at Financial Services didn't show up for work today."

Her legs felt like liquid, ready to melt in any direction. She leaned forward to ask him to repeat what he'd said. He caught her as she stumbled and held her tightly. At some point, she heard him shouting for Eileen to call 9-1-1.

THIRTY-ONE

Sint Michiel, Curaçao, Thursday February 2, 2023

Annika checked in with Fidelia when she returned from completing her assignment in Aruba. She reported that Earl Boyante had taken the bait as expected, followed her to the room reserved in the name of Suzy Smith, and had no pulse when she left the room. As instructed, she'd called the pilots. They brought her back, and her mission was complete.

What Fidelia didn't expect was her request to leave.

"I want to go back to Barbados. I'm not cut out for this stuff. I'll dutifully sleep with anyone that Luigi or you need me to sleep with, in Washington or anywhere else. But I can't handle the pressure of these other assignments. I want out."

Fidelia studied Annika's face before replying. The woman looked ready to break into tears. Haggard was a good word to describe her appearance. In the soft light of the fixtures surrounding the pool, she seemed to have aged in hours. She showed no evidence of the bright, smiling image she had projected that morning. With her emotional state and current appearance, Annika would serve little further purpose.

"Okay. I get it. Are you alright traveling to Barbados on a commercial flight?" She waited for Annika to nod. "I'll ask Mia to book a flight for you tomorrow. Get a good night's sleep. You'll feel better. And thanks, Annika. I really appreciate all you've done for us."

Fidelia watched Annika head toward the huge house and the room she shared with Mia. They crossed paths as Mia headed out to receive new instructions from Fidelia. The pair chatted for only a few seconds before each continued on her previous path.

"Did she mention that she's leaving?" Fidelia asked.

Mia nodded with an uncomfortable, grim expression.

"Go ahead. Book a flight for her tomorrow morning to Bridgetown. And make it first class," she added as an afterthought.

Once Mia had left the poolside area to carry out the instructions, Fidelia pressed the speed dial for Mateo and gave him his orders. He agreed to complete the job with no hesitation.

Fidelia stood up from the comfortable poolside lounge chair and stretched. She needed to relieve aching muscles caused by too much tension. Before she could complete many bends or stretches, her secure phone rang. It was Luigi.

"Did ya hear somb'dy took out Disputas?" His tone of voice was more than questioning. It carried a tinge of bewilderment or uncertainty, and the working-class accent was back.

She waited a moment before responding. When enough time had elapsed to convincingly convey shock, she breathed in heavily and added desperation to her tone. "Disputas? Dead? What are you talking about, Luigi?"

"Jus' heard. Cops in Aruba said he washed up on shore missin' a kneecap. Ya heard anythin'?

"Nothing. What's he been up to in Atlanta to get himself killed?"

"No idear. Tried a couple guys workin' for 'im. He jus' signed a new contract with Multima nob'dy on his team wanted, but none of his gang are outta the country. Nob'dy there with 'nuff money to hire out. I'm fuckin' pissed at it all."

"You should be, Luigi. It sounds to me like somebody's trying to encroach on your territory. Maybe you should get a guy down there and find out what's going on."

"Isn't Aruba where Knight and yer Germ'n friend 'r workin' now?"

"Yeah, I'll talk to them and see if they've heard anything. But they aren't doing anything for The Organization there. I'm letting them start a separate new business. I still think it would be wise for you to have one of your people see what they can find out. I'll let you know if I learn anything from Howard and Klaudia."

"Ya know I don' trust that bastr'd. If he's dun' somethin' to Disputas, he's gotta go. By da way, wer' ya at now? Still 'n da Bahamas?"

His display of nerves had grown more frayed as they spoke. She had to be careful not to push too hard. "No, I headed south again until your guys find out why the FBI and Immigration people are watching for me. What's happening on that front?"

"Nothin' yet. I'll push 'em 'gain."

"Keep me up to date on both issues, Luigi."

Klaudia was probably sleeping at that time of the night, but Fidelia called anyway.

"Have you heard from Howard yet?" She used a tone of urgency.

"No. Sorry, I'm a little groggy here. I just fell asleep." It sounded like Klaudia was buying some time. "Still nothing from Howard since I called you today. The Aruban police say they're no longer holding him but won't say anything else. I've tried his phone, but it just rings and rings. No voice mail message. Nothing."

"Have the police told you when they let him go?"

"No. Everyone I call gives the same answer. 'We're not holding anyone with that name.' It's like someone ordered them all to say the same thing."

"How about Earl? Has he heard anything?"

"The last time I talked to him, he was partying with his usual crowd at Surfside Beach about three this afternoon. He hadn't heard anything and seemed distracted by some new woman friend. He only gave me a couple minutes. Said he'd call if he heard."

"Klaudia, I want you to get off the island. Something's going on and I think you're in danger. Let me send my plane to pick you up and get you out. You won't need your passport if you use my jet."

Her friend took several seconds to think about Fidelia's offer before she replied. "No. It's all right. I'll lie low for a few days to see where this is all heading, but I won't let you drag me back into The Organization again. I just won't."

The call ended before Fidelia could ask about the woman's progress with the electronic plants in the US, but now wasn't the time to pursue it.

THIRTY-TWO

Willemstad, Curaçao, Thursday February 2, 2023

It was almost midnight. Howard Knight sat on a bright yellow plastic chair facing a wall-mounted screen. Undercover Agent Leonardo Garcia sat beside him again after making another pot of strong, black coffee and placing two fresh cups on the stubby, gray plastic table between them.

Together, they faced a camera that videotaped their conversations as they looked at Agent John Burke, who continued to pose one question after another from Washington. He also made extensive hand-written notes, so the process was long and cumbersome. But Howard had experienced all this before. Twice.

Leonardo shrugged his shoulders and smiled sympathetically while they waited. He was clearly the designated "good cop" for the interview. He'd flown from Curaçao, where he worked as an undercover FBI agent, to gather Stuart McGregor from the Aruban police. In fact, it was only during the past couple hours that he'd stopped calling him Stuart.

Howard liked the guy. When they'd first met in the office of the police chief in Aruba, Leonardo quickly signed the documents his counterparts requested, formally transferring custody of one Stuart McGregor.

The guy was efficient, too. At the airport, Leonardo did all the talking with the airline and immigration authorities. He flashed an FBI badge when necessary and explained that Stuart McGregor was traveling undercover.

Of course, neither Stuart McGregor nor Howard Knight was part of the FBI. They'd created the fictional name and fake passport when Howard entered the FBI witness protection program—for the second time. Now someone had screwed up with the Canadians, exposing him again.

When Howard had told Agent Burke he was "ready to come in" during the call from Aruba's police chief's office, he used the code to let Burke know his identity was compromised and he needed help. But it also carried a far more critical subtext that prompted the FBI agent to act decisively to get Howard out of there.

That simple phrase told Burke that Howard had new information and that he would share it with the FBI. Both understood well that he'd only be willing to do that if the situation was dire and the information of value to the FBI.

So Howard continued to sit in a plain, modestly furnished, second-floor apartment of a brightly painted orange building in the Otrobanda quarter of Willemstad, Curaçao's largest city.

"Tell me again how The Organization skims its money off cryptocurrency accounts," Agent Burke said. It was the third time he'd asked Howard to explain it, and the fellow knew it was growing tedious, so he smiled for the first time, then waited.

Howard took a sip of his coffee, then launched into the explanation once more. Burke had a pattern of questioning he liked to use. They went through everything three times so he could check the accuracy of Howard's memory, the plausibility of each explanation, and receive input from FBI agents Howard couldn't see but knew were listening off camera.

He'd already gone through this process when he described Luigi's role in the US since Giancarlo Mareno's murder. Again, when he recounted the names and last known addresses of each of the leaders who headed up the illicit activities of The Organization in the drug, payday loan, gambling, escort, and auto theft businesses.

Although the FBI already knew Howard's memory was just shy of photographic, they planned to use this information to prosecute people in court. So they had to be sure they had the correct information.

Howard also realized he'd need to do all this again in Washington—or wherever they housed him while they prepared their court cases. Today's grueling sessions were only to determine if they'd give him another identity and continued support in the witness protection program.

So, he took a deep breath, reminded himself he wasn't working with financial geniuses, and patiently walked them through the cryptocurrency mess a third time, making sure his names, examples, amounts and other material facts stayed the same as the previous two rounds.

It was almost one o'clock in the morning before Agent Burke called it a day.

"Okay, Howard. That'll do for today. Leonardo has you well secured there in Curaçao. We have people in the ground-floor rooms, the apartment upstairs next to yours, and the ground-floor suite at the rear doors. We'll keep you there for a few days." He paused.

"You've given us enough. HQ approved our request for a new identity, and it'll be ready Monday. I'll fly down Tuesday and bring your temporary new passport with me. Then we'll spend the rest of the week debriefing. By then, decide where you want to live."

Burke left unsaid the brutal reality that Fidelia Morales would use every resource at her disposal to track Howard down and kill him for this monumental betrayal. Would it really matter where he chose?

THIRTY-THREE

Montreal, Quebec, Friday February 3, 2023

Fortunately, Suzanne had arranged a RAMQ card when she decided to work from the new headquarters in Montreal. RAMQ was the acronym for Quebec's government health insurance program, *Régie de l'assurance maladie du Québec*. A mouthful even for French speakers, the card was essential to receive prompt and free health care in the Canadian province.

When she'd collapsed in her office two days earlier, Serge had rummaged through her bag and had the card ready for the paramedics. They rushed her to the McGill University Health Centre. It wasn't the nearest hospital, but the paramedics agreed it was the best place to take her for a suspected stroke.

Suzanne recalled only scattered bits of the brief trip. She heard a siren at some point, felt a jolt or two as the ambulance hit a pothole or something, and realized someone had administered some sort of treatment. She tried to speak, but words wouldn't come out of her mouth clearly or logically.

When they arrived at the hospital, she was groggy. People jammed the emergency care area. Since the pandemic first arrived, hospitals worldwide were overloaded with patients. They often lacked staff or space for treatment. What Suzanne hadn't realized was the expertise emergency health professionals had in triaging or prioritizing health cases.

With a suspected stroke, they rushed Suzanne to the head of the line and began assessment and treatment within minutes. She had slept much of the time, but Serge was there. She heard his voice a couple times and caught glimpses of him looking down at her lying in bed. That gave her some hope that all would be right again soon.

It was a transient ischemic attack, a doctor explained sometime later. Commonly called a mini-stroke, her condition was temporary. It hadn't affected her brain permanently, and she'd feel fine again within a day or two.

"But, it was a warning sign," the doctor had said in a grave tone. "You should meet with your doctor soon and discuss changes you can make to your lifestyle to reduce the risk of a recurrence or a stroke. About one person in three has a serious stroke after experiencing a transient ischemic attack."

That morning, Suzanne felt normal, but Serge had persuaded her to work from her new home in the Laurentian Mountains instead of the office. Eileen Lee would superbly screen her calls downtown. By mid-morning, her phone had sat idle since her brief chat with Eileen before the office opened.

She called Gordon Goodfellow at Supermarkets' Atlanta headquarters. He knew about her health incident and confirmed she was really all right.

Suzanne dove in. "What's happening with the Disputas case?"

"The FBI is involved. There's concern organized crime is behind it. The way they blew apart his knee before he drowned. We had an agent here yesterday for a few hours."

"Do they suspect someone at Multima is involved?"

"Hard to say. Agents interviewed all the members of the negotiating team and me. They asked questions about the negotiations, the final agreement, how his team behaved, and Disputas's frame of mind. It seemed to me they were grasping at straws, looking for something to help them connect the dots." Goodfellow's tone seemed calm and analytical.

She changed the subject. "Did the PR people complete the focus group yet? Any feedback on the *49 Minutes* interview?"

"Yes, on both counts. They did sessions in Orlando, Atlanta, and Pittsburgh. Used our usual method with ten participants, two-way mirrors, and a moderator. When we finish, I'll send you a summary of the outcomes, but nothing was shocking. Increasing the cost of everything pisses people off. They think we're making far too much money, but your message seemed to resonate positively. Each group had vocal participants who embraced your assertion that other forces were also at play. There was general agreement that the police and government authorities should take your warning about organized crime more seriously."

Suzanne smiled ruefully to herself. "How have sales held up the past few days?"

"Still strong. The month is starting as well as last month ended." Goodfellow had ratcheted up his enthusiasm, probably remembering Suzanne's health issue and wanting to end with a positive message.

Later, Serge wandered into her home office from the kitchen carrying a fresh cup of coffee. He was still concerned about her health and studied her up and down before he smiled.

"Your concept of taking it easy today apparently includes phone calls." His admonishment used soft tones and his smile broadened.

"Don't worry, Serge. I'm feeling fine. I'll follow the doctor's advice and limit my calls and activity for the next few days."

"It's against my better judgment, but James Fitzgerald asked me to relay some info to you. Can you handle some bad news?"

Suzanne nodded, but her shoulders slumped in anticipation.

"They found Judy Jones. They discovered her body last night in South Chicago. Fentanyl. Drugs have apparently been a problem for a while."

"Oh, my God." She reached for her phone. "Stay here. We need to talk with James."

THIRTY-FOUR

Sint Michiel, Curaçao, Saturday February 4, 2023

Everyone had adjusted to the time zone and climate, so Fidelia gathered the group poolside at her beachfront mansion on the waterfront. Mia had found a local woman and her daughter to prepare meals and serve drinks. They wouldn't offer any alcohol during the time she set aside for meetings, but juices and water would flow freely.

She called them together to change her plan, made necessary by Disputas's incompetence and a rapidly unfolding situation in Japan. The day before, Tak Takahashi had received word from his contacts that fifty million US dollars in cryptocurrency had moved from Tokyo to an account in Gibraltar.

Fidelia already knew about the amount. Tak had alerted her to what was going on. Since August, the head of The Organization in Japan had skimmed two million per month from the commissions he owed Fidelia. Until Friday, those funds had accumulated in a secret Japanese account. Tak felt he should make Fidelia aware because Luigi Fortissimo knew all about it, and Tak had found it unsettling that his boss, Sugimori, would connive with the US crime boss to short-change Fidelia that way. He'd sworn loyalty to both, of course, but Fidelia was the kingpin of The Organization now.

Once he'd shared the information, she'd pulled Tak out of Japan and brought him to Curaçao as soon as she could, and he was grateful beyond words. She smiled when he sat close to her as they gathered around the poolside table.

The weather outdoors was a typical day in paradise. She'd noted that every day on the island felt the same, and the high and low temperatures displayed on her weather app validated her impression. They sat in a circle under a covered canopy, in comfortable beach chairs, a low table covered with bottles of water in the middle.

She looked around before she spoke. No one laughed or joked. Instead, there was total silence. The evening before, Mia had summoned each of the guests to Fidelia's master suite. Each came alone and spent less than fifteen minutes in the room, but all left with a slightly dazed expression reflecting something between fear and awe.

Fidelia had been straightforward. The reason she'd summoned them was a need for each to swear personal loyalty to her alone. She asked each person to affirm that he or she would carry out every order she gave them, whether or not they supported it. After they agreed to obey, she asked each person to swear they were prepared to die to protect her. Finally, she demanded they keep secret all the information she shared with them about future plans.

Fidelia had prefaced her demands with promises of unimaginable wealth and power if they swore their loyalty. No conversation took longer than the allotted fifteen minutes. Before those private sessions, she'd let Mateo share with his guys a vivid description of Annika Wentz's misfortune on her way to the Curaçao airport a few days earlier, after she chose not to show unwavering loyalty to Fidelia.

Mateo had encouraged his guys to pass along this gem of information as casual poolside gossip. A more somber mood had developed around the home within hours. That morning, it appeared all the participants in her gathering were both mindful and attentive. Still, she had to choose her words carefully and divulge only what they needed to know to perform their individual tasks.

"Mia will collect all your personal phones now and give you new ones. She'll save all your current information on the phones and keep them secure. At the end of our mission, we'll return them to you. Be sure you transfer now any numbers you think you might need because you won't have access to them for a few weeks."

That process took about an hour. Mia delivered the new phones to everyone, made sure they worked, and gave them time to program any personal numbers they needed into the phones. With a unique app, she recorded all the numbers for each device, keeping a database for each personal number added. Then she collected and labeled each of the handsets entrusted to her care.

"The new handsets are all secure burner phones. They can't be traced. When you send a message by text, it's encrypted. When you talk, it distorts your voice. Use the phones only when necessary."

Fidelia made penetrating eye contact with each participant as she delivered her instructions, remembering the counsel of Giancarlo Mareno: "Watch carefully anyone who can't make and keep direct eye contact. Eliminate them if necessary."

Marie Dependente looked most vulnerable. She held Fidelia's eyes but her lower jaw tightened more than usual. The daughter of one of France's wealthiest billionaires probably realized she was far out of her element now. Hanging out with the head of an escort business, who then became the boss of the entire outfit, had probably appealed to a rebellious spirit in the rich girl.

But she was an intelligent woman. Fidelia had sensed a momentary hesitation when she called upon her long-time ally to take the oath of loyalty. She'd been a source of trustworthy information about high society in Paris and Multima's European business but was never involved in The Organization. Last night, she'd said the necessary words but hadn't shown as much fear as Fidelia expected. It was time to test her.

"Mateo, assign one of your men to work with Marie for the next few days. Marie, the guy Mateo gives you will be your partner, and you'll work as a couple. Mia has a room waiting for you at the Renaissance Resort in Aruba. Here's a picture of my friend Klaudia Schäffer and a guy named Howard Knight. He uses the name Stuart McGregor and travels with a Canadian passport."

Fidelia reached across the table with the photo as she spoke. "Here's an address we know they used for an office and an apartment we think Klaudia rented in Oranjestad. We had a locator on her phone, but she's a technology whiz. I'm guessing she discovered a way to shut off the locator or ditched her phone, so we can't find her. Bring her back to me, alive and well. I need her."

Fidelia watched Marie's reaction. She nodded at the appropriate spots and seemed fully attentive.

Fidelia switched to Howard Knight. "The last we heard, police in Aruba were holding him for questioning related to a murder on the island. We don't know what happened to him. Did he escape police custody? Did they let him go? You need to find out what happened and where he is now."

Fidelia knew Mateo's guy would have no hesitation, but she wanted to see how the high-society woman reacted. "I want Klaudia back. With Knight, it doesn't matter. Do you understand?"

Marie Dependente didn't flinch. "Mateo's guy will take care of it?"

Fidelia nodded. "The jet will take you over. Get packed for a few days and be ready to leave in a half hour. When you get there, Mateo's guy will know how to reach someone named Jose. He'll get you on the island without an immigration check and get you out again when you've got Klaudia."

"What do I use as a reason for her to come back with us?" Marie's tone was matter-of-fact, neither fearful nor apprehensive.

"Say anything you want. Mateo's guy will also have some stuff to make her drowsy, should you need it."

THIRTY-FIVE

Willemstad, Curaçao, Tuesday February 7, 2023

Howard's insomnia was back. It wasn't unexpected. Sleep had been a continual challenge every time he needed to escape. It started first with Giancarlo Mareno, now again with Fidelia running The Organization. Fear of torture and death did that to a guy's mind.

But the current circumstances in Curaçao added more complexity to his quest for rest. First, the FBI's undercover agent Leonardo Garcia and his guys refused to let him away from the housing they'd arranged. They guarded the front and rear doors of his second-floor apartment and the doors of the ground floor. Another one watched the door from a courtyard behind the apartment that led out to a side street.

His only direct sunshine came from brief visits to a small balcony behind the apartment or to one of the wooden lawn chairs in an enclosed courtyard. Someone stayed by his side every moment he was outdoors. That limited physical exercise to some stretching and climbing up and down the stairwell. He missed the long walks along the beach that he'd enjoyed every day in Uruguay and Aruba. His muscles stiffened and ached.

They kept all the windows of the apartment closed. It was bad enough that the glass held in recycled air-conditioned air all day and night, but the windows had wooden slats that also blocked out all the natural light. Howard could have lived with all those inconveniences and still slept somewhat normally, but he couldn't adapt to the traffic.

The neighborhood was residential, yet the street in front of the apartment was busy. It carried traffic from the downtown Otrobanda district to the only bridge crossing to the Punda district on the other side of the bay. Cars, trucks, motorcycles, and buses passed the apartment at virtually all hours of the day and night.

The crowning touch was a speed bump directly in front of the apartment. Those who slowed down for the bump invariably sped up as they left, often burning rubber on the road or exercising exotic exhaust systems that sounded like rapid-fire automatic weapons.

Howard cringed in annoyance with every departure. Those who didn't slow down generated another kind of noise, with rattling springs and suspension systems squishing together, creating a metallic ruckus as off-putting as the loud mufflers of the other guys.

Leonardo said his hands were tied until Agent Burke arrived. If he agreed, they'd try to find another spot, but it would be tough. The people of Curaçao would celebrate Carnaval in the next few days. Rental apartments and hotel rooms were scarce.

Burke had just arrived, and Howard wasted no time.

"I need another place. You want to debrief me, but I can't sleep. If I can't sleep, I don't remember as well. If you want my best information, you need to find somewhere else to do this."

Leonardo signaled for Burke's attention, and the two wandered out the back door and down to the courtyard below. They chatted with their backs turned for a few minutes while Howard stewed on the balcony overlooking their hushed conversation.

When Burke returned, his tone was assertive and his expression unwavering. "There's nothing else available that'll work. It's too risky to move to a hotel or resort. Leonardo's guys tried every rental service on the island. So we're going to stay right here, and you're going to cooperate, or this passport and the new identity that comes with it go back to Washington with me on the next flight out. Do we understand each other?"

Agent Burke dramatically waved an American passport as he spoke and held it up to tempt Howard while he considered his options. Of course, there were none.

Officialdom would now know Howard as "Benjamin Castello." The newly issued passport was just one component of his new identity. Naturally, Burke also provided a social security card, a driver's license issued by the State of New York, and a twenty-page document Howard would commit to memory in the coming days.

That document was essential. It included details such as the schools Benjamin Castello attended, his grades, the sports he played, and whatever other educational information might come up in conversation that a curious questioner might check for accuracy. Expert hackers had added all those details to legitimate schools and universities' formal records and data banks.

He skipped to the part summarizing his grades and courses to earn a master's degree in business administration from Harvaard University. He smiled. Howard Knight had also attended that college but had failed to graduate.

Quickly skimming through the information package, he also learned that Benjamin had worked for three different companies over his career and had served as treasurer, risk manager, and chief financial officer. In each of those jobs, most people simply called him Ben.

Now, the guy was enjoying early retirement, drawing a monthly pension the FBI would pay into an account in Panama using the name of a legitimate US pension fund manager. Not mentioned in the summary: the FBI would also withdraw that pension weekly to make it look like Ben was using his pension. The US government was recovering every dollar paid out. They called it recycling.

Ben was a sports fan, too. Over the years, he'd held season tickets for the Yankees, Jets, and Islanders. Anyone checking would see that Benjamin held tickets for at least three seasons with each team. That meant Howard would need to learn more about hockey. He'd never paid much attention to the sport before.

"I'll leave it all with you in good faith," Agent Burke offered with a half-hearted smile. "You can start memorizing at your leisure, but it'll all evaporate if you don't give us enough over the next few days. We'll start in the morning. Use earplugs, music, air conditioning in the background, whatever you like. But after your breakfast and coffee tomorrow morning, be ready for several hours a day for the rest of the week."

Agent Burke's smile had disappeared entirely, and he wore an expression suiting a high school principal warning that the next mistake in behavior would result in suspension.

THIRTY-SIX

Montreal, Quebec, Wednesday February 8, 2023

James Fitzgerald had assured Suzanne that Judy Jones's unfortunate death had involved no compromise of Multima data. They'd lost a good employee who'd veered off track in her personal life at some point, but there was no evidence of any attempt to access the databases their technical guy had blocked. Serge had concurred.

Suzanne had asked Alberto Ferer to join their Zoom call, and he advised James and Suzanne to make no public comment at all. If contacted by the media, he suggested they instruct their respective PR teams to reply that her death was a tragic personal matter. Multima would have no comment other than to express condolences to her family, friends, and colleagues.

He said it would also be okay to convey that their thoughts and prayers were with all those people if that made them more comfortable.

Despite some discomfort, Suzanne had agreed to leave it that way for the weekend. So far, there had been no calls from any media outlets.

James called again that morning. "A local FBI agent called and requested an interview with Judy Jones's immediate superior, Natalia Tenaz, and me. I told her I'd get back to her."

Suzanne instructed Eileen to connect Serge, Alberto Ferer, and Edward Hadley to their Zoom call. Her chief legal officer confirmed they should meet with the FBI if requested, answer questions honestly, and share any information required. It was a legal obligation. He advised James to relay that information to affected staff and not coach them otherwise.

Edward Hadley thought it best to issue a media release confirming the police would interview some Multima employees, and the company had instructed everyone to cooperate fully with their investigation.

Serge was more cautious. "From my policing experience, I find it curious that the FBI is involved. Usually, with a drug death, local police and forensic investigators would handle the investigation. They're also asking to speak with a fairly large number of people. Do they really expect James or Natalia to provide useful information unless they have reason to suspect one or the other is involved?"

No one responded immediately. The culture at Multima was to cooperate with legal authorities, just as Alberto had said from the beginning. But Serge posed a good question. They discussed the pros and cons for a few minutes but agreed they needed to decide.

Serge proposed an alternative. "Let me call someone in Washington I interacted with during my RCMP days. She'll find out what's up and give us some good advice. Sound all right?"

Suzanne agreed immediately, with no objection from the other participants. *Was that a twinge of jealousy when Serge said "she"?*

There was little time to consider the possibility that their relationship may have been more than professional, as another call from Washington was waiting when they finished the Zoom discussion.

Beverly Vonderhausen was calling. "A bit of follow-up to the bad news I shared with you last week about Fernando Disputas. Another body surfaced down there in Aruba. There doesn't seem to be an obvious connection, but police on the island are treating them as related because of the proximity. They discovered the other body first, in a partially sunken boat. It took a while to identify the guy. Someone blew his head apart, and sea life had consumed much of the corpse."

"Spare me any more of the gory details, please. Who was the corpse?"

"A two-bit actor from California with a history of corporate espionage. Name was Joe Montebank. Ring a bell at all?"

"I'm afraid not. But what do you mean by corporate espionage?" Suzanne's interest was piqued instantly. She sat upright, pulling her shoulders to attention.

"I'm not sure exactly, but I expect he stole confidential information and corporate data for a fee. Why?"

Suzanne paused a second to assess the wisdom of sharing some information. "Please keep it to yourself, but we learned recently that someone tried to buy some human resources info from an employee in our Financial Services division."

"Are your employees in that division unionized?"

"No."

"That might explain a connection. If Disputas was trying to organize another union, might it be useful for him to seek human resources information?"

Suzanne weighed the pros and cons of sharing with Beverley that Serge's illegal wiretaps suggested the call for information came from Aruba. She chose not to divulge it, just in case.

"I guess it's possible, but it sounds like a stretch to me. Why wouldn't they just call a few employees and see if there's any interest in forming a union? And why would both men end up dead? But I'd appreciate you keeping your ear to the ground on both cases. If there's any relationship with Multima, I'd value a heads-up. Anything else going on in Washington that might interest Multima?" Suzanne laughed casually as she posed the question.

Beverley guffawed in return before she added one final bit. "I have little information so far, but yesterday one of my associates heard a senator is trying to break up Jeffersons Stores with an act of Congress. She claims the guy's working with a group of about twenty in the House of Representatives to make breaking up Jeffersons Stores part of any debt limit negotiations. He thinks it's something the president might accept."

"It does sound ridiculous, but I've learned that ideas hatching these days in Washington can move from 'ridiculous' to new law alarmingly quickly. Please let me know if you learn anything." Suzanne gazed off as she considered what such an improbable development might mean for Multima.

THIRTY-SEVEN

Sint Michiel, Curaçao, Wednesday February 8, 2023

When Marie Dependente reported to Fidelia that their search came up empty in Aruba, alarm bells rang.

The business address Fidelia had given them, where Howard and Klaudia supposedly worked, remained locked every day. One of them had watched the building around the clock and saw no one go in or out of the office.

Marie had contrived a story and gained entry to the furnished apartment Klaudia had rented. There were no clothes or other personal effects anywhere in the unit, and it shocked the landlady that Klaudia had said nothing about leaving.

Marie and Mateo's guy used The Organization's fellow, Jose, for some inquiries, and he seemed well connected to more authorities in Aruba than they'd realized. They praised his knowledge to Fidelia, who encouraged them to squeeze every bit of information possible from the guy.

Curiously, a couple hours after their morning conversation, Marie reported that Jose was also working with one of Luigi's guys out of New York. Did she know about that?

Fidelia drew a blank. She'd talked with Luigi about the deaths. To add credibility to her posture that she wasn't aware of the deaths, she'd suggested he send a guy to Atlanta to learn more.

Shit! He must have misunderstood and thought she'd wanted him to send the guy to Aruba, not Atlanta.

She barked out new orders after a moment's consideration. "Get Mateo's guy to give Jose a few hundred dollars, with orders to keep Luigi's guy occupied and out of the way a few days. Tell him to keep the lout drunk and incommunicado with New York till you track down Klaudia and Howard. You'll have to do it alone, without Jose. Keep me posted on your progress every few hours. It's a tiny desert island, for *chrissake*!"

That strategy should shine a light on Luigi's intentions quickly. If Jose was successful and got Luigi's guy out of the way, Luigi had probably misunderstood her suggestion and sent a flunky to kill a few days there. If the guy didn't take the alcohol bait, he probably had more specific orders, and she'd have to decide what to do with him.

She had Mia try both Klaudia's and Howard's phones every hour. With his history of running off, he was the bigger concern and had been missing for over a week since leaving police custody on the island. *The bastard is probably trying to run again.*

By mid-morning, the news became worse. A paid—and consistently reliable—resource with the Washington offices of the FBI confirmed a team of agents had landed in Aruba. A serious investigation was underway to determine the causes of death and the relationship between Fernando Disputas and Joe Montebank. Aruba's police were cooperating.

The source learned that someone high in the FBI hierarchy had ordered the investigation. Before she signed off, the woman added another bit of information. Her same gal near the top of the ladder with the FBI had started some sort of investigation into a drug-related death in Chicago. It involved someone at the big corporation Multima, and the company was pushing back.

That sounded curious. *What could the FBI want with Multima related to the death of a drug user?*

Tak Takahashi added to her wall of worry shortly after lunch. His sources in Japan told him the real estate deal for the properties owned by Jeffersons Stores had heated up. The people from Mizuto had received firm offers for all the land owned by Jeffersons in the states of California, Oregon, and Washington. The offer was in the billions, with an expiry date of March 31. Sugimori and his people were studying the proposal seriously.

Fidelia watched his mannerisms as Tak shared this development with her. He appeared more nervous than usual. Brown eyes flitted from side to side as he spoke. His voice was just above a whisper. It was hard to read whether he conveyed fear or alarm.

"Is there anything else I need to know about over there?"

He started wringing his hands as she spoke, then looked downward. "Not in Japan. Gibraltar. The fifty million in cryptocurrency disappeared overnight."

THIRTY-EIGHT

Willemstad, Curaçao, Thursday February 9, 2023

For three full days, Howard reluctantly spilled information. What else could a guy do? It was almost certain Fidelia was already plotting his demise. If he didn't cooperate, the FBI would surely ship him back to the jail in Aruba. And, if they thought he was holding back on them, the essential new identity might disappear. So he cooperated.

Agent Burke and his associates took turns asking him questions. Everyone sat around a wooden table about eight feet long and three feet wide on four gray plastic chairs. Two on either side. A light on a curved pole, shaped like a beehive, hung over the table. A pitcher of ice water sat in the middle, and the participants refilled their glasses as needed.

To his chagrin, Burke had insisted they didn't need to waste the Agency's money on bottled water. Tap water was perfectly safe. In his preparation for the trip, he'd read that the island desalinated the drinking water from the South Caribbean using modern technology and sophisticated testing. That should be good enough for everybody, he said.

That comment caused Howard to wonder if the cost of water was that important, how much money could he expect them to advance when they eventually freed him to the outside world? He didn't dwell on it, though.

They set up two videorecorders, one on each side of the table, behind the participants. Howard almost knocked one over the first time he stood up for a bio break, but no damage was done. Agent Burke sat facing Howard for each of the three days of grilling. The undercover agent, Leonardo Garcia, sat beside him. The other three agents from Leonardo's team took turns sitting in the fourth chair.

Rotating in and out, the guys took lots of notes as they listened, so they probably used the sessions for training. Despite the confidentiality of the witness protection program, the FBI liked to use opportunities like this to groom its people.

The questions started with the simple stuff, the low-hanging fruit Burke called it. Since Giancarlo Mareno's death three years earlier, what US businesses did The Organization dabble in? How were they organized? Who were the key players? How much money did they generate?

Each morning, Howard had started with his standard disclaimer that he hadn't slept well, so there may be gaps or errors in his memory. Miraculously, each day, after the second cup of black coffee, he found answers to most of their questions.

On the first day, Burke started with the drug business. The FBI was taking a lot of heat because of fentanyl deaths and opioids. He wanted to know where The Organization's drugs came from and posed dozens of questions about the people involved and where they all fit.

Burke often asked the same questions in two or three different ways. Howard realized this was to test his recall and the veracity of his answers. Then he let the 'trainees' ask away. Often, they'd repeat some of Burke's questions and, frequently, Leonardo had to translate because all his guys were Latino, with English as their second or third language.

Leonardo appeared to control the clock. He'd propose a break for ten or fifteen minutes mid-mornings, a full two hours for lunch, and another break towards four in the afternoon. Each day, they wrapped up around the dinner hour and gave Howard the evening to watch TV on the wall-mounted screen in the living area or to read in his room.

By the end of the first day, they had completed only the drug and prostitution businesses. Howard chuckled to himself that none of the questions posed to him used the word "escort," as Fidelia liked to refer to the business. The FBI's interest tended more toward human trafficking of the women rather than the business numbers. Howard had never been directly involved in recruiting the women for the business, so Burke probably found that session less productive.

The FBI agent started the second day with the payday loan business. There, they focused on numbers, and the questioners all seemed shocked at the enormous profits The Organization generated with small loans at usurious interest rates to people down on their luck.

That second afternoon, questioning moved to gambling, where

Howard remembered and shared information about the massive numbers of dollars earned in casinos and backrooms across the US. The agents immediately connected the dots between gambling and the payday loan business. The extent of The Organization's holdings in legal casinos—some even trading on the New York Stock Exchange—appeared to shock even Burke. They ran longer that day, but he appeared satisfied.

Today, questions started with The Organization's activities outside the US. Burke began with Japan. They suspected The Organization controlled Suji Corporation. He wanted to know how they pulled the strings at Jeffersons Stores and how the money flowed back to Japan.

Howard drew charts on sheets of paper to show how Jeffersons Stores laundered cash through offshore accounts and back to Japan to finance illegal activities there before forwarding a percentage to The Organization's bank accounts in the Cayman Islands.

In the afternoon, Burke's focus switched to Europe and Russia. It took hours for Howard to persuade him that The Organization had no links to the Russian Mafia and wanted to stay as far away from it as possible. Even then, the FBI agent asked a few fishing questions to determine The Organization's relationship with other criminal elements operating in Europe and the Middle East.

Finally, they dealt with the subject Howard dreaded the most: Fidelia.

The two had been lovers for years. Later, she'd hunted him, used him, and rewarded him. At one time, she probably genuinely loved him. If Agent Burke hadn't brought a new and revised agreement to confirm the agency wouldn't prosecute Howard in return for testimony, he could never have thrown Fidelia under the bus. Its wheels would have crushed him too, for much of her success in the past five years carried his fingerprints.

Well before his request to move to Aruba, where she would let him run his own semi-legitimate business with Klaudia, Howard had considered the consequences of selling her out again. Of course, she would use every device at her disposal to track him down. And there was no doubt this time she'd aim to kill him.

In the end, he'd known it would eventually come to this. The only possible path to buying a few more years of life was to sell his information to the FBI in return for their protection. Hopefully, they'd find and incarcerate her. That might buy a little more time. He was prepared for the outcome, regardless.

So the FBI learned about the roles she played with criminal elements around the globe, the massive fortune she had accumulated, and her homes in Uruguay and Singapore, her apartment in New York, and the compound in Muynak, Uzbekistan. With his near photographic memory, Howard provided addresses when he could.

And, when it wasn't possible, he described the buildings, locations, and road directions for getting there. If Fidelia visited any of those facilities in the coming months, it would be hard for her to avoid arrest—unless the local police were so tightly under her control, they were prepared to defy an Interpol Code Red. Which was not out of the question.

As Agent Burke and Howard wrapped up the sessions in Curaçao, the FBI man said he wanted to tie up loose ends.

"You've given us enough to work with. Everything you've told us is checking out, so the folks back at headquarters approved your cosmetic surgery. Leonardo and his team will take you to Costa Rica in the morning, and you'll be in protective custody while the surgeon reconfigures your face. As soon as it heals, we'll get another photo for your passport, then get you settled somewhere else."

"After that, I'm good to go on my way?" Howard asked.

"We'll have to bring you back to somewhere in the US, probably Washington," Burke replied. "I'll need you for another week with the attorneys who will try the cases for those we arrest. Then, we'll set you up with new, final documents, using the post-surgery photos, and local country ID. Wherever you choose. So, where do you want to live?"

His first choice had been on a yacht. As part of the deal six years earlier, the FBI had bought him a cabin cruiser, and Howard had lived on the water for a good number of months. They wouldn't have nabbed him again if he hadn't caught the mumps from a hooker in Uruguay. While he was hospitalized, someone tracked him down. Then, the FBI had to rescue him again as he recovered from surgery in Quepos, Costa Rica. Someone blew up his boat, almost catching him in the explosion.

Early in their negotiations, Agent Burke had made it clear the FBI only provided one yacht per informant. So, Howard had to choose an alternative on land.

"Portugal." It wasn't perfect. But, combined with some time in Brazil, it might work.

THIRTY-NINE

Montreal, Quebec, Monday February 13, 2023

Serge barged into Suzanne's office before she finished her first cup of coffee, closing the door tightly behind him. Even trusted Eileen wouldn't overhear their conversation.

"I tried to reach that FBI contact from my RCMP days this morning. She hadn't gotten back to me with anything about the goings-on in Chicago, so I followed up. There was no answer or voicemail, so I tried a couple other people I'd worked with in the past. One wasn't available, but the other told me my contact had disappeared!"

His eyes bulged below deep furrows in his forehead, with arms raised above his shoulders, as he shook his head and spoke more quickly than usual. "This woman is well up in the FBI hierarchy, and she hasn't shown up at the office in almost a week. No calls, no messages, nothing. According to my third contact, they'll issue a missing person report and bulletin later today."

Suzanne was unsure how to react. Clearly, Serge was upset by the news. However, she had no insight into his relationship with the FBI woman while he'd served with the RCMP. Were they colleagues and nothing more? She probed carefully. "That must be very shocking for you. How well do you know the woman?"

"Quite well. On a professional level, of course. We probably traded information two or three times a month for several years. As her influence within the FBI grew, she became more and more useful to us in Canada. I hadn't talked with her for months until I inquired about the Chicago issue."

Good. He probably hasn't slept with her then.

Suzanne shifted in her chair to signal a change in direction and motioned for Serge to sit in the chair beside her desk. "I'm sorry to learn about your missing contact, but what about James Fitzgerald and the team in Chicago? Did you get any information to help them with the request for interviews?"

"Yeah. That too is shocking. There's no longer an FBI investigation taking place in Chicago. Apparently, someone higher up heard about the agency's involvement in the case and killed it immediately. Sent it back to the city police to handle."

Together, they called Fitzgerald and shared the news. Of course, he was relieved, but wanted to discuss where they should go with the suspicious recordings and attempts to get information from Judy Jones.

"Should we report what we learned from the recordings to the police?" James wanted to know. "I realize we recorded the conversations without consent, but should we make the police aware, regardless?"

His question didn't surprise Suzanne. His commitment to ethics and good behavior was legendary, but she let Serge handle a response.

"The more I've thought about who would benefit from that information, the more I've become convinced only a competitor would find it of value. The question is, which competitor?"

Suzanne had reached the same conclusion and intuitively preferred to avoid the police. "We know the caller was specifically interested in getting names, titles and so on for the Supermarkets division. Serge, are you suggesting we should try to identify which Supermarkets competitor it might be? Or might we fall into a trap, focusing our attention there when their true target might be James's division?"

They debated the merits of both positions for a few minutes, then Suzanne gave them instructions.

"James, Natalia can lead a team of financial experts in your offices. Let's get them to identify any likely takeover suitor and test whether their balance sheets would be strong enough to take a run at you. I think this might be helpful in the longer term anyway. She might identify somebody we'd like to take out. I'll have Gordon do the same with a team down in Atlanta for Supermarkets."

She'd just completed that Zoom conference when Eileen buzzed. Beverly Vonderhausen was on the other line.

"I'm not sure how much comes from your *49 Minutes* interview, if any, but there's some gossip from a contact I have in the FBI this morning. A massive investigation into organized crime is underway. They're doing everything they can to keep a lid on it, but it seems they've found a source of information that's got some of the agency's hierarchy rubbing their hands with glee."

"Interesting. Any scuttlebutt related to the food business?"

"Jeffersons Stores is attracting some attention. My contact expects the FBI will announce an investigation into its foreign ownership. They got a tip that something was amiss in Japan. Maybe a connection to The Organization they didn't know about previously."

Suzanne listened intently. Her run-ins with The Organization had been traumatic, and she still suspected they'd had something to do with the bombing of her home in Atlanta. It had all started when that coward Howard Knight tried to take over Multima Corporation before John George Mortimer outsmarted him. It seemed the nefarious bunch had tried some form of coercion every year or so since then. *What else does Beverley know?*

"Is your source of information high enough in the hierarchy to see names?"

"Yeah. She's near the top, and the FBI still doesn't pay its people well, not even the higher-ups. We officially have a budget for entertainment, but we use it to thank folks inside for giving us a heads-up. She's a frequent and grateful recipient of our generosity. Speaking of no ethics, I heard more gossip about that wayward senator who's trying to break up Jeffersons. Word is, the lever he's using to bring onside the twenty far-right members of Congress is five million dollars each, paid to offshore accounts."

"Seriously? Someone's willing to pay a hundred million dollars to get legislation that breaks up Jeffersons, and some government officials will accept that?" Suzanne's tone was incredulous.

"Seriously. Someone saw a draft document sent to the president linking this breakup to his debt ceiling battle with Congress. His people are thinking about it."

FORTY

Sint Michiel, Curaçao, Monday February 13, 2023

Almost another month had passed, and Fidelia's plan had barely advanced.

Luigi continued to stall. The bastard claimed his people in Washington—inside the FBI or on the periphery—couldn't find out why someone had dispatched agents to Teterboro, anticipating Fidelia's planned arrival in November. His usual sources cut lines of communication and clammed up. She wasn't sure if what she detected in his voice these days suggested he knew more than he was sharing.

The listening devices she'd asked Klaudia to install could have identified the cause of his uncertainty if she'd put them in place as directed. But, for the first time in the over twenty years she'd known Klaudia, her supposed friend had defied those orders. Worse, she hadn't heard from the woman in weeks. It was time to pull the plug with Marie Dependente looking for her over in Aruba.

She and Mateo's guy had been thorough. For several days, they had called every few hours with updates. They'd visited every hotel and resort on the island, questioned dozens of people working in the tourist industry, and watched Klaudia's former office and apartment. They'd even poked around at the airport.

The only decent lead they found was a tiny inn in a residential area. Marie had spoken with the owner, Sandra. The woman was cheerful and accommodating and even recognized the photo of Klaudia they shared. Yes, the woman they were looking for had stayed there for a few weeks in December but had moved to an apartment after that.

Marie claimed she pushed for more, and Mateo's guy had threatened Sandra's well-being should they learn she'd held out on them. To no avail. The woman didn't change her story, and they found no evidence of Klaudia on the premises.

As Fidelia waited for Marie to pick up her phone, she prepared to order them back to Curaçao.

"We just got a lead this morning," Marie Dependente started.

"One of Jose's friends in the fishing business. They were out drinking last night, and Jose asked if the guy had any unusual requests lately. Apparently, that fisherman occasionally got weird appeals from tourists who wanted to rent his boat and a driver to go skinny-dipping in the ocean or have sex on the boat while the driver watched or took pictures. That sort of thing. They usually enjoyed a good laugh about his stories."

"What's the lead, Marie?" She was tired, and the story seemed longer than necessary.

"Well, the guy said he had an inquiry from a single woman to take her to Curaçao one night last week. Jose showed the fellow a photo of Klaudia, and he recognized her immediately. The guy claims she paid him a couple thousand US dollars to take her by boat, in the middle of the night, to a beach near Westpunt. He left her there all alone with a big backpack."

Fidelia smiled. She had taken care not to tell either Klaudia or Howard where she was. Neither knew she had aborted her trip to New York nor about her eventual purchase of a home on the island of Curaçao. Her friend had unwittingly chosen a destination that put her closer to Fidelia's reach, not further away as she undoubtedly had hoped.

Fidelia set the wheels in motion immediately. Mia dispatched the private jet to Aruba to pick up Marie and Mateo's guy.

Fidelia summoned Mateo to her secure area. "Your guy, Jose, in Aruba, deserves a reward. He found where Klaudia was headed. Give him a weekend with the girls and a few hundred bucks to feed his booze habit. But first, get your guys to find the local passport artists here. All of them. The police in Aruba kept her passport, so she hired a boat to bring her to Curaçao last week."

A grin appeared on Mateo's face as he made the connection. Satisfied they were on the same page, Fidelia continued.

"She landed at the northern tip of the island, but Klaudia's a big-city girl. My guess? She hailed the first taxi that passed after daybreak and headed toward Willemstad. Look for forgers there first. She'll probably try to buy an EU passport.

"Then have your guys contact the hotels and Airbnb. She usually carries lots of cash and probably paid that way with no passport."

Nadine Violette knocked gently on Fidelia's door, then poked her head around it, asking permission to enter. Fidelia nodded okay, and the beautiful young woman entered wearing only the bottom of her bikini, as many French women liked to sunbathe. Her tan was exquisite from hours of inactivity poolside and droplets of oil or perspiration enhanced her allure. It was easy to understand why she was Pierre Boivin's favorite. But Fidelia liked her for her brains.

"You asked me to reach out to some of Klaudia's old friends in Europe to see if they'd heard from her. I came up empty, mainly. But this morning I heard from Bernadette in Lourdes. Do you remember her?"

"Our madam there, right? She's been there forever. One of my first recruits in Europe, I think."

"That's the one. A sweetheart. I worked for her for a few months before I caught Pierre's attention. She's old school. She doesn't carry a phone with her and relies on email when she's home and can access an old desktop she uses to keep all the books."

Again, the story ran long. Fidelia gave her a nudge. "What's up with Bernadette?"

"She got back to me today and said she saw Klaudia last week in Aruba." Fidelia sat up straighter and tilted her head for Nadine to give her more. "She paid for an air ticket to Aruba to help Klaudia with some sort of telephone project. When she got there, the deal was off. They had closed the company. Howard Knight had disappeared, and Klaudia was planning to do the same."

Fidelia looked suitably surprised by the details but hoped for more. "That sounds very odd, doesn't it? What did Bernadette do?"

"She stayed there for a week at a resort, then returned to Lourdes."

"Nothing else?"

"Not much. She said she had a good time on the beaches there and enjoyed spending time with Klaudia. Said she sent her away with another couple thousand for herself and an envelope for safekeeping. Bernadette thought Klaudia might head back to Germany."

It wasn't as much as she'd hoped, but the gossip might prove useful. "Remember our conversation the other evening about loyalty?"

Nadine's expression turned to horror, and she covered her bare breasts reflexively.

"Call one of Pierre's guys. Tell him to visit Bernadette and get whatever Klaudia gave her for safekeeping. If she doesn't cooperate, have them do what's necessary. And remind her to get in touch with me directly should Klaudia make any contact for any reason. No permanent damage, but enough pain that she'll remember where her loyalties lie."

FORTY-ONE

Miami, Florida, Thursday March 30, 2023

Agent Burke had originally ordered Howard to Washington, DC., but his superiors saw the wisdom in asking the attorneys to travel instead to Miami, Florida. The guys at the top feared a leak might damage the entire operation, and the nation's capital was the worst place in the world to keep a secret.

Besides, they owned a comfortable three-bedroom condo in Miami for just such circumstances. Howard looked around the luxury suite where they had deposited him with two agents for protection. He shook his head at the use of taxpayer dollars. This spot was far better than the one where they'd parked him six years earlier for a similar grueling couple days.

Floor-to-ceiling tinted glass all the way around made for a pleasant start. An outdoor terrace off the living room overlooked the magnificent yachts in Miami Harbor. Outdoors, it looked like a view of paradise, while the twelve-foot ceilings made the interior look palatial.

Howard wandered around as though he might buy the place, touching the elegant European cabinetry and marble counter surfaces in the kitchen and opening the stainless-steel doors of the refrigerator to peek inside. Agent Burke pointed him toward the main bedroom with its king-size bed and private bathroom, then handed him a large brown envelope.

"The guys upstairs want to give you the five-star treatment for whatever reason. You can use this room," Burke said with a touch of disdain or envy. One could never be sure. "The lawyers have landed and will be here in an hour to start. They want to finish by the end of the day Saturday, so be sharp and consistent. Any major variances from the interview in Curaçao and our deal is off, got that?"

Howard nodded. It wouldn't be a problem. He'd slept well his last night in the condo where he'd lived for over a month in Costa Rica. It had been a quiet, out-of-the-way spot where he could recover from cosmetic surgery the FBI had arranged to reshape his appearance.

As Burke wandered off to check the technicians setting up recording equipment in the ample living space, Howard first peeked at his new look in a full-length mirror mounted on the back of the bedroom door.

He was pale. The surgeon had insisted Howard stay entirely out of the sunlight for a month while his face healed. But the beard had grown in nicely. It featured many more gray hairs than he preferred, but it effectively hid the scars and rawness of his skin. The color of his eyes had changed again. Now he used contact lenses that gave them a blue hue rather than the brown that came with his Italian heritage.

They'd changed his ears, too. In the last surgery, they'd made him look like a pale Steve Urkel from the nineties TV show *Family Matters*. This time they drew the ears back, closer to his skull. Now, he looked more like the newly crowned King Charles III of England.

Howard bent his head forward and checked his hair in the mirror. He saw a lot more of it. There was no trace of the previously receding hairline and balding on the top of his head. A hair transplant procedure was doing the trick. But he hated the nose. The surgeon flared it wider and added fat, making him look more Russian than Italian.

From the mirror, Howard retreated and plunked himself on the edge of the massive bed. It had been years since he had enjoyed such a space to himself, and the firm mattress felt inviting.

He opened the brown envelope. Inside, he found a new European Union passport, issued by Portugal. He was still Benjamin Castello, with the same history, but now a retired American living abroad.

Tucked inside the passport, a plastic identity card also featured his new and improved appearance, with all the details needed to travel freely within Europe. Once again, it looked like a genuine card issued by Portugal.

When he shook the envelope, a driver's license slid out. It showed a fictitious address in Lisbon used by the government for exceptional cases like Howard's. The Policia Judiciária there had worked with the FBI to provide all the documents, but Burke assured him they could be trusted.

"They're the national agency we work with regularly for matters concerning organized crime, terrorism, kidnapping, cybercrime, and financial crime. We figured you fit in there somewhere."

Tucked inside the fold of the envelope and joined together by a paper clip, Howard counted fifty one-hundred Euro bills. It wasn't much, but the FBI knew he was financially independent. This cash was for incidentals like his breakfast while in transit through Madrid, taxi to an apartment or hotel, tips, and those sorts of things until he could access his stash in the Caymans.

The last item in the brown envelope was an air ticket, economy class, to Madrid Saturday evening, with a connection to Faro, in Portugal, Sunday morning. Burke had told him earlier that entering the EU through Madrid would be better. They'd still recheck his documents in Faro, but much less thoroughly than in Lisbon.

Howard ambled to the window and looked at the brilliant sunshine in a cloudless blue sky. His gaze dropped slowly to the city's waterfront, the boats in the harbor, and the sailing yachts floating offshore. He drew a deep sigh and cast a long view in a semi-circle, silently appreciating the sights before him.

Just as he had every day since he took this massive gamble with his life, Howard wondered if he was taking in a view or experiencing a special moment for the last time.

FORTY-TWO

Montreal, Quebec, Thursday March 30, 2023

Three pressing crises for Supermarkets because of runaway inflation, Multima's extraordinary profits, and the *49 Minutes* interview had slowly crumbled into everyday concerns. They needed watching but no longer occupied the media's attention or sapped Suzanne's valuable time monitoring, listening, and managing events for the best outcome.

Over at Financial Services, they didn't forget Judy Jones's death, but it, too, had become less important with time. Serge continued to monitor phone conversations with his sophisticated software, looking for code words, but no suspicious calls came in after her death.

At last week's board of directors meeting, Suzanne won approval to appoint Natalia Tenaz as president of Multima Financial Services, effective April 1. James Fitzgerald had agreed to stay on as an advisor to Natalia until the end of June to ensure a smooth transition, and they announced that decision to generally favorable media coverage.

Still, some far-right media in the US focused more on Natalia's Puerto Rican heritage than her MBA from Yale, fluency in three languages, and the outstanding business plan she'd crafted for the coming years. One even had the temerity to suggest she'd do better in a senior role over at Supermarkets, which focused on things of more interest to women.

There remained lots of work for women to level the playing field in the world of business. In the Multima universe, Suzanne drew satisfaction from the current stable environment and resoundingly successful business results. The time seemed right to tell the world about her secret relationship with Serge.

At Stanford Business School, they hadn't taught her that the law drove decisions in nearly every aspect of American companies, but she'd learned that lesson early and quickly in her career. She realized news about her relationship with Serge would draw scrutiny from the media and the legal community. Her first conversation was with

Multima's chief legal officer, Alberto Ferer.

"You'll raise some eyebrows for sure," Alberto began after a clipped word of congratulations. "Society accepts the reality that many personal relationships develop in the workplace. But most relationships are among peers or associates on different teams, among employees who enjoy a reasonably equal status. Those that draw the most attention are those where the balance of power in the relationship is most pronounced. I think some people will find unequal influence with a CEO in a relationship with her chief of security."

Suzanne listened and watched his body language. His discomfort was apparent. The power balance in their business relationship probably caused him some unease as they discussed an issue touching on her personal life. Still, it was rare for Alberto to choose his words so carefully. He'd touched a forefinger to his collar twice while sharing his opinion, as though the shirt collar was too tight. And was that a bead of perspiration on his forehead?

"Relax, Alberto. I won't sue you if your advice proves wrong." She laughed and watched him do the same, though his was more restrained.

"We're serious. No thoughts or discussion of marriage or anything like that, but I sense it's better to make our relationship public. I think it'll be better for the company and for us in the long term. How should we do it?"

Alberto tutored her for about an hour. Before announcing anything publicly, he urged her strongly to get a legal agreement with Serge. He warned about state laws affording far greater rights to unmarried spouses than people realized—even if the relationship proved short.

He also asked her whether Serge should continue in his current role.

He wondered out loud if she'd thought about how Serge's outlook toward her safety might change if their relationship turned rocky. How might she react if Serge's negligence one day put her in danger's way? Could she manage media stories about the news of their relationship? Would morale change among employees at Multima, or would the company's leaders now think it appropriate to have relationships with their subordinates?

A candlelight dinner with Serge in the privacy of her new home in the Laurentian Mountains provided the right mood and environment. They were alone, except for Florence Carpentier, her cook and housekeeper, who prepared and served their exquisite dinner.

She asked Florence to prepare a Chinese fondue, thinly stripped morsels of beef. Suzanne and Serge would cook the meat themselves in a pot of seasoned broth using long, specially designed forks. A fondue took time to prepare each mouthful and stretched conversations she could lead in many directions while they enjoyed a delicious meal with superb wine.

Serge guessed her intention to have a meaningful conversation almost immediately. After a long sip of wine between the French onion soup and firing up the fondue pot, he smiled ruefully.

He spoke softly, but his dark eyes were intense. "The last time we had a fondue together was in 2006. In a small, dark French restaurant in Toronto. You told me you were leaving for Atlanta the following week to become the president of Multima Supermarkets. You said we wouldn't be able to see each other for a while. Will you deliver a similar message tonight?"

"Only if I've misread your intentions every time we've made love over the past year." She leaned in, closing the space across the table, and smiled invitingly. "I have no intention of going anywhere, and I want the world to know how much I love you. As we agreed at the beginning of the year, it's time. We just need to be sure we're on the same page as to how."

"Where do you want to start?"

They talked far longer than any conversation Suzanne could remember. Florence had extinguished the flame of the small cylinder heating the broth, served a scrumptious dessert, refilled their glasses of wine three times, and bid goodnight before they finished.

Suzanne hadn't used a checklist or anything like that, but one by one, she had introduced for discussion the various concerns Alberto Ferer had raised. Serge welcomed each subject, listened carefully while she explained the issue, then offered his thoughts respectfully and articulately.

In that two—or maybe three—hours of meaningful conversation, she felt they were equal. The power imbalance of their corporate roles seemed to evaporate. Serge suggested concerns Alberto hadn't mentioned and proposed solutions they might both find acceptable.

Neither was ready to consider marriage, but they discussed ways their relationship might become more permanent. They explored where each intended to go with their careers and the timeframes each envisaged.

They laughed, held hands across the table when emotions grew more intense, and looked deeply into one another's eyes often throughout the evening. When she was sure they had covered it all, a few tears unexpectedly trickled from the corners of her eyes. She reached to wipe them away, but Serge stretched across with his napkin and dabbed her cheeks gently.

"I hope those are tears of joy." His smile reflected his own happiness as she nodded her head vigorously, too overcome in the moment to find the right words.

FORTY-THREE

Sint Michiel, Curaçao, Wednesday April 5, 2023

Howard Knight must be behind this!

Text alerts woke Fidelia first, shortly after she fell asleep around midnight. Police had arrested Antonio Verlusconi at his home in Milan at four in the morning. In towns across Italy, the Carabinieri also snatched a half dozen of his lieutenants from their sleep.

Minutes later, Fidelia received a call from a distraught wife, notifying her that police had spirited away Juan Suarez while his family slept in their vacation home on the Mediterranean. The woman emailed later, adding that other wives in Spain reported authorities had also stolen their husbands from their homes.

An hour later, Nadine Violette banged loudly on the door of Fidelia's bedroom before she burst in, screaming that the police had snatched her lover, Pierre Boivin, and held him in Aix-en-Provence. They wouldn't let her—or his lawyer—speak to him.

In a matter of hours, law enforcement had detained her three most powerful allies in Europe. Police knew where to find them all. Worse, they must have worked in coordination with someone, someone who'd provided information so accurate and easy to verify that they could boldly take out so many in such a short time. Only Howard Knight and his cursed photographic memory had the knowledge to feed police authorities enough info to grab so many of her key people so boldly.

Fidelia quickly dressed, made coffee, and sat beside her phone in the newly completed secure area of her Curaçao beachside mansion. She didn't wait long.

Luigi Fortissimo's wife was the first to call from the Americas. At three in the morning, New York time, police shattered the doors to their home in the Hamptons with a battering ram, terrifying his family. They used a SWAT team armed to the teeth and yelled at everyone in the house to cooperate as children screamed and begged their parents to protect them.

Mia got up early, too, and fielded some of the calls from across the US, Canada, and Latin America. At the same time, Fidelia responded to texts and emails as quickly as her fingers allowed. She could do little but express her sympathies to the victims, assuring them everything would turn out okay, and remind them to give no information to the police.

The disaster unfolding looked just as she imagined it had when Knight had spilled his guts to the FBI in 2016, just before she escaped to the safety of her compound in Uzbekistan.

Back then, it was she who had also sold out a significant number of European leaders of The Organization. That's how she'd put her just-arrested allies in power. It was the defining event that had helped her eliminate Giancarlo Mareno and seize his powerful criminal outfit.

Now, it appeared to be collapsing on a grand scale. The Organization's lawyers were among the best in their profession, but it would take time to free the guys on bail, and millions, maybe even hundreds of millions, to minimize convictions and jail time.

Determined not to panic, Fidelia called her motley crew around her poolside to let them know what happened. She put on a brave façade with an exaggerated smile, her chin high, and used only cheerful tones. Then she put the team to work.

Mateo and his guys handled all the Latin American communications and rousted lawyers from their beds, demanding immediate results from Mexico to Argentina.

Tak Takahashi handled Asia. She had brought him to Curaçao not only for his protection. She'd had her interests in mind, too. In times like these, he could work capably with leadership on two or three levels within The Organization in Asian countries from Japan to Australia.

After Mia gave Nadine a couple Prozac, she regained enough control for Fidelia to let her work the phones in Europe and ensure lawyers in each country assisted everyone arrested.

Fidelia took care of the US personally. If she handled this disaster correctly, she might help solve another lingering problem and solidify her power and control at the same time.

If she failed, she'd either end up dead or in prison.

Her first call was to The Organization's mole inside the FBI. The woman was hiding in her apartment in Washington. She'd heard about the raids and was too terrified to go to her office. Instead, through sobs and tears, she told Fidelia she'd had enough. As they spoke, she was packing her bags and on the way to Dulles airport. Delta had a flight leaving for Buenos Aires in two hours and she planned to be on it. She'd disappear somewhere in Patagonia.

Twice the woman hung up on Fidelia. On a third attempt, she was able to reason with her.

"If you run, they'll know. Flying time to Buenos Aires is almost twelve hours. They'll have enough time to notice you're missing, ransack your apartment, and find out from the airlines where you're headed. If you run, they'll have people waiting for you on the ground in Argentina. If that happens, you're on your own. I won't spend one cent to defend you."

Fidelia let that settle in before she carried on. "Go to your office. Act normal. Volunteer to help in any way possible with the extra work this roundup creates for your colleagues. Then call me every night with updates."

The woman listened with occasional sobs but without protest or interruption. Still, Fidelia let the woman consider the possibility before she moved to close.

"I'll have a special phone dropped off at your apartment while you're working today. Our calls can't be traced. Your voice will be distorted. Help me with information, and tomorrow I'll drop a quarter-million dollars into that account you use in the Caymans."

FORTY-FOUR

Seville, Spain, Wednesday April 5, 2023

There was no reason to wake up at any specific time that morning, so Howard Knight slept until his body told him it had enough. He reached for the burner phone the FBI had given him a few days earlier and noticed it was past noon. Sun glared through a gap in the heavy black curtains he hadn't closed entirely before turning in for the night.

But there was no reason to beat himself up. The few weeks he'd just endured were among the most stressful he remembered. Today, his heart rate seemed slower. He breathed more freely. Muscles aching a day earlier magically became more limber, and he even looked better as he caught his image in a mirror across from the bed.

He didn't bother to dress. First, he needed a coffee to clear the waking fog. Then he needed to find out what was happening in the world that fine day. Once the hotel's tiny Nespresso machine bubbled, he touched the power button of a TV remote, and the screen brightened to highlight the CNN news logo. Above it, an animated Luigi Fortissimo, shouting and cursing, dominated the video.

A camera must have been inches from the US crime kingpin's face. As the camera moved further away, it became apparent that the action had occurred at night, and at least four heavily armed men in uniform surrounded their prey. One man on either side grasped his elbows solidly, almost dragging him as they pressed near the camera.

Howard turned up the volume.

"... in the early hours this morning. According to police sources, Luigi Fortissimo is the most powerful person in the US operations of The Organization. Law enforcement arrested over fifty of his cohorts in similar raids across the US, and we have reports of dozens more arrests in Europe, Canada, and Latin America. Authorities call this the biggest organized crime roundup in the past six years."

Howard lowered the volume again and pressed the power

switch off. He glanced downward as he set the remote on a counter. His left hand trembled slightly and he rubbed both hands together as steadied himself, then plunked himself down on the end of the mattress.

The vengeance he had unleashed was well underway.

Four days earlier—as soon as the lawyers finished with their questions and videos—Howard learned the expression's true significance when Agent Burke used the term "protective custody" one last time.

"You satisfied the attorneys with your answers, and we all appreciate the information you provided. We're finished. When I leave, you're officially released from protective custody. You have the Benjamin Costello identification, the air ticket to Faro we agreed upon, and the promised five thousand euros. Here's a burner phone if you need it. We've loaded it with one hundred international minutes. You can call us for help from anywhere. Good luck."

Burke held out his hand for Howard to shake, then followed the lawyers and Leonardo Garcia's team out the door. For the first time in weeks, Howard was alone.

Unless there was an FBI leak right out of the chute, he was in minimal immediate danger. Until law enforcement acted on the information he'd provided, it was unlikely Fidelia or her lackeys would pull out all the stops looking for him. She'd know he was missing, but he'd promised her never to cooperate with the FBI again. She'd probably give him the benefit of the doubt for a couple days. But not much longer.

Burke had promised no action until Howard was out of the country on Sunday. The safest course of action, before he traveled to the airport, would be to stay in the FBI's condo until he needed to leave for his flight. But he had one more preemptive step to take.

Howard pulled the baseball cap he'd been wearing since Costa Rica down over his ears, pulled on an N95 mask only a few folks still dared to wear, added sunglasses, and took the elevator from the FBI condo to the ground floor.

Burke had told him the phone was a burner, but Howard assumed it included a tracking device and maybe a recording app. Either possibility forced him to pay an exorbitant twenty-five euros to a security guard in the lobby to borrow her phone for a local call.

One benefit of a memory just short of photographic is the ability to recall useful names and numbers. He punched in the digits.

"Are you still in business, Smidge?" It was the only name the guy ever gave him.

"Yes," the voice answered.

"Can you meet me at Starbucks at Bayshore Landing, in Coconut Grove, in thirty minutes?"

"Yes."

"Red Cap, sunglasses, N95 mask."

Once Howard returned the phone to its owner, he left the lobby and walked to South Miami Avenue, where he hailed a cab, confirmed the driver would accept euros in payment, and directed him to Starbucks, Bayshore Landing.

Smidge found him, right on time, seated at a small table in the corner, away from the Saturday evening crowd.

"Can you do a Canadian passport today?" Howard asked without ceremony.

"Two hours and one grand."

"Can a thousand euros work?"

With a nod, Smidge pointed toward the men's room. Howard followed, then watched the kid slam a wooden wedge under the door right after they entered the restroom. He pointed for Howard to stand next to a plain white wall and motioned to remove the cap and mask. The guy drew out his phone and two flashes followed almost instantly.

Howard wandered around the neighborhood for a couple hours, his first long walk since the day he and Earl had walked from Sandra's Inn to the beginning of the nonsense with the Aruba constabulary. He'd plotted and schemed about his next steps for that entire time.

Smidge delivered the final product as promised. Howard inspected the Canadian passport with his current photo and the alias Mario Bartoli he'd used the last time Smidge created a false identity for him. He paid the fee, still silently cursing his currency conversion losses. Breakfast in Madrid might be only a bottle of water at the rate he was going.

It was that passport Howard presented to the immigration officer when the flight arrived in Spain early Monday morning. The officer didn't request either a boarding pass or a ticket. With a yawn, he stamped the Canadian passport and wished Mario Bartoli a pleasant stay in Europe.

Howard had no plans to visit Portugal immediately. It was merely a guise to set those who might benefit from an FBI leak on a fruitless chase. That wasn't paranoia at work. It was prudence. Four years earlier, a leak in the FBI had compromised his identity as well as that of the beautiful young woman he lived with in the Netherlands.

The Organization's thugs had captured him for a while. Luckily, he escaped. They chased him through five European countries before it all ended with the tragic murder of his lover by that bastard Giancarlo Mareno. Howard would have suffered the same gruesome end if Fidelia hadn't saved him by taking out Mareno with one bullet to the kingpin's face.

He'd owed Fidelia, but he also considered that debt long repaid.

He expected she'd already contacted her plants in the FBI and surely offered them tons of money to let her know his new identity. He'd need to lie low for the next few weeks. For a few days, she'd have her hands full with the chaos he'd caused by divulging all that incriminating information to law enforcement. But he knew the woman well. His betrayal would only intensify her rage and passion to eliminate him.

Seville was a good place to disappear while he waited for her anger to force a careless mistake.

The CNN news story about rounding up The Organization's guys prompted Howard to tweak his previous plan. That he was running low on cash was another factor.

Hotel Alfonso XIII was indeed one of the splendid hotels in Seville. In the old city, right next to Universidad de Sevilla, the hotel boasted luxury in every respect. Outside, it reflected a Neo-Mudéjar style of architecture that looked comfortably at home in Andalusia. Lots of decorative features, yet understated in color and finish. Inside, arches and columns projected wealth and status befitting the royalty and celebrities the place had attracted over the past almost one hundred years.

But staying there cost 457 US dollars a night. Before incurring another night's charges, he checked out of the luxury hotel and walked the streets until he found a tourist office.

"I need a place to stay for a couple nights. I lost my credit card but have a few euros to pay in cash. Do you know an Airbnb owner who might rent to me for cash until my new card arrives?"

Of course she did, right in the quarter of the old city he'd pointed to. Within thirty minutes, Howard met a young fellow named Daniel, who offered to carry his backpack while they walked to his apartment near the Basílica de Jesús del Gran Poder. It turned out to be a twenty-minute walk. On arrival, the apartment's owner led the way as they climbed three flights of stairs to reach a tiny apartment divided compactly on two floors.

Howard looked around, nodded, and handed him the agreed eighty-two euros for one night. Daniel said he'd return the following morning to pick up payment for the rest of his stay.

Fortunately, on their walk, they'd passed the Seville branch of the TVB Bank. Howard knew precisely where to go next.

FORTY-FIVE

Montreal, Quebec, Wednesday April 5, 2023

They had used the few days after their candlelight dinner to prepare for today's planned interview with *La Presse*. Suzanne dressed in a soft pastel pink business suit and wore her recently dyed-blonde hair cascading over her shoulders and partway down her back. She applied limited makeup but aimed for softness in her face as well.

Serge dressed in a brand new dark blue power suit and fiddled uncomfortably as he wrapped a bright red tie around his neck for the first time in a while. She helped him with the final touches, making the knot just right and centered.

Both followed Edward Hadley's advice. They'd agreed that a Montreal newspaper would be the best public-relations vehicle to break the story of their relationship. It was Serge's idea initially, and the team quickly bought his argument that a Quebec newspaper would probably treat their reveal more sensitively than other media in Canada or the US.

"Since abandoning the domination of the Catholic church in the middle of the last century, Quebec has become the most socially liberal society in North America. With the lowest percentage of couples choosing marriage and the highest divorce rate, people here have a much more relaxed view of relationships. Our media tends not to sensationalize changes because Quebec consumers have little interest when the media tries to titillate them with stories like ours." His confidence sealed their direction.

Before that morning's interview, they also carefully crafted a subtle change to his image. The business suit was part of it, but they also updated the Multima Corporation website to show photographs of Serge sitting around a table with the board of directors. They tweaked his job description, highlighting "Chief of Security" in bold letters, pointing out his responsibility for the safety of employees and customers in Multima stores and offices around the globe.

They expanded his background on the site, highlighting his senior roles with Canada's national police force and mentioning his earlier position as chief of security for National Grocers, once Canada's largest supermarket chain.

Before they sat down with the business editor for *La Presse,* Hadley had done his best to portray Serge and his role as almost equal in importance to the chief executive officer.

He also masterfully explained their strategy to the board of directors as they met via Zoom an hour before the scheduled interview, so it would surprise no one when the story broke later in the day.

"I've positioned the interview with the editor of *La Presse* as an opportunity to create an exclusive story about how moving Multima's headquarters from Fort Myers to Montreal has created exciting opportunities for the city, plus a human-interest angle about how senior management is making a new home in Quebec."

Suzanne revealed to the group that part of their story would be about her and Serge setting up a home together. They hoped a thoughtful media story might reduce interest in their relationship and avoid distraction from the core Multima businesses. She pointedly didn't ask for approval or comment. Just like Alberto Ferer had suggested, she was informative, factual, and confident.

There were no questions. A couple directors thanked her for the heads-up on the planned interview and the strategy for managing this recent development. Everyone smiled, and no one appeared nervous or alarmed. The director from the Bank of the Americas offered congratulations with a chuckle as he signed off.

Minutes later, Suzanne and Serge sat side-by-side in comfortable leather chairs facing Nicole Gagnon of *La Presse*. They were all in the alcove off the main office Suzanne used to perform her duties as CEO of the company.

Nicole brought a photographer with her. After the introductions, they all posed for shots from various angles and chatted in French until he left with his camera.

"It's odd for a corporation like Multima to offer the CEO and chief security officer for an interview. Usually, it's a CFO who joins these interviews," she noted.

Suzanne answered without hesitation and with a broad smile. "We think we're part of your story. While our company has set up a new home in Montreal, we are doing the same. Together."

Nicole took a second or two to process the message, then smiled in return. "Congratulations, I guess. But I'm not in the habit of writing human interest stories. I'm a business editor. So, if you're counting on me to break your news to the world, I'm not your gal."

"We're here to talk business. Our company has been successful in its transition to this city and province. How much or how little you deal with our personal circumstances is up to you." Suzanne maintained a professional, confident tone as she shrugged and smiled with ease.

Sitting a few feet behind the reporter with his recording device, Edward Hadley smiled and gave a thumbs-up.

The interview lasted over an hour. Nicole came prepared and asked good, pointed questions about why Multima had moved its headquarters to Montreal and about the challenges that move created.

Suzanne took care to answer precisely half of the queries, deferring to Serge on every second question.

As they wrapped up the conversation, Nicole commented wryly about how skillfully the CEO had managed the interview. "It was an interesting few minutes for me, Suzanne. I never realized so much of Multima's business strategy revolved around security." She looked directly into Suzanne's eyes, then allowed a faint smile to form before she said goodbye.

From the interview in Montreal, they rushed to Pierre Elliott Trudeau airport, where the Multima jet whisked them to New York in less than an hour. The American Supermarket Products Association had invited Suzanne to deliver the keynote address at its annual convention.

In the limousine from Teterboro Airport to the downtown hotel hosting the convention, she checked *La Presse*'s website. Their story was up. Nicole Gagnon had written a balanced and informative article about why Multima chose the city of Montreal for its new headquarters, touched upon the company's business issues, and mentioned her blossoming relationship with Serge. It was low-key and moderate, just as Serge had predicted.

Suzanne switched to Twitter and found a completely different landscape. *"CEO of Multima Sleeping with Former Police Officer,"* screamed a *Wall Street Journal* headline. *"CEO Simpson Affair*

Uncovered," a *Fox News* article said. "*Multima CEO now More Secure?*" a little-known Canadian business journal taunted. She shared them with Serge, who shrugged and said he guessed it came with the territory.

Two hours later, she stood on a fifteen-foot-high platform before a crowd of almost one thousand people, most related to Multima's supermarket business, and drew a deep breath before speaking. What kind of reaction should she expect?

"I hope the thoughts I share with you today will generate as much media buzz as the salacious stories of my personal life." She smiled with the most charm she could muster and shrugged her shoulders in mock exasperation.

The crowd laughed, then applauded enthusiastically and for longer than she expected.

Relieved, Suzanne launched into her speech with passion and enthusiasm. "The story far bigger than the goings on in my personal life is news breaking all morning about dozens, maybe even hundreds, of arrests of suspected members of the criminal element known as The Organization. Candidly, I'm gratified that law enforcement officials have taken action to get these people off the streets and out of our business lives!"

More applause. She paused until it faded.

"But we all know The Organization is only one of the organized criminal elements attacking our businesses and weakening society. Last week I read a news report about the federal government imposing punitive fines against a cleaning service used by many of the country's meat suppliers, maybe even some of you in this room. It shocked me that the cleaning service used thirteen to seventeen year olds to clean equipment in meat processing plants.

She shook her head in disbelief. "Some of those children worked night shifts, often until well after midnight, and at the minimum wage or below. Most of those kids had to attend school the next morning. What has happened in the executive suites of that cleaning company and its customers? How has such flagrant flaunting of child labor laws been tolerated for so long?"

The room went silent. Suzanne had touched a nerve. The audience appeared to consider her message. She paused briefly for dramatic effect, then spoke for another fifteen minutes with her audience spellbound.

She addressed her outburst on *49 minutes* about organized crime. Then she summarized ways The Organization or other criminal elements had bombed Multima supermarket locations multiple times. She reminded them about the tragic kidnapping of the founder of Farefour Stores, their French subsidiary. Suzanne spoke again about the bomb attacks on the home of the former CEO of Jeffersons Stores that killed her competitor David Jones and his wife. She finished with a description of the aftermath of her own destroyed home in Atlanta.

Her call to action was dramatic, so she intentionally softened her tone to show resolve rather than anger.

"It's time for each of us to do our part to stop this scourge in our society. If we know a company we deal with is paying so-called protection to criminals, we should find another supplier. If they threaten us, we should call the police. If our suppliers break laws or take other shortcuts that endanger their employees, we should find alternative sources for their products. And if we have management or employees aiding those criminals, we must weed them out. Let's all resolve to do everything we can to help law enforcement wipe out this miserable contamination of our values, our security, and our future."

She glowed as the crowd rose as one, applauding and cheering her message with thunderous enthusiasm.

FORTY-SIX

Sint Michiel, Curaçao, Monday April 10, 2023

Most of the guys were now out of jail on bail or by other means of commitment to appear in court to answer the charges laid by law enforcement in more than a dozen countries. Fidelia listened as her little group summarized the details.

So far, The Organization had paid out more than fifty million dollars to get temporary freedom for over ninety guys incarcerated after the raids. That was almost double the amount Giancarlo Mareno had to raise during Howard Knight's previous shenanigans. She'd get most of it back eventually, but there was little doubt a good number of these guys would soon face more time in prison. And their court cases would cost a fortune.

She'd have to name replacements for some, but there would be time to deal with that later. She had more significant headaches this week.

Over in Japan, Sugimori had raised five billion dollars by selling all the real estate beneath Jeffersons Stores on the US west coast. That happened in March. One billion of that price was profit realized over the years as the land appreciated, and a chunk of that money had already evaporated.

Tak Takahashi walked her through the timeline. The deal had closed on the fifteenth of March. Jeffersons Stores paid down all the outstanding mortgages on the properties the next day. During some recent bad times, Jeffersons had borrowed against the land's value too, leaving only five hundred million.

Jeffersons Stores converted half of that amount to cryptocurrency two days later. One hundred and fifty million showed up on the Suji Corporation March monthly report to Fidelia, together with her commission of thirty million from Suji's stake. One hundred million was missing, and Tak hadn't found it yet.

She knew Sugimori well. He'd have an excuse manufactured to send her off on the wrong track, then move the funds elsewhere. There was no point confronting him until Tak found the missing money. Probably, it would be better just to steal it back.

But without a top-notch technical person, stealing the money was more difficult. Klaudia had worked with Howard to hack crypto accounts. He understood how crypto worked. Klaudia had the hacking expertise. With both out of the picture, Tak had tried to bring a Japanese ace to Curaçao. Mia even had flights arranged, but the damned police in Japan had rounded up lower-level people like him in their raids rather than kingpins like Sugimori.

Tak's guy was out on bail, but the authorities now held his passport.

A ton of techies worked for The Organization in California, but Fidelia lost direct access to them when she gave the US to Luigi. Silently, she cursed her judgment and generosity in ceding so much power to her former primary protector, but it was too late for regrets.

Her secure phone lit up. The bastard must have felt her thinking about him.

The phone that was ringing was secure but traceable. Since the FBI could track Luigi—and he too might have reason to track Fidelia—she waited until the ringing stopped. She called him back on another device that didn't leave a digital trail. It simply erased all evidence of a call on digital networks as she stole time from the networks for her untraceable calls.

"Where da fuck's Knight?" Luigi bellowed into her ear. "Dat bastard did 't again. We're up ta 'r ears in shit here 'n I wanna see dat fucker dead."

No need to monitor his stress level by his accent during this call. Fidelia let him spout his anger for another minute until it appeared he'd finished venting and was prepared to talk. She used a forceful tone to remind him to whom he was speaking.

"Good morning to you as well. Now that you've got that off your chest, let me suggest you should know better than I where Howard is. Hasn't your guy in Aruba found him yet? Haven't your people inside the FBI given you any reports? Aren't those folks the same insiders who were supposed to tell you months ago why I'm on their radar? So cut the crap. Have you got all your arrested people out now?"

"Couple guys 'n Florida still 'n jail. Drug dealers caught with stuff durin' da raids. They'll be there awhile." His tone calmed.

"Folks inside say da FBI bilt some kinda digital wall 'round da informer. Nobody's able to get inside dat wall ta confirm. Sounds like Knight, though."

Fidelia took another tack while his manner was calmer. "What's going on over at Jeffersons Stores? I'm hearing rumors of a real estate sale. What's that all about?"

Luigi paused just long enough to suggest that he had to make something up. "Real 'state? Why'd Sugimori wanna get rid of good American real 'state? Who'd ya hear a story like dat from?"

If Luigi was prepared to mislead her like that, she'd need to move faster. "I thought my source was reliable, but I'll drop it if you've heard nothing to validate the rumor. What did your guy in Aruba find out? About Howard? Or Disputas? Or Montebank?"

"Sumbitch did'n lern nothin'. Got drunk. Dis'peared fer two weeks. Came back empty. Had da boys 'n Atlanta arrange 'n accident."

Fidelia held the phone to her ear and waited a moment.

Luigi offered nothing more.

"Are you able to travel?" she asked.

"Nope. Cond'tion of bail. No fuckin' passport."

"We need to meet in person. I went through all this legal crap when Howard raised a ruckus with the FBI the last time. I can help you save a bunch of guys with a lot less expense. But we need a few hours together with a couple lawyers from your team. Where can we do that safely? For both of us?"

"Nowhere. Got a' ankle bracel't. Plus, at least one tail. Can't go nowhere."

"Then I'll have to come to you. Your office is still in Mareno's old spot in the back of the restaurant?"

"Yeah, but ya sure ya wanna take a risk like dat?"

"Friday. Your office. Seven in the morning."

FORTY-SEVEN

Seville, Spain, Tuesday April 11, 2023

Fortunately, Howard had established a rapport with his new Spanish landlord, Daniel, on their walk from Hotel Alfonso XIII to the tiny apartment in the city's old section. It turned out the new fellow at TVB Bank was not nearly as efficient as his predecessor—the one who threw himself out a window in the tall corporate headquarters building in the Caymans a couple years earlier.

Curiously, the new fellow also called himself Mr. Fernando and claimed to be the dead man's cousin when Howard first contacted him. All remote transactions conducted with TVB Bank in the Caymans were by phone because Howard accessed his small fortune using voice recognition software.

He also used his voice to gain entry to the TVB office located across Plaza Almeda and a couple blocks closer to the Canal Seville-Bonanza. Once inside the office, Mr. Fernando used voice recognition again to verify Howard's identity before agreeing to discuss any transactions.

The software worked well at each step, but Howard still didn't have the fifty thousand euros he'd asked Mr. Fernando to release.

The story had shifted slightly with each visit to the Seville branch of the bank. First, the fellow told Howard they had blocked his account temporarily because there'd been no activity for several months. Once Mr. Fernando was able to confirm "Mr. Smith's" identity again, he said he could release the funds in forty-eight hours.

Howard returned two days later, as they'd agreed. Voice recognition again identified him as Mr. Smith, but there was a fresh twist. Someone had contacted one of Mr. Fernando's superiors to lock the account once more. That person had reported to TVB that Mr. Smith had been involved in an unfortunate accident and was under emergency care in a hospital.

Mr. Fernando expressed his regret about the misinformation but again needed forty-eight hours to reactivate Mr. Smith's account. He insisted it was a security feature the bank used to protect its clients.

Of course, the TVB Bank people didn't work on weekends, and the forty-eight hours extended into Monday, so today was the day his money should become available.

Daniel, his temporary landlord, thought he should accompany Howard to the bank. After all, seven days and nights had passed since his new tenant had first promised payment for two weeks "the next morning." Daniel leaned against a utility pole on the other side of the street, trying to be as inconspicuous to observers as possible as he watched Howard enter the TVB branch office.

An attractive, tall woman with long brown hair opened the door after "Mr. Smith" identified himself using the voice recognition software. But her cheerful smile through the glass door affirmed that she already recognized him from previous visits.

"I have some euros for you." Her smile broadened as she greeted Howard in Spanish and led him toward an elegant black leather chair in her private office. "Mr. Fernando apologizes again for the delay, but I have the fifty thousand you requested. Will one-hundred-euro bills be all right?"

She quickly counted out the money for Howard, inserting stacks of one hundred bills in small white envelopes, sized perfectly for the purpose. When she finished, she gathered the five envelopes, tapped them into one neat pile with practiced efficiency, and slid them across the bare desktop.

"Are you comfortable taking them with you all at once?" she asked. "If not, I'd be happy to open a lockbox for you if you plan to stay in Seville for a few days." As she asked the question, she tilted her head inquisitively and turned on considerable charm with pouting lips and a fluttering of her long eyelashes.

Howard caught her signals, but he proposed another solution instead. "Rather than using the lockbox, would it be possible to take half the amount and load it onto a prepaid credit card?"

She nodded and wandered away to another area of the office. His eyes followed the sway of her hips and her confident stride in heels higher than usual for an office.

When she returned, she flashed another inviting smile and handed him a new Mastercard with a flourish of accomplishment.

He leaned closer and asked in a murmur if the attractive woman might like to join him for dinner.

Without a moment's hesitation, she whispered an address where they could meet at nine o'clock that evening.

FORTY-EIGHT

Montreal, Quebec, Tuesday April 11, 2023

Back at headquarters in Montreal after an extended Easter weekend, Suzanne dug into her review of the previous quarter's financial statements, prepared by her CFO, Pierre Cabot. Investors worldwide were eager to learn if Multima continued to rack up extraordinary profits. Although the media and consumers might have complained about the company's phenomenal success because of increasing prices, investors loved it.

Multima's share price had increased over 18 percent during the past twelve months. That meant Suzanne's considerable wealth had increased by the same amount. Astute, Pierre Cabot knew that might mean negative publicity for his CEO again, but he was also smart enough to know there were options in how they reported the results. He had an idea.

Suzanne thought it wise to engage Natalia, her new president at Financial Services, along with James Fitzgerald, who was still serving as an advisor for the next few months. When their faces appeared on the Zoom screen, she motioned for Pierre to share his proposal.

"You guys have generated some impressive numbers again. But I'm recommending we take substantial reserves for losses. With the Fed and other central banks continuing to raise interest rates, the economy will undoubtedly slow. You're well within the two percent of loss exposure we usually reserve, but I'd like to double that reserve this quarter... to be prudent."

Natalia Tenaz looked at the camera and smiled. "Why?"

Pierre appeared flustered. The reason probably seemed evident to him, but Suzanne said nothing, leaving it to him to justify his rationale.

"If we double the reserve, we'll shield the company from accusations of gouging consumers and hoarding profits. You'll probably never realize those losses. We'll just convert the reserves back to profit at a more convenient time."

"But I have two acquisitions about to close. Big ones that will make lots of money for us in the future. If you increase our loss reserves, our balance sheet weakens, and lenders who committed the funds we need to complete those acquisitions can increase their fees or interest rates. Where's the win for Financial Services here?"

Suzanne looked at the screen and back to Pierre. Natalia was right, but Pierre looked out for her interests and the company's. Her new president at Financial Services needed to learn that lesson.

She used a soft tone but left little room for negotiation. "You'll get whatever support you need to close those two deals. That's the way it works here. But first, you'll take one for the team. Pierre gave you a heads-up. Use that timing advantage to prevent any lenders' squeamishness."

James Fitzgerald remained silent but nodded in agreement. The call ended soon after Pierre thanked everyone for their support.

The morning was still young, and Eileen let Suzanne know Gordon Goodfellow was holding for a Zoom conference. Suzanne motioned for Pierre to stay once she noticed that Bessie Forsia, CFO at Multima Supermarkets, was also on the call.

"You know we track the balance sheet over at Jeffersons Stores every quarter, and Bessie discovered something odd," Goodfellow began, then apparently thought some justification might be necessary. "You know I'm interested in monitoring what they do in case you let me buy them at some point, right?"

Suzanne nodded but didn't encourage him. Instead, she focused on Bessie, who started with some background.

"I keep a phantom balance sheet reflecting the changes they announce publicly. I know they might adjust them later. But this one's odd."

She looked into the camera, checking that everyone had followed her story so far. "Suji Corporation announced they sold five billion in real estate on the west coast. That deal closed in March. That info is all public. From their March-end financials, we see they paid off mortgages and loans related to the properties. They realized a profit of five hundred million dollars. Now, it gets tricky. When we look at their balance sheet, it appears they used half that amount to buy some cryptocurrency."

Bessie was taking her time to get to the point of the call. Suzanne nodded and added a prompt. "And then?"

"Well, Suji Corporation also released its end-of-March statements. We see one hundred and fifty million dollars attributed to the sale of real estate in the US. The other one hundred million just dropped off the balance sheets of both companies!"

"Could there simply be an entry error?" Suzanne asked.

"It's possible, though not likely. We think they laundered the cryptocurrency and used it for purposes other than Jeffersons' or Suji's businesses."

The group mulled over the implications of that possibility for a few moments. The securities and exchange authorities might find the discovery of interest. Even the FBI might have reason to investigate if someone shared the facts. However, no one on the call seemed comfortable about what—if anything—they should do with the information.

"Let's sit on it for a bit," Suzanne declared. "Good work on picking up this anomaly, Bessie. Continue your monthly monitoring. If they don't make an adjustment next quarter, we'll decide how best to use this."

"There's one other development over at Jeffersons you maybe haven't heard about." It was Gordon Goodfellow, and his tone was grave. "CNN just carried a story out of Japan. Jeffersons' new CEO, Grace Benedict, fell from the balcony of a penthouse suite at the Limpton Hotel in Tokyo and died yesterday evening."

"Oh, no!" The news shocked Suzanne, and she took a moment to recover. "It was she who tipped you off about the potential sale of Jeffersons' real estate back in January, wasn't it?"

"Yeah. As you suggested, I followed up with Amber Chan in China to see what she could find. Amber came up empty. Her Mizuto contact said he couldn't learn a thing. I never heard from the woman again."

"Until we hear another credible explanation, we should probably assume her 'fall' was not accidental at all." Suzanne chose her words carefully. "Let's keep digging on this. Maybe check with some of our Japanese suppliers to see if they've heard any rumors. I sense something is going on at Jeffersons that we ought to learn more about."

Suzanne made a note on her phone to talk with Serge about the news over dinner that night. Before she could even set down her device, Eileen burst into her office.

"It's the White House calling, the president's chief of staff," she announced with unrestrained enthusiasm.

After a brief and cordial greeting, the president's aide got right to the point. "If you can be in the DC area this Friday, the president would like to invite you to a brief meeting, just fifteen minutes. He'd like your opinion about some legislation he's considering. Would 2:45 p.m. work for you?"

FORTY-NINE

Sint Michiel, Curaçao, Tuesday April 11, 2023

Luigi was becoming an increasingly troublesome problem. First, the wayward senator. Then skimming money off her commissions in cahoots with Sugimori. Something was amiss with his FBI plants. Now damaging scuttlebutt surfaced that he had diverted money and resources usually used to traffic girls for the escort business into a new and dangerous venture. All without letting her know.

Mia had picked up the news while she was helping The Organization's Latin American victims of those early morning arrests and arraignments. A lawyer they used in Guatemala provided details. Thousands of children left the ravaged country every day. Naïve and desperate parents entrusted their children to local gangs affiliated with The Organization. Those rogue operators smuggled the kids to the Mexican border with the US.

With a recent federal government decision to let immigrant children into the country if they had sponsors, Luigi's guys took control of hundreds of desperate child immigrants. They diverted the girls suitable for the escort business to sponsors under the direct control of The Organization, but Luigi's guys had also discovered an entirely new source of income.

They charged the kids a fee for getting them into the US, more fees for finding a sponsor, and even further fees for finding them a job to repay their debts. As a result, most of the child immigrants owed The Organization thousands of dollars. To repay their obligations, Luigi and his minions forced the kids to hand over most of the money they earned as laborers. Effectively, they became enslaved.

With Central American countries suffering severe economic hardship that left people starving, Luigi had seized an opportunity that had even greater potential than payday loans. At the same time, American businesses had become so desperate for scarce labor resources that they looked the other way and hired the children at bargain-basement wages.

That news touched Fidelia more deeply than she could have imagined. The captivity and abuse the children encountered didn't disturb her much. After all, she'd become accustomed to effectively owning her girls in the escort game. They'd get used to it and probably still live better than they would have in the streets of their home countries.

What she truly feared was the backlash and outcry when The Organization's role was discovered. It was only a matter of time before some bleeding-heart journalist would find the connection to Luigi's guys. That backlash could make the round-up they'd just experienced look inconsequential. It could disrupt the escort business for years.

She didn't sleep at all the night after she delivered her dictate to Luigi to meet her at his office early the coming Friday. Instead, she stewed over every potential outcome.

Using the methodical thought processes they'd taught her at Columbia Law School, she considered the immediate consequences of any action she might take, then tried to think of as many potential secondary outcomes as possible. After all, understanding every issue, from every perspective, allowed an excellent lawyer to argue either side of an issue with equal skill.

In her case, every potential outcome could end her life violently, perhaps with great personal suffering.

She thought about the strengths and weaknesses of each member of the motley team she'd assembled in Curaçao. Then, like solving a puzzle, she mentally shifted each character in and out of her plan until she decided the roles they fit best.

With The Organization's human resources charts on the screen of her laptop, Fidelia assessed their probable reactions to each of her alternatives and considered how best to bring them into the process. And when.

Despite her relative comfort with technology, some processes just worked better when she set aside the laptop and put her ideas on paper. Scrawling on a sheet of paper, she developed a list of all the little details that could go wrong and pondered workable solutions should they occur. Her list grew by the hour, but she plodded onward, meticulously assessing the probabilities, the risks, and potential outcomes. Rather than tiring, she grew energized.

At daylight, on another piece of paper, she scheduled meetings with each of her team members, individually where appropriate and combined with others when necessary. Every bit of information had to be shared on a need-to-know basis only, and she considered the timing and sequence that would maintain confidentiality until the last possible moment.

The only people missing from the first phase of her plan were Marie Dependente and Mateo's guy assigned to finding Klaudia Schäffer. She'd weave both of them into the action once they had her long-time friend. She had arrived on the island of Curaçao. They knew that. It was only a matter of time before they captured her, but their task on Friday would become immeasurably easier if she could make her German friend part of her scheme.

We must play the cards we're dealt. Giancarlo Mareno's consistent counsel each time she'd encountered a new challenge popped into her mind as she considered her current hand. She shook her head to clear the cobwebs of fatigue and tension and refocus on her current reality, then knocked on Mia's door to wake her.

Once they'd finished a cup or two of coffee and Fidelia had outlined her assistant's orders for the day, she headed back to her bedroom for a nap before her team meetings started. It wasn't much rest, but she'd managed on less before.

Mia knocked on the door even before she could sleep.

"One of Mateo's guys thinks they may have a lead on Klaudia."

Although it was only seventy miles between the two islands, the small fishing boat Klaudia had hired took almost five hours to cross the South Caribbean from Aruba. Waves were much higher than she expected, forcing her driver to keep their speed low to avoid taking on water over the bow. Initially, constant motion made her nauseated, but gradually she became more comfortable.

It was cloudy that night, with only glimpses of moonlight, making it harder for someone to spot their boat on either departure or landing. But the driver warned her more than once that the coast guard patrolled regularly. He couldn't guarantee a safe landing. As they approached the steep rock cliffs of the shoreline, Klaudia's unease grew.

"How can I climb those rugged cliffs?" she asked him.

"I know a place. I'm lining up with those three huge white balls you see on the top of the mountains. Across the bay from that landmark, a new housing development is under construction. They've built a stairway to the beach. You can climb up easily. There's a security guard, but he's usually asleep at this time of the morning. To be sure he doesn't see you, cross the field outside the fence surrounding the development. It should take you only five or ten minutes to get across, with little danger of discovery."

He shut off the engine well before the shoreline. Tall, gentle waves had nudged the tiny vessel toward land. Then the driver used an oar to steer it parallel to the shoreline, just below a metal ladder leading to a stone stairway to the top. The driver grabbed onto a crevice in the granite wall and held tight with one hand while Klaudia hoisted herself over the edge of the boat and stepped onto the rocky beach with water above her ankles.

It was still dark, about four o'clock, according to her phone. The boat driver confirmed they were at the island's northern tip, near a village named Westpunt.

She turned on the flashlight app on her phone the moment he'd drifted offshore and restarted his engine. With care, she climbed the ladder, then felt her way to the top of the cliff one step at a time. She never experienced a sense of danger but worried regardless. What she was doing was illegal and could have consequences should they discover her out there without documents.

She paused at the summit to take a deep breath and slow her heart rate.

Before leaving Oranjestad, she'd topped up her phone with Digicel voice and data after they assured her both would work in Curaçao. Reception was poor at the cliff's edge, but the maps app eventually loaded to reveal her current location. For directions, she keyed in the name "Willemstad" and pressed an icon for walking directions.

The app pointed her toward a road leading to the principal town. But first, she had to pass through the vacant field beside the new housing development that her driver had described. Weeds, shrubs, and knee-high grass covered the vacant lot. That terrified her.

That environment undoubtedly harbored snakes, lizards, iguanas, and who knew what other slimy reptiles. Maybe mice, rats or groundhogs too. Since childhood, the only morbid fear Klaudia had was an illogical—but paralyzing—fear of vermin. From her backpack, she yanked a small plastic bottle and sprayed herself with insect repellent, hoping that might keep the pests away too. She took a few deep breaths and vowed to keep calm.

The narrow shaft of light disturbed lizards and other slithering creatures, scattering them in every direction as she walked. Her skin crawled with revulsion and unease, but she paused from time to time, inhaled to calm her nerves and continued with hands trembling and knees weak.

Eventually, she wended her way through the field until she discovered a dirt pathway. More confident, she scooted along it at a quicker pace until she reached the road. It had taken only a few minutes but felt far longer.

The road was paved and wide enough for two cars to pass comfortably. It appeared in good condition, so she felt safe walking along the shoulder as she wound her way past several resorts and apartments, most with limited or no light. In less than fifteen minutes, she came upon a shelter with a small sign marked *Bushalte*. Dutch for bus stop—not that different from the German. She curled her feet up on the wooden bench to wait.

A gentle honk woke her sometime later. She'd dozed off, and a small, old, dirty white bus idled in front of her, with a driver waving from inside. He said something to her in Papiamento. She didn't understand it but recognized the indigenous language of the Dutch Antilles Islands from her stay in Aruba.

"Can you take me to Willemstad?" She called out in English, pronouncing the city name as Dutch-like as possible. He waved for her to get in.

"How much?"

"Two dollars," he said with some effort, holding up two fingers for clarity.

She paid and sat on the bus immediately behind the driver. One row back, two women sat, chatting in Spanish or Papiamento or a mixture of both.

With three or four more stops, they took on another few

passengers. The original women behind her got off in front of one resort before the driver continued to speed along the highway with quick, frequent stops. It took almost an hour before she saw a concentration of lights on the horizon, with houses and stores.

The driver turned to her. "Otrobanda or Punda?"

"Otrobanda, please." Before fleeing Aruba, her meager research suggested the city's historic section might be a good place for her to avoid attention and apprehension most easily. The quarter had a few tourists and visitors from cruise ships but reputedly had areas where visitors were welcome but scarce.

Three traffic lights later, the driver pulled into a bus station across from the Renaissance Resort and parked among a dozen other vehicles of all sizes and descriptions. He waved for her to move forward and get off before she stepped down from the bus with her backpack in hand.

Although it was still early in the morning, the area around the parking lot was active, the sun was bright, and a warm breeze blew off the harbor just a few hundred yards away. She headed toward the sea and the Renaissance Resort. At a Starbucks on the corner of the complex, she stopped for breakfast and coffee. There, she chatted with an American at the next table, who said she'd just stepped off a cruise ship minutes earlier.

"Are you from the ship?" the American woman asked with a friendly smile.

"No, I have an apartment," Klaudia lied. She didn't know the names of any other hotels and knew nothing about the Renaissance. It seemed like a suitable answer.

Undeterred, the woman carried on, and they chatted about the weather and the woman's cruise. Then she switched her focus to the town. Klaudia knew it was time to leave and said farewell, hoisting her backpack and heading toward the waterfront again.

She asked a hotel security guard for directions to the downtown, and the woman pointed to a street a few hundred yards away. She motioned to the left as she spoke in Papiamento.

At the main thoroughfare, Klaudia noticed a smaller street heading up a slight incline where there appeared to be a hotel or something a hundred yards ahead on the left. Entering the gates, she found no lobby. Instead, there was a museum, a restaurant and bar, plus a winding alley that promised more of the same. The only hotel in sight was a casino, a tourist magnet.

She wandered along the stone pathway open to the sunlight and discovered more boutiques, restaurants, bars, and a small park. It was warm, inviting, and comfortable. However, she needed a place to sleep after a night on the ocean.

Eventually, she found a path back to the main street heading away from the waterfront. Walking briskly, she passed souvenir shops, clothing stores, a Chinese supermarket, a couple banks, restaurants, bars, and snack stands. There were two more casinos, but nothing resembling a hotel or hostel where she'd comfortably avoid crowds of tourists.

When she eventually reached a large hospital, she turned right onto a side street heading up a sloping hill toward a large church at the end of the roadway. A hundred yards from the church, she spotted a small inn that looked perfect. The neighborhood appeared to be mainly lower-income residents, with a few tourists. Attached to the large church, she noticed a series of schools, divided by ages or grades, she supposed. Immediately across the street from the church, a planned parenthood office thumbed its nose.

She paid cash for a room for a week, dropped off her backpack, and set out on her mission. Back on the main street, a guy she'd noticed earlier hanging out beside a bar still leaned against the building's brick wall. He greeted every man who passed with a fist bump and every woman with a sly smile.

"Hello, can you help me?" Klaudia asked.

"Do you need some weed?" he replied with a leer.

When she told him she did, he pointed down an alleyway. She followed him behind the building to a corner darkened by an overhead balcony. There, he named his price for three ounces of marijuana, and she paid him with US dollars. Mission accomplished, she returned to the inn and spent the rest of the day in her room.

She returned to the same guy outside the same bar the next afternoon and made the same deal. On her third day, Klaudia asked him if he knew someone who could make her a passport. He smirked knowledgeably and, for twenty-five dollars, agreed to show her where in Punda she'd find just such a guy.

They walked together across the pontoon bridge that crossed the bay, then continued along the main street on the Punda side for about a quarter-mile. Beyond the City Suites Hotel, he pointed left, and they veered off the main road into an alleyway with a bar on the corner. About halfway along, she noticed a Chinese variety store and a small printing shop beside a laundromat.

The printing shop was closed, but the dealer led her through the laundromat into a back room where a short Chinese man sat at a desk burdened with papers, envelopes, and empty food containers. The laundry guy asked questions. The marijuana guy translated. Klaudia eventually handed over two hundred and fifty US dollars, agreeing to pay the same amount when she picked up a passport issued by Germany the following Tuesday.

They entered the closed printing shop through a locked doorway from inside the laundromat. There, the Chinese fellow took a photo and carefully printed the name and other information Klaudia provided in block letters on a scrap of paper.

For the next few days, Klaudia left her room at the inn near the church only for food. She used a different restaurant each day and ordered only takeout, then ate in her room. She knew Fidelia's tentacles reached everywhere, and her friend would search tenaciously for her and Howard. That whole Aruba fiasco would be their fault in the mind of the powerful crime boss, and she would definitely seek revenge.

As agreed, Klaudia headed back to Punda and to the laundromat in the alleyway the following Tuesday. The fake German passport was ready and looked perfect. She could book her flight to Düsseldorf that very day.

She set off toward her room in Otrobanda on the other side of the bay.

When Klaudia turned the corner from the alleyway onto the main street, she noticed a woman walking casually up the alley about a hundred yards behind her. She looked like a tourist, wearing sunglasses and a short, bright blue sundress blowing up around her thighs in a breeze from the water.

Klaudia carried on but glanced back again later while she slipped through an outdoor café that split its tables on either side of the walkway. That same woman was following her at the same pace.

Klaudia suddenly veered right down the first side street and picked up her walking speed to almost a jog, increasingly concerned.

When she ducked left down the next street and reached its end, the woman in the blue dress was turning the corner, now clearly in pursuit. Klaudia increased her pace, and her heart rate quickened, too. She reached the main street along the waterfront and headed toward the pontoon bridge only a few yards further along. Suddenly, she heard an alarm bell ringing continuously and noticed it was coming from the pontoon bridge.

She ran. The bridge was only a few yards away, but a tall, green, sliding metal fence was already beginning to close as engines powering the moveable bridge revved loudly for departure. Klaudia strained with every ounce of energy she could muster and squeezed through the closing metal gate, tearing the sleeve of her T-shirt in the process.

The operator of the bridge yelled and waved at her to go back. Instead, she dashed toward the wooden platform now separating from the concrete wall. There was a gap of more than a yard already. Regardless, Klaudia sprinted. With a final desperate lunge, she landed on the moving platform but kept her balance. She looked up at the shoreline, and no longer saw the woman in a blue dress.

Klaudia ambled as nonchalantly as possible toward the other end of the bridge as it swung across the bay to dock on the Otrobanda side. At the end of the bridge, she stopped at the midway point and watched two freighters chug slowly out of the bay to the ocean.

As the bridge swung toward shore, she surveyed a growing crowd waiting behind another green metal fence on the wharf. Cautiously, she scanned faces to see if there was any reason for concern. She saw none. A mix of local people and tourists milled patiently about as a street entertainer serenaded the growing crowd, hoping for meager donations.

When the pontoon boat locked into its fixed position again, and another alarm bell sounded to signal the opening of the green metal barrier, she walked casually toward the opening gate. She blended into the oncoming crowd rushing to cross in the other direction.

She felt only a pinprick, almost like a mosquito bite, then a strong arm squeezed around her waist, pulling her close to a giant of a man. Her world turned dark.

Fidelia watched as the effects from the Propofol injected by one of Mateo's guys into Klaudia's thigh gradually wore off. Her friend was almost comatose when they'd first carted her into the beachfront mansion. Fidelia worried the thug had administered too high a dose and briefly considered finding a doctor. Ultimately, she decided involving a medical professional would raise too many awkward questions. Her friend would have to survive on her own.

After a while, Klaudia stirred, which was followed by some twisting and turning to find a more comfortable position on the sofa tucked in one corner of Fidelia's bedroom. A few groggy groans escaped. Then her eyes opened. She blinked several times as though adjusting to the bright afternoon light, then raised her head, looking around to see where she was.

"You should have accepted my offer," Fidelia said with a neutral tone. But her words carried enough gravity to make sure it was the first message Klaudia received.

"Where am I?" Disorientation, fear, and confusion were evident in her tone. "What's going on?"

Fidelia didn't answer immediately. Her friend needed time to become more alert and aware. It wasn't the time to either inform or assure. Instead, she sat comfortably on a nearby chair, crossed her legs, and waited for further reaction.

It took several minutes before Klaudia screamed out, "What the fuck have you done to me? Where are we? Why did you drug me?"

Klaudia struggled to hoist herself upright and off the sofa. She lunged furiously at Fidelia, making guttural sounds like a wounded animal.

Before Fidelia could react, her friend had covered the short distance between them, slapped her hard on the side of her head, and then clutched her hair with both hands. With considerable force, Klaudia yanked Fidelia forward and downward, thrusting her onto the marble floor, then pressed down on her back with a muscular leg as she pummeled both sides of her head with closed fists.

Fidelia screamed for help, but it took time for Mia to hear her cries, see what was happening, and shout out for help from one of Mateo's guys. Drips of blood appeared on the floor beneath her pummeled face.

Two of Mateo's men finally subdued Klaudia and restrained her flat on the floor while Fidelia regained her bearings and found the strength to lift herself to her knees, then to the chair. She looked down at her subdued friend in bewilderment and disgust. After several moments, she spat out her message, blood from her nose and mouth spattering Klaudia, who was below her on the floor.

"That will cost you more than you might imagine." Unsteadily, Fidelia hoisted herself from the chair, then used it for balance after she was on her feet. "Snap some zip ties on her hands and feet and leave her there."

After cleaning up and calming herself from the trauma, Fidelia changed her mind and ordered Mateo to drag Klaudia out of the bedroom and park her on one of the lounge chairs by the outdoor pool. She pointed toward a place beneath an umbrella offering protection from the sun, then tossed him a bottle of water to leave with her.

After the dinner hour, Fidelia felt better. Mia had provided some home remedies to ease the pain from the beating of her face and head. The bleeding in her mouth had stopped, and a bit of sleep relieved tense muscles and stiffness. Her brain was again dealing with facts as she tried to strip the emotion from her thought processes.

The situation with Klaudia was dire but not yet disastrous. Her friend reacted unpredictably and irrationally, but it was important to look beyond that. She now had all the leverage, so immediate revenge wasn't foremost in her mind.

The rest of the team was anxious, occasionally glancing at Klaudia lying outdoors all afternoon, but dared not question Fidelia about her intentions. She occupied them with group discussions and planning for their trip to New York the coming weekend. Every conversation identified a potential weak point or fine-tuned extra details.

When she dismissed the group for the night, she motioned for Mateo to stay behind. "Tell two of your men to tear off her clothes. They're covered in urine and excrement. Burn them on the sand down by the beach while she watches. Then throw her into the sea to clean up. When she's clean, bring her back here. Leave the zip ties on a while longer."

Mateo's guys followed their orders and carried out their assignment roughly. They dropped her once on the stairs to the beach and then threw her into the water at the edge. It was shallow where she landed, and Klaudia cried out with pain as she landed on her back with her hands and feet still tied. Sharp rocks and stones below the surface scratched and bruised her, making every tiny movement more excruciating.

The guys let the waves splash over her body for several minutes, cleaning away some of the filth. But they only paid attention when she struggled to avoid coughing and gagging as the waves pushed water into her mouth and nose. When her naked body was acceptably clean, they fished her out of the water, dragged her up the stairs to the pool area, then rinsed her down again with cold water from a hose.

When she was adequately humiliated, they dropped her back on the lounge chair Fidelia pointed to beside her.

"What were you thinking?" Fidelia asked after the men left the two women alone beside the pool. She didn't expect a response and didn't get one.

Klaudia looked at her defiantly, with an ugly sneer and cold eyes.

"That's the way you treat a friend of thirty years?" Again, she didn't expect an answer.

Klaudia blinked her eyes and swallowed, showing some acknowledgment of their previous warm bond. The sneer gradually morphed into relaxed lips. Fidelia fought back a temptation to explore them again with her tongue.

"I've been patient with you these past few years and tolerated your distaste for The Organization. I even allowed you to work at cross purposes to the escort business for a while, hoping you'd get it out of your system. When I let you and Howard start the new business in Aruba, I told you I'd hold you responsible should anything go wrong. You're accountable, remember?"

This time, she required an answer.

"Answer me. Do you remember?" Her voice raised, with narrowing eyes and a threatening tone, she left no doubt about her intentions. Then she waited.

"You probably arranged the entire mess. A couple murders to draw the attention of the police? Settling some old scores at the same time? Casting a net wide enough to trap Howard and me, then drag us back under your thumb? Now, will you blow away my brains like you shot Giancarlo Mareno? With a clear conscience? I know you too well, Fidelia."

Several minutes passed as Fidelia weighed her options and chose her words carefully. Her German friend lay naked on the lounge chair and closed her eyes calmly, as though she expected the worst and was ready for it.

"Where's Howard?" Fidelia suspected chances were slim the woman could help, but she had to try.

"No idea," Klaudia said in a monotone, adding a slight shrug without looking up. She was probably telling the truth.

"Well, if you can't point me to Howard, you don't want to help me with The Organization, and you try to beat me to a pulp for picking you up off the street, give me one good reason why I shouldn't put you out of your misery."

No reply.

Fidelia stood up and walked away from the pool area without a further word. The woman needed more time to think. Maybe by morning she'd be more pliable.

Mateo stood out of sight in the house's shadow, waiting for instructions.

"Leave her out there uncovered. No food or water. She has a phobia of reptiles. No lights, so you don't scare the critters away. Have someone go out every thirty minutes or so and just stare at her. If she asks any questions, ignore her. Don't touch. Just stare at her in the dark."

Returning to her bedroom, Fidelia fell asleep almost immediately. She awoke to a knock on her door. It was four-thirty in the morning, according to her phone, and she threw on a negligee before answering the knock.

"She's asked to talk with you the last two times my guy went out to stare. I think the lizards have her spooked. She's blubbered a lot out there and seems distressed. Want me to do anything?"

Mateo was smart. Fidelia thanked and dismissed him, then wandered nonchalantly toward her captive.

"Mateo says you're ready to cooperate."

Klaudia nodded once, not with her usual solid German resolve. Instead, her gesture conveyed defeat. With her eyes closed and tied hands covering her pubic hair, the woman appeared ready to listen.

"I love you, Klaudia. I always have. And I value the technical skills you bring to the table. I'm willing to overlook your errors in judgment this time. But I'll do that only if you're prepared to swear an oath of allegiance to me, just as you swore it to Giancarlo Mareno. Absolute and unquestioned loyalty. Complete obedience. Unfailing execution of orders. Do that, and I'll treat you with love, compassion, and respect. If you don't swear the oath of loyalty, I'll go back in the house, get a weapon, and say goodbye to you now, forever. What's it going to be?"

Klaudia swore the oath of loyalty slowly and hesitantly, her eyes focused on Fidelia as she had demanded.

Fidelia waved for Mateo, again in the shadows beside the house.

"Cut her loose. I'll give her some clothes to put on, then take her and two of your men to wherever she was staying in town. Get her computer and any other personal stuff. Bring her back as quickly as you can. We have work she needs to finish before we head out to New York."

FIFTY

Seville, Spain, Tuesday April 11, 2023

It was just after midnight. He'd offered to see the woman home at such a late hour, but she insisted she'd be fine. It would be less complicated if she arrived alone.

Howard gave her polite farewell kisses on each cheek and said goodnight. Her command of English was excellent, but they'd chatted mainly in Spanish once she heard his fluency. She teased him good-naturedly about his Latin American accent and odd expressions.

She proved to be an excellent conversationalist throughout their dinner, able to talk comfortably about business, the arts, culture and the bit of philosophy they strayed toward after they started the second bottle of wine. Midway through their meal, something more than dinner looked promising. Her smile grew warmer; she touched his hand on the table often and held it there twice.

Neither shared information about their relationships with others in any detail, so her comment about making it less complicated if she arrived home alone implied someone already occupied her bed. He didn't press it.

From the restaurant, it was about a fifteen-minute walk to his apartment across the Plaza Almeda and up a couple smaller back streets. Dozens of people were still either dining outdoors in the patio restaurants along the route or walking about leisurely. Howard set off toward the tiny apartment at a brisk pace and with a comfortable demeanor.

It struck him as he turned right off the Plaza onto the first side street toward the apartment.

During that tense conversation with Fidelia in Uruguay back in November, she'd said, "Even after your contact, Mr. Fernando, jumped from a balcony outside his office?"

How did I miss it?

In all their years together, he'd never shared with her the name of his contact at TVB Bank. He was sure of it. And he'd certainly never shared the information about Mr. Fernando's death with her or anyone else. Fidelia must control someone within the bank, and it was probably that person who was responsible for the delays in getting his money over the past few days.

Instantly tense and more alert, Howard turned onto the second side street and looked carefully in both directions. He spotted only one younger couple strolling on the sidewalk a hundred yards or more along the road. Quickly, he covered the distance to the next side street and poked his head carefully around the corner before he entered what was no more than an alley in width.

All was clear as he strode towards the doors to his apartment entrance, the key already in his fingers, ready to unlock the door or defend himself, whichever came first. He stepped inside the building entrance, which also served as the doorway to a parking area.

Several cars sat in the poorly lighted indoor space, but no one appeared to be around. Howard marched past the rows of vehicles to the stairwell and peered inside before tentatively approaching the stairs. He flipped on a switch, lighting the stairwell all the way up to his apartment on the third floor.

He listened for any sounds as he climbed the stairway and heard nothing.

Was paranoia setting in? Had he treated his immediate security too casually?

Inside the apartment, Howard turned on all the lights and checked every nook and cranny on the main level.

When he climbed to the upper floor, he examined the sliding glass door that opened onto a small balcony. It was slightly ajar. Alert, he opened the door entirely, threw on the outdoor light switch, and dashed to the outdoor metal staircase that served as an emergency escape. Almost at the bottom of the stairs, he spotted a form dressed entirely in black jumping from the stairway. Then, like a shadow, it disappeared into the night.

Howard left the outdoor light illuminated, returned inside, and locked the doorway behind him.

Without hesitating, he reached for his backpack and jammed his few possessions into it. Within minutes, he fled the downstairs parking lot again and walked as quickly as he dared back toward the plaza, looking over his shoulder every few feet. At Plaza Almeda, he spotted a taxi discharging a passenger. He ran up to the car before the door closed and asked the driver to take him to Plaza des Armas, the inter-city bus station.

The street ran almost in a straight line halfway to the terminal, with one right turn for the other half of the trip. There was virtually no traffic at that time of the morning. Still, he checked out the rear window discreetly several times but saw nothing suspicious behind. In less than ten minutes, the driver pulled into the taxi stand at the side of the sprawling complex. Calmly, Howard stepped out of the car, paid the driver, then surveyed the landscape to check again if anyone had followed.

From the taxi stand to the main entrance was less than fifty yards with a few steps to climb. All looked clear to the front, and Howard strolled as aimlessly as his tension would allow. Inside the massive hall, all the shops and snack bars were closed. No one manned the information counter either.

He wandered about the virtually vacant hall, keeping the half dozen other people in view while he tracked down an electronic monitor. He found one hanging over the escalator down to the levels where buses parked and stood to one side to read the departure schedule, still keeping an eye out for anyone approaching.

No buses were scheduled until five. However, he heard at least one engine idling on the lower level and ran down the escalator. Midway along the line, a driver was finishing a cigarette and flicked it to the ground just as Howard approached and called out in Spanish.

"Where are you going?"

"Salamanca, I hope. They fixed the engine, so I should make it that far." His mood was surly. He didn't look at Howard and started to climb back onto the bus.

"How much is a ticket?" Howard stepped closer to the man who had reached the top step.

"Don't have a ticket already? You don't go. Buy a ticket tomorrow when they open."

He reached out, showing the driver a one hundred Euro note in the dimly lit doorway of the bus. The fellow nodded, took the bill, slipped it into his pocket, and sat in the driver's seat, set for departure.

Howard scrambled inside and worked his way toward the rear of the bus. He noted every face as he passed the rows of seats, surprised by the number of people on board at that time in the morning. The bus was more than half full. No one had followed him down the escalator to the bus departure area, but it was always better to sit right at the back where he could watch passengers boarding and debarking throughout the journey.

Seated with his backpack on the seat beside him in case of an emergency, Howard took stock of his situation.

It was lucky he'd stopped yesterday at that hole-in-the-wall shop on the path back from TVB Bank to the tiny apartment. He'd bought a burner phone from them with unlimited data for a month, so he didn't need to use the FBI phone that might be able to track him.

Once the bus was in motion, Howard yanked the new phone from his pocket and fired it up. His first stop was Google Maps. He needed to find out where the hell Salamanca was.

FIFTY-ONE

Washington, DC, Friday April 14, 2023

They told Suzanne she could bring two guests to meet with the president. Naturally, she needed to provide details in advance about James Fitzgerald, Serge Boisvert, and herself, including copies of their passports, COVID vaccine status, and a health questionnaire. Eileen had emailed everything requested.

Suzanne and Serge traveled from Montreal to Dulles International using the Multima corporate jet, while James flew from Chicago's Midway airport on the Financial Services plane. On the tarmac, they met in her corporate aircraft three hours before the scheduled meeting.

Every day since the invitation, her excitement had grown, almost like a child readying for a memorable trip. Suzanne had devoted considerable time with her colleagues, speculating about what possible legislation the president thought might impact Multima Corporation.

Those few minutes at the airport were their last opportunity to prepare for as many eventualities as they could devise. Their goal was to state succinctly any appropriate Multima objections or encouragement to proceed.

Was Congress considering price controls to get inflation under control? Were they considering legislation to increase the minimum wage nationally? Might some financial interests be lobbying to relax or tighten credit card or mortgage lending rates or standards?

Suzanne and James had contacted all their lobbyists and industry associations to discreetly ferret out what potential legislation might be under active consideration. Of course, they had to make those inquiries without divulging the president's invitation. Any breach of confidence about the private meeting before an announcement by the White House might scuttle the event.

In the final analysis, the only rumor that seemed to have any foundation was the off-the-wall idea first reported by Beverly Vonderhausen, the one about the rogue senator from New York trying to pass a law to break up Jeffersons Stores. The Washington lawyer continued to insist her sources were serious and a draft of such legislation was with the White House.

James and Serge, as well as Alberto Ferer and Gordon Goodfellow, had all discussed with her the possibility of such legislation over several Zoom conferences. Until now, they hadn't decided whether a development like that was good or bad for Multima.

Goodfellow had been positively ecstatic about it. "That would let us swallow up all the good parts of the company for a song and not waste time on the garbage," he said in one conversation.

James saw little positive for Multima and lots of downsides. "Precedent is a dangerous opiate for those in power. If they can break up Jeffersons that easily, who's to say Multima isn't next on their list?" he asked during the same call.

Today's smaller group took another run at a consensus, but a final decision would have to wait until the actual meeting.

"We only have fifteen minutes with him and it's his agenda, so we likely won't have a chance to raise any new issues. But if we can, I want to make every minute count," Suzanne said.

They identified topics they'd be ready to discuss if the opportunity arose. James wanted to press to harmonize financial reporting standards with Latin American countries. Serge wanted the white house to push the FBI for even more action on organized crime. Suzanne agreed with both.

Three hours before the start of the meeting, one of Serge's security people met them in the reception area of the private aircraft section of the terminal. They scrambled into a limousine and headed out. The tension was palpable.

At a snail's pace, Serge's man maneuvered them past the iron fences, some steel vehicle barriers, and three security checkpoints on the White House property before dropping everyone at the instructed doorway to the West Wing. Suzanne glanced at her watch before smiling at Serge. What one would expect to take thirty minutes to an hour had left them with just ten minutes to sign in and meet with the president.

He was a gracious host. Suzanne had met the man briefly at a fundraising event in Atlanta during the Obama administration. She doubted he would remember the encounter, but his memory or advisor served him well, as he greeted her by name with a broad smile, a formal handshake, and a hug.

She introduced Serge and James. As he shook Serge's hand, the commander-in-chief blurted out that he was one lucky guy. Suzanne tried hard to avoid a wince but wasn't entirely successful. The president gently touched her shoulder and winked before he reached out to shake hands with James.

Seconds later, they sat in a small circle in massive leather chairs. The president wasted no more time on pleasantries.

"I'm told you all signed the confidentiality undertakings and agreed not to discuss today's meeting with anyone, including the media, until we authorize you to do so. I want to underscore the importance of that condition." He watched as they all nodded before he continued.

"At first, I dismissed this proposal out of hand. I find the idea somewhat repulsive, and it grates my sense of fair play. But I'm under enormous pressure from my closest advisors to not only consider breaking up your competitor, Jeffersons Stores, but sign into law a statute to do it. I'm curious what you think about that."

"May I ask why you're considering it?" Suzanne asked politely.

The president nodded to his chief of staff seated next to him, "Of course."

"A bipartisan group in the House of Representatives has drafted a bill to force Jeffersons Stores to divide itself into five separate companies by region within the country. They believe each company would be forced to compete more vigorously for consumers' dollars, driving retail prices downward and breaking the back of inflation," the chief of staff said. He turned away from Suzanne as he finished, reverting his gaze to the president.

"I'm curious why you chose Jeffersons Stores." She needed to pose the question carefully. "After all, Jeffersons is the fourth largest supermarket chain. If the goal is increasing competition, why not break up Walmart, Costco, or Target?"

"That was my question precisely!" replied the president.

The chief of staff stiffened uncomfortably in his seat. "As we advised the president, Jeffersons Stores isn't nearly as powerful as some in the marketplace, but Congress believes breaking up the number four company might signal to other players, including Multima, that they better take more care to bring inflation under control ...."

"Or the government might choose to break up other companies, including Multima?" As she interrupted the chief of staff, her face flushed. She took a deep breath to regain her composure. "Look, I'm no fan of Jeffersons. We're arch competitors, after all. But if bringing us here today was to garner our support for your legislation, that kind of rationale won't do it."

The president expressed no emotion and made no effort to support his aide. He, too, waited for a retort.

"There are also lots of rumors out there about Jeffersons' parent company in Japan and the unsavory company Suji Corporation keeps. Over the past months, you've made speeches about criminals in the food chain and a need for governments to act. We thought you might be amenable to breaking them up as a way of reducing the company's influence." The chief of staff tilted his head slightly and looked over the frames of his eyeglasses, apparently pleased with his counterargument.

Suzanne was ready. "We've called for government action to make police investigation and prosecution a priority. We don't support any legislative action to solve the problem, just enforcing laws already on the books. And the federal government can exert its influence on states to enforce their laws and foreign governments to do the same. Breaking up Jeffersons Stores simply establishes a precedent other governments can subsequently use to attack Multima Corporation or any other major publicly traded company."

"So, we don't have your support, regardless of the benefits Multima might realize from weakening a competitor," the president said.

"Not only do we not support such measures, but we will also adamantly and vociferously oppose the proposed legislation the moment it becomes public."

Suzanne looked at the president sternly, but his eyes softened, and a smile formed. He glanced at his watch, then at his chief of staff as he stood up. Stepping toward Suzanne, he reached out to shake her hand. His trademark presidential grin was prominently displayed, and his blue eyes sparkled.

"If ever you decide to leave the business world, you should consider a career in politics. We'd welcome you."

"But that welcome would probably depend upon which country

I choose, right?" Suzanne matched his humor as she spoke, then broke into a full laugh. The president giggled all the way to their farewell at the door.

"We still don't know what he'll do with the proposed legislation, do we?" Serge asked as they walked toward the area where they would meet their limousine.

"I think we do," James replied. "The old dog would have fought much harder for the bone if he wanted it. Suzanne reinforced his preference, just as he'd hoped."

FIFTY-TWO

Morristown, New Jersey, Friday April 14, 2023

Fidelia brought the entire Curaçao gang on the jet that morning, including a subdued Klaudia Schäffer. During the five-hour flight from Curaçao, she reviewed every element of the plan to be sure each person knew their role. She felt like the director of a live performance, emphasizing timing, dialog, and interactions with other players.

It was a complex exercise, more complicated than any she'd tried before. Dozens of moving parts in her charade could go wrong should any of her motley crew forget, make a mistake or betray. Any one of those possibilities could result in death.

One hour prior to touchdown, Mateo took Nadine Violette to the rear compartment. There, he wired up the young woman who was the lover of her first-in-command for France. A barrette on the top of her head secured a microphone, and a thin black wire threaded through her long dark hair and down the back of her collar to a device connected to a video camera so tiny it appeared to be a button.

Mateo undid the top three buttons of her shirt to encourage any eyes scanning that area of her body to focus on her cleavage rather than inspect for hidden devices.

They installed the same technology on Nadine as they'd used in the fiasco that killed Fernando Disputas. Nadine wouldn't use a speaker in her ear this time. That would be too easy for Luigi or his guys to spot. Fidelia could listen to any conversations and see what was happening, but couldn't intervene with any comments in Nadine's ear. It wasn't ideal, but Fidelia could at least observe the woman's interactions and tweak the plans to deal with any unexpected developments.

Tests in the jet worked fine. Fidelia gave a thumbs up after she listened in on a conversation between Mateo and Nadine.

When the aircraft landed at Morristown Airport in the New Jersey town of the same name, Nadine exited down the steps, followed by Mateo's guy Joe. Both climbed into a black Lincoln stretch limousine, which immediately sped off from the tarmac area.

As they'd agreed, Nadine and Joe continued chatting with the driver to be sure their technology worked. Fidelia listened and watched their travel progress toward New York City as the pilots prepared the jet for immediate departure. They informed the air traffic control tower that their flight was headed to Buffalo and pointed in that direction once cleared for take-off and in the air. Over the next two hours, they would change their destination three times in flight and refuel on the ground once.

Thirty minutes after the private jet left New Jersey, Fidelia watched the limousine pull up at the back door of the Manhattan restaurant Luigi Fortissimo used as his headquarters for The Organization's operations in the US. She recognized it from a distance because she'd visited there often when it was Giancarlo Mareno's office.

At precisely seven o'clock, a driver pulled up behind the parked limousine in a matching black Lincoln and Luigi stepped from the rear seat when the driver opened the door. The other car's doors opened and Nadine and Joe approached him as he headed toward his office.

"Luigi!" Nadine called out cheerfully and waved with enthusiasm. Fidelia also expected she'd use her high-powered smile as male bait. It worked well for her.

Luigi's driver reached inside his jacket for his gun, but Luigi waved him off as he recognized Nadine. Giancarlo had gifted her to him for more than a few nights, and his broad grin suggested he remembered those nights instantly.

"Nadine, whatcha doin' 'n New York?" he asked as he wrapped his burly arms around her, blocking the camera momentarily.

"I'm working for Fidelia. She's here but can't come to your office. Said you'd understand why. She wants you to come with Joe and me to meet her. We're unarmed. Your guy can check, and you can reach her on the secure phone to confirm."

Luigi stepped back from them and looked Nadine and Joe warily up and down. Then he motioned for his driver to pat down both visitors for weapons as he reached for his phone.

"Ya said ya'd be here at seven, not Nadine. What's goin' on?"

"Good morning to you, too, Luigi. Change of plans. I'm in the air and will land shortly. Nadine knows where I'll land. Can't take any chances naming the location now since you haven't found the leak among your guys."

"How long's it gonna take?" His tone was surly, but she detected no resistance. He also looked annoyed on the video, but he managed his voice effectively.

"The car will have you here in thirty minutes. We'll need about an hour. The driver can have you back at your office within two hours."

"I'll use my driver 'n car."

"Okay, bring no one other than your driver. Joe will give him directions. Give your phone to him and I'll explain."

He passed the phone to Joe.

Fidelia carried on when she saw the exchange complete. "Joe, he wants to use his car. Give his driver directions, one turn at a time, as we rehearsed. Clear?"

Joe returned the phone to Luigi, and Fidelia made one further parting comment. "I've got a few other people from my team with me. They'll be present but won't participate in our meeting. None of them are armed, so don't be alarmed."

She watched him process that comment and scowl. Luigi wasn't used to interactions where he wasn't entirely in control.

He shook his head. "Don' wanna do that."

"Luigi, I've got to protect myself. You know that. There's only one reason I can't meet you at your office. You've got a leak somewhere. I asked you to fix it over five months ago. Now get in the car. Come meet me and get me comfortable about a few concerns, or ugly stuff will start happening, and it will start happening as soon as I give the word."

He squirmed a bit while he silently weighed her threat. Their long relationship had been complex, ranging from his help to seize control of The Organization, to infrequent nights of passion away from his wife. Nadine's camera picked up an image of a man torn between his better instincts for personal safety and her potential wrath.

It took several long seconds. Finally, he said, "Okay."

For exactly twenty-seven minutes after their conversation, Fidelia watched them travel back to Morristown and listened to their conversations. Joe gave the driver step-by-step directions and Luigi and Nadine chatted, Luigi inquiring about France and Pierre Boivin. His subsequent efforts to pry information about Fidelia's intentions from both her operatives failed.

About a mile before they reached the airport, Nadine asked a question. "How does that ankle bracelet thing work?"

Fidelia smiled the moment she heard the question. Nadine had asked it as a pre-arranged code. Her question confirmed that Nadine had digitally deactivated the GPS monitor attached to Luigi as a condition of bail. Fidelia called the pilots on the aircraft intercom and instructed them to start the jet's engines and let them idle, ready for takeoff.

She stepped down the stairway from the jet and met Luigi's car the instant it stopped on the tarmac.

"The plan changed. We'll talk up in the air. It's safer that way." She led Luigi by the hand until he balked at the foot of the stairs.

"Can't. They're trackin' me. Can't leave da state."

"They lost your signal fifteen minutes ago. Nadine disengaged it with a special app. Police are probably on the way to where they lost you and might come here eventually. We should get up in the air, have our discussion, then drop back here later when they've given up any search."

"An' if they don' give up?"

"We'll drop you at another airport. When they check for you at home and you finally meet up, they'll simply see a malfunction that they can restart with the same app and chalk it all up to a technology glitch."

Luigi grimaced but didn't challenge her authority. He dismissed his driver before they stomped up the stairway. One pilot on the ground waited until everyone had passed through the doorway before bounding to the top and sealing the passenger compartment.

Fidelia pointed Luigi toward the rear of her jet and watched as he made his way there slowly and uncertainly. He made eye contact with every member of Fidelia's team seated in the first two sections of the jet as he worked his way back.

In the rear compartment, Fidelia slid closed the floor-to-ceiling door behind her to seal them off from the rest of the team. She pointed for him to sit on the loveseat, sat down in her chair beside it, and buckled for take-off. The jet had started its taxi before she heard it click shut.

"I have a long list. Let's get started."

Luigi nodded without smiling, his face muscles tense with either anger or frustration.

"Let's start with your sinister senator. Did you hear the news this morning?"

Luigi shook his head in reply.

"The FBI rousted him from bed at four a.m. and perp walked him in sweatpants before the TV cameras. They plan to charge him with three or four counts of fraud. Two questions. First, why haven't your people at the FBI told you about that? And second, what do you plan to do with the asshole?"

"Ya shut down my phone. Can't get calls from anyb'dy. Ya know that."

"We shut off your phone at seven when you got in the car. That means your plants had three hours to inform you. They didn't. Just like they never got back to you with why the FBI and Homeland Security were waiting to arrest me at Teterboro five months ago. I recommend you have a strong word with them. Now that the FBI has arrested him with what they call an open and shut case, what will you do with your senator?"

"Dunno. Haven't had time ta think 'bout it."

"I have. My informant tells me the Shadow sold out your senator. A tip came from a call using a burner phone at his Florida compound, followed by an email routed through the middle east that originated from the same Florida compound. Your guy did something to piss off the Shadow and now you're out a few hundred grand, and the little worm may try to take you down with him. Figure it out. I want your answer before we land again."

Luigi's expression morphed from anger to discomfort. It must have dawned on him that he should've been giving that information to Fidelia, not hearing about it from her first. She didn't leave him time to mull it over.

"Now, tell me about the kids from Central America." She used a flat, inquiring tone with no hint of disgust.

"I was plannin' ta tell ya 'bout that when ya came. It's workin' out great. The senator tipp'd me ta the opportunity."

His grin projected confidence, but the deepening accent more accurately revealed his stress and apprehension.

She waited for him to continue.

"The Feds need ta let some immigrants inta the country. The Shadow told 'm 'bout some guys 'n Guatemala who get fam'lies ta pay transport ta the border. Then, the senator found some ways ta get visas 'n spons'rs. We're chargin' the kids ten grand for travel 'n ten grand for visas. They pay us back from jobs our guys find for 'em."

"How old are these kids, Luigi?"

"All ages. Teenagers, students, adults. It's a gold mine. Take 'bout half what they earn. We're chargin' 'em fifty percent interest. Figure we'll get 'bout twenty grand per imm'grant b'for they start ta pay down the loan. Plus, we're gett'n two grand each from the employment service who puts 'em in jobs. Figure we make 'bout fifty grand each."

"How much is going back to the Shadow?"

"Ten percent."

"And to the senator?" She locked on to his eyes as she asked the question.

Luigi paused before he said, "Nuthin'."

"That's bullshit and you know it." She unbuckled her seatbelt, stood up, and leaned down toward his face. She scowled.

Luigi met her gaze and said nothing. A small bead of sweat surfaced near his hairline, but his facial expression remained neutral.

She waited a minute or longer before he finally replied.

"We help da senator 'n other ways."

"Like funding an act of Congress to break up Jeffersons Stores?"

He blinked and twitched nervously but remained silent. His face turned red, and a vein on his throat bulged with increased activity.

She raised her voice. "Like misappropriating one hundred and twenty million dollars of my money to pay off some crooked members of Congress?"

She didn't see it coming. Her former protector lunged up from the sofa in a fraction of a second and swung his massive fist into her mouth and nose, knocking her backward into her chair and banging her head hard against the wall.

She raised her arms to protect herself while he tried to punch her face again with both hands. As she slipped down from the seat to the floor, he continued to pummel her face. A tooth broke and she spit up blood that sprayed everywhere.

Luigi bent over her again. With surprising force, Fidelia managed to kick open the door to the rear compartment and saw Marie Dependente shriek in horror as she lunged inward.

Just before reaching them, Marie swung in a rapid half circle and raised her leg to catch Luigi's head with her foot with enough force to cause him to stagger and step backward. Before he could react, she used her other foot to kick him in the balls.

He screamed and grabbed his groin as his legs buckled.

Marie seized his shoulders with both hands near his neck.

Luigi's mouth gaped open but no sound came out. His eyes bulged as his body stiffened, immobilized. His legs folded beneath him, and he tumbled slowly toward Fidelia, who sprawled, still covered in blood, on the floor of the jet.

She reached out with her arms to shove Luigi off to her side. Marie continued to grip his neck and shoulders with her hands. With his last breath, his bodily functions stopped with a final release of urine and excrement.

Marie released her grip on Luigi, clasped Fidelia's hand, and helped her to her feet, pulling her away from the mess.

Mateo came into view, gripped one of Fidelia's arms, and wrapped it around his shoulder for support as they guided her toward a forward compartment and into a chair. Mia waited with a handful of wet towels in one hand and started to wipe Fidelia's face. Nadine arrived with a first aid kit, and both worked to stop the bleeding and relieve the pain.

A pilot stepped out of the cockpit to use the restroom and glanced toward them, then stopped in his tracks and gawked open-mouthed. He moved toward the group huddled near Fidelia, then looked around them toward the rear compartment. His eyes widened in shock when he saw the body.

He turned back toward Fidelia. "You're injured. What happened?"

It was Marie Dependente who replied to the pilot's question. "We'll get to all that later. First, you'll need to change course. How long can we safely fly with the fuel you have? Check that now and come right back to us with the answer."

As soon as the pilot returned to the front, Marie turned to Fidelia. "Where's the best place to dispose of the body?"

Fidelia looked to Mateo.

"I've got people we can use at Cartagena in Colombia."

"What kind of people?"

"We move stuff through there to Mexico. Got people in air traffic control, on the ground, refueling, baggage handling, and ground transportation. We should be able to get it off the plane and disposed of without detection."

"Should be able to? Or can you do it without detection?" Fidelia pressed.

Mateo nodded with confidence. "We can do it. Do you think you can live with the stench for that long?"

The pilot returned with the news that they had enough fuel to last five hours.

"It's cutting it close," he said when he heard the preferred destination. "You mind if I reschedule our destination for The Bahamas? Refuel there, then report a destination of Cartagena?"

Fidelia liked the way this guy thought. She smiled the best her bloody mouth with a missing tooth would allow and nodded. "The Bahamas. Then Cartagena."

As the pilot turned away, she gave Mateo his orders. "Get your guys in Columbia moving so we spend as little time on the ground there as possible. Get Tak to help you drag the body further into the rear compartment and seal the door the best you can.

"Mia!" she called out. "Find a dental clinic I can visit tomorrow in Curaçao."

FIFTY-THREE

Salamanca, Spain, Friday April 14, 2023

For almost a week, Howard recovered from his panic in Seville, leading to the early morning bus escape to the city of Salamanca in northwest Spain. By mid-week, his heart rate and blood pressure returned to normal. His concern about both had been significant enough to seek a pharmacy where he could test his blood pressure every day or two.

While the functions of his critical organs may have normalized, Howard's anxiety about his freedom intensified. TVB Bank had become a problem. He'd analyzed the situation from every perspective possible. It seemed clear Fidelia had compromised someone at the bank, and that someone had let her know where to find him.

That made it difficult for him to access his money. If he used the Mastercard the bank issued to him in Seville, they would know where he was. If he visited a TVB Bank office anywhere in the world, the voice recognition software would identify him and his location.

What good is it to have a few hundred million dollars in a bank account if you can't use it?

With just under fifty thousand dollars in cash on hand, he wasn't yet poor. But it was time to plan for his future survival, and Howard couldn't devise a plan that allowed him to stay in Salamanca.

Howard had known nothing about the city before he fled there. It was the only travel option available to escape immediately from whoever was spying on him in Seville. So he'd hopped on a bus and traveled through the night without further threats. Google research on the bus helped him identify a quaint spot a short distance from the bus station in the center of the city of about 150,000 people.

For a hundred euros a night, he got a basic, functional penthouse apartment where he could cook his own meals, work at a small white desk, and sleep comfortably in a bedroom at the back of the apartment. He made sure it had Wi-Fi and called the owner the morning he arrived. She agreed to accept cash, with payment for one week in advance.

During his week there, Howard left the apartment only when necessary to buy food at local grocery stores or check his worrying blood pressure. He used a different store each outing to avoid any patterns, and each time he bought enough supplies for a couple days.

The rest of his time, he plotted his next steps—the actions he needed to take to access his small fortune in the TVB Bank in the Cayman Islands. Online, he created one new account at another bank in the Caymans using the Mario Bartoli identity—one that was also linked to European banks and allowed digital transfers.

Using the Benjamin Castello identification provided by the FBI—and a small firm that acted as an intermediary between Cayman banks and people who wanted to remain anonymous—he created yet another account that would link to the Portugal address provided by the FBI. Using the fake Canadian passport he got from Florida again, he created a third account in Singapore.

With alternate accounts ready to accept money, his plan launched.

He started that day by dressing differently. Wrap-around sunglasses. A floppy hat that covered his head and much of his ears. He even toyed with the idea of wrapping a newly purchased European-style scarf around his throat, but the day was too warm to make that work.

Early in the morning, Howard left the key to his penthouse apartment on the kitchen table, slipped on his fully loaded backpack, and walked fifteen minutes to the central train station. He paid fifty-one euros in cash for a one-way ticket to Lisbon, Portugal, on the fastest train available. He was in his seat for the nine o'clock departure and dared not sleep for the seven-hour trip. Instead, he read a fifteen-year-old John Grisham novel, the only English book he could find in the station's convenience store.

He hailed a taxi outside the railway station on arrival and instructed the driver to take him directly to Lisbon's international airport. It turned out to be a seven-minute ride at breakneck speed, so he arrived with more than adequate time to kill after check-in and security clearance.

His British Airways flight left Portugal on time, headed toward London. He silently cursed his original choice to take the cheapest flight available to save his limited cash. The seat he chose sagged with worn-out padding in the bottom, and a mother with a crying child sat directly behind him for the almost three-hour flight.

On the ground, Howard headed for the exit, then realized he was in a long queue for immigration. He cursed again, out loud this time, as he realized there was no longer a seamless border between the European Union and the United Kingdom. The Brits had opted for Brexit and now checked every passport of the several hundred passengers arriving on his flight and others. As a result, he checked in at the Hyatt Place London Heathrow Hotel just before midnight.

Exhausted, he fell asleep within minutes of arrival.

A gentle knock on his door two hours later woke him from a deep sleep. Howard leaped from his bed and cautiously trod toward the door. It had a peephole. He silently lifted the metal cover and put his eye close to the glass. Standing about three feet from the door, a giant hovered behind a cart carrying a covered silver platter.

The fellow wore the white shirt of a waiter, but it was too small for him. The buttons didn't close completely, and chest hair poked out at the top. He wore blue jeans and running shoes. The picture didn't look right. Howard stepped back from the glass as the guy approached the door, knocking again as he called out, "Room Service."

Howard called back that he needed a moment, then scrambled for the telephone beside the bed and called the front desk.

"There's someone outside my room claiming to be from room service," he whispered into the phone. "I didn't order anything. Send security immediately."

Once the front desk attendant confirmed he'd notify security, Howard rushed to put on some clothes. He shouted out a couple times that he was on his way and would be just a moment longer. Dressed, he heard running in the corridor and dashed to the peephole again.

No one was visible. The same cart sat in front of the doorway, unattended. He waited and heard voices over a radio or walkie-talkie and more footsteps in the hallway before a uniformed security guard entered the area and knocked on the door. Howard swung it open to talk.

"Are you all right, sir?" The security guard tipped his cap as he greeted Howard.

"What's happening?" he replied.

"Thank you for alerting the front desk. There was an intruder. I found one of our staff unconscious in the stairwell as I ran up here. Someone dashed off before I got to your room, but I've called the bobbies. They should be here soon. Please stay in your room until they arrive. I must check on the waiter now."

The security fellow backed away from the door as he spoke, then ran toward a stairwell. As soon as he was out of sight, Howard scurried back into the room, gathered up his belongings, stuffed them into his backpack, hoisted it onto his shoulder, and dashed from the room.

Walking as quickly as possible, Howard headed to the stairwell opposite the one the security guard took and ran down the steps two at a time until he reached the ground floor. He slammed down on a bar to open a fire escape door and ran into a parking lot. There, he reverted to a brisk walk and headed toward a roadway where police cars with flashing blue lights—but no sirens—rushed into the hotel's front driveway.

Howard walked along the side of the road toward the airport in darkness. It was a cloudy night with no moon or stars in the sky. Only streetlights lit the way along Perimeter Avenue toward Heathrow Airport's terminal five. He used a leisurely pace, knowing he needed only about forty-five minutes to reach the terminal for a flight scheduled to leave eight hours later.

As he walked, Howard searched his memory for any clues. How had someone learned he was at a hotel in London? He'd shown the FBI-issued Portuguese passport at immigration and to the front desk clerk as he checked in to the hotel. He paid cash and didn't use his credit card for either identification or a security deposit.

In Salamanca, he'd reserved the flights with a local travel agent, paying cash from his precious and depleting reserve, and showing the FBI-issued passport.

The only common denominator Howard could identify was the FBI.

He stretched the walking time to about an hour, but hanging around the terminal until flight time was too dangerous. As he approached the airport, he looked for the arrivals area and found a taxi with its driver snoozing at the wheel in a queue, waiting for passengers.

"Good morning, take me to Belgravia. I'll check my hotel details while you drive." Howard pulled out his phone and searched for a hotel as the driver slowly departed from the curb. Google responded immediately to the prompt for a hotel in Belgravia. "The Clermont, please."

Upon arrival at The Clermont, Howard paid the driver, who reluctantly accepted payment in euros only after he sweetened the offer to almost double the pound equivalent. He headed toward the entrance until the taxi driver was out of view, then changed direction to find a coffee shop instead.

None were open, so Howard wandered around the neighborhood until daylight, when he found another travel agency. By then, a nearby coffee shop was also available so he could eat, refresh, and do more research. He used the burner phone he'd bought in Salamanca to do his work.

Using Google, Howard found another routing that could work. Around nine o'clock that morning, he located a British Airways office, hailed a cab, and arrived moments after it opened. Within a half hour, he left the office with about two thousand fewer euros in his wallet but a revised ticket in his pocket. On foot, he wandered the streets of London for another hour, deciding what to do about the FBI-issued phone.

Ultimately, he walked toward the Thames River and found a quiet stretch of sidewalk where he was partially blocked from the view of curious passersby. There he set the FBI phone on the cement sidewalk, stamped on it aggressively until the plastic case shattered, then dropped the pieces into the Thames.

Satisfied that he'd broken the link to the FBI, Howard still had an entire day to wile away in London. He could have flown to Grand Cayman later that day by way of Miami, but even transferring through a US airport posed unacceptable risk.

Instead, he hauled out the burner phone, found an out-of-the-way inn near the airport, and hailed a cab. An hour later, he'd checked in for some desperately needed sleep.

This minor delay wouldn't impact his plan to get his money from TVB Bank in the Caymans.

FIFTY-FOUR

Montreal, Quebec, Monday April 17, 2023

Suzanne's day started like most others. At her desk in the Montreal headquarters before seven in the morning, she reviewed emails, already sorted and prioritized by Eileen, who usually arrived an hour earlier. From eight until nine, she read a package assembled by Edward Hadley's team that included media clippings about Multima and other news deemed important for her to know before the business day was fully underway.

Then she began meetings booked in thirty-minute increments by Eileen with business unit leaders, direct reports, directors, politicians, and other vital business contacts. She tried to stay on schedule, but something almost always derailed Eileen's meticulous plan. That morning it was an urgent call from Gordon Goodfellow on her personal cell, bypassing Eileen's usual screening. So it must be important.

She excused herself from a meeting with CFO Pierre Cabot, motioning for him to stay seated where he was. Suzanne rose from her desk, retreated into the alcove, and greeted the president of Supermarkets.

"What's up?"

"Hang on to something solid because this will shock you," Goodfellow said. "I just got off the phone with someone named Akira Sugimori. He claims to be with Suji Corporation and says he's just stepped into the role of CEO of Jeffersons Stores. He wants us to make an offer to buy his company outright."

"Whoa, there. He wants to sell Jeffersons to us? Why?"

"He claims supermarkets no longer fit their business model. Says he won't give the company away, but he'll make a fair deal if we're interested and act quickly."

"Why do I smell something rotten?"

"I know. My trouble antenna jumped to full alert as well. But the guy was persuasive. Claims their real estate sale was just the first step, and the people around him want to sell their entire investment in Jeffersons as soon as possible. He wants you to discuss it with him in Hawaii Wednesday morning."

"Wednesday morning? That's ridiculous! How can we prepare for such a crucial meeting on such short notice?"

"My team doesn't need any preparation. Remember, we've been working on this for months already. I can have them ready to fly within hours."

"Get your people together in your conference room. I'll ask Eileen to link us in on Zoom. Pierre is here with me, but I want to include Serge and James before we decide on a meeting. Candidly, this just doesn't feel right."

Thirty minutes later, they were back in conference, Eileen's carefully planned schedule for the day in shambles.

After thanking everyone for joining the Zoom call on short notice, Suzanne mentioned an unusual guest. "I want to especially thank our director Abduhl Mahinder for joining us so early in the morning out there in California. I imagine we must have interrupted your breakfast at this hour."

Everyone around the table smiled, including Abduhl, who was also the Bank of the Americas CEO.

"Gordon, please lead it off with a recap of your conversations earlier with Suji Corporation and with me a few minutes ago."

He was prepared and provided a brief, succinct summary of the two conversations. Serge was the first to express a concern.

"Before we get too deeply involved in the discussion about a possible deal, I think it's important to make everyone around the table aware that Akira Sugimori is reputably one of the world's most dangerous criminals. He's CEO of Suji Corporation, but he's also the leader of the Japanese Yakuza. We built an extensive file on the guy when I was with the Canadian RCMP. You don't want to know about some of the sordid stuff he's involved with, from pachinko parlors to human and drug trafficking. Anything we do must keep this profile top of mind."

Serge's tone was professional. He sounded like an airline pilot briefing passengers for take-off, but his expression was grim. He glanced toward Suzanne more than once to be sure she understood his message.

"Great point," Suzanne said. "Should we even consider discussing a proposal with a criminal?"

"Suji Corporation is a publicly traded company." It was Abduhl Mahinder who answered her question, and he was the same director who had threatened to resign during the meeting in Montreal if Multima bought Jeffersons back then.

She waited for more.

"If we exclude publicly traded companies whose shareholders or executives have unsavory reputations, the universe for lending or trading might become small indeed. If Jeffersons is a clean company—operating within the law—nothing should prohibit you from considering the merits of buying it. As a director of Multima and a lender to the company, I'm more focused on the impact on profitability for Multima. Is it a good deal that Multima can afford, or not?"

Suzanne glanced at James Fitzgerald. He too had opposed Gordon Goodfellow's earlier proposal to buy their competitor. He caught her glance.

"Nothing grates me more than dealing with someone who doesn't play by the rules, but Abduhl's right. If we eliminate dialog with all the bad guys, we're left talking to a very small group. My concerns with entertaining a proposal to buy Jeffersons relate specifically to the impact it might have on Financial Services' ability to borrow at competitive interest rates. If you can negotiate a deal with Suji Corporation that keeps Multima Corporation's debt to manageable levels, I won't oppose it."

Interesting. Both previous strong objectors to a deal had softened their opposition. Suzanne's danger antenna remained elevated.

"Gordon, walk us through what you propose again."

For almost an hour, the president of the Supermarkets division presented the same proposal he'd introduced in Montreal months earlier. He had updated his numbers to reflect his target's current financial position, operating results, and the financial benefits a merger might bring to Multima. Both were moderately more favorable because of Jeffersons' lower debt and higher cash position resulting from the recent real estate sale. But his concluding comment drew the most attention and interest.

"As we all know, most acquisitions pay a premium to shareholders over the current price per share on the stock exchange. Today, Jeffersons' shares are trading at eight times the company's book value. I recommend we meet with Sugimori and offer to pay precisely that amount."

After the initial shock of that suggestion, and a hearty debate, those around the table eventually agreed with the wisdom of that strategy as an opening negotiating position. After another hour of discussion, a tougher negotiating posture evolved. The current price per share should be the only offer. Take it or leave it. If Suji Corporation was unwilling to accept that price, Multima should walk away from a deal.

With the high-level offer decided on, the discussion shifted to the best way to present the offer to buy Jeffersons.

Serge preferred to send an email. "You already know I'm uncomfortable dealing with Sugimori and his crowd. They're outright criminals. From a security perspective, I'd rather not have a personal meeting until it's time to sign a deal, if then." Again, he glanced in Suzanne's direction.

With an inquisitive expression, she looked at the faces on the screen and those in the room.

"I don't think that will work," Gordon Goodfellow said softly, with a grim expression. "Sugimori asked to meet in Hawaii Wednesday in person. He was very clear. I get that we have to swallow hard to deal with the guy, but I think we must respect Japanese culture. I fear he'll take offense if we send an email after his specific request. Respect and 'saving face' are so fundamental to Japanese men. And he might already find the offer we're preparing insulting. If we're not comfortable meeting in person, it's better not to make an offer at all."

There was more discussion about the quality of the offer, meeting in person, and the value of the deal to Multima. As the conversation pointed toward the conclusion that Suzanne should lead the delegation, Serge showed signs of increasing stress. His face reddened. His voice raised a notch higher, and his glances toward Suzanne became increasingly frequent.

Finally, he drew his line in the sand. "I'll cooperate with a personal meeting, but I'll need to leave almost immediately on a corporate jet with a team of fifteen. We have to scour the hotel for listening devices and assess any other risks."

He quickly punched some numbers into his laptop, scrawled

some notes on a piece of paper, then read out his results.

"Okay. If we're going to do this. I'll leave in two hours—if a jet can be ready. That gets my security team to the hotel this evening. We'll do our research overnight and tomorrow, then be ready for a meeting at 9:00 a.m. Wednesday. Suzanne, I prefer you come later, closer to the meeting time. Leave about midnight tomorrow. Sleep on the plane. That will get you in about five in the morning, allow time for a good breakfast at the airport, and give you a cushion if there are headwinds, air traffic or ground delays."

Suzanne nodded her agreement and looked at James, who said, "Sure. We'll bring the Financial Services jet to Montreal. We should be there and fueled for departure within a few hours. Serge can use it for as long as necessary."

"Gordon, confirm the meeting with Sugimori. Let's see how cheerful he is when you wake him at two in the morning. Then, get your people organized and up here to Montreal by tomorrow morning. We'll use the corporate jet. Bring up to nine people if you need them, and a couple changes of clothes, just in case."

FIFTY-FIVE

Sint Michiel, Curaçao, Monday April 17, 2023

Two full days had passed since they'd dumped Luigi Fortissimo's body in Colombia. So far, nothing appeared in the news, no inquiries from people within The Organization, and no hint of law enforcement discovering the body in a shallow grave where airport workers buried it a few miles away.

A two-day lull had been essential. Fidelia's mouth still bled whenever she tried to eat. The area surrounding her broken tooth remained painful; her face a bruised mess from the punches she'd received from her once-loyal primary protector. Sleep eluded her over the weekend, with only brief naps when her body simply couldn't function any longer.

She used the time to reconsider her original plan for the US. Her inclination from the beginning—back in November when she'd first detected things were amiss—had been to replace Luigi as her top-in-command there. Intuitively, she'd sensed his loyalties had shifted, whether it was the age-old problem of male greed for power and money, or the Shadow more subtly influencing Luigi's thought processes as he had so many others.

She'd devoted dozens of hours thinking about a better person to run her US operations and had narrowed the candidates to two. She called out to Mateo to join her for a walk along the beach. They could talk privately and candidly, and in Spanish.

She chatted with him about the sandy beach, the beautiful high white clouds in the sky, the limestone rocks lining the shore, and the perfect temperature of the warm air with an ocean breeze.

When they were well clear of hearing distance, she got to the point. "What do you think about the United States? Ever thought of living there?"

"Yes, I've thought about it. Who hasn't? But do I want to live there? The answer to that question is no. When I visit the US, I feel like a foreigner. Their sense of superiority. The widespread racist belief that white folks are somehow God's chosen people with special insight into what's right and wrong in the world. If you're thinking of sending me there, I wish you wouldn't."

"You're doing a great job with Latin America and all the special help you've given to execute our plan. I wanted to give you full consideration if you were interested in the US. If you're not interested, how about me adding Mexico to your sphere of control? Same twenty-five percent for me as the rest of your territory. You'll make the change?"

"It's a deal. I appreciate your confidence, and you know I'll grow our activities there as much as I can." Mateo's smile was genuine. His eyes sparkled with satisfaction.

"I know that. But I want you to kill the immigrant import stuff immediately. Cut it off in Guatemala, Honduras, Mexico, or wherever Luigi's guys are doing it. Nothing will create more trouble for us in the long run than selling kids into slavery for twenty or thirty years or until some media bleeding heart makes it a cause célèbre, and the government runs us out of the country."

"I'll get it done, but give me a few months. It didn't start last week, and I can't shut it down tomorrow. There are already thousands in transit."

"Until the end of summer. But stop new recruiting right now." Fidelia met his eyes directly until he blinked and nodded acceptance.

"If you're still considering options for the US, you might want to consider Marie Dependente."

Fidelia stopped walking, smiled, and turned to face him directly. "Why do you say that?"

"My guy who worked with her in Aruba was impressed. Says she's the smartest person he's met. Did you know she speaks Spanish as well as French and English? And you saw how she took down Luigi with only her hands and feet."

They started walking again. After a moment or two of silence, Fidelia thanked him for his suggestion.

Upon her return to the beachfront home, she allowed an appropriate amount of time for Mateo to disappear into the guest house and start working on his additional responsibilities for Mexico. Then she called out for her first choice for the job as a kingpin for the US.

When Marie Dependente arrived, she invited her to walk together.

They headed off in the opposite direction along the ocean. This time, the path was more rugged, with large limestone rocks jutting out from the shoreline, beaches made of natural pebbles, and tree roots desperate for water jutting out above and below the surface. They didn't talk for a while. Marie waited for Fidelia to reveal what she wanted to talk about. Fidelia gave the matter her final consideration.

"How did you feel when I asked you to swear an oath of loyalty?"

"Surprised. Confused. Scared. Though I know I've given you information in the past, I'm just a French businesswoman, not a gang member. I didn't know what to expect or why you made the request."

"Do you understand better yet?" Fidelia used a warm tone, inviting discussion and openness.

"Not really. I was of limited help finding your friend Klaudia, but we eventually found her. When Luigi Fortissimo attacked you on the plane, I was able to help. But I doubt you asked me to swear an oath so I'd help another woman in distress. You haven't asked me a single question about Multima or its French subsidiary, which I do know something about. So you might say I still don't understand what you want from me."

"Your oath to me made you part of The Organization. You're one of us now. Maybe you think you're not a gang member, but when you swore allegiance to me, you accepted that I might ask you to do something illegal. You must have known that. Would you swear your loyalty to me again?" Fidelia stopped walking and turned to face Marie as she posed the question. She focused on the woman's eyes.

"If I chose not to swear allegiance, I think it's clear what my fate would be." She smiled ruefully as she replied. Her eyes showed confidence, not fear. "I'm not a fan of violence, and I'm not sure I ever could become comfortable with it. But if you strip away the violent aspects of The Organization, your world is not that different from the world of business."

"How so?" Fidelia tilted her head with genuine curiosity.

"You build a structure. You surround yourself with a team of people you can trust. You look for opportunities and build a plan to realize them. You try to stay off the radar of police and tax authorities and find a way to smooth out the path should they catch you. Candidly, it's not much different from the corporate world. Just take away the violence."

"That's why I want to make you the leader of The Organization's activities in the US."

Marie gasped in surprise. Her eyes widened, and her posture stiffened. Her mouth opened, but no words came out for several seconds. She stuttered when they finally came. "W-what are y-you saying?"

"I want you to leave tomorrow for New York to take over Luigi's office behind the restaurant and run the American show. You bring all the qualities I seek, which is why I invited you to the island in the first place. You're smart. You can take care of yourself if you need to. And you've got the skills to make our criminal activities respectable businesses."

"Respectable businesses?" Marie appeared genuinely confused.

"Yeah. People everywhere have weaknesses. For some, it's sex. Others need drugs. Some develop a gambling habit. Others just can't manage their money. We perform a service in each of those businesses. They'll all become legal and accepted eventually."

"How does that relate to The Organization?"

"My old boss, Giancarlo Mareno, dreamed of making The Organization, and his family name, respectable—like the Kennedy and Bronfman families did when booze became legal. We already control casinos and marijuana companies that trade on the New York Stock Exchange. Luigi wasn't flexible enough to adapt to that vision. That's why he had to go. Now, I want you to make all our businesses respected profitable ventures that continue to pay me a few hundred million a year."

"A few hundred million dollars?"

"Yes. I'll keep others out of your way and help you when you need it. Every month, you'll transfer twenty-five percent of your tax-free stake to an account I'll designate in the Caymans. You'll keep the rest and become one of the richest women in the world within five years. If you do your job right, the companies you control will send me dividends as your efforts become more respectable." Fidelia used air quotes to emphasize her words.

Marie appeared to process the information. Her manner was

calm, thoughtful, even reflective. After a long moment or two, she took a deep breath before she uttered just one word with a defining nod. "Okay."

When a solid rock formation along the waterfront blocked them from continuing, they followed the outline of a path back to a paved roadway toward the beachfront home. As they walked, Fidelia described the outfit's organizational structure in the US, where Marie would find all the computer drives and files she'd need to study, and gave an overview of all the key players by activity and region.

Fidelia assured her she needn't remember all the details immediately, just where to find them. They talked about complying with US immigration requirements, getting a necessary visa, and the importance of learning both the legal and political systems in the US. She told Marie where to find the names of experts she should meet and consult with.

Marie absorbed the information even more quickly than expected but surprised Fidelia with one question. "Who is this person I hear people refer to as the Shadow? And where does he fit into The Organization?"

Fidelia recoiled. "I refuse to use his name. Just think of the one American reviled by more people around the globe than any other and you'll have it." Fidelia turned to face Marie and underscored the importance of her advice with a grim expression. "Have nothing to do with the bastard. Stay far away from him."

Marie nodded her understanding before they carried on toward the house.

As they arrived, Fidelia gave her final instructions. "I'll tell the team about your new role now. Ask Mia to get you a flight tomorrow to New York. I'll work the phone with the main regional and business leaders tonight and tomorrow to break the news. Start getting oaths of loyalty from the guys the first day you're on the job. Call me when you need me."

Fidelia called out for everyone to gather around the table poolside, where she made the grand announcement about Marie to congratulations and pledges of support from the entire team. When she finished, she glanced around the group and noticed Tak Takahashi raise a finger to signal a need to see her privately. She nodded for him to follow and headed inside.

"Bad news," he blurted when she closed the door to her secure room. "Sugimori plans to sell Jeffersons Stores. He's leaving shortly for a meeting in Hawaii Wednesday with the CEO of Multima Corporation. My source says he plans to have an agreement for Multima to buy the entire company before the end of that meeting."

"What the fuck? When did you learn that?"

"Just before you called us to meet outside. My usual source texted me. He's leaving on the flight with Sugimori."

The low-life plans to sell one of the most significant assets of The Organization in America? Fidelia reached for her phone and barked out orders, first to Mia. "Get the pilots to the airport, and the plane fueled. I want to leave for Hawaii in an hour."

A click to end the call and an aggressive press of a speed-dial number followed. "Mateo, load all your guys in the van and be ready to leave on a mission in thirty minutes."

Another click and another call as she started to throw clothes into a backpack. "Nadine, we're leaving now. All but you and Marie. She's headed to New York tomorrow. I want you to fly back to Europe. I'll break the news, but I want you to talk personally with every leader there about her taking over the US activities. I'll talk to you from the jet."

One final call as she shoved her toothbrush and makeup kit into the backpack. "Klaudia, you're leaving with me for Hawaii in fifteen minutes. Pack your bag. Bring your technology."

FIFTY-SIX

Grand Cayman, Cayman Islands, Monday April 17, 2023

Surrounded at a distance by Cuba, Jamaica and Mexico in the Caribbean Sea, the tiny Cayman Islands have long been a British protectorate.

Howard always found it intriguing to know that Grand Cayman has more than six hundred banks—including branches of forty-three of the world's largest—serving a population of fewer than seventy thousand people. Clearly, he was far from alone in stashing his money there out of the reach of tax authorities and other curious parties.

With jet lag, Howard didn't need the alarm he'd set and had already showered and brushed his teeth before it sounded. Despite the early hour, his nerves tingled with anticipation. It was time for the next stage in his mission to recover his money.

He left the small Airbnb suite he'd rented for a week. Its location on the waterfront appealed to him, not because of the view, but because it featured a digital lock. Once his payment for the suite had arrived in Grand Cayman, the owner texted a four-digit code to access it. Howard wouldn't see the owner during his stay.

He started his morning with a long walk while it was still dark outside. Following the waterfront for about a mile, he circled several small streets around the TVB Bank offices, scoping out the environment. It was exactly as he remembered it during his last personal visit six years earlier.

The bank opened at nine o'clock each morning, but Howard knew the woman he wanted to see arrived at the office much earlier. By seven o'clock, he'd secured a table at an outdoor coffee shop with a direct view of the employee entrance. Employees swiped a card through a device at the side of a nondescript, windowless brown door just around the corner from its main entrance.

He sat at the small round table wearing his sunglasses and cap, blending in with other visitors to the café while he sipped a strong black espresso to stay alert. The first bank employee, a tall black fellow Howard didn't recognize, arrived within minutes. He carried himself with authority, so he must be a manager of something at the bank.

A couple drove into the parking lot a few minutes afterward, exchanged a long kiss before leaving the car, and strode towards the employee entrance laughing and giggling, both carrying bags that looked as if they might hold a computer and some documents.

At about seven-thirty, she arrived on foot. Dorothy Bodden was her name, if he remembered correctly. As she walked toward the office, Howard studied her carefully. Tall, slim, with a long confident stride, just as he remembered. She looked more mature, wearing a pale blue blazer and navy pants. Her shoes had heels less adventurous than those she used to wear. She'd cut her hair shorter, but curly, blonde locks still caught at her shoulders and bounced as she walked. He was confident it was her.

When Howard had last visited TVB Bank in 2017, he'd noticed Dorothy sitting at a desk outside the office of Mr. Fernando, who managed his account. Just days before, the FBI had released him from protective custody for the first time—that time he'd persuaded them to buy him a yacht.

That day, too, he'd needed to withdraw cash from his account. While Mr. Fernando fiddled with his computer and keyboard, arranging the cash and prepaid credit card, Howard watched the attractive young woman outside the office and speculated.

After a while, his interest became apparent, and the banker said, "Not a chance."

Howard laughed, threw back his head and asked what didn't have a chance.

"You're in for a disappointment if you have your eye on Dorothy. She just left a convent. Something happened that she won't talk about, but she lives alone, doesn't go out, and now seems to think money is the only God worth worshipping."

"Is she a good employee?"

"The best. Usually, one of the first here in the morning and one of the last to leave at night. Manages her accounts meticulously and never complains."

When Howard recently concluded that someone at TVB Bank was under Fidelia Morales's influence, making it more difficult for him to get to his money and perhaps even feeding his whereabouts back to The Organization's kingpin, Dorothy immediately came to mind.

In Spain, he'd contacted a private investigator in the Caymans and hired him to find out if she had debts, bad habits, or any known connections to the underworld. He found none. Just like Mr. Fernando had described it, her life was boring, lonely, and fixated almost entirely on her job.

He'd also paid the private investigator to check out the new Mr. Fernando. That guy looked more like trouble. Three days in a row, he went directly from work to his favorite casino and played well into the early morning hours before returning home to a dark apartment driving a top-of-the-line BMW 7 series sedan.

Howard decided to use Dorothy to regain access to his small fortune.

After coffee that morning, he returned to his Airbnb, slept for a few hours, and ate again. By five o'clock, he was back at the coffee shop at the same table with a perfect view. He knew he'd have to wait a while if she was still the conscientious employee the first Mr. Fernando had described, but he was patient.

A little after six o'clock, she closed the employee doorway tightly behind her and set off in the direction she'd come from that morning.

Howard followed her.

She lived only a few blocks from TVB Bank and soon arrived at a modest three-story apartment building that looked to house a dozen separate units. The entrance door swung open when she pulled the handle. It didn't seem to require a key.

Howard watched and waited. It took only a few seconds before he saw lights go on in a ground-floor unit a few feet away from the building's entrance.

That was enough information for the first day. Tomorrow they'd talk.

FIFTY-SEVEN

On the Multima Corporate Jet, Tuesday April 18, 2023

All fifteen seats on the jet were in use, including the two sofas in the rear compartment. Suzanne's first task, once they boarded, was to lay down the ground rules for the overnight trip to Hawaii. Anyone could use the sofas in the rear to nap for an hour or two. Eileen would keep time and roust back to work anyone who overslept, making space for the next exhausted soul.

The group laughed, so she added another couple rules. "Eileen is with us tonight for her first flight on the jet. Don't get any ideas about coffee or refreshment services, however. She's here to add keyboarding skills and relief for Alberto's legal secretary, Marlene. If you need food, water, coffee or other refreshments, serve yourself."

Again the team laughed and made mock expressions of disappointment.

She let the laughter die before she continued. "Alberto and Pierre will anchor the oval table. They'll share responsibility for building the formal offer we'll present. Gordon and Bessie will speak for Multima Supermarkets. Sit close to the other members of your team for the quickest consultations when necessary. James and I will use the seats in opposite corners. He'll exclusively use line one to keep the board of directors, Natalia, and the Financial Services team in the loop. I'll use line two when needed. Edward will build a PowerPoint to deliver our opening offer and conditions. Give him the seat in the middle of the table. Any questions?"

She looked around the plane and watched the team begin to follow her instructions without questions or discussion, then she thought of one last detail. "The captain tells me flying time today should be about eleven hours. Let's shoot for the final offer in seven hours, with the presentation ready for a walk-through at the eight-hour mark. Eileen, you're in charge of time management for the table and the sofas."

After another murmur of humor, Alberto called for everyone's attention as the engines revved for taxi and take-off. Before the wheels lifted, half the people at the oval table clicked furiously on their keyboards. The others reviewed the rough first draft Alberto had already copied from a template in Montreal for discussion.

When the plane reached cruising altitude, Suzanne beckoned the youngest member of her team, a Japanese American named Yuki, to take the vacant seat beside her. They'd worked together a few years earlier when the now-deceased founder of Suji Corporation first proposed a transaction between their two companies. Suzanne had rejected that overture but remembered Yuki had provided valuable support with translation and her knowledge of Japanese culture. She'd insisted the young woman join the team for this trip.

"Remind me of every cultural sensitivity I need to respect during these negotiations," Suzanne instructed with a tension-breaking laugh. "Assume I forgot everything you taught me the last time."

Yuki reminded her about bowing during initial greetings and how important it was to bow more deeply than her adversary to convey respect. She reminded Suzanne about the benefits of speaking softly, even in anger, and spent considerable time discussing the long-held subservient role women play in Japanese society.

She pointed out the areas where attitudes had improved and underscored where biases remained. When Yuki finished, Suzanne asked if it might be better to let one of the guys lead the negotiations while she adopt a secondary role.

Yuki looked down and nodded.

Culturally re-sensitized, Suzanne called Serge in Hawaii. His team had settled in at the beautiful and luxurious Prince Waikiki on the waterfront, nestled along the lagoon and harbor. Part of a Japanese hotel chain, Sugimori's people liked to use the Makiki conference room there for their meetings.

"They're setting up the room now," Serge said. "You'll love the view overlooking the tops of the palm trees out to the ocean. I'm told the Suji people requested a U-shaped setup of the tables to accommodate thirty people, fifteen on each side. They plan to have their backs to the splendid view. I'm not sure if that's Japanese courtesy or possibly intended to create a distraction for our folks."

Suzanne smiled at Serge's attempt at levity with his trademark dry humor. "Any sign of an advance team from Suji Corporation?"

"Can't tell. There are hundreds of Japanese visitors staying in the hotel. It's impossible to know who might be working for Sugimori. I've instructed our security team to assume anyone they see or interact with might be with the 'bad guys'."

"Will you still be able to plant listening devices?"

"Yeah. But there's a good chance they'll be discovered when Sugimori electronically sweeps the breakout rooms. He might also change the assigned breakout rooms at the last minute, so my team is working on a way to get devices into meeting rooms in other ways."

"Any sign of devices in our breakout room?"

"Not yet, but they still have lots of time. Our sweep an hour before the meeting will be more conclusive."

"Keep me posted if you discover anything I need to know. Love you."

FIFTY-EIGHT

On The Organization's Jet, Tuesday April 18, 2023

Fidelia worked two secure phones on the jet from the moment they reached cruising altitude. She had only a few hours to reach all the key players in The Organization around the world, letting them know about Luigi's demise and Marie Dependente's appointment as his replacement.

Because she disturbed people's sleep, or perhaps interrupted some sexual activity, and also because Fidelia didn't like to be kept waiting, Mia used one of the phones and dialed the numbers on the list Fidelia provided, tracked down the names on that list, and then kept them on hold until another call finished. Then, they switched phones and repeated the process.

Fidelia knew her people well. So she tweaked the message, her tone of voice, and the degree of reassurance. But her calls all conveyed the same basic message.

To those in the US, she didn't mince words. "Luigi's gone. He made a fatal mistake. I've decided Marie Dependente will run the US. I expect you to pledge loyalty to her and send her the agreed percentage of the take starting this week and every week until she instructs otherwise. I won't tolerate any dissent. Can I count on your support?"

So far, there hadn't been a single objection. Who would be foolish enough to attract her ire during a phone conversation? Still, she sensed hesitation from a couple guys who stretched way back with Luigi. Guys that had probably started out with him. She made a tick by both names. If their weekly payments didn't arrive by Friday, she'd order Marie to eliminate them.

Her new chief in the US already knew about The Organization's munitions expert and where to find him. If she were forced to act before the weekend ended, any dissenter would be eliminated and his office destroyed. Should one defy her orders, every other guy in the outfit would realize his likely destiny. Before the end of the month, things would be stable, with money flowing uninterrupted into her Cayman accounts.

Outside the US, her messages used a softer tone. Some might even think she grieved for the callous bastard. They all knew her former primary protector had been an occasional lover. Everyone knew it was she who had elevated him to kingpin in the US. She couldn't care less if they started looking over their shoulders and wondering if they were destined for the same fate. No, outside the US, she simply needed to make sure that no one got any ideas about seizing new ground in a power vacuum.

So, her message was more moderate. "Sorry I have to be the one to let you know we just lost Luigi. It sounds as if he made some mistakes and disappeared. Don't worry. It's business as usual in the US. I appointed a French woman to replace him. She's smart as a whip and knows how to take care of herself. Should she contact you for information or help in your territory, I'll appreciate you extending her every courtesy. Can I count on your support?"

By the flight's midpoint, Fidelia finished her calls and motioned for Tak Takahashi to change places with Mia. She also woke Klaudia, who was dozing in the seat across from her, and swiveled her seat around to face them.

"Klaudia, I'll need you to perform your magic and penetrate some systems. Listen to what Tak's learned so far. Then we'll decide what you can do."

The German woman no longer acted like her intimate friend. She sulked like a teenager, spoke only when necessary, and used the minimum number of words possible to respond. This time she just nodded. A moment after enduring Fidelia's glare, she lifted her shoulders more upright and tilted in to listen over the constant hum of the engines.

Fidelia signaled that Tak should begin.

"According to my source, Sugimori has a dozen armed men in his security detail. Most left on a commercial flight earlier today and plan to case the Prince Waikiki Hotel when they arrive. He guessed that it would be about three in the morning in Hawaii. A second flight carries the business contingent and has two more security guards for Sugimori, along with a dozen other businesspeople from the finance, legal and technology departments. They're scheduled to arrive about seven tomorrow morning and plan to meet with Multima at nine."

"Have they booked individual rooms or suites?"

"He doesn't think so. For some reason, Sugimori insists they must reach a deal by the end of the day Tuesday. He's told that to everyone on the team."

"Do they know about Luigi?" Fidelia used an offhanded tone but watched Tak's response carefully.

"My source asked me if I had any idea where Luigi was. Sugimori has asked a couple times since Friday."

"And?" She crossed her legs to divert any sign of concern.

"I told him we never met up in New York. Like you instructed, I told him I was headed there with you to meet him."

"How did you explain why we didn't meet him?"

"The best I could think of was telling him you ended up shopping for some new clothes all weekend. Maybe we'd meet Luigi later in the week."

Fidelia smiled. It was an answer that all the sexist buffoons in The Organization would easily believe.

Clearly, Sugimori had no intention of discussing his plan to sell Jeffersons Stores—an investment that generated annual sales of over seventy-five billion annually, bringing in a profit greater than four billion dollars each year. Worse, he planned to sell a company that paid out over thirty-five million yearly in dividends to The Organization. Maybe it wasn't as lucrative as the escort business, but it wasn't small coin she was prepared to lose.

"Klaudia, if Tak reaches his contact by phone, can you install the software that makes the phone a microphone, relaying live conversations and surrounding noises?" Fidelia asked.

"I can't if it's an iPhone. Should be able to if it's Android."

"How much conversation time do you need?"

"Never done it with two phones in the air, but I guess it should take three or four minutes."

Fidelia shifted toward Tak. "Figure out with your contact when he can get five minutes to talk. Maybe he can go into the toilet or something. Tell him we're installing some software to track him. Say nothing about the speaker's capability. It's best to hear what he's saying too, and he might clam up."

She shooed Klaudia and Tak off to complete the download mission and switched her focus to Mateo and his guys in the middle compartment of the jet.

Laptop computer screens in the center of the table displayed maps, photos, and detailed floor plans of the hotel for the dozen security guys either standing or sitting around the table. In Spanish, Mateo was figuratively walking them through the Prince Waikiki Hotel, pointing and assigning his men to different positions on different floors.

The men dressed like tourists, the same outfits they had worn for their day out exploring Curaçao a few weeks earlier. She didn't see any weapons or pockets to stash a gun from sight and made a mental note to question Mateo about that when his guys weren't around.

Fidelia watched Mateo coach his guys on the story each would use if accosted by hotel security or law enforcement. Mateo had them practice their explanations in English polished enough to pass for a South American visitor on his annual holiday.

Then it was her turn.

She was brief. She spoke slowly and entirely in Spanish to avoid any possibility of misunderstanding. She warned that they were dealing with a highly trained and violent unit of The Organization that had misbehaved and must be punished. For several minutes, she emphasized the importance of accomplishing their objective without hurting or killing any innocent bystanders.

Her last message—and the most powerful by far—was an announcement. If the men were successful, they would each find one hundred thousand dollars in their bank accounts the day after completion.

FIFTY-NINE

Grand Cayman, Cayman Islands, Tuesday April 18, 2023

Howard found a vacant children's playground down the street, with a direct view of the entrance to Dorothy's apartment block. The little parkette also had a wooden bench, probably to offer a few moments of comfort for parents or nannies supervising the kids. It suited his purposes as he waited and watched for her to leave her apartment for work.

Shortly after seven, she stepped out of the building and securely closed the door before she headed toward the bank. He rose nonchalantly from the bench and headed leisurely toward the sidewalk where she'd pass in a few seconds. Before they intersected, Howard took off his hat and waved it toward Dorothy with the friendliest smile he could muster that early in the morning.

"Hello, Dorothy. Do you remember me? Mr. Smith? Account number 243876A?" He continued to smile and move slowly toward her, although she'd stopped in her tracks to scrutinize him.

"Yes, I remember you. One of Mr. Fernando's clients." She nodded uncertainly as she spoke but showed no inclination to smile or welcome more conversation. "Why are you here?"

Howard moved a step or two closer, continuing to smile confidently. "May I join you as you walk to the bank? I want to ask for your opinion and advice. I prefer we do it outside the bank."

She nodded again, so he stepped beside her and they headed off.

"I have a concern. Recently, I've had trouble accessing my funds on time. There seem to be delays of some sort. Do you have any idea why that might be?"

"Sometimes, an account executive will buy some time to double check an identity if there hasn't been recent activity on the account. That's the only policy I'm aware of, and it usually takes less than an hour to verify if the voice recognition software is working properly."

"Have you had any voice recognition incidents in the past month?"

"No," Dorothy replied quickly. "It's been at least a year."

Howard looked at her as they continued to walk. Her eyes looked downward. She seemed ill at ease.

"Are my questions making you feel uncomfortable, Dorothy?"

"A little. I've never had a customer approach me on the street this way."

"Would you prefer I leave you alone and discuss my concerns with the management of the bank?"

She shook her head no, stopped, and looked directly at him. "I know you're an important bank customer, Mr. Smith. I don't mean to offend you, but your questions make me nervous. You bring back all the horrible memories of that day Mr. Fernando fell from the balcony outside his office."

"I know you worked closely with Mr. Fernando and understand how shocking that must have been for you. But is there another reason for your unease?" Howard looked intently into her eyes, sympathetically inviting her to share her concerns. He was ready to give up after a few seconds, when she blurted out her fear, almost in tears.

"A new client met with him that day with the door to his office closed. Only a few minutes after that meeting, I saw him jump suddenly from the balcony with morbid fear or desperation on his face. By the time I ran to the balcony, he was already on the ground, a bloody, crumpled mess. When I ran back into the office screaming for help, she had disappeared."

Howard stopped walking, turned to Dorothy and said, "She? The new client was a woman?"

Dorothy nodded.

Howard stood there in silence. He had no photographs and she purposely avoided the public eye so there might be nothing there. Still, it was worth a try. He yanked his phone from his pocket and Googled her name.

"Come on. Come on," he pleaded with the Internet.

Dorothy watched him impatiently. As she stepped away to carry on, a digital photo of a newspaper article materialized with a headline related to an arrest of Fidelia for procuring from the New York Times in the late nineties.

"Is this her?"

Dorothy leaned in closer and squinted to see the black-and-white photo. "Yes. The woman looked about twenty years older, but I'm sure that's her."

"Did she ever become a client of the bank?"

"No. There was no record of a woman entering the bank that morning, no record of a meeting in Mr. Fernando's calendar. The police didn't believe me and thought I imagined things in my shock. They never tried to find her."

Howard digested that information. They started walking toward the bank again and were only a few yards from where she would turn onto the street for the bank. He stopped and asked her another question.

"Mr. Fernando Number Two, the current Mr. Fernando, did he work for the bank at the same time as Number One, who fell from the balcony?"

"No, he joined the bank a few weeks after Mr. Fernando died. I heard he was a cousin or something, and the president of the bank hired him."

Howard looked directly into Dorothy's eyes again and spoke slowly but calmly. "I need your help. I know the woman in that photo." He paused. "She's trying to kill me. Will you join me for dinner after work and let me explain how you might help me survive?"

She hesitated, then nodded. They agreed on where to meet to speak privately, confirmed a time and set off in different directions.

One more thing occurred to Howard and he turned back. "Please check all the balances, in every currency, for account 243876A before we meet. It will help you understand my request better."

SIXTY

On the Multima Corporate Jet, Tuesday April 18, 2023

Fully confident that her chief legal officer and chief financial officer had the experience and expertise to draft a purchase agreement that would benefit Multima Corporation, Suzanne popped Melatonin pills about three hours into the flight. Usually skeptical of the benefits of sleep aids, she compromised this time with a hope that she might get four hours of sleep. That amount of rest usually allowed her to function at peak efficiency.

Leaving the sofas in the rear for others, she reclined her seat to a position just slightly higher than completely flat, raised the footrest even with the seat bottom, and fell asleep sooner than expected.

She awoke when Eileen gently touched her bare arm, said it was time, and offered her a steaming cup of black coffee. Two hours remained on their flight to Hawaii.

A few minutes later, Alberto Ferer reached across from his seat and handed her his laptop. "I'll nap for an hour while you read it. Make any comments or highlight concerns right on the document. I'll review and discuss them with you when you're finished."

The agreement to purchase had thirty-five pages and forty-thousand words, she noted at the bottom of the screen—too much for even a quick reader to absorb in an hour. So she ignored the mumbo jumbo of legal definitions and jumped right into the deal.

Subject to extensive conditions, Multima Corporation agreed to buy all Jeffersons Stores' publicly traded shares as of the date of the agreement. The agreement assumed all 2,197 store locations and a dozen regional warehouses spread across thirty-two states from the Southwestern US north to the Canadian border were included. As the new shareholder, Multima also would take over all of Jeffersons' remaining real estate and the mortgages still owing on those properties.

When the New York Stock Exchange had closed hours earlier, the last trading price for the day was $19.91 per share, and Multima proposed to purchase all five hundred and forty-nine million shares. Multima would spend over ten billion dollars to buy its larger competitor but would become the third-largest supermarket chain in the US. Suzanne shuddered as she considered the enormity of the deal.

She skipped down to the conditions of the agreement outlined in the last three pages. She scrolled until she saw the reassuring legal jargon that released Multima from liabilities in case she couldn't raise the financing. Although Abduhl Mahinder, her director from the Bank of the Americas, was confident the consortium of banks he put together would raise the amount needed, it was all happening far more quickly than anyone preferred. She needed an escape, and it looked as if Alberto had added adequate protection.

Under the conditions section, she scrolled to the financial audits. Gordon Goodfellow's team had tracked the financial statements published by Jeffersons Stores for years and had questions and concerns.

Good. She found three long paragraphs that dealt with exceptions and adjustments. No doubt they'd need to show some negotiating flexibility to get Suji Corporation's agreement to all those clauses, but it was an appropriate place to start.

It was boring, meticulous detail some would expect to be handled at a pay grade lower than CEO. But Suzanne had learned early in her career that successful chief executives were always the best negotiators. To negotiate expertly, one must have command of all the issues, and recognize where latitude to concede exists and where compromise isn't possible. Tired or not, she had an obligation to know the contents of that document as well as anyone sitting around the table.

So she studied, reviewed, and made digital notes in the margins until Alberto resurfaced and sought his laptop. As she passed the device to her chief legal officer, Suzanne glanced over to where James Fitzgerald and Natalia Tenaz were huddled in animated conversation. She watched as her new president of the Financial Services division bent the ear of her predecessor, Suzanne's long-trusted advisor.

With all the key executives around the table for the final hour of the flight, she expected disagreements, tension, misunderstandings, and perhaps even some problematic moments before they touched down. She first called on Natalia to share her views from the Financial Services perspective.

"Jeffersons Stores has a loyalty card program and a Mastercard credit card with US Mega Bank Inc. We'd like that business for *our* credit card group. Can we add to the agreement a provision that Jeffersons will unwind its agreement with Mega and pay any early cancellation fees or penalties before Multima closes the deal?"

"Great catch." Suzanne calculated quickly. That move would almost double the number of cardholders with Financial Services—a massive win if she could get it. "Unless you see a problem, Alberto, let's add that to the agreement. But I want to warn you this may be a clause they won't concede. I'll do my best, but no promises, Natalia. Any other issues?"

There were no further asks from Financial Services, so she shifted her gaze to Gordon Goodfellow and his team. "We'd like to see stronger language for auditing the financial statements. Bessie tells me our accounting firm needs almost two months to audit our stores effectively. She estimates up to four months might be required to dig through and verify all the Jeffersons records."

Suzanne looked around the table at knowing nods of agreement.

"Okay, we'll tighten the agreement language, but there's no way we'll get four months to close if we get our price. Put three into the document, Alberto. We may have to give up more. Bessie, you should probably get OCD Accounting working on a plan to complete the audits in less than sixty days. They can start planning today. We'll pay them extra for their time if we don't get a signature."

For almost an hour, Suzanne chaired the discussion, listening to requests, debating concerns, and making decisions they'd have to live with if they made a deal. It was time to wrap up the discussion and get dressed to meet their adversary.

"Other issues before we get into the room with them?" She used a tone that signaled her intentions. She moistened her lips, straightened her posture, and looked around the jet's oval table one last time. "I want Alberto to carry the ball for our first round. We know Japanese men still aren't comfortable doing business with women. I'll jump in only when necessary."

Despite her confident demeanor, Suzanne continued to worry. Suji Corporation was a front for the Japanese Yakuza. Only recently, she had urged an audience to avoid doing business with companies known to be part of organized crime. How might that audience react if a deal was announced? Should she trust the clever Sugimori, or might he have some hidden agenda?

There are still so many questions.

SIXTY-ONE

Honolulu, Hawaii, Wednesday April 19, 2023

Even in the wee hours of morning, it was far too risky to check into the Prince Waikiki with both Sugimori's team and the Multima Corporation delegation prowling around. Mateo had pointed out to Fidelia the law enforcement background of Multima's chief of security and his special relationship with the CEO. There was little doubt he would be in the hotel with a large contingent of bodyguards, and they already knew Sugimori had a dozen armed operatives poking about.

So Mia had made reservations at The Modern Honolulu right next door. Stepping from the limo, Fidelia noted that it took about two minutes to walk from one entrance to the other. Tak, Mia and Klaudia trailed her into the hotel. Mateo and his guys had followed in rental cars in case they needed to leave the hotel quickly or pursue anyone.

Avoiding attention as much as possible, Fidelia and Klaudia walked up to an attendant at the front desk. Mia and Tak found another host to serve them. The Penthouse suite was cleaned and ready because Mia had booked it for arrival on Tuesday, but poor weather and a refueling stop in Los Angeles delayed them. The hotel would bill them for the extra night, but Fidelia didn't begrudge paying an additional $2,260.04. At least they could start immediately.

The attendant who checked them in guided them up to the suite and walked through it, describing its benefits and perks. It wasn't the most luxurious accommodation she'd seen, but it was good enough.

Floor-to-ceiling windows looked out over the glistening Pacific Ocean. There was only one master bedroom, but they probably wouldn't have a chance to use the bed. The advertised formal dining room turned out to be a round wooden table with four comfortable chairs that would work as her office for the mission. The massive terrace was more than she expected, with plants, outdoor sofas, and spectacular ocean views.

Fidelia tipped the hotel attendant with a twenty-dollar bill and ushered him out of the suite as quickly as possible.

She sat Klaudia down for a chat before the others arrived.

"Tak says he's getting good reception from the software you installed on his buddy's phone. Any way we can get that app onto a phone of one of the Multima team members?"

"I doubt it. Remember, I need three to four minutes. Unless you know someone on the Multima side well enough to engage them for that long, I can't do it." Her manner remained aloof, and it grated on Fidelia.

"Fair enough. When we find out which rooms the two teams use for breakouts, are you still confident you can plant listening devices as we discussed?"

"If Mateo gets me a cleaner's uniform, I can have both planted within five minutes. I'll set both up to transmit back here."

"Okay. Have the Multima room broadcast into the master bedroom. Tak can listen in on the Suji gang from the dining room table. We've still got time. They start about nine, but there won't be any breakouts for at least a few hours."

Klaudia nodded nonchalantly without making eye contact. Fidelia waited, silently staring at her friend. She could feel her blood pressure rising. Her face became red, but the woman still ignored her. When Klaudia finally lifted her eyes from the floor, Fidelia sprang to her feet and lunged.

She grabbed her friend's throat and squeezed tightly with both hands, shaking the woman's body violently as she spat out her words. "If you intend to leave this island alive, start showing me some respect. I've had it with your juvenile behavior. You think your technology skills are indispensable. You resent me for snatching you from the streets in Otrobanda. But you forget. It was me who saved your ass from the Russian secret service and the FBI in Guantanamo. I have loved you passionately but won't hesitate to leave your body here if your attitude doesn't change immediately."

A quiet knock on the door saved Klaudia from more. Fidelia dropped her grip and backed away, glaring furiously. Mia and Tak were at the door, and she wordlessly let them in.

Tak blurted out the news as soon as the door closed behind him.

"The broadcasts from my contact's phone stopped. I think they've compromised him."

"What do you mean compromised?" Fidelia snapped, her tone louder than necessary.

"The last thing I heard were loud, animated conversations between Sugimori and one of his security team. They had picked up signals of someone transmitting voice data from the room. It sounded like they were running about the room checking phones, TV cables, loose wires, that sort of thing. Suddenly, someone demanded to know who was using their cell phone. My contact started to say something, but someone interrupted him and yelled, 'I've got it.' Then the broadcast connection died."

Another knock at the door. Mia checked the security eye, then opened the door for Mateo and three of his men.

Once the door closed again, Fidelia shared the news in Spanish. "We've lost the broadcast. It's urgent that you get Klaudia into the breakout rooms. Do we know which ones they're using? Did you find a uniform?"

"We know the breakout rooms and I've got a guy over there now stealing a uniform. He should be here in a few minutes. It's the same guy who got the room names."

Continuing in Spanish, Fidelia threw a look at Klaudia, silent on the other side of the room. "Your guys will have to watch her carefully. She's still rebelling and may try to escape again. Get your guy to steal a uniform for himself and be sure he sticks with her. Send another man along to lurk in the background, ready to help in case she runs."

She turned to face Klaudia. Composed, her tone became softer. "Mateo will take you over to the other hotel. He'll have uniforms for you and one of his guys. Take your technology tools and be sure you get it done without attracting any attention."

Without waiting for acknowledgment or confirmation, she spun on her heel to speak with Mia. "Call Kai. He's on the spreadsheet I gave you under Hawaii—Escort. I talked with him last night, and he agreed to get a couple guys over once we settled in. I want them here within the hour. Tell him I also want his guys to bring two girls. Japanese speakers. Gorgeous, bright and seasoned."

SIXTY-TWO

Grand Cayman, Cayman Islands, Tuesday April 18, 2023

Dorothy was sitting at a table in the farthest corner from the entrance to the outdoor patio when Howard arrived precisely on schedule. He greeted an inquiring server with a smile, a nod, and a wave toward the bank employee. She still wore the same outfit as earlier that morning when he'd intercepted her on her path to work.

Her choice of tables was excellent. Behind her, six-foot tall shrubs blocked any view from the street or sidewalk outside. The angle of her chair let her see every person entering the patio area, and a black box mounted on a pole among the shrubs implied excellent reception from a nearby Wi-Fi router.

About a dozen tables on the patio were spaced at least six feet apart. Each had tall flower arrangements in the center, and a rubberized all-season carpet covered the cement floor. Voices might travel, but not far. Only half the tables were occupied, the guests spread out comfortably.

Surprisingly, Dorothy rose as he approached the table and leaned toward him for kisses on both cheeks with a sensuous smile. Howard, too, smiled wryly. The woman was smarter than he expected, positioning their meeting as social for any curious onlooker. Howard maintained the ploy and sat beside her rather than across the table. He added a hug of her shoulder as he settled in.

"Thanks again for coming. I know you're taking risks."

"I checked the account today as you suggested. It had four sub-accounts in various currencies. When I total those current balances in US dollars, euros, Canadian dollars, and Swiss francs, the US dollar equivalent is $403 million and change. Is that what you expected?"

Howard nodded. His query on the account the previous week totaled slightly less than that amount, but currency values change constantly, and he'd surely earned interest in the meantime. But it was too early to talk business.

When a waiter arrived, he ordered a bottle of red wine—one of the more modestly priced varieties on the menu to conserve cash until his plan played out. Then they chatted about living in Grand Cayman, travel, and the books they liked to read, while ordering dinner and enjoying three courses served slowly over two hours. When she swallowed the last morsel of a chocolate-coated French pastry for dessert, it was time.

"For a woman who left a convent only a few years ago, you have highly elevated social skills." He smiled mischievously, watching her reaction.

She laughed. "Is that the line he used?" Her laugh morphed into a giggle. "I've heard that was the story he told whenever a client showed some interest in me. He never wanted to find himself in a position where he had to share me."

"You mean ...?"

"Yes, I was the other woman. For a few years." Her smile disappeared and her voice softened to a whisper. "That's why I found it so hard when he jumped."

"And why you're bitter about no one bringing to justice the person who caused him to jump."

She nodded.

"The woman in question heads up a criminal ring, one of the biggest in the world. She has the technology, resources, and will to use any information to any end she chooses. My guess? She had some photos of Mr. Fernando Number One. Maybe photos of you and him together. She has no inhibitions about using those kinds of tactics to get what she wants. Currently, I'm in her crosshairs."

"Why is she after you?"

"To be honest, we used to be lovers. I ran when I no longer wanted to be part of her lifestyle. I've been running since." Honesty, of course, was a relative term. She only needed to know the parts that might evoke sympathy at this stage.

"Why do you think I can help you?"

"I fear she's compromised someone else at the bank. When I use my credit card or visit a TVB Bank branch, weird things happen in the following days. I think someone is feeding her information on my whereabouts. I need to move some of that money to other banks to survive. If I do that with Mr. Fernando Number Two, I fear details about those banks and accounts will also find their way back to her."

"So you want me to transfer your money?"

"Yes, I'd like your help to move part of the money. I'll leave a significant portion with TVB Bank so you wouldn't sell out your employer. You'd just be helping a client improve his chances of surviving in an unfair world."

"But it puts me in a precarious position. They'll find my digital fingerprints on every transaction, no matter how much I might deny helping you. At the very least, they'll fire me. Worse, if Mr. Fernando Two is in cahoots with your former lover. My life might be in danger."

"And that's why I'm prepared to share. Can you access the main server and make transfers to other banks from your home?"

"Yes, but it would be too dangerous for me."

"Here's what I propose. Tonight or tomorrow, set up your own personal accounts in Gibraltar, Malta, or wherever you choose. You know how to do that, right?"

She nodded and tilted her head. "I'm listening."

"Once you have personal accounts ready to accept transfers, you bring your laptop home, and we move the money together. I give you the deposit details and amounts and watch you complete the transactions. When you've finished, I watch you transfer ten percent of the original amount to whatever personal accounts you choose. Ten percent of the original amount means you will earn over forty million dollars for helping me. Enough to live anywhere and never work again."

She considered the idea. After a few minutes, Howard wandered to the men's room to give her some space. He took his time, stopped on the way back, and chatted with a server before he asked him to bring the bill in five minutes.

When he returned to the table, she looked up with a smile and excited eyes. "It's too dangerous to do any of that from home. The bank can track digital footprints to a location. Where are you staying?"

"I have an Airbnb a few minutes from here. You're welcome to come there."

"Call a taxi. Bring me to my apartment to gather up a few personal things. Then we can go to your rental."

It took most of the night for him to guide Dorothy through the mechanics of setting up offshore accounts. They had to abort three initial choices because of documentation requirements or timing restrictions but had two accounts set up and ready to accept cash later that day.

When they finished those tasks, Dorothy stood up and wrapped her arms around his neck, pulling him close to her. Howard bent forward to kiss her, and she leaned in and welcomed his tongue for a few seconds, then broke away.

"Thank you, Mr. Smith. But that's enough for tonight."

SIXTY-THREE

Honolulu, Hawaii, Wednesday April 19, 2023

They sat in the Multima jet on the ground for a couple hours, one idling engine generating enough energy to power the air conditioning system. Winds had been favorable across the Pacific, so they'd landed a few minutes earlier than scheduled.

Before leaving, Eileen had astutely tracked down a company catering to the airlines and arranged hot first-class breakfasts, and a small vehicle delivered them to the jet a few minutes after they landed. Everyone had wolfed down their allotted meal and enjoyed a cup or two of coffee within an hour.

Serge wanted Suzanne to arrive at the hotel precisely ten minutes before the meeting.

The concept of arriving slightly early to show respect was a long-established Japanese business practice, as was the rule that arriving too early showed inadequate respect for the value of time. From Serge's perspective, it also allowed him to usher the team quickly from the front door to the meeting room to avoid hanging around in the lobby or other crowded areas. His law-enforcement background still influenced his mindset and attitude about dealing with a known criminal.

Four SUV limousines formed a line around the aircraft, waiting to load their passengers. Inside the jet, Suzanne's team chatted in groups of two or three, reviewing small details about the deal and calculations related to the proposed agreement.

The driver of the lead limousine climbed the steps to the aircraft at precisely eight thirty and signaled they should leave for the hotel. Twenty minutes later, Suzanne swept into the conference room and headed toward Sugimori.

He was easy to spot in the crowd.

Slightly taller than the rest, he stood erect when he noticed her crossing the room. He took three steps forward from the group around him and bowed deeply. His head seemed to be as low as her knees, but he looked upward directly into her eyes as he said, "Welcome, Suzanne Simpson."

Suzanne aimed to lower her head to the height of his knees as well and looked upward as she responded in Japanese, *"Sugimori-san, arigatōgozaimashita. Anata ni o ai dekite kōeidesu."* Thank you very much, Mr. Sugimori. It's a pleasure to meet you.

One at a time, her team members stepped forward and bowed ceremonially. Suzanne examined Sugimori more closely as she introduced each person to him.

Sugimori looked younger than she expected. Handsome, with a warm smile and welcoming eyes, he projected the air of a Japanese ambassador, but flaunted conspicuous wealth. His dark blue, custom-tailored suit probably cost ten thousand dollars. The Louis Vuitton black shoes about the same. His white shirt was more brilliant than she'd seen anywhere, and the pale blue tie appeared to be one-of-a-kind.

Afterward, the process reversed, and Sugimori introduced each of his colleagues to Suzanne.

When the introductions were complete, he asked Suzanne a few polite questions about their flight and jet lag while all the other meeting participants silently stood around. The man's command of English was excellent. His accent was pronounced, but even with small talk, he showed a clear understanding, robust vocabulary, and ease with the language.

After a few moments, Sugimori gestured magnanimously toward the row of seats facing the windows and suggested they all sit down and get started. Suzanne let him take the lead.

He addressed the room in Japanese, with a woman he'd introduced as his assistant translating every few paragraphs. This avoided any misunderstandings for such a meaningful discussion, he told everyone.

His message was short and succinct. His predecessor had proposed merging Multima and Jeffersons five years earlier with a vision of creating one of the world's largest supermarket chains. Part of that founder's vision was influenced by a stark realization that Suji Corporation didn't have the internal knowledge and expertise to lead Jeffersons Stores to optimum success. In the five subsequent years, they changed US leadership three times, with no improvement in operating results.

He believed Multima and Jeffersons Stores would be great

partners with an excellent cultural fit. Since Suzanne wouldn't entertain a merger, he wanted Suji Corporation to sell the entire company to Multima—if they could agree upon a reasonable price, terms, and conditions. Such a result would allow Suji Corporation to focus on other businesses it was more comfortable managing, and with greater success.

However, he emphasized that if an acceptable agreement wasn't achievable, Suji Corporation would continue to support Jeffersons Stores until it achieved satisfactory results. His tone seemed moderate, but while his assistant translated, Sugimori's eyes locked on Suzanne and his face tightened.

Suzanne maintained her polite smile and eye contact, unperturbed by the implied threat that he might double down in the American market. When it was clear that he'd finished his opening remarks, she focused first on Sugimori, then worked her way along the table.

"We respect Jeffersons Stores as a fierce competitor and often admire your company's innovations. Culturally, we agree with Sugimori-san that we could be a good fit, drawing on the strengths of both companies. We have experience integrating a major acquisition. You'll remember we acquired the European company Farefour after I told your founder five years ago that we didn't feel the time was right to merge with Jeffersons Stores."

She watched how the people across the table reacted to that gentle reminder. Only Sugimori's eyes didn't drop downward.

She continued. "We know how to make a major acquisition and what we must do to make it work. We are seriously interested in purchasing all the company's outstanding shares, and we'll present you with an offer we hope you will find reasonable and fair. We're also somewhat uncomfortable about the speed with which you'd like things to happen, so we'll propose some conditions that make us more comfortable acting more quickly than usual."

She paused to let that point sink in before she continued, seeking some levity. "Our chief legal counsel, Alberto Ferer, has a presentation he'll walk us through to explain our position. You know how we Americans both love and fear our lawyers. They seem to rule our lives some days."

Everyone across the table except Sugimori gave her knowing

smiles, so she focused on him. "We're prepared to discuss our proposal, but our room to maneuver is minimal. You'll see we have considered every aspect of the deal. We've carefully studied and discussed our options, so we hope you'll find the proposal Alberto explains one you can accept."

Sugimori nodded without a word, a smile or any other indication of how he received her implied threat to walk if they didn't take the deal as offered.

It was nine thirty when she asked Alberto to begin his presentation. He patiently clicked through a dozen slides for about an hour, building the Multima offer bullet-point by bullet-point.

The Japanese team listened intently, made notes and studiously avoided communicating anything through their body language.

When he finished, Sugimori thanked Alberto for the presentation. He said his team needed to take a break to discuss it, and proposed they each use the breakout rooms for the next hour and reconvene at about eleven thirty.

Serge waited for them inside the breakout room and pointed to the location of the hidden microphones he had discovered. He held up a sheet of paper stolen from a printer. On it, he'd scrawled a message with a red sharpie. He raised a finger to his lips as everyone looked in his direction.

They're Listening & Recording Everything.

SIXTY-FOUR

Honolulu, Hawaii, Wednesday April 19, 2023

Kai brought over the two Hawaiian escorts and two additional security guys. Mateo ushered all five visitors into Fidelia's suite where she monitored conversations from the Multima breakout room with Klaudia. It was mainly dull and unproductive.

When the Multima group assembled, there was a round of congratulations for Suzanne Simpson and Alberto Ferer on how they led the discussions for the first session. Then everyone switched gears and started talking about ice hockey, of all things! They knew someone was listening in.

There were only four or five different voices, suggesting the key players were holding meaningful conversations elsewhere.

Fidelia needed to get the girls over there quickly. "A little less makeup, ladies. Use my bathroom to tidy up before you leave. Look more business-like. Keep the short skirts but add a blazer. Mia will get you a couple from our luggage that should fit."

Mia scrambled away while Fidelia held up her phone, displaying a picture of Akira Sugimori. "Here's the man I want. Mateo will walk with you to the hotel next door, get you in, and show you where to find him. He runs the escort business in Japan, so you'll know how to get his attention. Separate him from the rest of his people. Tell him I'm here, I sent you, and I want to see him for a few minutes."

She studied both women as she spoke. Not everything rode on the success of their mission, but it would become much more complicated if they failed.

"Use only my first name, Fidelia. If he refuses to come back with you, use this phone. Hit 'one' on speed dial. I'll talk to him and give you any further instructions after we speak. Got it?"

Both nodded and followed Mia toward the door, where Mateo waited to accompany them to the hotel next door. Before they left, one of Mateo's men knocked on the door and had a whispered conversation with him.

"What's the problem?" Fidelia sounded impatient, so she

tempered a follow-up comment with a smile. "Anything new to report?"

Mateo motioned for his guy to tell the story.

"We noticed two big Japanese guys helping a guy out the side door of the hotel from a stairwell. He wasn't unconscious but looked woozy and couldn't control his legs. A white van pulled up to the door and the big guys threw the injured one into the back, then jumped in after him. The van took off."

"Did we lose it?" Fidelia wondered.

"No. We had a guy on the second-floor patio, and he watched the van circle outside the property, then drive it back to the corner of the parking lot closest to the harbor. It's still there. Should we check inside?"

Fidelia nodded. "Get your colleague to break in there quickly. Call when you're inside and let me know what you find."

Mateo led the escorts away while he talked with his guy.

Meanwhile, Fidelia motioned for Tak, who was wearing a headset and listening at the dining table, to join her. "What's going on in the Suji breakout room?"

"There's chaos. Sugimori thinks the proposal's a good one and wants to accept it. Some of his guys are trying to persuade him that the price is too low. They've warned him you'll be furious when you find out the details and they don't want any part of it. They've been yelling at each other for more than half an hour."

Fidelia smiled. Tak should play the role well.

"The girls should be there any minute. Continue listening. As soon as Sugimori steps out of the conversation, wave to me. Then change into your business attire and have an energy drink or something to keep fully alert."

Mateo's guys reported back from the van moments later.

"The Japanese guy is okay. He's in zip ties and needed some water. Doesn't speak any Spanish or English."

"Hold on." She strode to Tak's table while speaking into her phone. "Put the guy on."

Within seconds, Tak nodded that they had his contact on the line and listened with one ear as the guy spoke, then raised a finger to get Fidelia's attention.

"Two things," he finally explained. "Sugimori just left the room.

More importantly, my contact knows why he's trying to sell the company so quickly."

She turned to Mateo's guy. "Get him up here now."

Fifteen minutes later, her secure phone rang. She picked up on the first ring. Without any greeting, she said, "When did you plan to tell me?"

"Fidelia! Your ladies told me you were in town. I didn't believe them."

"We need to talk. Now."

"I'm rather busy at the moment. May I call you back this evening?" His voice remained pleasantly defiant. He needed a nudge.

"You're trying to sell a ten-billion-dollar company that belongs to The Organization without consulting me. That won't happen. Come here immediately with the girls. Your jet is currently disabled at the airport. I have a dozen men around the hotel. You won't leave Honolulu alive unless you meet with me immediately. No weapons."

Tak walked into her room as she ended the call. He looked like a CEO. "He's on the way over. Do you have the documents ready?"

SIXTY-FIVE

Grand Cayman, Cayman Islands, Wednesday April 19, 2023

Howard didn't sleep at all that night. It wasn't because he wasn't tired—he was exhausted. Rather, he forced himself to stay awake to monitor Dorothy Bodden. He couldn't let her out of his sight until his money was transferred from the TVB Bank to his newly created accounts.

He would have preferred to finish it all last night after she agreed to the arrangement. Unfortunately, Dorothy informed him she couldn't do it until the current-day business transactions uploaded to the central server overnight. If she made the transfers in the wee hours of the morning, they might still upload with the previous day's activities and alert management at the bank before they could leave the island.

The other reason he still schemed well into the evening was the problem of what to do about Dorothy. For over a week, he'd wrestled with the dilemma. Once she made the transfers out of TVB Bank into the accounts he directed, she'd know how much money was there—and the passwords to get at it—until he could move the money to different banks again himself.

Two options remained. His preferred course of action was to complete the transfers, then finish off Dorothy. Therein lay the problem. Howard had killed only one person in his entire time with The Organization. He'd shot and killed a guy to pass the loyalty test.

When it happened, Howard immediately became violently ill. He threw up multiple times, felt his body temperature soar, shook like a leaf in the wind, and almost collapsed with the trauma of what he'd done. Fortunately, there were no witnesses. However, he had to take a photo of his victim for Giancarlo Mareno and vomited again when he clicked the camera.

The situation with Dorothy was worse. Not only was he loath to kill someone, but he didn't have a gun. Unlike the US, in the countries he'd been in the last few days—Spain, Portugal, the UK, and the Cayman Islands—it was almost impossible to buy a gun. Even the black market operated so far underground that a guy needed connections to buy a weapon illegally. He'd checked the possibilities online and on the Dark Web with special software he'd purchased in Spain.

Killing her with a knife was equally out of the question. He didn't know how to do it and imagined the blood and gore would be worse than a shooting. As he watched her stir in his bed that morning, he planned to book her on his flight to Cuba at 6:40 that evening.

If he didn't find a way to get rid of her before then, at least she'd be with him until he transferred the money without her involvement. At that point, she'd only be a witness with no specific details to connect to him.

The idea of using Cuba only came to him while he was in the UK. While waiting for a flight, a fellow passenger wanted to chat. The man was a Canadian returning to Toronto from business in London. What caught Howard's attention was the fellow's plan to leave again a few days later for Cuba.

The rogue island had been off the radar of US tourists for years because of government restrictions on trade and travel. Americans simply couldn't go there. However, Canada never respected that US ban and Cuba welcomed thousands of Canadian visitors every year. Even more helpful, Cuban immigration authorities don't stamp passports, so travelers avoid any possibility of blacklisting when they might later enter the US.

For Howard, it was perfect. He could easily get to Brazil from Cuba when he was ready to leave the island. His Portuguese passport would be helpful in southern Brazil and neighboring northern Uruguay. There was a good chance he could evade Fidelia and The Organization for a considerable period of time.

But first, he had to get it right with Dorothy.

He woke her as the sun rose about six and offered her a cup of coffee. When she was alert, they sat at the kitchen table of the Airbnb side by side and he explained his plan.

"When we're done today, I want you to come with me."

She shook her head and grimaced.

"It's not only because I want to make wild and passionate love with you to celebrate our success when you're done. You've got to come with me because I can't trust you with the valuable information you'll have when we finish. You understand I have no intention of giving you forty million dollars and the tools to strip out the remainder when I go to the bathroom. So you have to stay by my side continuously until at least tomorrow when I'm out of the country and able to transfer those funds somewhere else. Got it?"

Dorothy listened without interruption, then processed the message. "I understand. You don't know me. I'd never try to steal your money, but I can accept going to Cuba and staying there with you for one more day."

"First, we'll book you on Cayman Airways flight number 834 to Havana at 6:40 this evening. Book seat 2C, right next to me, with payment in cash when we arrive for the flight. If they won't accept that, offer to drop over later this morning with the money."

He made another coffee while she tried unsuccessfully to book online, then waited while she called the airline's office and eventually confirmed her seat on the flight.

"Now, we're going to transfer my money."

For almost an hour, he sat beside her and watched more than three hundred million dollars flow digitally from TVB Bank into the newly created offshore accounts. He took pictures of the screens with his phone and also made notes. His spirit became buoyant and soared higher with the completion of each transfer. Freedom was genuinely exhilarating.

Dorothy became almost giddy. Her smile broadened with each transfer, and her hands trembled in anticipation when Howard told her it was okay to start her own transfers of the agreed ten percent.

He verified each amount with the calculator on his phone before nodding for her to press the send button. Each time, he retook pictures of the screen, just in case. He was resigned to losing the forty million as a cost of gaining his freedom from Fidelia and The Organization. It was a lot of money, but he wouldn't miss it in the grand scheme of things.

When she finished with a whoop of joy, Dorothy threw her arms around his neck and embraced him with such passion it tempted Howard to find another solution for her.

When she drew away after a moment or two of delicious interaction, he said, "I've got to be out of here by eleven. Let's find a nice beach, take a swim, and get to know each other better before our flight."

She answered with another long, passionate kiss.

SIXTY-SIX

Honolulu, Hawaii, Wednesday April 19, 2023

Suzanne first became suspicious when a low-level member of the Suji negotiating team knocked on the door to their breakout room and asked for a one-hour delay. Mr. Sugimori had been called away unexpectedly on another urgent matter. Perhaps she and her team might like to enjoy lunch while waiting for Mr. Sugimori to return to the hotel.

Unfortunately, that information confirmed a tip-off Serge had whispered into her ear only moments earlier. One of his security team members had spotted Sugimori headed toward The Modern Honolulu Hotel with two young women.

Suzanne seethed.

She followed the advice of the Suji Corporation emissary and had Eileen order lunch for everyone. She also held up a piece of paper on which she wrote "Entertainment." Her team smiled, with a couple almost giggling at the stupidity of it all. But conversation gradually switched from hockey to the Oscars, then to upcoming concert tours.

The low-level emissary returned almost two hours later, red-faced and apologetic. There had been a further change. Mr. Sugimori would not return to the meeting. Mr. Tak Takahashi, another Suji Corporation executive, would take his place. There should be no concern as Mr. Sugimori had delegated to Mr. Takahashi all the authority necessary to enter into an agreement with Multima Corporation.

However, there were a few details they needed to discuss further.

"We'll need some time to discuss this change. It will probably take about two hours. May I suggest you also order lunch for your team?" Her tone dripped with sarcasm. Unsmiling, she spun on her heel and pointed to Yuki, Alberto, James, and Gordon to follow her out of the breakout room.

Back in the main lobby of the conference rooms, she spoke into the microphone attached to her bra. "Serge, meet us outside the front entrance with a couple folks to keep an eye out for us."

Silently, the group descended the elevator to the ground floor and marched out the front door.

"Let's keep walking until we're sure we're far enough away from any listening devices," Suzanne said.

They stepped briskly but silently. Serge led the entourage. The rest followed informally in pairs or threesomes until he pointed toward some shade from an overhanging billboard almost a half mile from the hotel. They huddled in a loose circle.

"We probably look as odd as we feel standing out here in the heat, but I need your advice, and this is the safest place to get it." She laughed nervously and looked toward Serge for assurance.

"Yuki, you first. From a Japanese cultural perspective, is there any explanation for what we just heard?"

"None. I've never heard of such a thing happening. Japanese executives are usually thoughtful, considerate, and measured—even when they strongly disagree. I think something extraordinary happened back there."

Alberto jumped in. "Legally, we need to understand exactly what authority the new guy has and how it was conferred on him. If we don't know that, regardless of what he says and what he agrees to, we might have a legal challenge that could cost millions."

Gordon Goodfellow was pale. His long-sought acquisition opportunity was disappearing down the drain. "Look, it's weird. I don't have an explanation. But we've all flown about five thousand miles and lost a lot of sleep. Let's listen to what the fellow has to say. I admit it's a stretch, but there might be a logical explanation we can get comfortable with."

James Fitzgerald simply nodded his support for Gordon's plea.

Suzanne looked at Serge as all eyes turned reflexively in his direction.

"From my days in law enforcement, I have no alternative but to recommend we leave—the sooner the better. I think Yuki said it well. Something extraordinary happened back there. My best guess? There's been a power struggle in either the Japanese Yakuza or The Organization. Maybe both." He paused to make everyone think about that for a moment.

When he continued, his tone was grave and his voice dramatically soft. "Your lives are at risk if you go back in there. My team and I will provide you with the best support we can, but we're not armed to defend against a gang war. I'd prefer you call Eileen, ask her to bring up the limousines, and we all head for the airport before the new guy shows up."

They continued discussing their options for a few more minutes in the shade of the billboard. Words changed slightly. Emotions remained in check, but no consensus developed. It would rest with Suzanne to make the decision.

"Let me think about it while we walk back." She turned and led her procession back toward the hotel. Serge eventually joined her there. "Any chance personal concerns are affecting your judgment?"

"Absolutely. I love you more than anyone or anything in the world. If the risk of danger were far lower, I'd still urge you not to do it. I don't like the smell of this situation at all. However, I know you have more at stake than personal safety risks. If you decide to go back in there, I'll protect you with my life if necessary."

"If you're right and something sinister is happening with these guys, I think it's unlikely they'd risk drawing attention to themselves by harming me or any other Multima people. Remember, only a few weeks ago, I talked passionately about the need to fight back against organized crime, especially in the food chain. If I can buy Jeffersons Stores, clean it up and make the company a respectable part of Multima, I'd be doing my part in that war. If we can't do a deal, I think it unlikely they'd harm us because that would draw in law enforcement worldwide."

"So you want to go back into the meeting?"

"I don't want to, but I will."

SIXTY-SEVEN

Honolulu, Hawaii, Wednesday April 19, 2023

Once Tak Takahashi's mysterious contact from the white van identified himself, and Fidelia realized he was The Organization's financial wizard in Japan, the fellow confirmed the scope of Sugimori's treachery beyond any doubt.

With a borrowed laptop and a USB drive from his pocket, he brought up spreadsheets that showed the billions of dollars involved. A file of photos showed over one hundred exotic cars, valued in the millions. Files followed with addresses and land deeds for more than a dozen mansions spread around the globe. Another entire digital file contained several emails from the government of Japan, demanding payment for unpaid taxes.

The final straw was an email from the Prime Minister of Japan threatening to close every pachinko parlor in Japan, using the armed forces if necessary, should Suji Corporation not pay all delinquent corporate taxes before the thirtieth of April. For generations, successive governments had turned a blind eye to the goings on in the parlors' backrooms in return for paying corporate taxes on revenues from the games. The pachinko run was over if they didn't pay their taxes.

Sugimori at first deflected, then defended, and finally—like a blubbering baby—pled for forgiveness for his incompetence and greed.

Tak's contact served as a witness while Sugimori signed over a dozen documents transferring his authority in the Yakuza to Tak Takahashi. That included all power related to Suji Corporation, Jeffersons Stores, and Japanese companies that dealt with businesses as diversified as dodgy pachinko parlors and chains of lucrative hostess bars.

The moment Sugimori signed the last document, Fidelia motioned for Mateo. He pricked Sugimori's outer thigh with enough midazolam to induce sleep for at least three hours. They had more if needed.

Then she summoned Klaudia from the bedroom to wire Tak

with a camera, microphone, and earbuds to let Fidelia participate in the meeting unseen. His long hair covered his ears entirely, but she inspected him closely to ensure they wouldn't easily be detected.

She gave him his orders as they installed and tested the technology. "Go into the meeting room. Tell them we find their price acceptable, but we'll only move forward if the deal closes before April 30. Your contact is right. Our pachinko parlor business in Japan is finished if they bring in the army and shut us down. You must find a way to get an agreement signed today for a closing date before the government moves. We need that cash. They'll probably object, so you may have to concede something in the price. Keep talking and listen for my instructions."

With Tak on the way to the other hotel to resume the meeting with Multima Corporation, Fidelia set other wheels in motion with Mateo. "Be discreet. Start with the top Suji bodyguard and take them all out with the drugs. Commandeer a staff elevator and get them out the hotel's back receiving doors. Stash them with zip ties in our two white vans. No civilian casualties, please. Are you sure you have enough midazolam for all of them?"

Mateo nodded and strode away, punching numbers into his phone.

Fidelia popped another couple pain relievers. A headache had begun before they'd touched down that morning and progressively worsened. She looked in the bathroom mirror and winced. She looked as bad as she felt.

It seemed that dozens more lines creased her brow and around her eyes since the last time she'd checked. Her once flawless complexion looked dull, dry and rough, and her skin drooped in more places the longer she inspected. The bruises on her face still had a hideous purple hue. She dabbed lipstick on to at least brighten her visage and silently promised herself a facial and massage when this mission was over. She made a mental note to have Mia schedule something the day after they returned to Curaçao.

She grabbed another coffee and sat at the suite's dining room table just as her phone showed her the room Tak had just entered. He strode confidently to his assigned place at the center of the table across from Suzanne Simpson and bowed deeply and respectfully as he introduced himself.

Then he stood at the table and spoke in English, addressing the CEO of Multima and her team sincerely and apologetically. Once he delivered his apology, and Suzanne Simpson accepted it with a gracious nod, he began to sell.

SIXTY-EIGHT

Grand Cayman, Cayman Islands, Wednesday April 19, 2023

Dorothy suggested West Bay Beach near the island's northwestern tip and told Howard they could take a bus there in about a half hour. There were resorts nearby, so they could have a late lunch, then catch a later bus to the airport.

Spending the day at the beach was a good idea. If the opportunity arose, he'd find a way to eliminate her. If it looked too dangerous, or he lost his nerve, they would be out of sight of most people and harder for the authorities to track down if something triggered at TVB Bank.

Since the island was compact and travel quick to any part of the island, they had time for breakfast. His first three coffees of the day had worn off. Without sleep for the past thirty-six hours, he needed an energy boost and suggested they stop at a patio restaurant near the bus stop Dorothy had pointed to just down the road.

Howard ordered the largest omelet on the menu, not knowing when he might have his next meal. Dorothy chose a healthy muesli mixture. While they waited for their food, they chatted about the weather, where they would stay in Cuba, and locations she should consider for safe harbor when they eventually separated.

Howard talked about some of his travel experiences, asked about her interests, and pried into her personal life when he could do so tactfully. Dorothy intrigued him. Forty million dollars was a powerful incentive to leave a good job on a lovely island. He'd been confident the woman would help him get to his money, but the ease with which she made that big decision was still a bit unexpected.

He also wondered about her demonstrations of affection. He supposed big hugs would be a normal reaction to show one's appreciation for the lavish commission he'd bestowed upon her. But the passionate kisses, inviting much more, seemed premature, almost out of place. As they talked, it became more apparent. He should do everything possible to eliminate the woman at the beach.

Just as the server brought their bill, her phone dinged. Howard had confiscated the phone from her as a precaution and pulled it from a pocket in his shorts.

"What's this mean?" He pointed to a text message asking where she was.

"It's the bank. Human Resources wants to know where I am."

"Tell them you're sick. Can't come in today."

Dorothy quickly keyed in the message and received another one moments after she had pressed the send button.

"I need to give the code to open the vault. It's my turn to open this morning."

Howard scrutinized her face. Nothing seemed out of order. She showed no signs of nervousness or discomfort. Her tone of voice seemed simply to relay a message. He nodded okay and watched her enter a series of numbers in a blur of activity, then press the send button. He reached for the phone to check what she had written.

12 then 19.21.60 then 81.24.60

"It's digital. Those are my personal codes." Her eyes made direct contact with his, and he detected no subconscious blinks of discomfort or deception. No messages followed, so he tucked the phone back into his pocket.

"The bus passes here on the hour. We should hurry over to the stop." She was already standing up as she made her suggestion, so Howard dropped thirty dollars on the table and followed her.

The day was warm. The sun was bright. It took a while for a bus to arrive. When it came, their ride was uneventful. Still, Howard couldn't relax.

All the way from the bus stop to West Bay Beach, as Dorothy chattered about the scenery and views of the ocean they passed, he continued to fret about the best way to do the necessary deed. Drowning was the best he could come up with, but he realized that, too, could be ugly.

When a passenger pulled a cord to signal the bus driver to stop at the next roundabout, Dorothy casually suggested they get off one stop later. It would be closer to a more secluded beach, away from the main visitors to the popular spot. Howard nodded.

The roadway after the roundabout was paved but became

narrower. Two cars would have difficulty passing, but he saw the water only a few hundred yards in the distance. The ride took longer than he expected, maybe ten minutes or longer, before Dorothy pulled a cord to get the driver's attention.

When they debarked, Dorothy led the way. She took his hand and smiled mischievously when he glanced at her. She continued to chatter as they ambled toward the water at a relaxed pace.

As he took in their surroundings, the place indeed met Dorothy's description of secluded. No other people were in sight, and no cars were parked near the road. As they drew nearer, Howard noted no lifeguards or snack bars around. The only sign of civilization he noticed was a shack, barely standing, neglected and in disrepair.

It looked like the perfect spot for him to eliminate the woman. He steeled his resolve and plotted the most opportune way to arrange her drowning. As they passed the run-down shack, Howard released her hand, reached for his backpack strap and pulled it off his shoulder.

"Stop!" a harsh male voice shouted out from behind a corner of the building. Howard glanced toward the sound but saw no one.

"Dorothy, move away from him," the voice commanded. "Now!"

Fernando Number Two!

With that realization, Howard spun and lunged toward the voice. As he twisted, he heard only a series of pops, followed by a searing pain in his face and head. But only for an instant.

Then there was nothing.

SIXTY-NINE

Honolulu, Hawaii, Wednesday April 19, 2023

Suzanne's initial reaction to the new Japanese fellow negotiating for Suji Corporation was a mixture of disbelief and incredulity. She'd participated in dozens of negotiations to buy or sell all or parts of companies, and thousands of meetings with suppliers, unions, and government officials. She couldn't recall any as bizarre as this one.

It wasn't shocking that Suji found the purchase price offered reasonable. After all, it was clear they wanted to sell quickly when they'd demanded a meeting so rapidly. What was truly shocking, though, was the fellow's insistent requirement to complete the deal in less than two weeks. Audits and verifications so critical to ensure the company was truly worth the price they were paying took time. To compress that process so dramatically seemed like a deal breaker.

But she listened intently until the man finished, then took charge of the process decisively and confidently.

"Frankly, I doubt we'll be able to find common ground. I find your requirement to close the transaction before the end of April almost impossible to conceive. However, I won't give you a definitive answer until I talk with my team. But be forewarned, Mr. Takahashi. Should we find a way to accept your requirement, the price we offer will drop—and drop dramatically."

She drilled in on his eyes. No surprise registered. No anger appeared.

He nodded very slightly, maybe not even enough for the members of his team to notice. "Our side will consider the possibility of a minor price adjustment if all other conditions satisfy us. I think both teams should move to our breakout rooms and discuss further. Shall we meet here again in one hour?"

"Make it two. Because you've bugged the breakout room, we'll need to walk about a half mile down the road to discuss our positions freely. That takes extra time." She stood up, unsmiling, then spun on her heel again as her team followed her out.

The parade walking along the roadway must have seemed

unusual to drivers or other onlookers, but Suzanne wasted no time. Once they were clear of the hotel, and Serge was confident enough road and other noises would make recording difficult, she motioned for James Fitzgerald and her CFO Pierre Cabot to walk on either side of her for a moment.

"I want you guys to recommend what sort of price we might come back with. Talk it over with Abduhl Mahinder while we walk. See if he can commit to the financing at that price before the thirtieth. But please give him only the details he needs. You'll be the first to address the group when we get to the billboard."

She let them carry on and slipped back in the procession to walk beside Gordon Goodfellow and Bessie Forsia. "Get OCD on the phone while we walk. Find out how much they'll charge to do the audits and sign off on them by April 25 if they start tomorrow. Get the rest of your team talking to each other as we walk and prepare a list of additional concerns we should address with such a short closing."

Again, she dropped further back in the walking group, pointing to Alberto Ferer and his legal assistant. "This may go nowhere, but I want a document ready if we decide to make a revised offer. Hail a cab for your assistant and give her your laptop. Have the driver stop at the first Starbucks or Denny's with Wi-Fi where she can sit and make changes. You'll have to dictate them to your assistant by phone. She can email the final product to us at the hotel when we're ready."

Eileen was last in the line, and she seemed almost giddy watching her colleagues traipsing in the heat ahead of her. "You promised me my first ride on the corporate jet. I never dreamed it would include an afternoon hike and an outdoor conference." She broke out laughing as she sputtered the last words.

Suzanne smiled in return. "You won't attend the conference. Please return to the hotel to set some wheels in motion. Sorry I couldn't alert you earlier. Arrange a printer at the front desk. If we move forward, we'll need to print an agreement quickly. Be sure the pilots have the jet fueled and ready for departure within two hours. Have cars standing by for the rest of the afternoon. We may want to leave very quickly."

Shade from the billboard covered a larger area on the ground, so everyone shared some relief from the sun. They gathered in a circle and Suzanne set out the parameters immediately. "I haven't made a decision yet. The deal currently looks bad, and we may have to walk away. But before we do that, I want to hear your views. Let's all be brief so we can get back to some air-conditioned comfort as quickly as possible."

Everyone smiled and nodded.

"Pierre, start us off with what you and James want to share."

"If we're entertaining a revised offer, we suggest starting with a twenty-five percent haircut. We suspect they're hiding something. It might not be a 2.5- billion-dollar problem, but there's always a risk that it's higher. We think that gives us a reasonable cushion to deal with unforeseen surprises," Pierre said.

"That's a big discount. If we buy Suji's majority stake at a significant discount, the value of shares held by other investors will drop moments after the deal's announced. If we don't compensate minority shareholders, won't they revolt?" Suzanne asked.

"They might," James answered with a knowing nod. "But Abduhl offered a possible solution. It would help on two fronts. Multima could offer to buy all the shares at either the lower cash price we agree upon or offer to exchange one half of one Multima share for each Jeffersons Stores share. Then, make it a condition of the agreement that Suji will take only cash for its position."

Suzanne nodded, signaling her understanding. "An elegant solution. We comply with the requirement to make the same offer to all shareholders, avoid alienating everyone but Suji, and don't need to borrow nearly as much money to finance the deal. Can I assume Abduhl and Bank of the Americas can guarantee the funds will be there if we need them?"

Both men nodded.

"So we just need me to agree to a massive dilution of my personal holdings. A quick calculation. If we give one half Multima share for each Suji share to owners of about half of the shares outstanding, my percentage of voting rights drops from 25% to about 16%. I'll have to think about that very carefully indeed."

She pointed to Gordon Goodfellow. "OCD wants twenty million dollars to complete an audit within a week. They'd only physically check ten percent of the stores and a quarter of the warehouses plus headquarters, with a guarantee of accuracy of only ninety percent. We'd need a billion-dollar reduction in the offer price to offset that cost and risk."

Her president of the Supermarkets business looked crestfallen. The opportunity of his career appeared to be evaporating the longer they talked.

"Any other operating concerns we should address?"

Bessie replied to Suzanne's question. "We know the operating system Jeffersons uses is antiquated. We'll have to invest about a hundred million dollars in updating their point-of-sale servers and technology to match ours. I realize a deal looks like a long shot here. But if we decide to make a revised offer, I suggest we build that hundred million dollars into our proposal."

Suzanne looked around the group again. Everyone looked tired and defeated. Some wiped perspiration from their brows. All looked toward her, realizing the only possibility an agreement might move forward meant her relinquishing significant control over the company she managed.

"It feels as if I'm rolling the dice with this one." She smiled as broadly as the circumstances allowed. "Alberto, is your legal assistant on the line ready to type?"

He nodded.

"Let's all start walking back to the hotel. Alberto and Pierre, let's walk together and dictate the necessary changes. We'll offer $6.28 billion and see how desperate they are. If they don't bite, we'll head for the jets."

She turned to James Fitzgerald. "Have Eileen raise a quorum of the board of directors for an immediate Zoom call. Tell them what we're planning and take a vote. Let me know if you don't get approval."

SEVENTY

Honolulu, Hawaii, Wednesday April 19, 2023

The moment the Multima Corporation team told Tak it was taking a walk outdoors to discuss their options, Fidelia's spirits lifted. Her greatest fear was Suzanne telling them to shove their opportunity and head back to Canada.

That they were still willing to talk held out a slim hope she wouldn't have to sell off a few billion in assets to satisfy the Japanese government and save the pachinko business. It also suggested they'd probably return with an offer, although it might prove totally unacceptable. She assigned Klaudia the task of hacking any printers in the Prince Waikiki that Multima might have access to.

Using Mia as a decoy at the hotel, they'd located and hacked the printer at the side of the front desk where an American woman from the Multima team sat waiting. Before the device started printing, a copy of the data it received had already landed on Klaudia's laptop. She passed it to Fidelia to read before the printer stopped spitting out the pages the American woman collected from its tray.

Before the Multima team returned to the meeting room, Fidelia had already explained what their adversary would propose to Tak Takahashi. She'd also given him marching orders and coaching on the theatrics he should perform.

The new twist about offering shares instead of cash to minority shareholders offered a tiny opening and she let him know she wanted to seize that opportunity.

With Tak wired up with Klaudia's technology, Fidelia sat at the table in her suite, watching it unfold in the main meeting room.

Tak listened attentively while Suzanne explained the specific changes they'd made to the revised agreement. He pretended to make notes. When Suzanne announced the final price they'd pay, Tak looked appropriately aggrieved.

He shook his head slowly and dramatically, remaining silent for almost a minute. "I'm sorry, Ms. Simpson. I appreciate that you've agreed we can get a deal done before the end of April. That's helpful. And I suggested earlier that we might consider minor revisions to the offer, but you've chopped the price almost in half. Jeffersons is a wonderful, profitable, growing company. The people I answer to will never agree to give up so many billions of dollars to make a deal."

"Shall we call it a day and leave then?" Suzanne Simpson appeared defiant but calm.

She still might move a bit. "Throw out the Multima shares suggestion," Fidelia whispered into his earbuds.

A few seconds later, as though a new thought suddenly occurred, Tak asked if Multima would consider allowing Suji Corporation to trade its shares for Multima shares like all the other shareholders.

Multima's CEO reacted angrily. She slammed her pen on the desk, stood up, and raised her voice menacingly. "Mr. Takahashi, I will never agree to Suji Corporation or any of its subsidiaries or affiliates ever holding a single share of Multima Corporation at any price. I'm not even that excited about owning Jeffersons Stores at the moment. I'll give you a few minutes to consult with your team. If you won't accept our offer as revised, my colleagues and I will leave for the airport."

Fidelia seethed with anger as she watched on her laptop as the woman turned from the gathering around the table and marched toward the door. Her dream of controlling Multima one day looked increasingly futile.

"Ask her for fifteen minutes," Fidelia ordered.

Once the demoralized Suji team assembled in the breakout room with fifteen minutes of grace, Fidelia spoke to Tak through his earbuds again. "We have to get something from her. Ask your guys what they think she might be willing to concede."

Tak repeated her question to the team members, and they shared their ideas. The consensus was to ask them to add back the hundred million dollars they had reduced to upgrade the Jeffersons Stores technology. They thought Multima might give on that less significant point, and it would offer an added benefit. If Multima had to spend money to upgrade the systems themselves, they might not do it immediately. With the current technology, it would be easy for Suji to hack the system because its people knew it intimately.

Maybe they could use that opening to recover another billion or two with a future ransomware attack.

When the meeting resumed, Fidelia watched on her laptop as Tak politely pulled Suzanne Simpson off into an empty corner of the large meeting room. He delicately proposed the relatively minor concession, explaining he wanted a deal but had to win something for his backers.

Suzanne Simpson stepped back toward the table and stopped to whisper something in the ear of another woman on the Multima team, who then nodded her understanding. She made another stop at James's chair, where he nodded and murmured something the microphone couldn't pick up.

When she returned to her place at the table, she remained standing. "I've decided to increase the Multima Corporation offer to purchase Jefferson Stores by one hundred million dollars to a total of 6.38 billion dollars. Mr. Takahashi, will you accept that offer?" He nodded. "Alberto, please change the price in the agreement. We'll sign it now."

Fidelia set the wheels in motion for departure. "Mia, order up the cars and tell the pilots to start the engines. Have them file a flight plan for New York. Mateo, send your team off to the jet first. Follow along with us after I meet with Tak."

SEVENTY-ONE

Honolulu, Hawaii, Wednesday April 19, 2023

Serge entered the meeting room seconds after the final signatures and waved for the Multima team members to follow him out. Suzanne noticed he wore earpieces in both ears, and his typically calm demeanor looked tense. Clearly, this entire affair with Suji made him ill at ease.

He led them toward the elevators at a brisk pace. One of his team had commandeered one and held the door open while everyone scurried inside. Another Multima security guard called out for the stragglers to hurry to another door he held open.

On the way down, Suzanne caught Edward Hadley's eye and mouthed for him to ride with her. At the ground-floor lobby, another of Serge's people waved for them to follow her toward the exit. The woman pointed Suzanne and Serge toward the first limousine, everyone else toward three other vehicles. Edward started to follow the crowd, changed course and yanked open the front door just as the driver had begun to drive off. He screeched to a halt as Edward hopped in.

"What's the rush?" Suzanne asked Serge with a touch of irritation after a long day.

"A gut feeling." Serge glanced toward Edward in the front. Suzanne gave a wave of dismissal, urging him to continue. "Something very strange just happened back there. My gut tells me that today's Suji Corporation charade isn't finished yet. Most of those Japanese guys hanging about are armed and dangerous. We need to get as far away from here as possible, as fast as possible."

Suzanne nodded, showing more tolerance than appreciation. The show wasn't over at Multima Corporation yet, either.

"Edward, you got a sign-off from Suji on the media release you drafted?"

He turned in his seat to face her in the rear. "Yeah, it was tucked in behind all the legal docs, and Alberto passed it to me on the way out. I also got a video of you and Takahashi signing, photos of your formal, ceremonial handshakes, and good shots around the table. You want it all released?"

"We need the media release out before we take off, so our deal is a headline in tomorrow's papers before the markets open. Most people will soon fall asleep back in New York. Once we're airborne, maybe you could make a few calls? *Wall Street Journal*? *Forbes*? *The Globe & Mail*?"

"Sure. Are you up for any interviews?"

"I think it's better to wait until we're on the ground again after some sleep. I'm fine with you providing the background commentary as an official spokesperson."

Their return trip to the airport took less than fifteen minutes as the daily rush hour had ended, with darkness setting in. A wide chain-link fence to the private aircraft area opened as the limousines approached, barely reducing speed as the entourage dashed around the perimeter of the tarmac toward the pair of jets awaiting the Multima team.

En route, they passed a white Bombardier Global 7000 parked a few hundred feet from the Multima jets.

"There's a hive of activity around that one. Must be getting ready to leave too." Serge relaxed as he made that observation, and a smile gradually broadened. When Suzanne arched her eyebrows for more, he turned away and the smile disappeared.

At the corporate jet, Serge and his team rushed people toward the jets, urging laggards to pick up the pace, helping those who struggled with baggage or equipment, and scurrying into one plane or the other as assigned. Everyone was on board less than five minutes after the limousines stopped abruptly at the foot of the stairways.

Suzanne still heard seatbelts clicking shut as her jet moved toward the runway. Gradually, the plane gathered speed as it moved from the tarmac to the main runway, then to the takeoff position. They never slowed down or came to a stop. She couldn't recall a departure so quick while several mammoth passenger aircraft sat idling at the sides of the runway awaiting permission to advance.

Why the preferential treatment?

She supposed Serge knew, but he'd been intent on traveling on the other jet with all his security people. They took off right

CONTENTION

behind Suzanne's jet on the Financial Services plane, a smaller one. But Serge had told her he'd arranged with the pilots to coordinate touchdowns, so the security team arrived in Montreal first.

When the plane reached cruising altitude, Suzanne left her comfortable chair in the middle of the aircraft, walked to the front, and knocked on the cockpit door. "I know we have a public address system or something on here, but I've never used it. Can you show me how?"

She smiled and shrugged as one pilot showed which buttons to push. "We'll be smooth for a few minutes now?"

Once the pilot nodded and said it looked good for a while, Suzanne tried out the new device. "Hi everyone. It's Suzanne here. Can I ask everyone to approach the forward compartment for just a few minutes? I've something to share with you."

Edward Hadley lifted his phone in the middle compartment to show he was on a call and needed more time. She smiled and waved to him, "No problem," then spoke when she could see everyone's faces. "Today, you have made one of the most remarkable achievements in corporate history. Together, you worked almost non-stop for over forty-eight hours. You analyzed an enormous amount of data, considered dozens of options and problems, and provided the information that let me agree to one of the best corporate mergers ever."

She paused to let the importance sink in. "Together, we've created one of the world's largest companies and the third-largest supermarket chain in the US. Our deal today laid the foundation for Financial Services to possibly double the number of credit card loans it manages and offer mortgages at preferred rates to millions of Jeffersons Stores' customers. On behalf of our board of directors and shareholders, I thank you with all my heart. Over the coming weeks, we'll have much to do, unbelievably quickly, to bring it all to fruition. I know I can count on your support. So celebrate your win today. Relax during the flight. Try to get some sleep sometime. And let's all hit the ground running tomorrow morning in Montreal!"

Her team exploded with joy. The plane rocked from side to side for a few moments while her gang jumped up and down and shouted congratulations to Suzanne and each other. They hugged, squealed, laughed, and patted each other on the back. They took pictures of Suzanne, then selfies with her or anyone nearby.

Eileen had found a few bottles of champagne somewhere in Honolulu and popped the corks for everyone with glee. The party continued for a couple hours before people began to tire.

Three hours after takeoff, only Edward Hadley still worked the phones. When he took an abrupt break and squatted beside her seat, he held up his iPad to show her the breaking news story.

SEVENTY-TWO

Honolulu, Hawaii, Wednesday April 19, 2023

Her wrap-up meeting with Tak needed only an hour of Fidelia's precious time. He got the concept of unquestioned loyalty, so she saw no reason to dwell on it. Most of their time focused on making changes to the Japanese reporting structure, fixing the broken relationship with the Japanese government, and taking steps to ferret out any other insubordination in the Yakuza.

To avoid any exposure to facial recognition software at the Prince Waikiki, she'd waited in her penthouse suite next door at The Modern Honolulu Hotel. She stood in front of the mirror of her master bedroom and expertly tied a hijab around her head, then added wrap-around sunglasses to complete the deception.

Moments later, with Mateo holding open the hotel's front door, she swept into the limousine SUV, where Mia sat waiting in the rear seat. Mateo jumped in front with the driver as they sped away to Honolulu's international airport and her leased private aircraft.

"They tell me all's clear at the jet," Mateo called back to Fidelia. "The guys are there, the engines are running, the air conditioner is working, and the pilots are set to fly."

She pulled out her secure phone to check the latest encrypted email messages. One caught her eye. *Reward Request,* it said. She clicked on the headline to read the message, then gasped.

Mission accomplished 12:19 pm 04-18-23. Photos and passports attached. Please deposit to usual account.

Her hands trembled, and her heart rate soared. Fidelia could feel it pounding as she clicked on the photo and saw the bloody remains of Howard Knight's corpse. She recognized only the bloodied, tiny cross he'd worn around his neck since his university days. She clicked on the two passport photos, one for Portugal and the other for Canada. The names were false, but the images were indeed of Howard.

She drew a long, deep breath to calm herself and gazed out the window reflectively. It was finally over. Their relationship for so many years was as close to love as she'd ever experienced. She thought of the times he'd touched her tenderly, spoke to her in whispers of genuine affection, and laughed joyfully as they schemed secret getaways from the wife he eventually deserted and Giancarlo Mareno.

Their love affair began to fall apart when Howard made his billion-dollar mistake and failed to win control of Multima Corporation. It unraveled entirely when he told her he was running from The Organization and asked her to run with him. Foolishly, she joined him.

But it truly ended when Howard first decided to enter the FBI witness protection program. At that point, she knew their values were irreconcilably different. She couldn't spend the rest of her life hiding in fear. Instead, she negotiated a release to Interpol, where she gave them just enough information to take out potential rivals in Europe before she orchestrated the events that would make her queen of The Organization.

She should have killed Howard earlier. Luigi had pressed her to eliminate him continuously for five years. But some part of her affection for him remained. She thought he might evolve over time and see the wisdom of her vision. But he never changed, and now he was gone from her life forever.

It surprised her to find a stray tear slip from her eye as she typed a return message of congratulations and promised payment to the banker's account in the Caymans the following day. She quickly wiped the tear away before Mia noticed.

When she looked up from her phone, they were already on the airport tarmac, motoring toward the jet.

Mateo called back with a final assurance. "Still all clear. Take off is scheduled in three minutes."

When the car stopped, he opened the rear door for her, and she stepped out at the foot of the stairs to the plane. She ran up the steps quickly. Neither pilot was waiting as one usually would, and the door to the cockpit was closed.

Probably taking care of final details for takeoff.

She ducked her head as she stepped through the doorway and headed toward her rear compartment.

It took a second to realize that no one else was in the forward compartment of the plane. When she turned to look back for the rest of her team, the cockpit door burst open. A massive hand covered her mouth from the rear, squeezed her shoulder tightly, and gruffly ordered her not to move.

She heard several loud pops. In her periphery, a body fell from the plane's stairway. A woman screamed in horror. Fidelia's mind went numb. She struggled to free herself from the iron grip on her face and mouth, but nothing budged.

She panted from both exertion and pain, but words wouldn't come out. Sounds wouldn't come out either. Desperation set in. She hadn't experienced fear like this since Singapore immigration had seized her from her jet a few years ago. Then, the extent of her predicament set in.

"Stop struggling. It's the FBI. You're under arrest." The voice sounded familiar.

She looked up to see a face peering around a corner of the jet's second compartment with a stern expression that gradually worked into a grin of satisfaction.

He's wearing the same rumpled blue suit he wore six years ago!

Fidelia, still struggling to think clearly and put it all together, remained silent as the agent read out her Miranda rights. The rumpled agent needed only to take a few steps from his hiding spot to stand immediately in front of her outside the cockpit. He took his time as he recited words he'd used hundreds of times before with a tone of boredom bordering on disgust. "Hold out your hands in front of you."

Slowly, she released her grip on the massive hands that secured her and lowered them to her waist, then offered them forward together. The agent snapped handcuffs around her wrists without speaking, then snapped zip ties around her ankles. He nodded to the man holding her to release his grip, but the giant still stood directly behind her, blocking any path to the doorway.

The agent in the blue suit gestured for her to sit in the closest seat. He remained standing and hovered over her menacingly.

Her legs trembled now, and her thoughts remained jumbled. She dared not speak as the agent glared down until he won a small victory. She couldn't tolerate it any longer and looked away.

"Why are you in Honolulu?" he asked, apparently satisfied with her meek compliance.

"I'd like to speak with a lawyer." Her tone was polite but assertive.

Without warning, and so quickly she didn't see it coming, the agent raised his right knee and slammed his foot down so violently on hers she could feel bones shatter. She screamed out in pain. Tears filled her eyes, obscuring her vision.

He let her cry for a few minutes, then repeated his question. "It's unfortunate you hurt your foot and broke the heel of your shoe trying to escape. I hope you will answer my question and won't try to run away again. Why are you in Honolulu?"

She weighed the alternatives. If she betrayed Tak and his people, the deal with Multima could be aborted and the lucrative pachinko business in Japan lost.

"I'd like to speak with a lawyer." She braced herself for the expected pain and the agent obliged, stamping on her other foot with substantial force and the same excruciating pain. While she screamed in agony, the agent wordlessly squeezed past the massive hulk guarding her and left the aircraft.

Sometime later, someone shut off the plane's engines and left her sitting in her seat in darkness. The cabin became progressively hotter, her throat drier, and the pain in her feet throbbed incessantly.

At some point, she dozed from exhaustion. She awoke when someone shook her. It took a moment to focus clearly and realize where she was and who was again glaring down at her. Before she could beg for a sip of water, he interrogated her again.

"Let's try a different question. Who's the Japanese guy your people dumped off a cliff outside town this afternoon?"

She tried to speak, but her throat was too raspy and her mind too cluttered to form words. Her mouth opened, but there was nothing there.

He carried on. "You need to understand my predicament. Despite the shit I recited to you about your rights, you'll never see a lawyer. You lost that chance when you screwed us at Guantanamo the last time. If you'd packed it all in after helping Interpol, we'd never be having this conversation. Instead, you began scheming immediately to kill Mareno and inherit The Organization. Do you think we're idiots? The first thing you'll tell an attorney is how horribly we treated you by holding you illegally at Guantanamo."